THE NIGHT OF SHADOWS

THE SECRETS OF SILENCE
BOOK ONE

MARKUS BITNER

RINGWARDEN PRESS

CONTENTS

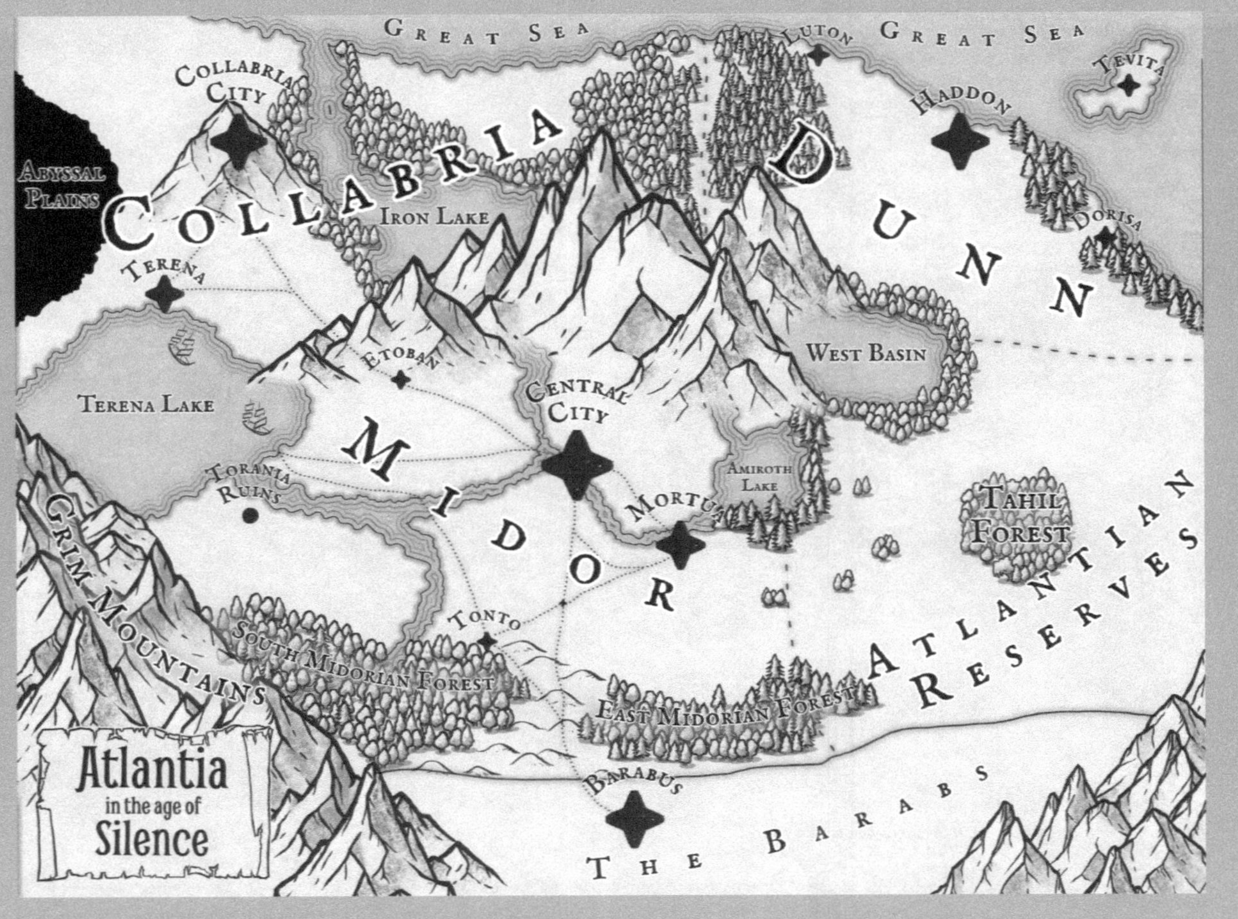

Great Sea
Luton
Great Sea
Tevita
Haddon
Collabria City
Abyssal Plains
COLLABRIA
DUNN
Iron Lake
Dorisa
Terena
West Basin
Etoban
Central City
Amiroth Lake
Mortua
Tahil Forest
ATLANTIAN RESERVES
Terena Lake
MIDOR
Torania Ruins
Tonto
Grim Mountains
South Midorian Forest
East Midorian Forest
Barabus
THE BARABS
Atlantia
in the age of
Silence

The night is dark, the shadows deep.
In every hour, the silence steeps.
The dawn is near, but not yet here;
Till then we yearn, and embers burn.

PROLOGUE

T he city of Torania was not always this way. Neglected, in ruins, despised. Once, it was a jewel. Once, this place would have beckoned him home.

Rastafus was not fond of darkness, but in this instance he would have it no other way. This city, betrayed by its own children, deserved to mourn its death. No, it would have no light. Not yet.

His breath shuddered into the chill night. The silence was more powerful than anything his human mouth could utter. Did the silence mourn? It was hidden from him. Did it laugh in mockery? He could not tell. But soon the silence would be pierced. The voices of man, beast, and nature would cry out again in pain and joy, and only then would the world mend. The silence needed to break.

Walking through the streets without fire glow, he could appreciate the light of the moon against the ruined buildings on his sides. They rose and fell, some towering above the mist and keeping watch over the city. The many spires and watchtowers once made Torania a spectacle, but only a few survived the storm that brought even the stone to ruin. They were witnesses to the passing of an age, and they would witness yet another.

Another gust of wind flew past him. He shivered. Though he was doing this for the sake of the Deep, he was still conflicted. The last time one had consulted the forces of darkness, that person had lost himself to unspeakable evil. But that was the point, wasn't it? To get someone else to use the darkness so he didn't have to? He could see no other way. Only the Abyss could bring about his goals, no matter what the Lightbreaker said.

Rastafus, a middle-aged man with a pointed orange-brown beard, hastened his eyes to the road on his right, where footsteps crept soundlessly towards him. They belonged to a figure in a dark cloak like his, though much taller. The man was slender, with long arms and a deep stride, and though a hood shrouded his face, moonlight glinted from his eyes. With every step, he scattered the mist, yet his movement was so smooth that he may have been the wind itself.

Rastafus gripped the black book in his left hand, clenched his teeth, and walked forward to meet the man. Baltashazar was his name. Cousin to the king of Barabus and the lord of the guard. One of the most intelligent people on the face of Atlantia, he also bordered on insanity. Age hadn't been kind to the man. Alas, if this meeting went as planned, Baltashazar would lose whatever sanity he had left.

The two stopped when they came within a few feet of each other, regarding the other in silence. Rastafus dared not break it. Now closer, he could see Baltashazar's long, sharp nose and his equally pointed chin. Frays of graying hair hung out from his hood, blowing in the gathering breeze. His breath, far shallower than Rastafus's, made no fog.

Baltashazar glanced at the book in Rastafus's hand. "I have given you secrecy," he said in a thin, gravelly voice. "I have left behind my king and people to meet with you, and I have done so without knowing your intent. Why did you desire to meet with me? And why in this distant ruin of a city?"

Rastafus met his eyes. "Fascination." His own voice, deep and full, permeated the mist, echoing longer than Baltashazar's had. He lowered it to barely above a whisper. "I have been watching you for a time, and I have seen you in your secrecy. I have seen your mind."

Baltashazar pulled back his hood, revealing his narrowed eyes. "Who are you?"

"One like you. One who delights to look upon the unpraised heroes of old. One who not only remembers Dreslen . . ." Rastafus raised the book. ". . . but reveres him."

Baltashazar's face turned to stone. For a moment, he said nothing, but as he gazed upon the tome in Rastafus's shivering hand, his mouth quivered open. "What is this?"

"It is yours." Rastafus extended the book. "I am intrigued, but I have not the will to go through with reading it. It is a dark thing, this book. But I am sure that for a man such as yourself, its shaded words would only bring illumination."

Baltashazar brought forth both hands, shaking. "He truly wrote this?"

"Indeed. But I would warn you . . ." Rastafus slightly retracted the book. "Once you read it, you may find yourself not wanting to return to your kingdom quite yet."

"And why might that be?"

Rastafus faced the northwest. "It speaks of the power he used to overcome Bein Mordecai himself. This book may teach you that power, or it may not, but I think we both know where he mastered it."

Baltashazar followed Rastafus's gaze. Far in that direction, a darkness beyond comprehension ruled the land. It was there that Baltashazar would go if he accepted this gift. There, he would destroy himself and be ruled by death.

After a sharp intake of breath, Baltashazar spoke. "I would not dream of it." His hands went back to his sides, but his eyes held fast to the book.

"Oh, but you do." Rastafus brought the book closer, almost holding his breath. "Remember Dreslen."

Baltashazar was still for a while. At length, he raised his shaking hands once more, this time grasping the book. "Remember Dreslen."

ONE

◆─◆○◆─◆

*"**Y**our sister will die again,"* the Voice said. *"She will fall to the same powers that killed—"*

"Enough!" Jacob said, leaning over the public watchtower's railing. "Lindina will be fine. She's just . . . not used to it yet."

Now, of all times, he needed a clear head. He would leave for Mortua tomorrow and wanted his wits about him. He took a deep breath, ignoring the Voice, and focused on his environment. It might be a few months before he'd see it again.

From here, Jacob had a perfect view of the entire town of Tonto, as well as the forest to the south and the rolling hills to the north. The sun set behind him on the southern horizon, giving a last few minutes of light and warmth before nightfall.

To the northeast, somewhere in the distance, the city of Mortua awaited. Little separated him from that place anymore. A day's journey, a bit of walking, nothing more. Finances were no longer an issue. By some strange chance, he had already secured a job there.

It had been two weeks since the chief librarian had visited relatives in Tonto—relatives who recommended Jacob for a job. Why the old chief obliged, Jacob still didn't know. Their meeting was brief, and the interview hurried. Still, he couldn't object. Jacob's dreams of becoming a publishing editor were far nearer than ever before.

"By all means, leave Lindina to her fate," the Voice said, using Jacob's mouth to speak again. At better times, it communicated by thought alone.

"She'll be fine." Jacob gritted his teeth. "Carl will take care of her, as will everyone else. It's for the better that I don't intervene."

"Yes, because last time—"

Jacob clamped his mouth shut.

Very well, the Voice said in thought. *I shall leave you to your folly. Reminisce about your beloved town before you forget it forever.*

"This isn't the end." Jacob looked down at the town square below. A gust of wind seeped through his grey tunic and chilled him. "I don't know when, but I'll return. I don't intend to give up on a library in Tonto, but for that to work I need a favourable position in the system. This is only the beginning."

"Perhaps, but you are still delusional."

Jacob sighed. When would he be rid of the Voice? Something told him he would bear this burden forever. But this burden, unlike the Deep, would not earn him death if someone discovered it. He really should be grateful to the Voice. Without it, his secret would have been discovered twice over, and he would not be standing here today with his ideal career in prospect. Two curses. One malicious but powerless, the other formidable but benign.

"You perceive your connection to the Deep to be formidable? You can barely summon a gust of wind!"

"Remember the sorcerers of old," Jacob whispered. "Remember how they shaped mountains, cast ruinous storms, and lit the sky with towering flames. Remember Dreslen."

"You are not Dreslen, fool. You are a simple Wayfollower who could barely use his power even if he wanted to."

"Even so, I would become dangerous if I were to practice wielding it . . . which is why I'll never do it again."

He didn't want the Voice to respond. Even thinking about that day made his stomach churn, but that moment of reawakening was the only reason he abandoned the Deep. *Thank the Silence for that.* Had he continued in the Deep, he may have become a powerful sorcerer that endangered everyone he knew.

All his thoughts were stolen away by a man in a grey cloak striding across the town square, paying no heed to the townsfolk. Despite his elevation, Jacob backed away from the railing and inhaled sharply. Every time he saw a Silencer, he felt a flash of panic. They were the law. They were justice. They were authority. They were the bane of Wayfollowers like Jacob, and there would be many more of them in Mortua. Yet Jacob, and everyone else, owed their peace and safety to these men. Were it not for them, Atlantia would have fallen into another war by now.

As the Silencer disappeared behind a building, Jacob relaxed. *If nothing else, they're warnings. The more I see them, the more careful I'll be.*

As Jacob was about to lean on the railing, a sound from behind caused his muscles to tense again. Turning around in a daze, he looked down at the trapdoor in the middle of the watchtower floor. Whoever opened it gave no heed to stealth, for it flew on its hinge and struck the floor on the other side with a terrible clatter. From the hole, a hand reached out to grip the floor, followed by a brown-haired head facing opposite Jacob.

"Jacob!" The head turned around, revealing Carl's face, his thick moustache styled more carefully than his wayward hair, as usual, but his eyes wider than ever.

"What?" Jacob stepped back. Carl hadn't heard Jacob talking to himself, had he? Even if he did, he was one of the few people Jacob trusted to keep it a secret. Jacob would have said that Carl was like a brother to him, but that would give his actual brothers too much credit. Only a few years Jacob's elder, Carl had treated Jacob like a sibling for as long as he could remember. There was barely a distinction between their families at all.

"It's Lindina." Carl climbed out of the entry hole and kicked the trapdoor shut, ignoring the rattle. He stood, panting, looking at Jacob.

"What?" Jacob asked. "She's come back?"

"Still missing." Carl averted his eyes. "I've got half the town looking for her in the forest. Someone said they saw the monster again too."

"You know it's not real." Jacob looked beyond Carl to the forest at the edge of Tonto. Those woods were as much his home as the town.

But Lindina, Carl's sister, was a different case. She was only eleven years old and never had a taste for risk. Lindina, like Carl, was like a sibling to Jacob, and she looked up to him as much as her own brother. She took after Jacob well—perhaps in more ways than she knew.

Books had always been Jacob's greatest passion, and it seemed Lindina was the only one who shared it to the same degree. Yet Lindina was content to read under the safety of a roof or on the stability of a bench. Unlike Jacob, she did not seek the thrill of adventures in the woods—which only made her disappearances the last month more confounding.

"The monster's real." Carl reached down and effortlessly pulled the trapdoor open again. As he lowered himself through, he paused and looked at Jacob. "You're coming to help, right?"

Jacob sighed. "I—"

"You're moving tomorrow," Carl interrupted. "I get it. But isn't that all the more reason to see her one last time? To say goodbye?"

Jacob looked at the forest. Carl was only partially right. He *did* want rest, but he wanted to find Lindina more. What held him back wasn't laziness, but fear. Fear at what he'd done in the past . . . what might happen again if he wasn't careful.

"Fine then." Carl disappeared beneath the tower floor without closing the trapdoor behind him. The ladder's groans echoed through the hole, quieting with each second.

Jacob sighed and closed his eyes. This was *not* how he and Carl would say goodbye.

I'll be back by midnight. Jacob walked to the hole and looked down. At the bottom, Carl let go of the ladder and walked to the watchtower's door, disappearing from view.

"You'll do none of that, fool," the Voice said. *"Leave the search party to the searching. Lindina is* not *your responsibility."*

Jacob ignored the Voice and lowered himself onto the ladder, grabbing the top rung with one hand and reaching up for the strap on the bottom of the trapdoor. Pulling it shut and nearly hitting his head on it, he descended through the tower. Waning light fell through the open windows in the stone bricks, wrapping around the old wooden ladder and resting on the dirt ground.

At the bottom, the tower door was still open. Jacob smiled. It was just like Carl to expect to be followed every time he left the room. For Jacob, at least, it wasn't an unrealistic expectation.

"You care too much," the Voice whispered as they walked through the watchtower door and carefully closed it behind them. The sentiment contradicted his mood, but the Voice tended to be that way. No matter how Jacob felt, the Voice was the opposite.

"So you've told me before." Jacob looked to his right, towards the forest and the setting sun. "And so I've chosen to ignore."

"Then—"

"No!" Jacob jogged down the dirt road to catch up with Carl. "Don't say things like that."

Burn them all. Get rid of your cares, then live in sorrow.

"I said, keep quiet."

The sun was low enough that it was nearly red. The entire southern sky burned with hues of orange and purple, fading into the last blue light of day, on the other side of which was a darkening sky with glimmering stars.

The gap between Jacob and Carl diminished. His slumped, broad shoulders were unmistakable, even in this light. As soon as Jacob came within speaking distance, Carl's head turned around. He stopped and waited for Jacob to catch up.

"I'll look with you until midnight," Jacob said.

"It's good enough. I just wanted to know that you cared."

"Carl, you know I care about you both. I'm going to miss you two more than anyone else."

Carl's jaw relaxed. "You're not worried about Lindina, are you?"

"She takes after me. Perhaps she saw the joy the woods brought me and wanted to experience it for herself."

"Did she tell you that?"

Jacob paused, then shook his head. "She told me nothing. In truth, I don't know why she's been disappearing into the forest. But I do trust her."

What Jacob didn't say was that he had a suspicion. A theory he hoped was wrong. The last month, Lindina had been reminding Jacob of his younger self—when he had less control over his connection to the Deep. The secrecy, the sudden disappearances. All he could do for her was maintain her secret. Anything more than that and he'd be overstepping a dangerous boundary.

"It's the suddenness that bothers me," Carl said. "One day she's happily talking with both of us, and the next she's gone till nightfall. Then she comes back upset and doesn't tell us why. Then she swings back and forth for weeks without telling anyone anything. You still think she's okay?"

"I can't know. She's growing, I know that. Perhaps she'll open up to you soon. I had hoped she'd talk to me about it, but my time here is done. I haven't failed, though. I've given comfort even though I don't know what I'm comforting her from."

Carl exhaled. "You really think she's going to be alright?"

"I do. Otherwise, I'd be more persistent."

"She's got a secret. Sometimes, I can respect that. But it's tearing her up, Jacob. You've got things you won't tell me, and I've learned to live with it. But this is different. She's my sister." Carl looked at the ground. "But she needs her mother, and no one can give that to her."

Jacob bowed his head. The two approached his house at the very edge of the forest. No lamps lit the windows yet. Jacob's parents—Carl's secondary parents—may already be out in the woods looking for Lindina.

"How did it feel?" Carl said. "When you lost Junia?"

Junia. Jacob's skin crawled. Junia didn't exist. Lindina was the only sister he'd ever had, and the only one he needed.

"How big is the search party?" Jacob asked. A bead of sweat slipped down his armpit.

Carl sniffed. "Around seventeen people. We haven't heard any wolves for the last week and a half, but remember . . ." He looked at Jacob.

"The monster?" Jacob was tired of hearing about it. A black creature creeping around the forest, killing the wildlife without eating it and tearing the trees without reason. The legend had gone back ever since Tonto was established. No one paid any mind to it until a few weeks ago, when a group of boys Jacob wasn't too fond of came back from the forest in shock.

"Yes, the monster," Carl said.

"You know Gilroy's crew. I wouldn't trust their testimony if they swore on their lives."

"They have, many times. Old Ewan heard it too, you know."

"He heard it?"

"A very . . . unusual scream."

Jacob raised his eyebrows.

"Don't scoff." Carl's face was set. "You can't tell me it isn't real just because you haven't seen it."

"Oh, I can. I've been in the forest more than anyone else in town, and I've never even *heard* it."

"Revena says she saw it too."

"Oh? And what did she see?"

"A . . . black creature. It darted away when it saw her."

"A black creature? That's the best anyone can do?"

"Come on, Jacob. You're the one who fills your head with non-sensical stories each day."

"Stories, yes. It's because I read so much that I can tell the difference between fiction and reality. That's probably why Lindina doesn't believe in the monster, either."

"She's afraid of it, so I don't care what she says. Come on!"

They were now at the edge of the forest, but Jacob halted.

"Perhaps I ought to grab a torch." Jacob looked at his house.

"Jacob, she doesn't want to be found. She's only going to run harder if she sees you coming from two leagues away. Come on. We're going to split up. I'll go west, you go south. Good?"

"Fair enough." Jacob tore his eyes from his house and walked to the forest. The first line of trees was thin and spread out, consisting mostly of tall firs that shot up like poles with frail branches. Here, the ground was still covered in green grass and nearly devoid of fallen sticks.

"What was she last wearing?" Jacob asked.

"Yellow dress. Her hair was braided with yellow ribbons, too, but I wouldn't be surprised if she undid those."

Jacob nodded. They walked together for a short while longer in silence, listening to the wind shake the leaves and the calls of crows from every direction. As they trekked across pine cones, sticks, and dried leaves, Carl spoke.

"Here's where we'll split." He stopped and turned to Jacob, his brown eyes as sullen as ever. "This may be the last I see you for a few months."

"It may." Jacob looked at his friend and sighed. "If so, then I hope we part in peace. I'll do my best to find Lindina."

"Don't expect to find her. I only wanted you to show that you care. Besides, I didn't tell you this yet, but I convinced a Silencer to help look for her. One way or another, we'll find her."

Jacob's jaw dropped, but no sound came from his mouth. *A Silencer? What were you thinking, Carl! Fool! If she's a Wayfollower, they'll kill her if they find out!* But Carl couldn't know. Even Jacob didn't know. If his suspicion about Lindina was correct, Carl had just put her in death's path. What madness had overtaken him?

"Are you alright?"

"Just . . . sad to say goodbye." Jacob faked a smile for a moment. "I hope I can say a last goodbye to Lindina as well."

"Aren't you glad I was able to convince a Silencer to help? I thought that would be impossible."

"Yes, of course. Good job." He turned his head away, and his smile vanished. What now? Silencers were good at whatever they did. They were the best. The Silencer would find Lindina before anyone else, like that Silencer almost found Jacob years ago. But Lindina didn't have the Voice to get her out of trouble, and had to rely on her own wit. As much as Jacob feared to admit it, that wouldn't be enough to keep her alive, not when a Silencer was looking for her.

"Jacob?"

Don't commit yourself, fool, the Voice said. *You don't know whether she is a Wayfollower at all.*

No, but I do. Jacob's breathing quickened, and the wind wrapped around him. *I know why she seeks solitude in the woods. I know why she will not tell her most beloved ones this secret we all know she holds.*

Trust my intelligence, not your own! Have I not proven myself countless times over?

"Jacob, are you alright?"

"See you in a few months, Carl." Jacob broke into a run. He heard Carl's voice behind him but could distinguish no words. It didn't matter. All that mattered now was finding Lindina before the Silencer did.

As the last daylight faded from the sky, he heard a sound. A scream, piercing and choked, in the far distance. Never had Jacob heard anything like it. Somehow, he felt it deep in his gut, twisting within him, writhing and despairing.

Something is wrong. Jacob knew the monster wasn't real. Yet there was the sound, as described perfectly by the legends.

Suddenly, nothing felt real to him anymore. He ran towards danger with no sense of purpose except the vague hope of outdoing a Silencer, but he could not stop. His legs carried him onward, past reason, past the Voice's pleas.

Find Lindina, he told himself. It was all he could do. *Save your sister.*

The dreadful cry sounded again.

Find Lindina.

TWO

"This isn't very good tea, Jacob." Lindina squinted and looked down at her cup.

"Of course it is." Jacob sipped from his own cup and let the bitter tea sit in his mouth for a bit before swallowing. After it went down, he could still feel some fuzziness on his tongue and around his teeth. "It's just stronger than you're used to."

"It's stronger than anyone's used to." Lindina took another sip despite her adverse reaction. Her face contorted. "You actually like this?"

Jacob took another sip, swallowed, and contemplated the bitter aftertaste, narrowing his eyes and looking off into the distance. "Yes." He smiled. "But you're right. It's not very good, is it?"

"No, it isn't." Lindina set her cup down on the table. Jacob chuckled and continued to drink his own tea. The day was good thus far. A successful shift at the well digging site, a lunch of ham wraps and apples, and now tea with Lindina and, if he showed up soon, Carl. He was late, as usual, but Jacob couldn't blame him. The weather today was perfect—a clear sky with a warm sun, but a breeze cool enough to stave off excess heat. If there was any day to put extra work into the house, it was today. Still, Jacob hoped Carl would take a break at some point. The tea, good or not, was getting cold.

"How's the book I lent you?" Jacob said.

"Very fun." Lindina brushed back the a few strands of her light-brown hair from her slender face, brown eyes alight. "I didn't expect that any of those kinds of books could be funny."

"Well, that's historical comedy fiction. A rare find, and rarer still is a well-written one."

"Do you think it's disrespectful, though? I told Carl about it, and that's what he thought."

"Yes, well . . ." Jacob shifted and set down his cup. "He may have a point, but I personally disagree. The War claimed many lives and broke many families, that's true. We ought to remember and respect that with solemness. But they died for a reason. They fought for the peace and joy that had been taken from them. How do you think they would feel if we all held onto the misery? The darkness lifted. When Amiroth slew the gargoyle king, he changed the world, including how we remember the past."

"But you're not sure?"

"About making serious historical events into comedies? No." Jacob shook his head. "I don't think anyone's sure, but it makes you appreciate those who gave their lives in a different light. They were real people, not just grave soldiers."

"And sorcerers."

"Yes, we mustn't forget the Sirathim." Jacob took another sip. The more he drank, the more bitter it got.

"You don't think Amiroth might have been wrong in banishing the Sirathim from Atlantia, do you?"

"Ah, there's a controversial topic." Jacob tried to keep his hands steady. "I have thoughts on that, but for now I'll say that I agree with him. Magic is dangerous, and that's the end of it. Remember Dreslen."

"Remember Dreslen," Lindina said, reaching for her tea and setting it down again a moment later. She looked out towards the town with darkened eyes, brushing back more hair that the wind had displaced. If only Jacob could tell her all that was on his mind. Yet as grown as she was for her age, she was still a child. Her education was not yet complete, and though it pained him more than he could describe, she had to be indoctrinated that the Deep was altogether dangerous. She showed too much curiosity and openness for her own good.

Worse still, she was only eleven years old. Every time he spoke with her, she amazed him. This kind of maturity could only come from being literate at a young age. Already she was a girl with the intellect of a woman, yet without proper wisdom it would only lead to trouble. Jacob almost wished he'd never started reading to her when she was a toddler—almost.

"Do you think you'll ever write a book yourself?" Lindina asked without looking at him.

Jacob breathed relief for the change of subject. "Yes, I think one day I will."

"When will that be?"

"Once I know all there is to know about good writing. There's still so much I haven't read. You haven't been to the Mortuan library, have you?"

"No, but you told me about it. You don't think you'll be able to read *all* those books, do you?"

Jacob laughed. "Maybe someday. But first I have to work there."

"Is that what you'd be doing, reading books for a living?"

"Being a librarian is *far* more important than that. Books are the words of scholars and storytellers, and librarians are their heralds. They maintain accurate accounts, making sure everything is in order at all times. If false history spreads, it's often the fault of the librarian for not catching it. That could land one in deep trouble with the Silencers."

"It sounds stressful."

"Not at all. It's only . . . What should I say? One of the most important jobs in the world."

Lindina laughed.

"I mean it. Librarians bring knowledge to the masses, even more than professors. Where do the professors get their books in the first place? How can writers shape the world, if not for librarians? Yes, they sit down with a cup of tea and read a gripping novel now and then. But more often they are contenders for truth, wisdom, and beauty. I can only hope to be such a warrior someday."

"But you'd have to leave Tonto." Lindina looked at him without a smile. "Like your brother and sister." She turned away. "But I guess that's going to happen anyway."

"Lindina, I don't want to leave. The chances that I'd actually get hired at the library are small when you consider all the applicants in Mortua. I'm not going anywhere soon, if at all."

"But you would go if you could get the job."

"I don't know." Jacob's voice hushed. "It would be the most difficult decision of my life. I'd have to leave everyone I love behind."

"And everyone who loves you would have to let you go." Lindina was still. Hair blew into her face, but she didn't bother to pull it back. For a while, neither said anything. There was still no sign of Carl.

"Jacob . . ." Lindina's voice was low and cautious. "What do you think magic feels like?"

Jacob didn't have to imagine. He could tell her exactly what the Deep, or magic, was like. How it felt to be an outlier who carried its burden. How it filled him with such power yet made him feel powerless.

"I have no idea, but you shouldn't be thinking about that. It's the curiosity that starts you down that path."

"I know, but you've read more than I have, and . . ." Her voice faltered.

"I'm serious. There's a reason we remember Dreslen. He pursued the Deep—magic, sorry—with noble intentions. Then he went on to slaughter hundreds with it. You're still young and innocent. If anyone is prone to its corrupting power, you are."

But Jacob spoke without conviction. All he could do was protect Lindina at all costs by repeating the wisdom that all Atlantia had been indoctrinated with for centuries. The Deep was corrupting, if not outright evil. If only he could convince Lindina of it.

Lindina inhaled tersely. "Okay." With a smile that failed to reach her eyes, she looked at him again. "Thanks for looking out for me."

"Of course." Jacob smiled back. As much as he could, he wanted to protect her smile. To make it genuine and lasting. To make it reach inwards and fill her heart. She still had years ahead of her to grow and so many trials and pains to overcome. Jacob couldn't be there for every single one, but he would help carry her burdens as long as it was in his power to do so.

"Oh, there's Carl," Lindina remarked.

Jacob strained his vision to the right. A man with broad shoulders and a well-groomed mustache approached with a wave. "So it is." He looked at Lindina again. She was his sister in a sense that ran deeper than blood. He would see to it that her laughter became more common than her sighs. For her sake, and for Carl's.

⸻ ◆ ⸻

The memory faded as Jacob pummeled back to stark reality, collapsing to the ground from exhaustion. His mouth hung open, giving way to agonized breaths as his entire body heaved in pain. He hadn't run through the forest like this in weeks. But even if the last time had been yesterday, he should know better than to sprint for this long without taking a break. What absurdity had overtaken him?

Yes, I know. Jacob moved his mouth along with the words but spoke not. *I'm a fool.* He didn't need the Voice to tell him. Fear, more than anything else, drove him. Fear for Lindina. If only he'd asked Carl when the Silencer started looking, he might have an idea of his competition's progress. Alas, he could only assume the worst if he wanted to keep himself moving forward.

Forward where? Jacob didn't even know where Lindina was. For all he knew, he may be running in the opposite direction. Perhaps he even passed her while lost in memory. The only reason he ran in this particular direction was because of the "monster" scream he heard when he started running. But he paid less mind to it with each step he took. Chances were high that he hallucinated it, like everyone else who "heard" it. Thinking of the monster didn't get him any closer to Lindina, though. If only there was a way of tracking her that didn't involve the Deep.

You're out of options, the Voice said. *Look at yourself, you pathetic piece of heaving idiocy. Not only are you lost, you're slow. Even if you manage to find the right trail, you'll be crawling along the ground to get to her.*

"I . . . won't . . . use . . . the Deep," Jacob panted, grimacing and clutching his burning throat. If the circumstances were different, he might consider it. *Might.* But there was a Silencer in the forest at this very moment. A man trained to find and apprehend Wayfollowers. That, along with moral reasons, made the choice obvious. He would not give in. The only way to go was without magic.

Then get up, fool! the Voice said. *Go along your merry way then weep when your beloved sister is never seen again.*

Resisting the Deep's power was never easy when the Voice tried to coerce him into it. But for his own sake, and the sakes of those around him, he had to. *Remember Dreslen.* He would not allow himself to become like Dreslen, a noble sorcerer turned dark warlord. The only way to ensure that didn't happen was to resist the Deep entirely.

You cannot fight it forever. This is who you are, Jacob of Tonto. A child of the Deep. Fight it forever, and you will tear yourself apart. You will fall to madness. You will fall to me.

"I want . . ." Jacob got to his shaking feet little by little, still huffing. "I want to understand this curse I have. I want to give into its power and be one with it. I want—" A twig snapped in the near area, silencing Jacob. Night was upon the face of Atlantia, and he could see little more than ten feet ahead of him in the pale moonlight.

I want to be at peace. Jacob started walking through the woods again at a slow pace. Though he needed to recover his breath, he had to keep moving. *But peace is not a privilege I have been granted. The Silencers stand for peace, and they defend it well. I do not fault them for it. If I must live a life of turmoil so that others may have what I want, I would have it no other way.*

How noble of you, the Voice sneered. *What a shame that Lindina will not benefit from your selflessness.*

Jacob had no answer. He mustn't let himself become distracted by the Voice. This was about Lindina, so he must focus on her, not himself. Though the woods were dark, he was not sightless. He could still distinguish birch from oak, pine from maple, and stone from root. At a sense of movement, he would turn his head and strain his gaze upon the source. A few birds, a squirrel, and nothing more.

A breeze flew into Jacob's ears and disturbed the fallen leaves, whispering of secrets no man could understand. The Deep called to him. It often did by way of the wind when his breathing intensified. In this case, he could not help himself from panting. Though necessary for recovery, the it may ward off Lindina if he came too close. Tracking was a difficult business—but then again, he wasn't tracking. He was aimlessly walking in an arbitrary direction and hoping for the best.

Minutes passed, and though Jacob's breathing quieted, the wind did not. If anything, it became more persistent. Swirling around him, obtruding his sense of hearing. How long had it been since he last guided it? If he willed it, he could direct the breeze.

The breath of nature was at his command. Such a condemning power to have in this world of peace and conformity. No, he would not use it. He would heed what he said to Lindina.

"Remember Dreslen," Jacob whispered, stepping over a fallen trunk and running his hand along a rough pine tree. Sap touched his fingers and lingered after he wiped them on his tunic.

"*Stop,*" the Voice said. *Stop and listen. Think.*

I can think while walking, Jacob thought back, looking at the ground around him. The grass was overgrown, strewn with fallen sticks and stones wherever he went. There was no easy way to check for footprints. But what other signs might Lindina have left?

The Silencer will know what to look for, the Voice said. *You do not. Give in to the Deep, fool.*

"To do what?" Jacob stopped and realized he was still panting. "I'm no Sirathim of past eras. Even if I was willing to use the Deep, there's not much I can do with it. I can direct the wind and . . . that's it, not counting the weird tree thing. Anything else comes involuntarily."

I can help you.

"Absolutely not." Jacob cringed at the volume of his own voice. Turning around, he dropped it to a whisper. "I know you. You want nothing but evil. I don't know why, but—"

"*Oh, but you do.*" The Voice smiled with Jacob's mouth. "*You know very well what lurks in those shaded recesses.*"

Jacob clenched his jaw. It was an accident. Nothing more. "Speak no more, Voice." He clutched his head, turning around again and walking. *Focus on Lindina.*

"*So much hatred for me.*"

"I said speak no more!"

The Voice chuckled. "*Very well. I will say nothing of that day. But you know that without my power you cannot find Lindina.*"

"You don't know that. But I know that with it, you will destroy me."

"Now what good would that do me, fool? After all, I am you. A part of you, rather."

Jacob didn't engage. The Voice may be right about needing to use the Deep, but Jacob would not yield to the Voice's control of it. He sighed through his teeth, tilting his head back. *Why?* What was the point of all his self-debate, trying to convince himself against the Deep, if he was just going to surrender to it anyway? But he had to. For Lindina. *Just this once.*

But the Silencer! he told himself. *What if the Silencer sees you controlling the wind?*

It was a risk he had to take. But which way was she? He would have an advantage in speed with the wind at his back, but that was pointless without direction. *If I were Lindina, where would I be?* It felt like such a basic, useless question, but what else was there to ask? Based on what he knew, she had been in the forest for most of the day. That would give her enough time to get virtually anywhere. If Jacob was correct that she wanted solitude to practice the ways of the Deep, the centre of the forest would be a good place to check. But she also didn't want to be found. Was the centre a good hiding place?

Eighteen people, including a Silencer, were looking for her. If the original search party had been split up into strategic directions to cover more ground, then—no, Jacob didn't even know if they left at the same time.

It shouldn't matter. He narrowed his eyes. *What was it Carl told me? He'd go west and I'd go south.*

His eyes snapped open. "The river! If she went west, the river would cut her off. She'd have to travel south from there. But if she traveled along the river, her chances of being found would increase. *If I were her, I'd turn back from the river. That would lead me east. Southeast, probably.*" Jacob swatted a fly away from his eyes and looked around. No sign of anyone. "That would put her on the path in my direction."

Generally.

"But would she stay in the same place once she found a good spot?" Given that she had been in the woods for an entire day, it was unlikely. She could have moved around a single time or could have never stopped moving.

This is pointless, the Voice said. *Think all you want. Any idea you come up with will be no more likely than another. Why are you here, anyway?*

"Why am I here?" Jacob raised his eyebrows. "Is that a joke?"

"Why here? In this particular spot?"

"The monster scream. A fabrication of my cursed imagination, like you."

"Stop. Look around you."

"I am looking—" Jacob stopped. He was in a clearing but didn't recognize it. Based on where he imagined himself to be, there should be a few young trees in the midst of the older ones that surrounded the space. As he looked harder, his memories were confirmed—strewn along the ground, amidst the patched grass, were the splintered remains of those trees. When could that have happened? It was less than two months ago since he was last in this spot. Then, it had been a place of new life. There had even been flowers growing around some of the new trees. All that was dead now. Destroyed.

Mouth agape, he walked in a circle around the area and surveyed the wreckage. Something about this place felt cold. Unnatural. The grass was a different length in every spot he looked. Though a faint wind filled the trees, the leaves were still. *What in Silence?*

Jacob was so busy looking at the ground that he forgot to look at the surrounding trees themselves. They were no better off than the grass. Bark was torn off, branches ripped, and on some, if the darkness did not deceive him, black slash marks marred the wood. At a single closer look, he believed in the monster. The slashes were in groups, running deep and jagged. Like the claws of wolves but as vicious as death.

Jacob put his hand against a different tree to steady himself. Without delay, he began to feel weak and nauseated. Looking at where his hand rested, he saw to his surprise that it was on untouched bark, not dark slashes. He withdrew it, but saw for the briefest moment in his mind's eye a view of the area from above, as if he were watching from the top of one of the trees.

Do you remember? the Voice whispered. Everything, even the wind, went silent. *The Way of Life. A connection to nature through the Deep.*

Jacob looked at his right hand—the one he'd touched the tree with—and turned it over multiple times, bending his fingers. The weakness that beset him had already faded. He knew exactly what was happening. Rather, he had a vague sense of what was happening. Reading material on the ways of the Deep was sparse, to say the least. But he'd experienced it before. To connect with nature and the forces of life, he had to give some of his own life force. That left him feeling sick. The first and last time this happened, he ended up vomiting on the same tree that he connected with.

Do it again.

Perhaps it would do some good. Jacob extended his hand again to the same tree, stopping a few inches away. Should he engage in this? This was sorcery, the very reason why Lindina was in danger.

"Oh, forget your indoctrination!" the Voice hissed. *"Do it, fool! Find Lindina! See what the tree has to show!"*

Jacob did as the Voice commanded and put his palm to the tree as before. He breathed deeply, closing his eyes, letting the weakness return. His stomach began to feel empty, and his thoughts faded. As he felt his insides go cold as death, he saw through his closed eyes the area in which he stood, looking down from the high boughs of one of the trees. Everything in his vision was faint, but he could still separate objects from each other. Colours were almost all gone, and his point of view seemed to constantly shift in height. The eyes of the tree were his.

In the middle of the clearing, young trees stood and grew. Around them, flowers flourished. Jacob felt an intense pang of nausea as his vision went black. The skin on his stomach felt like it was being ripped off. As shadows writhed all around him, his focus vanished. There was nothing but pain. Then wings. Terrible, mutilated black wings and curved claws. A dark creature. It cried out, piercing Jacob's ears, and he fell from the vision.

All at once, he fell backwards and vomited. Somehow, he managed to catch himself before his face struck the ground, but the impact rattled his shoulders enough to collapse them. Before he landed in his mess, he pivoted to his left side and rolled to his back, heaving. He expected nothing less, but all the vision did was weaken him and confirm the monster's existence. What good would that accomplish him?

I believe that was the scream you heard earlier.

"I . . . think so." Jacob gasped, attempting to rise. It felt worse than getting out of bed after an exhausting night, yet he managed to do it by leaning on a tree—a different tree—for support. He'd had enough of the one he connected with. Standing again, he looked upon the clearing and imagined the creature he'd seen. Nothing like that should be here. The age of darkness was over. Dreslen was gone. The gargoyle king was gone. Amiroth had dealt with the last of their machinations. So what was this?

Danger, the Voice said. *You have to leave. You're already out of time. Get back to Tonto and rest before you leave for Mortua. Others will find her, and if the Silencer does, I trust she'll protect herself.*

"That's what I'm worried about." Jacob looked to his left. He didn't know why, but he had a feeling about walking that way. Perhaps it was a last message from the tree.

I feel nothing. Go back home.

Tentatively, Jacob stepped forward. There had to be something there. All he had was a feeling, but its inexplicability made it credible enough.

There it was. He'd found what he was looking for, and it made him as sick as the tree. A man in a light-grey cloak lay motionless in the darkness. His face was gone.

The Silencer's face was gone.

THREE

⊷○⊶

"*Keep your head, fool!*"

Jacob staggered and looked away from the body. *Of all the times to lose my head, I'm justified here.* The Silencer was more than dead. Deep, bloody gashes occupied the place where his face used to be, exposing flesh and bone alike. His grey cloak was now torn and stained deep red in several locations. Jacob didn't want to know how much blood was on the ground. Perhaps he was stepping in it right now.

"*Calm yourself, for Amiroth's sake!*"

A Silencer was dead. Right in front of him. How long ago had this happened? Hours ago? Minutes? Was the monster still in the vicinity?

"I need to find Lindina." Jacob shuddered. He looked ahead, but saw only the image of the dead Silencer.

"*Find what's left of her, then,*" the Voice said. "*Or leave now and save yourself. The longer you stay here, the longer you have to be found by . . . it.*"

What was he to do? The Silencer, a man trained in every capacity, had been slaughtered and left to rot. The monster didn't even bother to use him for food—it killed for the sake of killing. If it encountered Jacob, he was better off already dead.

"*You cannot think, but I can!*" The Voice spun him around so that he could no longer look at the body. "*Listen to me, fool. Let me take charge.*"

"We both know what happens then," Jacob whispered. What choice did he have? The Voice would not allow him to regain his reason. It waited for moments like this, moments when Jacob had no other choice than to turn to it. To give it power over him. But Jacob was powerless now. What could he do?

"We must turn back home. There is nothing you can do."

"I have to find her."

"You have no reason to believe you can *find her!"*

"All I have is a fool's hope." Jacob looked up at the sky, searching for the moon. Straining against the trees, he found it low in the sky. North. The direction of home.

"Then you have proven my point. Come along! When has Lindina not come home of her own accord? You were all so rash to insist on looking for her when she would inevitably return. Run! Get out of these woods!"

Jacob swallowed hard and glanced down at the Silencer again. There was a chance that he would share the same fate if he remained . . . but the same was true of Lindina. Of everyone else still in the forest.

Foolish girl! Jacob thought, walking towards the moonlight. There was no place Lindina was more likely to be than any other. He would walk home, and if he found her, he would force her to return with him.

A branch snapped behind him. He froze. Turning around, he looked into the shadows of the trees for the source of the sound. It came from the direction Jacob had before he encountered the Silencer's body. Around the ruined clearing.

Oh Dreslen . . . The Voice saw it before Jacob did. A shadowy figure with one arm against a tree, standing still. It was too far away to make any distinctions in the darkness, but it didn't look quite right. The head was wider than it should have been, not shaped like a human's.

Jacob's heart caught in his throat. Though he faced a different direction than his feet did, he dared not move. *It's looking at me. It knows I'm here.*

And now it knows that you know.

What do I do? Help me, Voice!

That is not my name.

Help me!

All was quiet as he stood there, locked in thought, observing the object of his terror. But as his fear heightened, so did his breathing. In times like these, the Deep was prone to interfere. The wind, before docile, hastened, filling the area with its whispers and eerie wail. A glint of moonlight appeared in the eyes of the figure.

"What are . . ." Jacob's voice broke, and he could manage no more than a whisper. *Oh, help me!* If he did not speak, he could not know. He needed to know. "What are you?"

Without warning, the figure removed its hand from the tree, turned around, and ran.

Thank goodness for that, the Voice said.

But the wind did not die. Jacob's breathing did not lessen. His fear did not leave him. In fact, it heightened. What was this will of his? He needed to know what that figure was. Based on how it looked when it turned and fled, it was a human in a hooded cloak. But why was he, or she, running?

"Don't you dare!" the Voice spoke out loud. *"Fool! You fool!"*

It was too late. Jacob was already running with his full strength. The only thing that slowed him were the trees covered by darkness, but even they were of little hindrance. His fear provided two things: adrenaline and instinct. With those, he could dodge and correct his path while still maintaining a good pace. He knew this forest better than anyone; he could outrun this figure.

What in Amiroth's name are you doing? the Voice cried.

Silence. Jacob couldn't afford distractions. All he could turn his mind to were his emotions. Fear. He was in a forest with a brutal monster, chasing down someone who may or may not be friendly. Given that they were running away, they likely were not. But the unknown plagued Jacob. Part of what fueled his love for reading was his desire—his *need*—to understand the world. Here was a mystery that would haunt him forever if he turned away. He needed to know.

Even if you risk death?

Silence! Should he use the Deep to propel himself forward with the wind? Like connecting to the trees, guiding the wind required personal expense. To become one with the air, he had to give up his breath. While doing that, he could run for longer but would tire more easily. *No.* Though speed was essential, there were simply too many trees. *Pay no mind to the Deep.*

So he ran. The sounds of footsteps were still directly in front of him—all the more reason to calm the wind. If the fleer changed directions, Jacob needed to know. It wasn't long before the shadowy form came into view again, running without looking back. Once, it darted to the right, but Jacob was able to alter his course without difficulty, all while keeping his eyes fixed on the figure.

It wouldn't be long before Jacob overtook him. He'd mastered the skill of running through the forest long ago. Based on what he saw, the cloaked figure could not claim the same. Nevertheless, his speed was remarkable; it wouldn't be enough to escape Jacob, but it was enough to challenge him.

The runner stopped and vanished from sight. Jacob approached with caution, minimizing his breathing and bending his knees. The pursuit could resume at any point, and it could go in any direction. In this darkness, he could not distinguish the figure from the trees. Yet the figure disappeared near the large oak tree less than a stone's throw from him. It was big enough to completely hide his silhouette.

"I'm faster than you," Jacob said. Whether founded or not, his fear was abated. "If you run, I will catch you."

"And if you run," a voice whispered from behind Jacob, "I will kill you."

Jacob froze for a moment. When he made to move, a thin piece of cold metal pressed against his throat.

"Who are you?" the gruff voice said, bringing his hot breath far too close to Jacob's ear. "What are you doing here?"

His jaw trembled. There was a blade against his throat.

"Who are you?" the man shouted, removing the blade and grabbing Jacob's throat. Darkness shrouded his black-hooded face, but his voice was gnarled enough to leave an impression. "Tell me who you are, or I'll stick you and leave you to the wolves."

He pushed Jacob back against a tree and placed the point of his blade on Jacob's torso.

Don't tell them! the Voice said. *Lie!*

"Jairus." Jacob closed his eyes and winced. "My name is Jairus."

So, my name is still that near to you? the Voice said. *Perhaps I can have it back, then.*

"What are you looking for?" The man gripped Jacob's throat harder.

"Lindina!" Jacob gasped, coughing. He didn't have time to deal with the Voice. "A girl named Lindina!"

The man relinquished his grip but kept the sword where it was. Opening his eyes warily, Jacob saw another figure emerge from the shadow of the large tree, his hand within his black cloak.

"Tell me, Jairus," the man spoke slowly. "How many others are looking for this girl? Or are you alone?"

Hearing the Voice's old name spoken out loud again was as uncomfortable as the blade on his stomach. Why he answered with Jairus's name, he didn't know. Why he didn't trust these men with his real name, he didn't know. But they were willing to kill. How much truth dared he share with them?

"I am not alone," Jacob said, his hands quivering.

"How many others? Lie to me and you'll taste your own blood."

"Seventeen, not including me." What choice did he have?

The man swore and turned to his companion. "You ran from this fellow?"

The other man nodded, withdrawing his hand from his cloak.

"Why couldn't you outrun him?"

"I've never run through a forest before. None of us have, except maybe you."

The man with the sword turned to Jacob again. "Is everyone as fast as you?"

"No one." Jacob recalled the Silencer. "Not anymore."

"They'll be fine, then," the man said, probably to his companion. "What are you going to say when you return home, Jairus?" The blade pressed harder against Jacob's stomach.

"Nothing." Jacob breathed as shallowly as possible. "I didn't see either of you."

"Well, there's only one way to make sure of that."

Jacob closed his eyes and prepared himself.

"The problem is all the other people in the forest," he continued. "If they find you dead, they'll cause an uproar. Especially if it's done by blade. We'll have to kill you and make it look like an accident. Sound good to you?"

"Not at all."

"Perfect."

I'll help you escape, the Voice said. *Give me my name back, give me control, and we'll live through this. If you still resist me, you will die.*

Jacob grimaced. On his own strength, he was a dead man walking. But with Jairus's help, there was hope. Jairus could use the Deep in ways Jacob could not. Yet Jacob had locked him away for a reason. If he resurfaced in all his power and malice, Jacob may be better off dead. It was a question of whether Jacob could control Jairus after he set him loose. Could he? Or would he be forced to relive that day . . . the one that never happened.

I can save you.

But what will you do after that?

"Get moving," his captor removed his sword from Jacob, instead grabbing his wrist. The skin on his hand was so calloused it may have been a different material altogether.

Ask their names, the Voice said, *and give me mine.*

I will not. The Voice was a shadow of what it used to be, its full strength locked away deep in the vaults of his subconscious. If Jacob resurfaced the name, all he did to contain Jairus's power would be undone. No, giving the Voice his name back was not an option.

"Who are you?" Jacob turned his thoughts to his captor. Only now was it fully setting in. He was going to die. He would not make the journey to Mortua to become a librarian. All his life led up to this moment. It would end within the hour.

"Captain Hazak," he said.

"Captain!" his companion whispered. "This man is not dead. He might escape!"

"If all you're going to do is reprimand me, I suggest you shut your hole. Know your place, Sorias."

This captain is arrogant beyond compare. The Voice laughed internally. *He tells us both their names as well as his own position.*

What good does that do me? Jacob had to pivot his entire body to avoid walking into a tree, but that made Hazak grip all the harder. He grimaced.

"Let's say you were running," Hazak said. "You went too fast, tripped, and bashed your head open on a rock. That sound good to you, Jairus?"

Try it, fool, the Voice said.

He was talking to me. Jacob looked his captor in the eyes. There was a laughter there, though no mirth on his lips. The hideous, grim laughter of a sadist. The kind the Voice was prone to.

"I assume you'll be the one doing the bashing?" Jacob said.

"If you're alright with that."

"*Oh, do your worst,*" Jairus said.

Not yet! Jacob pushed Jairus back down to the subconscious. Though he didn't admit it to himself, he knew what was going to happen. Once Jairus started to emerge, chances were good that he would completely take over Jacob in a matter of moments. Until then, they shared consciousness.

Hazak squinted at him. Finally, the smile showed up on his face. "Getting bold, are we? I'd be more careful if I were you. Doing my worst would be a pleasure. It's been a while."

"Captain," the man called Sorias whispered, drawing close alongside them. "Are you sure this is the best course of action?"

"Shut it," Hazak said. "If you don't like it, then get back to work. The sooner we find it, the sooner we can get home."

"*Find what?*" Jairus said. Jacob winced. Perhaps his fear was becoming too strong.

"Don't you dare tell him," Sorias said. "Do it, and I'll have Baltashazar know."

"Maybe I should kill you too," Hazak muttered.

They walked in silence. Sorias did not depart, despite Hazak's orders, and Jacob found himself cursing every story he'd ever read. Normal people didn't read stories like they ate meals, and normal people didn't get captured and killed by mercenaries—or whatever these men were. Who was it Sorias mentioned? Baltashazar? Someone from Barabus, no doubt, with a name like that. Why did Jairus care so much?

So I have returned, Jairus said. *You will let me kill them?*

No. Jacob regretted his decision more every second. *You are to disable them. Leave them alive.*

I cannot guarantee that. Jairus smiled. *You know me.*

"Remember Dreslen," Jacob breathed silently. This was a horrid idea, but it was the only way out. Jairus had the potential to kill these men if he used the Deep. Would he carry it through? Jacob could only hope that his own will was stronger than Jairus's.

Hazak stopped. "Sorias, hold your sword against this fellow's neck, would you?"

Sorias cursed, withdrawing a short sword from the inside of his cloak and bringing it to Jacob's throat. Hazak released his grip on Jacob's wrist.

"Here's a nice rock." Hazak bent down and rose with a large round stone in his hand. His eyes bore same glint of malice, but the smile was gone. "You want it?"

"Keep your rock," Jairus said, twitching his fingers. Control was his. Already, he could feel the currents running through him. They would both die. The fool with the sword was too cowardly to use it, so he could be dealt with after, and the fool with the rock was too arrogant to attack at a moment's notice.

"What do you think, Sorias?" Hazak turned the rock over in both his hands, stepping closer. "Should I throw it or strike him with it?"

"I'm standing right next to him!" Sorias said. "With your aim, I'd be better off jumping from a building."

"Alright then." Hazak gripped the rock in one hand. "Striking it is."

"Oh, you're right about that," Jairus muttered. Both men turned to him as if he'd just shown up. He smiled. *"Tell me one last thing, fool. What are you looking for?"*

Hazak grinned, taking a quick glance at Sorias. "Nothing you'll be concerned with in a few moments."

"Do not be so sure." Jairus clenched his hands into fists. The time was near. He needed all the energy he could get. The wind was silent. The trees watched. Did the Deep know of what would transpire? How far did the eyes of the Deep pry? Through stone and air without a doubt, but also of time and mind?

The moment Hazak raised his arm, Jairus pointed his right hand at him and grabbed Sorias's wrist with the other. As predicted, Sorias was too hesitant to slit his throat. Lightning channeled from the Deep through his hands, and he felt once again his old power. Bolts of blue light stemmed from his fingertips, freezing both Hazak and Sorias in tremors. Jairus laughed and let go of Sorias, but kept the lightning trained on him. How long had it been since he'd last done this? Since Jacob sealed him away? Too long, it would seem. Already he was losing energy.

He stopped with a cry and stood shaking. His enemies dropped their weapons and collapsed to the ground, convulsing. *"Fools!"* Jairus yelled. He didn't care if anyone else heard him. If they came, he would kill them too. *"To be so arrogant as to tell me your names. Such stupidity!"* He walked forward and kicked Hazak in the face. The man groaned. *"Now I'll kill you the way you would have killed me."*

Jairus bent down to pick up the rock Hazak dropped, but the moment he made to rise, a force came from behind him and knocked him to the ground. His hands hit the earth first, but he hadn't the energy to stop the rest of his body from colliding. As he tried to get up, he felt a hard impact in his stomach. He collapsed, winded. In the distance, a bell tolled.

In front of him, he saw Hazak getting to his feet. *This cannot be!* How could he have underestimated them? He was superior! Yet his face pressed helplessly against the cold grass and dirt. In a few moments, he would have regained his energy, but in a few moments, he would be dead.

Is that it? Jacob thought.

You will now taste death . . . fool. Jairus relinquished his grasp on Jacob's consciousness and fell beneath the surface. Only Jacob remained.

"Wait!" Jacob strained his voice. What was the point? "I can help you!"

"It's too late for that." Hazak's voice sounded equally hoarse.

"You've . . . received your warning." Jacob propped himself up with shaking arms and got to his knees. To his surprise, he was not knocked down. "I can see you. If you make another movement, I'll not show mercy this time." Jacob did not in fact see them, nor was he in a position to show mercy.

The bell tolled again. Where was it coming from?

Before he could consider any further, something hard hit his head. Everything, even his thoughts, went numb. Above him, m-uffled voices shouted incomprehensibly. There was no pain yet, but it would begin soon. He knew that much.

As he regained feeling, his head throbbed, feeling twice as heavy as before, yet his whole body felt lighter than air. Sickness filled his gut. All the while, men shouted and the bell tolled. Pain. Nothing but pain and chaos. It was the end he feared—the end Jairus promised wouldn't come. Death.

The bell kept getting louder. Deeper, higher. Pounding against his skull in tandem with his throbs. At first worsening the pain, but after a few moments subsiding it. He was numb again—or was he? He could hear clearly now. He could feel the grass beneath his body and the wind flying across his face. The pain was gone, but his head still throbbed, remaining in time with the bell. His entire body pulsed at the same speed.

Get up! Jairus was back, and with him all the energy he lost.

Jacob got to his feet without effort, looking at the two men who now stared at him with wide eyes. Hazak put his hand to his sword hilt, but Sorias remained frozen.

The wind picked up even more, circling around Jacob and howling like a lone wolf. Hazak and Sorias staggered, Sorias nearly dropping his weapon. All Jacob could do was watch. This was not of his own doing.

The bell tolled anew with a different tone, and fire sprang up all around Jacob. Yet even he was frozen in shock and could not force himself to move. The flames ascended the trees and lit up the night, blowing along the course of the wind and casting a red glow about the area. The sudden emergence of light should have blinded Jacob, but he saw without issue. Sorias fled, dropping his sword before the flaming winds could carry him away.

Hazak yelled and stared Jacob down, planting his feet in the ground and letting the fire catch his own cloak. The bell rang again, and the ground shook. Hazak, screaming, fell to the ground. Jacob felt everything at once. Fear, wonder, relief, pity. He could see everything, accessing the vision of each of the trees. Beyond the flames, Sorias cast off his cloak and watched in terror. Amid the flames, Hazak tried to get to his feet, but the trembling ground chained him.

The bell struck a final time, and this time Jacob felt pain. Lightning struck every tree around him at once with a deafening crash, filling his vision with nothing but light. The bell resonated on. He couldn't tell whether he was silently standing or screaming on his knees.

As the light faded, so did his thoughts. The last thing he saw was a man in green robes with gold embroideries depicting trees. He was old, with a small white moustache and beard, his hair sparse and frayed. His hazel eyes locked with Jacob's.

Then all fell to darkness.

FOUR

"**S**ometimes, I truly wonder why you were permitted into this profession in the first place."

"Same reason as any of you. I've done the work and study. The only difference is that I've studied philosophy as well."

Adriel leaned back in her chair and smiled as the conversation carried on around her. The entire throne hall was filled with a slew of voices from other tables, but those at her table, the doctors, knew how to raise their voices above the din without shouting. It had been a good while since the king had hosted a banquet at the castle, and exactly a year since there had been one of this scale. The War's End festival was a holiday for the entire people, but the upper class, such as herself, were privy to more elegant celebration than mere street games and raucous dancing.

For the first time in a while, she was enjoying herself. A surprise, considering she sat at the same table as Doctor Harold.

"You don't think we've all studied it?" Harold said, scoffing and looking around the table. His eyes rested on Adriel for a moment. "Well, perhaps not *all* of us."

"I should say not." Adriel kept her smile. As long as she assumed everything was simply for humour, the night would pass without tension. "But for some of us, it's better to live life than to study it."

"Oh, but studying *enriches* living."

"Yes, but look what happened to poor Dredding." She nodded in Dredding's direction, to which he raised an eyebrow. "Completely lost sight of what's important by dwelling on all the really insignificant details—not to mention his philosophy on pain."

"I think you've hurt him," Harold said, looking at Dredding. "But you enjoy that, don't you?"

"Far from it."

Dredding was the only one at the table not smiling. Really, they shouldn't be joking about him. A black scar from fairly recent events marred his face, but that was nothing compared to the emotional agony he had been forced to endure. Still, he refused help from anyone. Pain, he said, was like medicine. It healed the soul of immoral infections before they became fatal. Adriel didn't have a problem with that view on its own, but when he implemented it on his patients, she couldn't stand for it.

"You're all blind, you know," Dredding said, crossing his arms and looking down at his plate, now empty. "No perspective but your own. So much potential for light so needlessly wasted."

"To you as well." Harold raised his silver goblet to Dredding before bringing it to his lips and taking a drawn-out sip of wine.

Adriel leaned back, the smile gone from her face, and watched on as Harold laughed at a joke from across the table. She did not hate him, and yet . . . he was so infuriatingly arrogant. Whether he was truly the best doctor in the city, she did not know, but she had suspected that he only got the position of royal doctor because of his bravado. The job could easily have been hers, if only she had her wits about her a year ago. She only had Sorias to blame for that. But regardless of who was better, it was undisputed among the table—except for perhaps Dredding—that Adriel and Harold were the best doctors in the city. Where there was likeness, there was rivalry.

Sighing, she turned her head from the vain laughter and looked around the throne room of Castle Dreslen, at the heart of Barabus. Everywhere, she saw the same dark-grey, nearly black, stone. It was the substance of the entire city, and it was the material of the floor, the ceiling, and the massive pillars that supported it. On the ceiling were glass and metal chandeliers that bore no light yet reflected the glow of the torches fastened to the pillars. Dying light streamed through the unreachable upper windows, heralding the end of a long day and the dawn of night. The countless people in this hall didn't seem to pay any regard to the festival's end, instead carrying on in laughter and conversation as if it would last forever. Perhaps it would.

"What's the matter, Adriel?" Harold looked at her. His mouth was solemn, but she saw the raging mirth in his eyes.

"Leave Dredding alone for a few moments, will you?" Adriel took a sip of wine, refusing to look back.

"You're the one who brought him up."

"And I'll be the one who shuts this all down."

Harold smiled again, and Adriel reconsidered her previous thought. Maybe she *did* hate him. He had as much hubris as the worst of young men, despite being over fifty years old, and never apologized for it. One day, he was going to be the death of a patient.

"Thank you for sharing in my misery, Adriel," Dredding said. His eyes were sullen, but his mouth bore a faint smile.

"You're welcome, I suppose." Adriel tried to detach her mind from the table again, but could think of nothing but treachery if she did so; treachery against her, guarded by memory. No, she would not go there. Sorias held too firm a grasp on her mind as it was.

Minutes passed, and the tension lowered. None spoke any more of Dredding, who sat back and sipped water in silence. Conversation turned to political matters, mostly pertaining to the Silencers and Midor's control of their economy. It was the dullest thing imaginable for Adriel, but it was better than making fun of one of their own. To this day, she could not understand the minds of her peers. They lived in such a professional and strict field, yet displayed such immaturity whenever possible. At least they were honest about their true selves, which was more than most could claim. For that, she appreciated them. No lies, no masks. Only the blunt, bitter truth.

A hand on her shoulder made Adriel's head spin around, bringing into view a woman with braided brown hair. She wore a silver tiara with an emerald pressed into it, and her dress was black with silver embroideries. "Sorry," she laughed. "I didn't mean to startle."

"Not at all!" Adriel rose from her chair to embrace her friend. Syndria was taller than her by almost half a head, but that wasn't saying much. Since childhood, they had been like close cousins, and even when Syndria married the king a few years ago, their friendship had not faltered.

"How are we enjoying ourselves today?" King Baraz strode alongside Syndria and looked upon the crew of doctors. His hair was shorter than Adriel remembered it, falling only a little past his head. As was the custom for significant events, he wore his black uniform with gold buttons and a purple cape, armed with a longsword strapped to his left hip.

"Wonderfully, Your Majesty." Harold raised his goblet.

"Glad to hear it." The king smiled and nodded, regarding each of the doctors. Even Dredding lifted his eyes to toast to his king, forcing a smile. Finally, Baraz looked at Adriel. "I trust things are going well with you? No encounters?"

"Only one." Adriel took her seat again, sighing. "Really, it doesn't even trouble me much anymore. I don't know why you bother."

"Oh, it's no inconvenience at all. It makes no difference to me whether he patrols the south end or the east. I understand betrayals hurt, and I want to do everything I can to help."

"Thank you, really." Adriel took a small sip of wine and held onto her goblet. "I'm sure I'll completely heal, I just . . . I don't know when. Or if ever."

"Such is the curse of life," Dredding said. All eyes turned to him, and he shifted his position. "My apologies."

"No need," Adriel said, setting down her drink and biting her lip.

"Or . . ." Syndria put her hand on Adriel's shoulder again. "Perhaps your pain *will* die soon. You mustn't let go of hope."

"And neither should you hold—never mind." Dredding shook his head. "It would appear as though my advice is not sought after."

King Baraz opened his mouth to answer, but he stopped before any sound could escape. His eyes shifted behind Adriel, narrowing with each second as a low groan sounded throughout the great hall. Turning her head, Adriel matched his gaze and looked upon the great metal doors. Towering higher than most two-story buildings, they turned inward and clanged like a hammer on a giant anvil. Strange. The door was supposed to remain closed until the banquet's end.

"Is there a problem?" a doctor asked.

"We'll see." Baraz's eyes rested on the door for a moment longer before blinking rapidly and turning again to the table of doctors. He smiled. "Well, I have a few more tables to check in on before the day's end. Keep enjoying yourselves!"

"And you as well." Adriel raised her glass, joined by the entire table. As she drank and the king and queen made motion to depart, a short man in armour shot past a nearby table and stopped near Baraz. A shadow covered his eyes as he cast a fleeting glance all around him. Fortunately, or perhaps unfortunately, he stood adjacent to Adriel's chair. She heard every whisper as if it were at full volume.

"He's back."

"Pardon?" Baraz leaned in closer, and Adriel turned her back to them.

"Your kin. He's returned."

"Baltashazar? Now?"

"He's waiting at the entrance to speak to you in private."

Adriel looked around the faces at her table. They, like her, wore masks of disinterest and ignorance. It wasn't their business, nor would it affect them much, but this was intriguing. Baltashazar, Baraz's cousin and the lord of the guard, was rumoured to have gone missing over a month ago. Some said he was arrested by the Silencers for crimes unnamed, but in truth no one knew the reason for his departure.

Baraz said nothing, instead walking away with his cape fluttering behind him. Syndria remained standing next to Adriel. "Don't pay any regard to this." She looked at each of the doctors in turn with a frown. Adriel wasn't sure, but there may have been some panic in her eyes. "You heard nothing."

"We heard nothing." Adriel tried to give her a comforting look, but Syndria's eyes were already turned and her feet in motion towards her departing husband. Her poise and posture were gone, replaced with uneven steps and a slightly craned neck. Rather than guess why Baltashazar's return had such an impact on her friend, Adriel turned back to the table and looked around uncertainly. She couldn't shake the worry.

"What were we saying?" Harold cleared his throat and took a sip.

"Nothing of importance." Adriel tried to do likewise, but couldn't bring the goblet to her mouth. Something was wrong, though she didn't know what.

"Remember what the queen told you, Adriel." Dredding looked at her with unmoving eyes. "You heard nothing."

"Right."

"So drop it."

"I know." Adriel had a feeling that Dredding's warning wasn't solely for her. The group sat in near silence and watched as the banquet came to its end without the usual speech from the king.

Something was definitely wrong.

FIVE

Jacob woke up running. The realization hit him like a slap in the face. Once he understood what was happening, he cried out and put his arms out in front of him to avoid a full collision with a tree. *How is this happening?* When no impact ensued, he hastened his vision and took a good look around him. There were no trees around at all, just grass beneath his shoes and the night sky above his head. In the distance, to his right, a forest sprawled. Where was he?

It took him a few moments to gain control of his body enough to stop completely. When he did, he found he was hardly winded. Not only that, but his legs were far from sore.

Jairus? Jacob looked behind him. To his dismay, he saw what was most likely the South Midorian Forest in the distance. It was even further than the forest on his right, which he now assumed to be the East Midorian Forest. *Jairus, is this you?*

It is not, I assure you.

Jacob could feel Jairus's confusion, though he said nothing of it. No, Jairus was not lying. He may have returned to his former strength, yet something like this was beyond even him. But if not Jairus, then what? What could possess him to run away from the forest? Stranger still, why east? Home was hours away at this point.

"East . . ." Jacob turned his vision to the east horizon again. Understanding entered him as nausea. There were no Midorian settlements east of this point. If he continued, he would pass beyond Midor's border and enter the Atlantian reserves, a land where no one could legally dwell. Past the reserves was the border of Atlantia itself—beyond which was the territory of the Sirathim, followers of the Deep that Amiroth exiled centuries ago.

The Deep was not only calling Jacob; it was pulling him against his will.

He staggered, clutching his arms together, and recalled the moments before he went unconscious. Captain Hazak burning on the ground from the fire that erupted around them. A fierce whirlwind. Lightning striking down all the trees around him. A vision of an old man in a green robe. All summoned by the tolling of a bell. Jacob did nothing to bring about any of that. Did the Deep rescue him? So it would seem. All to unite Jacob to the followers of the Deep.

"I do not follow you," Jacob whispered into the night. The title of Wayfollower, given to all who possessed a connection to the Deep, was unfitting. In fact, were it not for his rescue from Hazak, he would hate the Deep. All it did was set him apart as dangerous. It robbed him of peace and gave him power instead.

Wind gusted around Jacob. He scowled at it. "Is it not enough for you to take my peace? Must you also take my home and life? It's because of *your power* that Dreslen nearly enslaved Atlantia. The world is scarred because of you. Leave us to heal. Leave me!"

Whether it really was the Deep guiding him, he wasn't certain. He didn't know much about the Deep at all. Could the Deep think and act, or was it merely a well of sorcerous power? Either way, it was dangerous, and it was destroying his life.

As he was about to turn around and start walking back home, a thought overtook him. What of Lindina? He couldn't figure out why, but it felt as though Lindina was out here, east of the forest, as well.

"Foolish notion," Jairus said. *"Lindina is most likely back home by now. You should return in time to leave for Mortua."*

"Wait," Jacob said. "Were you conscious for longer than I was?" It wouldn't be the first time.

"I went dark sooner than you did."

"Let's hear the truth." The one positive thing about Jairus sharing Jacob's brain was that he could almost always tell when he was lying. Their thoughts had the same roots.

"The truth is that you need to rush home," Jairus said. *"Otherwise, you will not make it to Mortua in time. We wouldn't want to jeopardize your future, would we?"*

"I'm right, aren't I?" Jacob looked around the moonlit field. He probably wasn't too far from the road leading south to Barabus. In all likelihood, he'd already passed it. Lindina couldn't have gone to Barabus, could she?

"Right about what?"

"Lindina's not in the forest anymore. She's out here somewhere."

"Why in Atlantia would you think that?"

"Because I can feel you thinking about it."

"Listen, fool," Jairus said. *"I didn't bring us out here. But if you won't get your head together, I will bring us back."*

"What did you see?"

"What?"

"After I went unconscious. What did you see?"

"I saw only—"

Jacob clamped his mouth shut, closing his eyes and focusing on Jairus's blurred thoughts. The more Jairus thought about hiding them, the more Jacob saw. Memories entered his head as if they were his own. Images from the eyes of the trees—only these weren't inside the forest. He remembered looking outward from the edge of the forest, eastward, at a young girl. She ran away, her head tilted up towards the sky.

"Yes, it's unmistakably Lindina!" Jairus said. *"But you cannot go after her. If she wants to abandon Atlantia and join the Sirathim, there's nothing you can do about that."*

"But—"

"Jacob, if you go after her, you forfeit everything! You know how competitive the library is. This is your one chance. They won't offer the position a second time."

Jacob put his hands to his head, exhaling. The wind was still, but the chills of night were at their peak. Even so, he could not shiver. Instead, he paced, sweating.

"You know what you have to—"

"Do I?" Jacob shouted. As far as he could tell, there was no one in the area. "If I want to serve myself, I know what I have to do. If I want to help Lindina and everyone who cares about her, I know what I have to do."

He knew the choice he ought to make. Yet why was the decision so difficult? He never considered himself to be selfish. But then again, he'd never been in any position like this before.

She's made her choice, Jairus thought, now trying to sound sympathetic for a change. *Yours is yet before you. You can leave Lindina to her own decisions and feel no guilt. You are not responsible for her.*

Jacob closed his eyes and exhaled. *Guilt.* Memories trickled back. Fire. Smoke . . .

No, he didn't remember that day. It never happened. His sister was alive, and her name was Lindina. He *would* save her.

"Nothing you do now can absolve—"

"I'm going to rescue Lindina!"

After a sharp inhale, he set out running. This time, he would conserve his energy. There was no telling how far away she was by now, so he needed to cover as much ground as possible. Still, the sooner he got home, the better. Perhaps there was still hope for becoming a librarian. But in order for that to happen, he had to listen to Jairus—he had to draw power from the Deep.

Not to run away *from home!*

Jacob prepared himself to direct the wind. Taxing his lungs would be worth it if he found Lindina. He found it strange that minutes earlier he was yelling in anger at the Deep, yet now he would use it once again. If his mind was really that erratic, his decision to go after Lindina may not be a one-time event—especially with Jairus plaguing him.

In. Jacob took a long breath, slowing his pace. Then, closing his eyes, he concentrated on the cold air around him. *Out.* He emptied his breath into the air and willed it forward. It had been a while since he last did this, but the wind responded without delay. It blew at his back with sudden intensity, forcing him to quicken his feet. Were he to stop, it would probably knock him over.

As much as he could, Jacob tried not to enjoy the thrilling speed. Joy led to attachment, which led to dependency, which could very well lead to corruption. If he was going to use the Deep, he needed to remind himself of the truth often. He would remember Dreslen every minute of this journey.

I'm coming, Lindina. He would not let her fall prey to the Deep. As long as his lungs had breath, as long as his legs had strength, he would not give up on her. She may not have Jairus to help her, but she had Jacob. *I'm coming.*

SIX

"Thus, the downfall of the Sirathim was accomplished, and the dark fate of the world sealed in the eyes of all who witnessed. Shadow wrapped around Mordecai's men, who were slain by the hands of Dreslen—by dravelords, by gargoyles, and by Dreslites. No honour was given for the valour of their past days, for a darkness lied heavy upon their hearts, so that they did not resist the enemy. The names of those who fell are forgotten, for in the end, their presence in the duel meant nothing but tragedy. To inscribe their names would be to humour the spirit of Dreslen, to give him the victory he so viciously desired."

Adriel lowered the book into her lap and ceased her whispers. Darkness and silence enveloped her but for the candle that glowed at her side. Her old allies. Even still, they haunted her with memories uncorrected by the light of reality. In shadow, there was calm and foreboding.

A soldier sat next to her, his gaze hollow. "Leave me," Adriel said. Alas, he was already gone, never with her to begin with. An illusion of company to one in most need of it.

"Treachery." Her whisper made barely a sound as she placed a mark inside her book and set it next to the candle, above her father's book of poetry—she dared not read it. There must have been something wrong with her, for no sane person would be troubled by the harrowing days of years past. Only in the dark silence, where she once found comfort, did the memories approach her again. For this, she kept the candlelight, lest despair overtake her once more.

She had no doubt that in the morning all this trouble would fade into the sunrise. It always did. Each day presented its own problems and patients, with joys and sorrows alike. It was her duty to attend to the matters of the present. In truth, although she grieved, these days were happier than the ones past. There was nothing to hinder her from becoming the doctor she had always dreamed of becoming. The walls that she dreaded were now broken, and the world was ahead of her.

In her mind, stone was struck. Metal on stone from below. The sound of her door being knocked. Who might it be? A sufferer desperate for healing? A friend forgotten, a beguiler of the truth? The perished walking to bring aid to their daughter? Yet she would not reach out and grant entry to those worries. Tonight, she needed peace.

The knock came again, forcing Adriel's eyes open. How long had she been in a state of slumber? The book still sat beside her, but the candle dimmed. The knock was real. Rapid. Urgent.

Releasing a long, shallow breath, Adriel rose from her padded chair and staggered, reaching out for a support that wasn't there. The last light of the candle faded, leaving her in total darkness. As drowsy as her mind was now, she couldn't tell whether she had fallen or remained standing. But when she moved her arm forward again and the surrounding air moved, she knew.

With a step forward, she groped along the smooth stone wall for the rod that controlled the blinds for the window. When it brushed against her wrist, she took hold and pulled, opening the way for a stream of starlight to wash into her room. The moon was behind her, for the night was old, and it had crossed into the southern sky.

On the other side of the window was a balcony overlooking her lawn. If she wanted, she could walk out onto it, lean over the banister, and see who was at her door. Even so, she would likely still be obligated to walk downstairs and open it anyway.

"Just a moment," Adriel muttered as the knocking sounded again. Her mouth was dry and her throat sore. All she wanted was rest. Nevertheless, she walked across the palely lit stone room to the top of the staircase, put her hand on the stone rail, and descended into further darkness. She was used to it now, of course. Living in the same house for two years without proper lighting equipped her with an intrinsic knowledge of the layout.

After the tenth step came the ground floor, and in front of her was the main living area with a round table in the middle, a couch, and a few chairs. One of the front window's shutters was open, allowing dim light to show the way to the door.

The knocking grew louder. Adriel almost tripped over her nightdress in her haste to reach the door, but when her hand closed around the handle, she stopped everything. A long breath. She closed her eyes.

"Who is it?"

"It's me!" Syndria's voice, though muffled by the stone door, was unmistakable. Adriel wasted no time in undoing the latch. As soon as she put her hand to the doorknob, the door swung inward, nearly hitting her in the face.

Adriel backed off and raised her hands. "What are you—"

"Shh!" Syndria jumped into the entryway and closed the door as quickly as she opened it, careful to make little noise. "There may be someone—or more—following me." She brushed the stray hairs away from her face and looked at Adriel in the near darkness, panting.

Strange. Adriel noticed Syndria was wearing a nightdress as well. Syndria's was finer, of course, being royalty. Light silver material as opposed to her green fabric—but that was beside the point. Why hadn't she changed out of it to leave the castle?

"Who?" Adriel put down her hands and tilted her head. "Who's following you?"

"Give me a moment." Syndria sat down on the chair next to the door, breathing heavily. No eye contact. No movement.

"You heard that Baltashazar is back." Syndria didn't look up.

"Yes . . ." Adriel remembered the night of the feast. After Baraz left the banquet to investigate the news about Baltashazar, he hadn't returned all night. As much as she tried to put it out of her mind, she couldn't. Everyone knew that something was off, but there hadn't been a good chance to revisit the castle to check whether Baraz had returned since then. *He can't still be missing, can he?*

"On the night of the banquet, Baraz followed that guard to go meet with Baltashazar," Syndria said under her breath. "I wasn't allowed to follow. Turns out I should have disobeyed that order."

"Baraz was ordering you?"

"No, the guard was. But Baraz didn't object, even though I did."

"Why didn't you insist?"

"I don't know. I guess I trusted Baraz so much that I forgot how much I didn't trust Baltashazar."

"What did Baltashazar do?"

Syndria sniffed. "He talked to Baraz in an alley, apparently. The next I saw Baraz was the following morning. He was sitting in his armchair in our room, looking more worried than ever. He'd told Baltashazar that he could live in the castle again."

"Why in Atlantia would he do that?"

"Baraz said he wanted to keep an eye on him, but I think the real reason is that he couldn't bear to turn him away. All his other family is dead from the Plague. His cousin is the only one left."

Adriel remembered the White Plague all too well. It hadn't infected her, but for the pain it caused her, it may as well have. She couldn't imagine how Baraz felt. Aside from Baltashazar, his older cousin by over thirty years, Baraz was the only one left of the Barabian royal household. If he and Syndria didn't have any children before they died—and it was looking unlikely—only the Deep knew what would happen to the throne.

"I hated seeing Baltashazar walking around the castle." Syndria's voice quavered. "Do you remember that shadow that always lurked in his eyes?"

Adriel nodded.

"It wasn't just in his eyes anymore. It was everywhere around him. Once, he smiled at me when he saw me across the hallway, and I felt my insides go cold. I don't think I'd ever been more terrified than in that moment."

"Is that why you came here?"

"No!" Syndria wiped her nose with her sleeve. "I . . ." She broke into quiet sobs.

Adriel watched in silence and felt her own jaw quiver. No one had ever been a better friend to her than Syndria. It broke her heart to see her suffer like this. If she was in physical pain, Adriel could amend that. If she was sick, she could treat it. She had no medicine for this. All she could do was share in her misery until Syndria finally told her of it.

"Baraz . . ." Syndria's cries grew louder. "My beloved!"

A tear fell from Adriel's eye, resting on her chin. "What's happened?" she whispered.

Syndria put her face into her hands and wailed, muffling her voice. For a few seconds, she did no more. Even in this low light, Adriel could see her body heaving with each cry.

Adriel's resolve broke, and she too cried. "What?"

"My Baraz is dead!"

Syndria's sobs worsened, and all Adriel could do was stand in a state of laboured breathing. *How? How could Baraz be dead?* No, Syndria must be mistaken. She had to be. She must be mistaken!

"How?" Adriel asked, her voice hardly a whisper.

"Baltashazar threw him off a tower, that's how!" Syndria stood up and sniffed through her ragged breaths. "Why didn't he listen? Why didn't Baraz *listen to me?*"

"Syndria . . ." Adriel didn't know what to say. What was there to say? Her best friend's husband had been murdered by his insane cousin . . . who now had a claim to the throne. Although Syndria was queen, it was only through marriage. She wasn't born in Barabus, which meant she couldn't rule on her own. In order for her to have any claim to the crown, she needed to be wedded to a true Barabian.

"Now he's gone!" Syndria said. "He told me he'd protect me no matter what happened."

"I'll protect you." Adriel took Syndria's hands and gripped them tight. "I don't know how, but I'll fight to my last breath to make sure . . ." To make sure what? That she wasn't brutally murdered like her husband? Saying that would be far from comforting.

"What's the point?" Syndria withdrew one of her arms to wipe her nose. "Why should I live now? Baraz is dead, and . . . and Baltashazar is . . . king." Her crying gave way to stunned breaths.

"I don't know how you'll keep going after this," Adriel said. Honesty, as difficult as it was to hear, would do more good than comforting lies. "But I know you. You've faced so much. Somehow, you'll find a reason to keep going forward."

"I've never faced anything like this. And you haven't either, so don't tell me you know what I'm going through!"

Adriel let go of Syndria's hand and hardened her face before remembering the depths of Syndria's pain. "You're right. I don't know exactly what you're going through. I can't imagine how terrifying it must be." She stepped forward and embraced her friend. Although she was covered in sweat and shaking, Adriel held her tighter still. "It's alright—"

"It's not!" Syndria tried to break away.

Adriel wouldn't let her go. "It's alright to be afraid."

Syndria finally yielded and let Adriel embrace her. She shuddered, letting tears fall onto Adriel's shoulders. "I'm lost . . . I'm so broken. If only I could have convinced Baraz to turn away Baltashazar, I could have—"

"Stop," Adriel said. "You couldn't have known anything like this would happen. What you did was right."

"And what was that? Standing helplessly on the castle grounds while I watched my husband's body get thrown off a tower and carried away by a dravelord?"

"A what?" Adriel must have misheard.

Syndria gave no reply.

"I don't know what you learned growing up in Collabria, but there are no more dravelords."

"I saw it. It's real. The point is, Baltashazar is so hideously evil, and I knew it and said nothing!"

"It's not your fault."

"It is! And even if it isn't, I could have stopped it."

This wasn't doing any good. Nothing Adriel said would convince her otherwise when she was in this state. "You need rest." She drew back from Syndria and looked her in the eyes. Syndria didn't look back. "I know you don't feel like it," Adriel said, "but we can't do anything about it right now. In the morning, we'll discuss everything."

"I can't." Syndria looked up at Adriel. "You sleep. I'll watch the windows."

Adriel sighed. "Do you trust me?"

"I don't know anymore."

"Then trust me again. You can sleep in whichever room you want. I'll keep watch at the window for you."

"I—"

"If you can't trust me as a friend, then trust me as a doctor. You need sleep. That's an order."

After a few moments of hesitation, Syndria nodded. Adriel embraced her once more before taking her hand and guiding her up the stairs to the guest bedroom. After the door was shut, Adriel looked around the darkness and walked away. Only when she was sure that Syndria was out of earshot did she cry again. Why did she have to live through so much pain? Why was everyone she loved taken from her?

"I can't do this," she said between breaths, taking her seat at the couch by the front window. Everything was cold, dark, and silent but for her quiet sobs. There was no one to help her anymore. The only people in all Atlantia who she could trust were either dead or broken. Who could heal her now?

Syndria couldn't have known how much her words hurt. To say that Adriel didn't understand disregarded all the pain Adriel had endured. Loss. Betrayal. Helplessness. Even now, Syndria could not possibly be suffering as much as Adriel had. But Adriel would help Syndria, no matter how much it hurt her. No matter how many times Syndria said she didn't trust her. They both needed healing, and Adriel would see to it that Syndria got hers.

It's going to be a long night. Adriel shuddered and looked out the window. All was still in the dark streets of Barabus. No guards running to her door, no extinct monsters flying in the air. Not yet, at least.

SEVEN

The moon waned, shimmering pale light onto the green grass beneath Jacob's feet. Pine needles cast silver reflections of the moon, creating the illusion of stars dancing within the trees. There was no fog to break the clear night, no clouds to shield Jacob from the vast ranks of stars. Jewels of pure light set in utter darkness, a reminder that hope inhabited even the blackest corners of the world.

Now, more than any time in his life, Jacob needed hope. It was all he had. Even the hopes he used to carry were now gone. Dreams of becoming a high-ranking librarian? Dashed. The possibility of finding Lindina soon? Already failed. He'd been running after her for an entire day with no sign of her. He was exhausted, famished, and finding fewer reasons by the hour to keep moving. If Lindina really came this way, shouldn't he have overtaken her by now? She was a child, an unathletic one too. There was no good reason Jacob couldn't catch up.

Running with the wind's aid, or windsprinting as he now called it, hadn't taken the toll he first thought it would. Still, with the little energy he now had, all he could do was walk. He'd woken up from his last rest with sore legs, his mouth was dry and pasty, and his stomach felt worse than hollow.

Continuing his walk, he emerged past the scattered tree line of the bush. He was in the open plain, the land set apart for future expansion, beautiful and untouched. There were no cities, not even a village to cast obtrusive light and sound into the already perfect night. Whatever men built, even the Sirathim, was not worth comparing to the splendor of nature itself, fashioned by a force more powerful and wonderful than he could comprehend.

For once in his life, all was quiet. True, the crickets still chirped, and the grass rustled slightly, but the silence was greater than any night prior. The Voice was gone, and that made all the difference. There was no one to call him a fool, no one to laugh maniacally at him. There were no feelings of utter despair, no convulsions of te rror.

If indeed he found Lindina, all this will have been worth it. The hunger, the exhaustion, the abandonment of his career . . . even the deadly meeting with Captain Hazak.

Memories of that encounter poured into his mind, saturating his thoughts. The chase, the rough voice, the sword at his neck. The return of Jairus, his near death, and ultimately his surge of power. That surge still confounded him. Given, he was still unfamiliar with the powers he somehow possessed, but it still seemed impossible. Why was his life so important that the Deep would intervene to save him?

His legs hurt down to his toes, but it no more than made him wince. With every step, he doubted. Was he running towards Lindina, or was this all pointless? Had Lindina returned home? Did she change her direction? Jacob didn't know. He couldn't know. All he could do was pursue her with the best of his ability.

After a few hours of running, with numerous breaks, the moon began to vanish, and the stars blinked out one by one. To the north, colours formed. At first, a glow of deepest red saturated the dark canvas. From its source came lighter auras, spreading along the entire northern horizon and disappearing behind the mountains. Orange followed, surrounding the red and consuming it as the rest of the sky lightened to a vivid blue. Ever so slowly, the sun penetrated the horizon, casting its rays on Atlantia and freeing it from the shadows of night.

As the sun ascended above the mountains, it revealed a patch on the eastern horizon. There, not too far off, was a forest—one that seemed to glow green with reflected light, despite the cold season. Even from this distance, he knew of the foliage that the forest adorned itself with. At least, he knew what the legends said of Tahil forest.

Something about the sight, though he couldn't place what, made Jacob pause. Then he remembered. The vision of the old man in a green robe. If he recalled correctly, the robe was embroidered with golden trees. It may have been a vision of a Sirathim of the Far East for all he knew, but instinct told him it had something to do with this forest. What if he wasn't the only one who had that vision? What if Lindina had it as well and sought answers in Tahil?

You search in vain, Jairus said wearily.

I hope not. Jacob didn't know whether Jairus was right. He very well could be—that terrified him. All this sacrifice *had* to mean something. He wouldn't accept otherwise until he had no other choice.

Hope is what drives you to madness. Even if you find her, you won't convince her to return with you. If Lindina truly has travelled this far, she's made her decision.

"I will make her return," Jacob said. "Too many people would grieve her. This isn't just about her."

Is it about you, then?

"If this were about me . . ." Jacob stopped wasting his breath and switched back to thoughts. *I would have stopped before I started and left for Mortua like I planned.*

Ironic. You said "I" three times in that sentence alone.

That's irrelevant, and you know it. He focused on his destination. The forest neared with each moment, and it wouldn't be long until he was upon it. Now that it drew close, he wasn't sure he wanted to pass through it at all, yet he needed answers to his vision.

The trees of Tahil rose into the air just as much as those in his own dreary forests. These were not oaks, nor anything Jacob had seen before. Some towered, others were eye-height, but all appeared to be of the same species. Their branches twisted and flowed, some interweaving, and there was no strict posture among their trunks. It was no wonder they were considered to be alive, for each had its own personality, its own distinct shape and features, though all shared the same dark-brown bark patched with moss.

As he neared the border, he noticed the leaves and wondered. Even those on the same tree varied from branch to branch, sometimes from leaf to leaf. Some were round and perfectly curved, with a small point at their tips, and others had multiple blades with large veins, rigid and sharp. Others still were long and slender like wide blades of grass. All were brilliant hues of green, some lighter, some more shaded.

"What do we think of this?" Jacob whispered, setting his hand to the tree on his right. The bark was rough and ridged, leaving a sweet residue on his hand. A light breeze wove through the trees and rustled the leaves, complimenting the songs of unseen birds.

Beside the tree's base was a patch of flowers, swaying gently in the breeze. They spread their yellow petals wide, each one complimenting the others in a coordinated dance. It was more breathtaking than any poem, painting, or song.

Jacob backed out of the forest quickly. He was not worthy to enter into such serenity, such perfection. Yet now that he was back in the open air, away from the warm sweetness of Tahil, he found himself panting. There was something about the air of Tahil that made him feel as though he *needed* it.

Already it poisons you, Jairus said. *Such are the enchantments of the Deep.*

I know. Jacob gazed with longing and apprehension. If he entered, would he ever want to leave? Worse, if Lindina was in there, would he ever convince *her* to leave? There was only one thing he could do.

He dared not run, but stepped carefully onto the forest floor again. This time, he avoided taking in the resonating beauty of the trees, grass, and flowers. The air was warm again, and his feet didn't hurt when they landed on the soft ground. He walked with as much distance between himself and the trees as possible, as much from reverence as his fear of enchantment. It was no wonder the Silencers forbade entry into this place.

Several birds flitted between branches, chirping their joyous songs. Insects flew in the air, some attending to the flowers, others finding their places among the rich grass, but none hindering Jacob. Normally, he would have swatted away any bug he found, but not in Tahil. No, even the insects of this forest deserved respect.

A movement in the distance caused Jacob to stop. Inching forward soundlessly, his arms stiff at his side, he drew nearer to the spot. With every step, his eyelids struggled to stay open, and his balance wavered. He dared not speak to keep himself awake.

Jacob pressed on slowly, darkness overtaking him.

When next he awoke, it was not under the leaves of Tahil.

EIGHT

A driel leaned around the corner, breathing forcefully. Heavy metallic footsteps approached. She retracted her head.

Don't move, she told herself, closing her eyes. Around the corner, muffled voices argued. Guards. Not ordinary city guards—ones from the castle division. They didn't normally stray this far from the castle gates, but this wasn't a normal time. She believed all that Syndria said, but still didn't know everything. That was what this trip to the castle was all about.

As the footsteps neared the corner, they stopped and turned away. Adriel realized she'd been holding her breath, then released it.

The building she now huddled in front of, a jewellery shop, was closed for Full Moon Night, as was nearly every building in the vicinity. The street was quite deserted but for a few stragglers. Most of the high class, the only ones who could afford to live this close to the city's heart, would be at home or at restaurants. Had Syndria not come last night, Adriel would be no different. Her favourite salad bar, the Dark Leaf, had its anniversary celebration over the next few days.

As a crow's shadow passed, Adriel couldn't help but think of what Syndria had described. A dravelord—almost as much legend as they were history. Dreslen used the giant birds in the War all those centuries ago, among other servants, but they were gone. Even before Amiroth slew the gargoyle king and ended the War, they had vanished from sight, as Dreslen himself had. If the drav-elords were returning, could that mean . . .

Adriel shook her head. She believed Syndria spoke what she thought to be the truth, yet in her state delusions were to be expected. Adriel had treated patients with these kinds of ravings before. Visions of Abyssal figures were not uncommon among them. But for Syndria to speak so *specifically* about what she saw, as well as to identify it . . . It was something Adriel had not yet encountered.

All this thinking and peering around the corner would accomplish nothing. She knew exactly what the street looked like. The wide road continued for three blocks, with rows of mansions on either side, then ended at the castle gate. Guards were stationed at each corner, leaning against the street lamps and conversing with each other across the street.

Adriel took a deep breath through her nose, checking her shoulders to make sure they remained steady. She was ready. She wasn't royalty, nor was she a part of the castle staff, but bringing Syndria along to gain entry was too dangerous—for all she knew, it could get them both killed. No, Syndria had to hide. Adriel had forced her to remain inside her house until she'd gotten more information. As far as either of them knew, Syndria's location was unknown to everyone else. The Deep permitting, it would remain that way.

They'll at least let me get near the gate, she thought, taking another look around the corner. The only person who paid her a glance was an old man with a cane walking down the street. *I may as well get that far already.* Brushing her hair behind her shoulders, she walked onto the main road. Square shoulders. Even stride. Unwavering gaze. She belonged here, and she had to convince herself as well as the guards of it.

The old man with the cane passed her without a word, though he gave her a narrow look. Was she drawing attention to herself?

A quick glance at the first guard on the left confirmed that. He'd dropped his conversation, looking at her with a blank expression. What was it about her? Did she dress too lavishly? Possibly. Her silver-blue gown was her most expensive dress, one she rarely wore.

No. She blocked out the guards and carried forward. *I have an appointment. I need to be presentable.* Of course, that would only get her so far. At some point, the guards would catch on and remove her—or worse. Fortunately, she only needed to get to Doctor Harold. His office was on the east side of the castle courtyard, connected to, but not part of, the castle. They weren't friends, but, resentment aside, they were close acquaintances.

As she approached the last set of guards, her step faltered. Hands shaking, she straightened her dress and looked at each of the guards in turn. The left guard—notably taller than the other—regarded her with a nod and a smile. The other gave a dark stare. She wasn't sure which unnerved her more.

Adriel didn't stop until the guard on the right held out a hand and called out. "No visitors." His voice was raspy but strong.

"You're not expecting me?" Adriel tilted her head and lowered her brow, hiding her shaking hands behind her back.

"No one is expected, and no one is permitted."

"I'd double check that, if I were you." Adriel spoke slowly, as much to assert authority as to avoid stumbling on her words. "I have an appointment."

"All appointments are cancelled."

"Lord Baltashazar himself requested it."

The guard went silent at this, looking over at the other guard, who no longer smiled.

Adriel held her breath. *So, the guards know about Baltashazar's new authority.* Good. Without it, her lie would mean nothing. The guards looked perturbed, but they'd have their wits back in a moment. Unless Adriel kept them away.

The right guard spoke again. "When did you—"

"I don't plan on delaying my presence, guard. You know Lord Baltashazar. He doesn't take kindly to tardiness."

The guard opened his mouth, then paused. "I was given no indication you'd be arriving. When is your appointment?"

"You should know, shouldn't you?" Adriel was losing confidence by the second, but she didn't change her demeanour. "Unless you lost your instructions?"

"I was given no instructions." The guard's hand moved to the hilt of his short sword. Was he sweating?

"He'll have both our heads if I'm not on time, guard. Well, yours for sure. I may get no more than a slash on the arm. Trust me, I do *not* want that."

"Would you give us a moment?" the guard on the left said. He wiped his forehead with the back of his hand.

"No." Adriel stepped forward, staring at the guard until he broke his gaze. "Send for an armed escort if you have to. I will *not* be late. If I am, I'll personally blame both of you. Understood?"

The guard on the left's eyes widened. "What do you know about Lord Baltashazar?"

"Excuse me?"

"Recent events. What do you know?"

"All that I need to. I know he's to be king soon, and he apparently needs me to meet with Doctor Harold." This was the most unconvincing part of the lie. Why would Harold, the most renowned doctor in the kingdom, need to take counsel with Adriel? She hoped the guards didn't pay attention to the ranks and specialties of doctors.

"But Doctor Harold is—" The right guard stopped himself, looking into the distance, then turned to his partner. "We need to let her in."

"Are you *mad*?" he whispered.

"It makes sense. Doctor Harold needs help at the moment."

"But—"

"Trust me, Gib!"

Gib. Adriel remembered that name. One of Sorias's friends. She'd probably met him once, though she had no memory of his face.

Gib looked as if he were biting his tongue. The smile was gone. When he said nothing, the other guard looked at Adriel and spoke again.

"I'll accompany you to Doctor Harold's office," he said. "How long is your appointment?"

"Baltashazar's message was brief," Adriel said. "He didn't specify that much." She could hear the tremor in her voice now. Something was off. Why was this guard so keen to believe her?

"I'll station some guards outside the office for an hour, then. You'll be free to go after that."

Adriel's stomach lurched. *Free to go?* Was she going to be locked up for an hour with Harold?

"Come with me," the guard said, turning.

There was something behind his eyes. She couldn't place what, though she knew it wasn't mirth. Whatever it was, it sickened her. She was supposed to be in control here, not him.

With a glare at Gib, she followed the other guard past the gate into the courtyard. For the first while, they walked along the path leading straight ahead to the castle. Not too far ahead, the path parted to both sides to wrap around the Victory Torch, which looked more like a gargantuan bowl on a thick pillar than a torch. It was positioned exactly halfway between the castle walls and the castle's main entrance. Even though the War's End festival had been days ago, smoke still rose from the top. Odd.

"This way," the guard said, veering leftward off the path and walking onto less-even, stony ground. He didn't bother to check if Adriel followed him.

Adriel gulped and walked after the guard. She never had gotten used to the castle courtyard. Statues—some broken, some maintained—littered the ground in irregular intervals. If they weren't works of Dreslen himself, Adriel might not have found them problematic. Even the gore depicted in some figures might be tolerable if its purpose was to pay respect to those who suffered. But no, Dreslen created these statues to boast of his own power. Gargoyles and men alike under his command, with those who resisted suffering and dying. Every statue told the same story.

Focus, Adriel told herself. *This has no relevance to your task.* Yet she couldn't help feeling it *was* relevant. If there really had been a dravelord, that meant the powers of Dreslen were returning. All this carnage around her in the form of broken, morbid statues, could be made real again.

It was just a delusion! Adriel couldn't trust what Syndria thought she saw. Not if she wanted any hope.

The guard looked over his shoulder. "Keep up."

Adriel hastened until she was nearly beside the guard. Guards always walked much faster than was necessary, but in this case she was grateful. The sooner they got through this courtyard, the better.

It took a few minutes to traverse the grounds. The only comfort she had was the sun. Often, she'd visit Harold's office in the evenings, when the castle rose in front of the sun and enveloped the southern courtyard in a spiry shadow. Now, at least, all was illuminated. Thanks to the sun's warmth, she had an easier time staying calm.

Adriel and the guard finally approached the doctor's office. Compared to the castle, full of spires and towering like a mountain, it was mundane. A simple slanted roof, a chimney, and a few round windows on all sides. Two hallways led out of it, one leading to the right, where it joined with the castle, the other leading behind to the large recovery room. Unlike almost everything else in Barabus, it was made from stone bricks rather than solid stone.

The guard raised his gloved hand to the door, ignoring the brass knocker and striking the wood itself. A hollow sound rang in the air. Wooden doors were incredibly rare in Barabus. It was dark, but next to the stone it may as well have been white.

Only a few seconds later, the door creaked inward. Adriel leaned forward to hear the whispers.

"What does he want?" a hoarse voice said from inside. Harold must have a sore throat.

"You have a visitor," the guard said.

"I'm not supposed to have any visitors."

"Apparently you are. Lord Baltashazar requested it."

"Which means he probably demanded it . . ." Harold opened the door a little more. "Then killed the person next to him to emphasize his power."

"Perhaps," the guard said darkly.

Adriel's throat felt constricted. Hearing it from Syndria, Baltashazar's wickedness was merely a tale. Someone else's nightmare. Now that Harold and the guard attested to it, she felt like she was in the same dream. Nothing felt real but the fear. The stone, the guards, her tremors, those could all be in her imagination. But the fear . . . *That* was real.

"Let him in, then." Harold opened the door halfway, but Adriel saw no form.

"It's a 'her', actually." The guard nodded to Adriel.

She nodded back, now realizing what was behind his eyes. She saw herself, and not just her physical form. His eyes were a mirror of her emotions. He was as terrified as she was.

"Send her in."

Adriel breathed deeply and walked into Harold's office. Torches lined the walls, but none were lit. The only light came from the sun streaming through the streaky glass windows. Running along the perimeter of the upper walls was a wooden shelf bearing boxes and bottles of various sorts. A stepladder rested on the far left corner, leading up to the shelf. On the far right corner was a bed with perfectly white sheets, with neither a headboard nor a footboard. Beneath it, where its legs should have been, she saw small wheels that would roll sideways if the bed were pulled. That would block the door on the far end of the room, but Harold could get at the patient's other side then.

At the side of the bed was a wheeled rectangular table with emergency medical supplies on it—bandages, disinfectant salve, anesthetic, and cloths, among other containers whose labels she couldn't read at this distance. Being the royal doctor, Harold didn't have to pay for any of this. He could just bring his list of required materials to the king and have them delivered without question. Adriel wasn't so lucky. When business faltered, so did her supplies. That meant lesser treatment for patients, which lead to lesser satisfaction and less business. A bad streak could mean the end of a career for a doctor. Reputation was everything in this field.

As much as it pained Adriel to admit, Harold deserved his reputation. He really was the best doctor in the city. She shouldn't feel bad about it, either. He was more than twice her age. Sure, he was prideful, but he wouldn't let it impede helping patients.

The door closed behind her, but Adriel didn't turn. Another deep breath. She could trust Harold. "Something new, I see?" She pointed towards the square-shaped bottle on the edge of the emergency table.

"Never seen it before? Neither have I."

"That's a terrible rasp you've got." Adriel walked over to the table and picked up the bottle. She had to face Harold eventually. For now, all she wanted was to stall. The label on the bottle read *Henorin (62) Ginashium (34) Yeminim (3)*. Each substance was followed by the percentage of the solvent it made up. "Thirty-four Ginashium?" Adriel swirled the light-brown liquid in the bottle. Black flecks rose from the bottom and darkened the entire solvent. "What could you possibly need this for?"

"Much has happened since the festival." He coughed. "Are you going to just stand there admiring Harold's vanities?"

Adriel turned her head to the back corner of the room. Harold wasn't sitting in his chair. "Dredding?"

The weathered doctor coughed again, nodding. His hair was messier than ever, falling in front of his eyes and ears. He wore a lazy black suit instead of his medical uniform, not bothering to do up all the silver buttons on the overcoat. Both his feet were flush against the ground, as were his arms to the armrests, hands dangling at the end, unmoving.

"But—" Adriel looked all around the room. No Harold.

"Surprised?" Dredding said.

"I—yes. Where is he?"

"Harold? Let's hope he's dead. Better off that way for him."

Adriel's stomach did a backflip. Dredding was pessimistic, sometimes even morbid—but he never wished anyone dead. He was a doctor, for Amiroth's sake!

"You should see your eyes," Dredding said. His own eyes were on the ground. "Probably what I looked like at first."

"Dredding . . ." Adriel's jaw quivered, her breath coming in quick, shallow intervals. "What happened?"

"Harold's been deposed. Last night, guards came to my door, told me I was the new royal doctor, then hauled me over to the castle. I saw a few demonstrations from our new king. A few disobedient guards mangled, one of them skinned alive. He smiled at me, then sent me here to wait. I already tried escaping. They caught me and put me back here, but not before Lord Baltashazar killed another guard for my misbehaviour."

Adriel put both hands to her mouth. The sweat chilled her lips, and the salt made her want to gag. *What is happening?* She would prefer a nightmare to this. In a nightmare, at least there was a hope of awakening.

"I think I know why I'm here," Dredding said slowly. "Harold thought I was a sadist. Now Baltashazar does too. Soon, I'll be the one skinning people."

"Dredding!" she gasped. What was there to say? "What's happening?"

"The king is dead. The guards say Lord Baltashazar ate the king himself. They say the queen is missing, but I think she's probably dead too."

Syndria? No, that couldn't be. Syndria was hiding at Adriel's house. If she were dead, Dredding couldn't possibly know about it.

"Dredding . . ." Adriel walked forward and dropped her voice to a whisper. She could hardly manage it with her terse breathing. "Queen Syndria is alive."

"How would you know? You haven't been here since the festival. You haven't had to watch Lord Baltashazar hold down a screaming man and shove his own severed finger down his throat."

"Syndria came to me last night. She fled the castle before Baltashazar found her."

"It won't be long. You'll see. Even the Silencers won't be of use."

The Silencers! Why didn't she think of that earlier? Why did neither she nor Syndria go to the Silencers and request aid? Adriel turned to the door.

"I need to go."

"Did you not hear what I said?" Dredding's left hand twitched. "The Silencers can't help."

"Why not?"

"The Silencers are gone. Dead."

"That's not possible. Even if he killed one or two, there have to be *some* left."

"He killed them all. Every Silencer in Barabus. Their cloaks are burning in the Victory Torch as we speak. The Silencers failed."

No. Adriel staggered. *They can't have failed. I have to hope.*

But there was no hope anymore. The Silencers *were* hope.

"Baltashazar's rise to power has not been publicized," Dredding said. "Which means you couldn't possibly know about it."

"I would if Baltashazar himself sent me a letter requesting that I meet with Doctor Harold . . ."

The guards know Harold is gone. But the one on the right seemed to believe her. He even said that Harold needed help.

"Is that what you told them? Soldiers aren't stupid, Adriel. Even if your Sorias was, he'd be an outlier."

"Sorias wasn't stupid. Not in that way."

"They were playing you, Adriel."

"But why wouldn't they turn me away? Why do they want me here?"

"How could you have found out about Baltashazar's power?"

"I—Syndria told me." Realization filled her slowly, like tar dripping into a bucket on a ledge. Every drop threatened to make her topple.

"How else could you have known?"

"I couldn't have." She could hardly breathe. "They know. They know where Syndria is. That's why they're keeping me here." She looked at Dredding, and he looked back. There was nothing behind those eyes. "I have to go."

"And do what?" Dredding said. "Stop Baltashazar's guards? No need to get yourself killed as well."

"She's going to die if I don't do something!"

"The queen is going to die, *period.*"

"Why would they keep me here, then?"

Dredding cursed. "You and your self-importance. All you doctors are the same. It seems I am the only one with a grasp on just how *futile* everything is. Pain and death come for us all. What point is there in fighting it? Nothing is as sure as death. *Nothing.* We may as well be trying to eat rocks. You think you can overpower death?"

"We're doctors, Dredding! It's our job. I thought—"

"Whatever you thought is stupid. Any bit of care I had was taken from me last night. I'm just a shell, and Lord Baltashazar scraped the last bit of soul off. Death has the final say, and we would do well to listen."

"I can't believe it." Adriel wanted to cry, but she was too shocked. This man had once been her friend. That monster Baltashazar . . . He was taking *everyone* from her. Why couldn't he have killed her to begin with and spared her this pain?

Dredding coughed. "I do not wish to see you dead. Though you have scorned me more than any other, you have also done so more gently than all others. Do as I say, and I can help you live." He stared at her, unblinking.

What did that *mean?* It didn't matter. She had to go. "I'm sorry. I can't let Syndria die." She walked to the door and put her hand on the knob.

"If you open that door . . ." Dredding's eyes were on the floor again. ". . . they *will* kill you. And I cannot promise that Lord Baltashazar will not do it himself."

Adriel froze. Life or death. Was her own life valuable enough to be worth saving?

"Stay, Adriel."

Her trembling hand slid off the doorknob. On the other side of this slab of wood, her best friend was about to be taken by soldiers. Syndria might be executed immediately or brought to Baltashazar. *There has to be* something *I can do!*

But there was nothing. Even the Silencers were dead. Who could resist Baltashazar?

"We have to get word to Midor," Adriel said. "We need the Silencers."

"'Remember Dreslen.' That's what we've been saying for centuries. Well, there's no need to anymore."

"Why? Now, of all times, we have to remember!"

Dredding shook his head. "Why remember someone who lives? Dreslen walks again, and his name is Baltashazar. He was not defeated last time, and he will not be defeated now."

"But—"

"Dreslen disappeared. Amiroth defeated the gargoyle king, not Dreslen himself. Now he returns, even if only in spirit and power. The dark lord of the Abyss. The master of the Deep. Atlantia has had its rest. Now the Silence will be broken by screams."

"But Midor—"

"Will fall as well. Syndria is dead, Adriel. You know this. But perhaps you can save me."

Adriel looked at him, but he stared at the floor, motionless. What did she feel for him? Sadness for her dying friend? Anger towards a traitor of medicine?

Save the dying, the Creed said, *and give little thought to the dead.* Was Syndria dead, or was it Dredding? Whether or not Syndria lived, Adriel knew she couldn't save her. But perhaps Dredding was right. Perhaps she could save him.

Adriel stepped away from the door.

"Wait, and I will instruct you," Dredding said.

Adriel waited.

NINE

J acob awoke to the sound of whispers above him. He kept his eyes shut. Better that they thought he was still asleep.

The air was warm, yet not as sweet as it had been before—musty, even. He knew from the dark shade of his eyelids that he was no longer in the open sun but beneath a roof. He rested on something soft, likely a mattress. His head sunk deep into a pillow, pressing around his ears and muffling the conversation above him.

A door opened, and the hushed voices fell silent. Jacob heard footsteps and the creaking of a wooden floor, but they stopped a short distance away from him.

"Blood of the forest . . ." said the voice of an old woman. "Another one?"

"We think he's the one." This voice was deep and soft but sounded young. "The man the Elder's looking for."

The one? Jacob was flat on his back with his arms touching his sides, but his yearning to move made the position uncomfortable. If he could adjust his position, he might hear better. Better not to risk it. As soon as they knew he was awake, they'd stop talking about him.

"What about the girl?" the old woman asked.

"We must respect his decisions," an elderly male voice said. "Even if we do not understand them."

The woman scoffed, muttering inaudibly.

"Careful, Eliana," the man with the deep voice said. "The elder didn't suffer your husband, but he's been far better to you than you deserve. After what you did—"

"Stupid boy." The footsteps returned, this time moving away, followed by the sound of a slamming door. All went silent.

Now would be a good time to wake up, Jairus said.

Agreed. Jacob snapped open his eyes to see a young man with curly red hair and a large neck standing beside his bed. When he looked down and saw that Jacob was awake, he offered a faint smile. His eyes were bright blue, and his skin fairer than usual. He wore a green garment with a brown strap over his left shoulder, extending across his torso.

"Good morning," the boy, possibly sixteen, said as Jacob propped himself up into a sitting position. "How was your rest?"

Jacob looked at him. There were two other people in the room, an elderly couple with white hair, wearing simple robes of brown with a symbol of a green tree sewn onto the front. They each nodded at him, and he nodded back.

"I'm . . . fine," Jacob said, swinging his legs over the side of the bed. The mattress appeared to have once been white, but was now discoloured and better resembled yellow. The surrounding room was of a dark wood, with glassless windows in all four walls and a simple door of a lighter colour behind his three visitors. Two wooden posts stuck out of the ground, extending through the rafters to support the roof, which slanted two ways and had a small window on one of its sides.

"Where am I?" Jacob eventually asked, though he was fairly certain he knew the answer.

"Tahil forest," the boy said, getting to his feet. "You fell unconscious near the border, so we brought you here."

From everything you've been taught, Jairus said, *there are no settlers in this forest.*

"Where exactly is 'here'?" Jacob asked.

"You are in the heart of Tahil, where our people dwell," the old man said. His voice showed no signs of wear. "Our ancestors made their home here during the Exile and kept their existence a secret from the rest of the world."

Jacob looked over his shoulder through the window next to the bed. Light streamed in and revealed the same foliage he had seen when he entered the forest, with the addition of vines. An insect flew through the window and buzzed over his head, landing on one of the posts.

"The Exile?" Jacob asked, still looking out the window.

"The exile of the Sirathim from Atlantia," the boy said. "Can I ask your name?"

"What?" Jacob's head snapped back around. Did he say his ancestors were the *Sirathim*? Did that make these people—

"I asked your name. Mine is Leroy."

"Jacob of Tonto," he said, extending his hand absentmindedly. How was this possible? The Silencers should have extinguished these people by now if they were Sirathim.

"A pleasure," Leroy said, shaking Jacob's hand firmly. He motioned to the couple on his left. "These lovely people are Freya and Herman."

They nodded again, and Jacob returned the gesture.

No, Jacob thought. *He must be lying. A poor joke, perhaps.* The idea was ludicrous. How could the Sirathim have been living within the borders of Atlantia all this time, the Silencers unaware of it? True, it was outside the borders of Midor, but the Atlantian Reserves were within their jurisdiction. There must be something about the forest, some sort of magic that kept them hidden.

Jacob recalled entering the forest; he hadn't gone a stone's throw before falling asleep.

Something like that could only be enchantment. This was most definitely the home of sorcerers.

Well played, Deep. Jacob gritted his teeth. Now he, a Wayfollower, was among others who practiced magic. The Deep would seek to keep him here, a place where he could pursue it without ill-consequence. *Well, I won't play along. If Lindina's not here, I'm leaving at the first opportunity.*

Was there even a chance that Lindina was here in Tahil? She'd run in this direction upon leaving the South Midorian Forest, but he still had no evidence that she stayed the course. It was a gamble, coming here, but something felt *right*. It couldn't have merely been his own insanity. He needed to ask about her to these people, but not before he found out who they really were.

"Why did you venture into the forest?" the old man—Herman—asked.

"Are you Sirathim?" Jacob ignored him. His blunt question yielded no response from the man.

"I'm afraid it's more complicated than a yes or no answer," Freya said. Her voice, even more than Herman's, sounded young. "Our ancestors were Sirathim before the Exile, but there has been debate over whether their decision to remain in Atlantia lost them that title. I believe the followers of the Deep are called something else now."

"Wayfollowers," Jacob said.

"That makes sense. So, call us what you will. We are faithful to the Deep, and that is all that matters. Titles mean nothing to us."

Jacob did not know whether to tell them yet that he was a Wayfollower himself. But was he even a Wayfollower? He only followed the Deep to get to Lindina. It didn't matter. Like Freya, his title didn't define him, but neither did the Deep.

"You still have not answered my question." Herman stepped forward and clasped his hands. "What were you doing in the forest in the first place?"

"I was looking for a girl," Jacob said. "Eleven years old with very light-brown hair."

The three Tahilites exchanged glances. Finally, Freya spoke up. "Lindina?"

Jacob's heart leapt. He bounded to his feet, and his visitors backed up. After all that running, Jairus was wrong—he wasn't a fool! Well, perhaps he was and got lucky. It didn't matter.

"Is she still here?"

"As far as we're aware, yes," Herman said. He stopped Jacob when he tried to push through them towards the door. "You can't see her yet, though. She's with the Elder."

"Your leader?" He needed to know more about this elder. From what he overheard in the bed, the Elder was looking for someone like Jacob. All he knew so far was that these people trusted him, while that other woman, Eliana, did not.

"Yes, our leader. His name is Haanon, and he will wish to speak with you as soon as he's finished with the girl."

"When will that be?"

"We have no idea." Herman looked worried. "When the girl walked into the forest, he said—Haanon said—he felt pain in the forest. Something about her caused the trees to wither slightly, the grass to blacken."

Jacob looked at Herman confusedly. What about Lindina could blacken grass? She was a Wayfollower, like Jacob, and he'd experienced nothing like that. Perhaps she had powers he was unfamiliar with.

"Haanon said she's a plague to the forest," Freya said. "We don't know what he's going to do with her. Personally, I would have sent her away, but he's been acting strange lately."

"The same would go for you, too," Leroy said. "We usually send away people who try to enter the forest. But yesterday the Elder told all the scouts to bring in everyone they found instead. Terrible idea, if you ask me, but I trust him. We all do."

Jacob frowned as he remembered Lindina. Freya's words echoed in his mind. *Haanon said she's a plague to the forest. We don't know what he's going to do with her.* He wouldn't . . . kill her, would he? Were it not for what Eliana said, he wouldn't have considered it. But some people, despite what Leroy said, did not trust Haanon. There had to be a reason for that.

"We'll give you a tour of our village while you wait for him to finish up with Lindina," Leroy said, walking to the door. It barely creaked as it swung open to reveal the forest Jacob had been waiting to see. "Follow closely. We don't want you running off."

Leroy disappeared through the door, and Herman and Freya turned to follow him. Jacob took one last look at the small quarters before heading out and closing the door carefully.

He stepped down onto the lush grass and felt his feet sink into the soil beneath it. The sweet air filled his lungs again, and warmth enveloped him. He felt . . . safe, like he was being embraced in the warm arms of nature herself. The group of three waited for him, and together they walked through the village. Why would they possibly worry about him running off? Who in their right mind would want to leave such a perfect place?

The enchantment is getting to you again, Jairus said. *Be on your guard.*

For once, Jacob agreed with the Voice.

The trees were thinner in this inhabited area, and small wooden houses littered the ground. Most of them were larger than the one he exited, some at least three times the size. There were no paths leading up to the doors of the houses, which were raised slightly higher than ground level, reachable by a single stair. Flowers dotted the ground in colours of all sorts.

It was almost disconcerting to see the houses placed with such disorder. The entrances did not face uniformly, nor were their sides parallel with one another. It was as if they had been dropped randomly from the sky and kept wherever they landed. In Midor, this kind of chaos would have been impossible.

And yet, it was just like nature. Trees did not naturally grow in straight rows with expertly trimmed branches and perfectly concealed roots; they sprang up wherever they were planted, twisting however they wished. When he thought of the houses in this way, they seemed as orderly as those in Tonto.

The four of them were not alone in this area. Some people went in and out of the houses, while others walked and ran between them, darting into the outer forest and not returning. The life wasn't only in the trees and the grass; it was in the people. Even the elderly moved with the energy of children, especially Herman. He left the group for a moment to chase a duo of little girls, who squealed joyously and scattered in both directions. Herman laughed and walked back to join the group.

"Right now," Herman said, still smiling broadly, "we're walking towards the centre of the village. This is where the simple folk live. As far as most of us are concerned, the forest is all the housing we need."

"Why build houses at all, then?"

"They shelter us when it's raining. Some of us want to stay dry, you know."

"You're going to love the next part of the village," Freya said. "It's far more orderly than these scattered houses."

They reached the edge of the open area with wooden huts, entering a thicker tree line.

Remember, Jairus said, *you're only to be here long enough to retrieve Lindina. Don't fall prey to the forest's beauty.*

Jacob hardly paid attention to Jairus. So enamoured was he by the forest—the soft ground, the sweet smell, the vibrant green—that all else seemed to fade. The only sound was the rustling leaves in the arched branches above him and the songs of birds near and far. This was nature as it should be—a land the war spared. A place where the Deep's power flourished. It was the only place in all Atlantia that he could have what he wanted. Peace.

Why should he force himself, or Lindina, to leave such a paradise?

Because you're not doing it for yourself, Jairus said. *You're not doing it for Lindina. You're doing this for the families back in Tonto who are grieving over the disappearance of their loved ones. Eyes up, fool! Look!*

Jacob realized he was looking at the forest floor, and raised his head at Jairus's command. They had passed through the trees, and he now saw the area of the village Freya had spoken of. She was right—he loved it.

The houses were larger and more complex here, each with its own balcony and a set of chairs and wooden beams rising to support canopies. They were set in rows that curved towards a point further down the path. Each set of two rows faced each other, but there was no road between them. There was no road anywhere. Only grass and flowers, like a giant lawn shared by the entire community. Each house had one tree planted in front of it, but aside from these there were no other trees inside this area.

Following the group, he passed through the central two houses on the outer circle. Leroy waved to a group of young men conversing on a balcony across the street, and they waved back far too enthusiastically.

"Back already, Roy?" one of them called out.

"I'm walking here, aren't I?" Leroy called back.

"Any reason they let you finish early?"

"Say hello to Jacob." Leroy looked at Jacob.

One of the men, notably older than the rest, got to his feet and walked off the open porch. He had chestnut-brown hair, and his eyes were bright green. Like Leroy, he wore a garment of green with a brown leather strap across his torso. He walked barefoot—bounced, more like.

When he stopped in front of Jacob, he held out his hand. "Good morning, Jacob. My name is Iven, son of Ilemek." He spoke in a rare, sophisticated accent used mostly by Midor's upper class.

Jacob took his hand and shook it firmly. "A pleasure to meet you." His grip was matched by Iven, an occurrence far too rare.

"We'll all have plenty of time to chat later," Leroy said, stepping between them and looking at Jacob. "Right now, we have to get you to Haanon's house."

Iven released his grip on Jacob's hand, smiled, and walked back to the balcony to rejoin his conversation. When he spoke, he used exaggerated hand gestures and laughed heartily when the time came.

"Come along," Herman said as they continued walking between the houses towards the inmost point of the semicircle.

As they passed through the last row of houses, Haanon's residence became visible. It was a large, circular building with a small porch and a few round windows. Like the other houses nearby, its door was green with a light wooden knob on the right. Wooden archways and lines of yellow flowers led to the front door. The arch closest to him had a budding branch sticking out of its right side, as if the wood were still alive.

"This is the Elder's home," Leroy said. "He'll be in there right now, if I'm right."

Leroy walked to the door and swung the silver knocker twice. It was shaped like a bell, but did not ring when it struck the door. Jacob stood beside Leroy on the doorstep at Freya's suggestion, unsure of what to do. Were there certain signs of respect he ought to show when greeting the Elder? Instinct told him that since no one said anything about that, it wouldn't matter.

Jacob heard approaching footsteps through the door and braced himself. The door swung open slowly, and the head of an old man peaked through. His eyes, vivid green, complemented his dark-green robes. His hair was grey and thicker even than Jacob's.

The man looked at Jacob thoroughly, as if able to see through his skin and into his thoughts.

"Good morning, Ilemek," Leroy said. "I found another intruder earlier today. Is Haanon available?"

Ilemek, Jairus said. *The father of Iven. He has the same eyes, too.*

"I am unsure." Ilemek looked at Leroy, his eyes suddenly filled with worry. "He has not left his study since taking the girl inside with him. And I heard . . . screaming."

"From Lindina?" Jacob interjected.

Ilemek nodded solemnly. "He will wish to see you once he's finished with her. Come inside while you wait, and remove your shoes."

Jacob removed his leather shoes and set them beside the doorstep. Barefoot, he passed through the door as Ilemek opened it wider. Leroy tried to follow, but Ilemek closed the door quickly behind Jacob.

"Haanon's house is not a place for all to enter," Ilemek said as he re-latched the lock. He turned to Jacob. "What brought you to the forest?"

Jacob was unsure how much to say. They would never let him leave with Lindina, of course. Tahil had been kept secret for centuries, and they couldn't risk Jacob exposing them when he returned to Midor.

"I'm looking for a young girl," Jacob said after a pause. There wasn't much point in lying.

"I see," Ilemek muttered. "Tell me, how did you know to look for the girl here?"

"I fell unconscious and woke up running in this direction." Only after he said it did Jacob realize how ridiculous it sounded. Perhaps lying would have been more believable.

Ilemek said nothing, however, and walked towards a set of wood furniture in the living area. He sat down on a chair, rested his elbow on its arm, and put his forehead in his hand. "Have a seat," he said, not looking up.

Jacob did as instructed and sat down across from Ilemek on a bench with a curved back. Between them was a short rectangular table of a reddish colour, on top of which were two white porcelain cups. He peered into the one closest to him, finding it empty. Next to it was a wooden pitcher filled with water. Oddly enough, he realized he wasn't thirsty. He couldn't recall drinking anything since a pond he'd come across while running.

"Sir?" Jacob asked after the silence grew uncomfortable.

"Hmm?" Ilemek said, drowsily taking his head out of his hand.

"How is it the Silencers haven't found this place by now?"

"That is one Haanon's many secrets. Although, even *he* may not know how our ancestors kept us hidden. I think it is best to revel in the mystery. Wouldn't you agree?"

Jacob opened his mouth to object, but stopped as he heard the faint sound of a door creaking open. Footsteps on a wooden floor followed. He turned his head in time to see a girl with light-brown hair and a tattered yellow dress walk towards the living space. Her frail arms tremored, and tears stained her slight cheeks. She stopped when she saw Jacob, fear frozen on her face. *Lindina.*

A man wearing a green robe stepped around the bend, stopping behind Lindina and putting his hand on her shoulder. His head was balding with strands of white, matching the colour of the facial hair covering his mouth. On the front of his robe was a tree set in gold, with branches that multiplied and curled in all directions. If Jacob wasn't mistaken, this was the man from his vision.

Lindina opened her mouth, but no sound came out. She looked at the Elder, who looked back expressionlessly.

"Lindina," Jacob said, getting to his feet. Tears threatened to fill his eyes. "I'm here."

"What is your name?" Haanon said.

"Jacob of Tonto."

"A Wayfollower from the South Midorian Forest?"

Jacob shook his head. "'Wayfollower' is an unfitting title for me. I am touched by the Deep, but I do not follow its ways."

"Yet here you are."

Jacob was about to argue that he'd come for Lindina, but the look on her face gave him pause.

Lindina looked at Jacob and confirmed his fear. "I don't want to go back home."

You're not doing it for her, Jairus said. *You're doing it for her brother and father. Bring her back!*

Jacob saw her tear-stained cheeks and swollen eyes. He remembered the air of the forest outside, its life-giving aura. This was a place where she could grow in her connection to the Deep, where she could be accepted as she was. If she stayed, she could have what Jacob longed for—peace. Only here could she find it. Only here could Jacob find it.

No! Jairus screamed. *Bring her home!*

I'm not doing this for Carl, said Jacob. *I'm doing it for Lindina. Now be silent!*

"No," Jacob said. All their eyes fixed on him. "I've come because I had a vision."

Lindina's tears stopped, but her face remained sullen. What had Haanon said to make her like this? If he forbade her to return to Midor, it should have joyed her.

"Follow me, Jacob of Tonto," Haanon said.

Jacob followed Haanon away from Lindina and Ilemek. On all sides of the hall were furnishings of carved wood, most of the same red colour as the tea table. There were vases of flowers scattered all throughout and candles that smelled of pine. Beneath his bare feet was a soft orange rug that ran along the hall and stopped at a green door.

What in the name of Dreslen are you doing? Jairus said. *You gave up your life. Future as an editor? Gone! Chance at building a library in Tonto? Gone! All to find Lindina and return her to Carl and their father. I've said you were a fool before, but those times were mostly half-hearted. This time I mean it. You're one of the stupidest fools, idiots, and imbeciles to walk Atlantia!*

You're wrong, Jacob thought. *I set out to rescue Lindina, but she's already been rescued. As it turns out, I've been rescued as well.*

Jairus left his thoughts in a fit of curses. He would return, but for now, Jacob enjoyed the peace and turned his mind forward.

Haanon opened the door and stepped through. "Enter," he said, looking at Jacob. "We have much to discuss."

TEN

Haanon's study was a circular room illuminated by a large round window on the right side. Lining almost the entire wall were bookshelves rising to shoulder height, each one filled with tomes. The books varied in colour and size, some being as small as bricks and others nearly half as tall as the bookshelves themselves. Empty vases, flower-filled pottery, and the occasional bell littered the tops of the shelves. Between all these were yet more books, their pages strewn open and calling out.

The sight of the books filled Jacob with pangs of regret. This could have been his life, had he not pursued Lindina. As many books as there were here, the Mortuan Library had more. He would have spent day after day immersed in their stories and knowledge, basking in their musty aroma and watching as others found joy in them. The life he'd dreamed of forever was within reach, but as he reached out to take it, Carl pulled him away. Now it was gone forever.

It was difficult not to resent Carl. He knew it was irrational, but he couldn't shake it. *He didn't force me into this,* Jacob told himself. *I chose this path, this exile.* Yet if Carl hadn't approached him on the tower in the first place . . .

No, he wouldn't think of that. The tower was gone. Tonto was gone. And they would remain that way, unless Jacob could convince Lindina to join him in escaping Tahil. Not only her, but *himself.* He wanted to stay here. But, like Jairus said, there were people in Tonto who suffered the loss of him and Lindina.

If Lindina didn't return, perhaps Carl's heart would shatter at the loss of the only person he had left to protect.

Jacob looked out the window on his right onto a lawn with a single young tree in the middle. Haanon's house—a giant wooden ring—surrounded the round patch of grass. Was there any escaping this place? These people were sorcerers. Even entering the forest had rendered him unconscious. He had as much a chance of escape as that tree in Haanon's yard.

"I imagine you have a great deal of questions on your mind," Haanon said from behind him, "but I implore you, save them for another time."

Haanon sat with his back to Jacob on a dark green armchair near the centre of the room. Across from the old man, with no table in between, was a short sofa of the same colour and material. The fabric was indented periodically by brass buttons pinned in the backrest. The armrests were rounded at the top, and the seat cushions were deep. How could the Tahilites acquire such professional furniture? Surely they did not have the materials or means to make it themselves.

Jacob walked across the lush green carpet in the middle of the room and took a seat across from the old man. The cushion was quite soft, and he sunk into it like a stone in lush grass.

"I would offer tea," Haanon said, his arms resting stiffly on his armrests, "but I'm afraid I gave the last of the hot water to Lindina."

"No, I don't need tea. Thank you," Jacob said, masking his disappointment. In a forest like this, their tea must be something extraordinary.

"Very well." Haanon leaned back in his chair. Jacob wondered how anyone could be so stiff and still neglect to straighten out the stack of pages on his desk. "Where shall we begin?"

Jacob wanted to ask how their enchantments worked, but held his tongue. That would draw too much suspicion. "I had a vision of you," he said. "When I was in the South Midorian Forest. Somehow, you knew I came from there."

"Yes, I saw you as well." Haanon's fingers twitched. "A work of the Deep, if ever there was one. Never have I experienced anything like that before, though I have tried."

"How did you know I was in the South Midorian Forest, though?" When Jacob had seen Haanon, he didn't recall Tahil in the background. Now that he thought about it, he didn't remember seeing his own environment either.

"I saw the dying trees around you. Quite distinctive."

"So you've been outside Tahil before?"

"My prior answer betrays me. Indeed, I have."

"Were you born outside Tahil?"

"We have other matters to discuss. But no, I was indeed born in Tahil." Haanon leaned forward. "I saw you in your forest. Not just you, not just the trees, but chaos. I felt the heat, touched the whirlwind, and was nearly blinded by the light. What happened? Tell me everything."

Jacob scratched his head and looked past Haanon. Painful memories filled him. The strange men in hoods. Jairus's return. His near dying, surge of power, and full healing. Waking up running. How much did he dare tell this man? What were his intentions?

"I was looking for a girl—Lindina—in the forest. At some point, I came across two men in cloaks. For some reason, they tried to kill me. I still don't know who they were. But as I was about to die, my powers—the ones given by the Deep—surged like never before. From what you described, you saw everything I was doing. Then I saw you. I fell unconscious, woke up running, and didn't stop until I came here."

"Is that all? Do you remember anything else?"

How much detail do you want me to give? Jacob thought. He'd decided to not mention Jairus. Better that Haanon didn't think him insane.

The bells, Jairus said.

"Yes, there was something else." *Thank you,* Jacob thought. "Before my powers started surging, and during, I heard bells. One bell, really. It kept getting louder, and it seemed to come from every direction."

"Curious. I heard the bell too. In fact, I was the one who struck it."

"But . . ." How far away must the sound have carried? That was impossible. Then again, he saw Haanon from the same distance.

"I was as surprised as you are now. More so, actually." Haanon leaned back and looked at the ceiling. "The *Tiris Aledon* was silent for centuries. No one, no matter how learned, discovered its origin or workings. A giant bell in the middle of the forest with inscriptions of an unknown language. Many a time have I struck it to be returned with silence.

"Two nights ago, I awoke to the sound of tolling. None but I and a few others heard it. I hastened to the bell, forgetting my mallet. As soon as I laid eyes on it, its ringing stopped. I must admit, I nearly panicked. Hastily, I picked up a fallen branch and struck the *Tiris Aledon* myself. Finally, it tolled. Again and again, louder each time. I found myself looking at you, hearing nothing but the bell and the sound of a hammer on an anvil. Light flashed with each toll.

"Then I saw you, Jacob. Such power as I've never seen before. But there is one thing you must tell me. What of the ground? I know of the lightning, the fire, and the wind, and I suspect our shared vision had to do with the Way of Life. But did the ground shake?"

"I would guess as much." Jacob could hardly remember the details. In such a state of chaos, who would pay attention to whether the ground was shaking? He probably would have perceived it to shake, whether it did or not.

"Do you know what this means?"

"I have *no idea* what this means."

Haanon smiled. He actually *smiled*. "The Way of the Deep is no longer lost. You've found it."

The Way of the Deep. Jacob knew little about the Sirathim Ways—they were outlawed, after all—but it sounded familiar.

"The Way of the Deep has been lost ever since the Exile," Haanon said. "Why do you look so indifferent? Do you not understand the significance of this?"

"Remind me again of the Ways?"

"Ah, I remember. You said you do not truly follow the Deep. That makes this all the more strange. Very well. The traditionally categorized Ways of the Sirathim are as follows: Fire, Wind, Life, Light, and the Deep. Those who chose to inhabit Tahil instead of leaving Atlantia were most proficient in the Way of Life, as I'm sure you have guessed. Even so, Fire, Wind, and in some rare cases, Light, have all been accessible to Wayfollowers in Atlantia. But the Way of the Deep, the most powerful of them all, which can transcend the laws of nature instead of merely bending them, has been lost—until now."

Jacob furrowed his brow. What did that make him? Why *him*? "The ground might not have shaken. I may just have imagined it in the chaos."

But he didn't imagine it. The more he thought about it, the more he remembered that detail. No, the ground was definitely shaking. He'd nearly lost his footing because of it. But Haanon didn't have to know, did he?

"But you *do* have a notion of it," Haanon said. He no longer smiled, but his eyes were still alight. "Have you experienced anything like this before?"

"No, and I don't intend to again."

"Jacob, look at me." Haanon's hazel eyes pierced Jacob even more than Ilemek's eyes had. "The Deep has chosen you. You were sent here for a reason."

"I came here for a reason, yes." Jacob's expression hardened. He couldn't deny that the Deep probably had a hand in sending Jacob to Tahil, but that wasn't why he came here. "I'm here to find Lindina and bring her back to Midor. She has—*we* have—family that are probably grieving our deaths. Either that or they're looking for us in vain. We have to return."

Haanon sighed, his expression softening. "I suspected as much. I also suspect you won't take no for an answer."

"You'd be correct." All Jacob's attachment to Tahil vanished, but he could feel Jairus's hateful eyes on him. He'd given away his intent and spoiled any chance of a stealthy escape.

"I'm afraid I cannot let you go. Neither you nor Lindina."

"Tahil's secret is bound with us. I swear by Amiroth that we'll tell no one of the forest."

"This isn't primarily a matter of Tahil's secrecy, though that is a concern. Jacob, you are the only one who has experienced the Way of the Deep in centuries. You *must* be trained. I believe that is why you are here."

"And Lindina? Do you intend to train her as well?" Jacob didn't hide the frustration from his voice.

"My reason for keeping Lindina here is between me and her. If all goes well, she may leave someday, though I cannot foresee when."

The problem was, Lindina didn't even want to leave. Tahil was perfect. So why bring her back at all?

Carl, he thought. He couldn't imagine the grief on Carl's face right now. If Lindina never returned, it would be perpetuated.

"Again, that is between me and her."

"She's like a sister to me. I came all this way to rescue her, and—"

"I assure you, she is rescued."

"Convince me. Tell me the truth."

Haanon clasped his hands and pursed his mouth. "How well do you know her?"

"Better than nearly anyone else." He didn't mention her disappearances over the last month. No one knew anyone about those, and Jacob suspected he was the only one with a decent guess.

"Do you know of her condition?"

"Of being a Wayfollower?"

Haanon raised his brow. "So she's a Wayfollower too? Lindina didn't mention it to me."

What? If she wasn't a Wayfollower, then why her disappearances? What "condition" did she have? Now Jacob was no better off than all the others trying to solve Lindina's behaviour.

"She assures me that no one knows," Haanon said. "And I will do my best to maintain that. You must trust me, Jacob. This is the best place—perhaps the *only* place—where she can heal. Take my word. I will speak no more of her."

Jacob frowned. "I have no reason to trust you."

"You will find it in time."

"I have no reason to stay."

"Would you contend with the will of the Deep?"

"I'm not here because of the Deep. I'm here for Lindina."

"Here we are again." Haanon shook his head. "It seems nothing I say will convince you. Is there anything you want to hear from me?"

Unlike every other elderly person Jacob had met in the village, Haanon's voice sounded old. Now, it even sounded tired.

"There's only one way you could convince me to stay, but I'm sure you wouldn't allow it."

"And what is that?"

"Let me send word to Lindina's family in Midor. They need to know she's not dead."

"You're right. I could never agree to that. The risk of exposing Tahil would be too great."

"Then we're done here." Jacob stood up. "Thank you for your hospitality, but I'll be leaving." He paused. Haanon had said that this was the only place Lindina could find healing. If what he said was true, then by returning her to Tonto he wouldn't really be rescuing her. He'd be doing quite the opposite. "I'll ask Lindina one more time if she wants to come with me. If she does not want to, then . . ." Saying it undermined his entire quest. It was painful, almost. ". . . I'll leave her here. But someone needs to tell her brother and father that she's alive."

Haanon's gaze hardened. "I cannot let you go. Your connection to the Deep is far too valuable."

"I'm not asking you to let me go." Jacob started walking, turning his back to Haanon and reaching for the doorknob. As resolute as he was, he couldn't banish the guilt and regret. He truly wanted to stay here and learn the Way of the Deep without the threat of the Silencers. But Carl needed to know Lindina was safe, and there was still a chance he might be able to apply for a position in the library again. A slight chance, but it was there.

Before Jacob could turn the doorknob, it moved of its own accord, and the door slammed into Jacob's face.

"Sorry!" A voice came from the other side, followed by a figure entering the room. Iven, if Jacob remembered correctly. His eyes were wide, and he regarded Jacob with a grimace. "Sorry again."

"Don't mention it," Jacob muttered, rubbing his upper-left cheek and forehead. If his head hadn't been turned when the door opened, it might have broken his nose.

"Perfect timing, Iven," Haanon said. "Our guest here was about to leave Tahil."

Iven ignored Haanon's remark, turning to him with even wider eyes. Jacob was surprised they remained in their sockets. "Death has entered the forest!"

"What happened?" Haanon rose to his feet abruptly. He looked at the ground, mouth open. "Great Scholar," he breathed. "I can feel it."

"It's the girl. Lindina. She's brought in a monster. A giant black bird with—"

"A dravelord." Haanon looked up. "Bring me to her. Now!"

Jacob froze as Haanon rushed out of the room with the speed of a child, following Iven. *What just happened?* He didn't wait to find out. Forgetting everything else, he left Haanon's study and ran after the two men.

ELEVEN

Ahead of Jacob, Haanon sprinted across the hallway, all poise replaced with frantic urgency. Jacob had a hard time not tripping over the carpet, which had bunched up after Haanon ran over it. He still didn't know what was happening. Lindina . . . bringing a *dravelord* into Tahil? Not only was that impossible because of the dravelords' extinction—it was unthinkable. Jacob knew Lindina. She was practically his sister. And yet, her behaviour over the last month was unexplained.

Jacob gritted his teeth as he exited the hallway into the living area, taking a sharp right to follow Haanon out the door. He wouldn't believe Haanon about the dravelord—not until he saw it himself.

The monster of the South Midorian Forest, Jairus said. *You saw it in your first vision, in the mutilated patch of forest. Wings and claws.*

It fit all too well. But why? *How,* for Amiroth's sake? This was what legends and folktales were made of. A return of Dreslen's powers. Dravelords and gargoyles lurking in the shadows. Stories to scare children away from the Deep by any means necessary. If Jacob remembered correctly, he'd even read a few of those stories to Lindina. Now they were living in one.

Ahead, Iven and Haanon ran down the arch-covered path towards a crowd gathered at its end. "Disperse!" Haanon said. Only a few eyes turned to him. "Go to the outer lodges!"

It didn't take long before Jacob caught up to Haanon, who slowed upon reaching the crowd. Iven broke through the crowd, repeating Haanon's shouts and pointing them in the correct direction. More heads turned to regard Haanon, their eyes as wide as Iven's. After the first person ran off as instructed, it didn't take long for others to snap out of their shock and follow. Soon, nearly everyone was gone, giving Jacob a view of what they had been gathered around.

Haanon was right. The sight tore at him, but this couldn't be anything else. Lindina stood in the centre of where the crowd had gathered, her hand on a creature almost twice her height. Its black feathers were patchy, revealing even darker glossy skin beneath. The beak was equally black, hooked like a sickle, sticking bluntly into the bird's misshapen head. Its eyes—Jacob could see them even from here—were palest white, with not so much as a pupil to give the illusion of life. Even looking at the dravelord nauseated him.

Lindina stepped in front of the creature protectively, looking at Haanon. At first, Jacob thought she looked afraid. But as her hands clenched, her wide eyes gave testament to something more.

"I said disperse!" Haanon shouted to the last remaining onlookers. He took a cautious step towards Lindina, his robes as stiff as his demeanor.

As everyone else fled, Iven included, Jacob wondered if he ought to as well. *No,* he thought. *I'm already disobeying him by planning to leave the forest.* Haanon would have to drag him by force if he wanted Jacob gone. Lindina, as far as Jacob was concerned, was still his responsibility.

"What is happening?" a voice said behind Jacob. He turned to find Ilemek, standing with his hands limp at his sides, stunned as he beheld Lindina and the dravelord.

Jacob said nothing, turning back to Lindina. Even if he knew what he ought to do, he was as stunned as Ilemek.

"Stay back!" Lindina held up a hand, walking backwards until the dravelord's beak was above her head.

"Why have you brought this upon us?" Haanon's voice, desperate but firm, no longer showed any sign of wear.

Lindina glanced at Jacob then turned back to Haanon. "You said I'd never be allowed to leave. If I can't go, then Zachii has to stay!"

What? Jacob looked at Haanon. Hadn't he told Jacob that he'd eventually allow Lindina to depart from Tahil?

"Lindina . . ." Haanon dropped his voice. Jacob stepped forward to hear better. "We agreed that you would abandon all ties. Including the dravelord. *You* agreed."

"But—"

"You broke your word not an hour after leaving my doors. In bringing this creature here, you've brought death upon this sacred forest. Your own curse is plague enough already. The trees will not survive the stench of this monster."

"His name is Zachii," Lindina said. Her fists tightened.

"We have already discussed—"

The dravelord screeched. Everyone but Lindina put their hands to their ears. Jacob's went up so fast that he scratched his cheek. Nothing could have prepared him for this. The screech was sharper than a nail scraping glass, colder than midnight air, and worse, Jacob didn't just hear it—he *felt* it. His entire body churned and spasmed from nausea, and he could think of nothing else. Even Jairus screamed internally.

"Yes, I told him!" Lindina stepped back from the dravelord and turned to it. Jacob could barely make out the words amid the pounding in his ears. "I don't care about that right now. We need to—"

The dravelord screeched again, this time more quietly. It still hurt, but Jacob could keep his footing.

"Not now, Zachii!" Lindina said.

Haanon lowered his hands from his ears. "What did it—"

"He," Lindina interrupted.

"What did *he* say?"

Jacob scratched his head, still breathing hard. The dravelord was *speaking?* How could Lindina—oh, bother.

Lindina hesitated, wincing. "Zachii wanted me to tell you earlier, but I thought if I told you, you'd think Zachii and I were involved, and—"

"Tell me."

Lindina breathed deeply. "The king of Barabus was brought into the Pits of Todoros. He's been there for almost a week, but Zachii says he's still alive."

"The . . . What?" Haanon, for the first time, was at a loss for words.

Jacob couldn't blame him. King Baraz, in the Pits of Todoros? He shivered. Until now, he hadn't even believed the place was real. Stories said it was Dreslen's worst prison—a dungeon filled with tar, deep in the stone. Some now said it was merely a tar mine, but even they couldn't deny the horridness of the place.

"But Zachii has nothing to do with it!" Lindina said.

"I should think not, if he's the one telling me." Haanon rubbed his forehead. "Please . . . tell me you're lying."

"I'm not."

"Does this not bother you?"

"It does." Lindina looked at the ground. "I don't like it when people get hurt. And the one who did this is going to hurt a lot more people."

"Who did this?"

The dravelord crowed softly.

"Lord Baltashazar," Lindina said. "Zachii saw him in the Abyssal Plains. Most of the dravelords did. But one of them flew to Baltashazar and joined him. Not long after, I found the . . ." She glanced at Jacob. "I found the pen, and Zachii left the Plains to find me."

If there were more dravelords, they were clearly not extinct. But living in the Abyssal Plains? No, living there was impossible. Whatever this creature was, it wasn't alive. Speaking, flying, thinking even, but as dead as a corpse. Those eyes could mean nothing else. But how had Lindina managed to get one to fly from the Abyssal Plains to find her?

"What happened, Lindina?" Jacob asked. *For Amiroth's sake, give me answers!*

Haanon shot a glare at him. "Now is not the time. There are more pressing matters."

"No, I'll tell him." Lindina sniffed. "He deserves to know." She turned to Jacob. "You did come all this way to find me, didn't you?"

Jacob nodded.

"I can't go back. Even if I don't stay, I can't ever go back home."

"Tell me what happened," Jacob almost whispered.

"Okay." Her breath shook. "I was walking in the forest like you used to do. I wish I'd listened to Carl and stayed close to him, but I wandered off. It could have been for hours; I can't remember. But I found this area with dying trees and a black spot on the ground. There was a black pen in the middle of it all, with gold edges and purple letters I couldn't read. I . . . took it, and the next time I went into the forest, Zachii found me.

"He told me he came from the Abyssal Plains. He'd been there ever since Dreslen went into hiding. When I picked up Dreslen's pen, it was like a call to him. There's a curse, you see. He can't die, and sunlight hurts him. He can't even be in sunlight unless he's serving Dreslen or someone like him. Someone who draws power from the Abyss. Like me."

Jacob's jaw dropped. *Lindina? A Dreslite?*

"I kept going into the forest to see him, but he'd often be away spying on Baltashazar and his dravelord, Uroku. I think he first came to me because he wanted to warn others of Baltashazar, but

I was so scared someone would take Zachii away." She looked at Haanon. "And you *do* want to take him away."

"Lindina." Haanon's voice was stiffer than ever, but his hands trembled violently. "What you've told me now, what you kept from me out of selfishness . . . This is more harrowing than anything else. We must contact the Silencers at once!"

"The Silencers?" Ilemek said, stepping forward.

"Yes, Ilemek. They are our best hope."

Lindina looked down at her feet and muttered something, but only Jacob seemed to notice. He could only guess she disdained the Silencers as much as Jacob—probably more. If they knew she was a Dreslite, they would show her less mercy than even a Wayfollower might get. Swift death without a trial, if she was lucky.

Jacob didn't even know how *he* felt about Lindina. Confusion more than anything, but what lay beneath? Anger? Fear? A good helping of each, probably, but he felt pity as well. He knew he shouldn't. Lindina had become something more detestable than he dared imagine. Was his sister dead, replaced by a dark sorceress?

No. There was pain on her face. Whatever this plight was, she seemed to treat it like a curse. But unless she remained a Dreslite, Zachii could not be with her. She loved the bird far too much for her own good.

"The Silencers can't do anything," Lindina said. Haanon and Ilemek stopped arguing to look at her. "They're dead. All the ones in Barabus. That's what Zachii said, anyway."

"Zachii must be mistaken," Haanon said. "The Silencers are a force of nature; like wind, they may disappear from all knowledge." He raised his hand into the air. Indeed, there was hardly a breeze in the forest. "But like the wind, the Silencers never truly vanish. Storms always come, and they can shake the earth. I trust the Silencers are alive and working in Barabus. In fact, they are probably moving against Lord Baltashazar as we speak."

Lindina shook her head. "You don't know how powerful Baltashazar is. He spent over a month in the Abyssal Plains. He's gotten really powerful. Even Zachii is afraid of him."

"He is but one man. The Silencers are many."

"Oh, yes they are." Ilemek forced a chuckle. "Many enough to nearly burn down our forest!"

"Nearly. But they did not."

"Not for lack of trying. They failed to thwart us, so what makes you think Baltashazar can't thwart them?"

"Because Baltashazar doesn't have—oh, Great Scholar, Ilemek! When will you learn to trust me?"

Ilemek pursed his lips.

Haanon turned to Lindina. "Your dravelord's news has distracted me. You have but three options, and I will not consider a fourth. First, and most preferably, you can banish Zachii to the Abyssal Plains and follow through with letting Tahil heal you. Second, we kill Zachii and heal you. Third, we banish you both. This bird *cannot* stay. The forest is dying because of it."

Lindina cursed. *Lindina.* Cursed. Something flashed in her eyes—no, not a flash. A flash produced light. This was a shadow. "Zachii will remain with me, and you will heal him as well."

Haanon stared at her, unmoving. "I am old and learned in the Way of Life, but I cannot match the power of Dreslen and undo his curse. Ilemek, go fetch my dagger."

"What?" Lindina shrieked.

"I gave you three options. It appears you've chosen the second. Ilemek, my dagger!"

"But Zachii can't die," Jacob said. That put a stop to Ilemek. "If he's cursed with immortality, what good will trying to kill him do?" He looked at Lindina. "You have to expel him from the forest. Lindina, you have to heal. Look at what the Abyss has done to you. Think of Carl."

Lindina's face didn't change. "I'm already dead to him. And he doesn't care about Zachii."

"This is for your own—"

"Would everyone stop saying it's for my own good? I know it is! But Zachii would have to go back to the place he hates the most. I can't do that to him!" She dropped her voice. "And we're the only ones who can stop Baltashazar."

All anyone could do was stare at Lindina, grass blackening around her feet, as she barely held back tears. The silence was almost worse than Zachii's screech. Every time someone opened their mouth to speak, they closed it again.

Was Lindina right? Was she really doing it for Zachii and not herself? It was the same question he'd been asking himself. Was he on this quest for Lindina's sake, or was he just serving his own conscience to feel better about himself? Worse, it was an adventure. He longed for adventure almost every day. Who was to say that wasn't his motivation?

Right now it was difficult, almost impossible, to assume the best of Lindina. Jacob and Carl had always known she was lying to them, but they couldn't have guessed it was to this extent. Her innocence was gone, taken from her by a bird thought long dead. His eyes turned to Zachii, suddenly hot. He left the Abyssal Plains to warn of Baltashazar, but why did he stay with her? Surely he could see that Lindina was dying—*worse* than dying. By remaining with her, it was *his* fault for all of this. He had to be banished, even if just as punishment.

Death would be too great a mercy for it, Jairus said. *As it would be for Lindina.*

Jacob tried not to think about Lindina's crimes. Tried and failed. She was guiltier than a Wayfollower could ever be. But he couldn't give up on her. Not yet.

Lindina stroked Zachii's mutilated feathers, basking in the silence. It was one of the few things she still enjoyed. Darkness, silence, and cold were the only things that didn't hurt. But even the silence hardly detracted from the pain of sunlight beating down at her skin, like an iron pressed over her entire body. She didn't bother checking for redness anymore. There never was any. Only scorching nausea all over her skin.

Even worse was the air. This blighted forest was so perfect, so warm and green, the air so sweet, that it made her want to die. She didn't show them the pain, though. Even though it felt like someone—probably Haanon—had shoved a bottle of acid down her throat, she stood tall and kept breathing. She needed the air. Without it, she would die, but with it she felt like she was dying. The Abyss was probably the opposite, but she kept using it anyway. It was the only way to lessen the pain.

She needed her pen back. The pen she had found a month ago in the forest, partially buried in the ground and surrounded by dead trees. The pen that she had accidentally pricked herself with, bringing upon her a curse. It felt horrid to use it, but she couldn't get rid of the craving now. The pen was far preferable to the growing agonies of light and warmth. She didn't know what would keep her alive anymore, and she was having trouble caring. All she wanted was to be rid of this pain. More than that, the curse itself.

Haanon told her this forest would heal her. When he seized her pen, he ignored her screams of protest and tried to convince her it was for her own safety. He calmed her down in that moment, assuring her of the life-giving trees of Tahil. She believed him then, but now doubted. Her need for the pen's darkness wasn't going away—it was consuming her like a starving girl's craving for food. If she didn't get it soon, she would die.

Lindina thought of her passed mother, that day that caused so much grief. After that day, Carl swore to protect Lindina. He tried so hard, but she outran him, and now he was probably crying in grief again. She didn't know if he would heal this time, but she couldn't return to Tonto. She was broken, and as long as she lived with her family, she was a threat to them.

As much as she loved Zachii, she wished he never brought her to Tahil. But where else was there to go? After waking up and killing the Silencer, she had been in tears. She was throwing up, trembling, and weeping for minutes before Zachii came and convinced her to go to Tahil. It seemed like a good idea at the time. She wanted to be free from her curse, but couldn't bear the pain it would require. She wasn't strong enough.

And then there was Zachii himself. The dravelord who had offered her friendship like no others had. True, it began only because he wanted to warn of Baltashazar, but it didn't stop there. He showed affection like many humans could not fathom. And without darkness in her blood, her greatest friend would be forced to return to the place he hated most, unable to die and find rest. Even if only for Zachii's sake, she had to renew the death flowing through her. She had to keep him in the light for as long as possible, even if it meant that she herself would fade.

She took a shaky breath in, shallowly filling her lungs with rich air. How twisted was it that the most life-giving substance in the world caused her such pain? To others, this air was a sweet delicacy, inhaled deeply to give strength to their souls. To Lindina, it felt like the pen, a self-inflicted torture necessary to keep herself alive. She needed the pen back, but Haanon had it in his pocket. He wouldn't give it back, even if she threatened to kill for it. He cared too much about her.

Haanon broke the long silence with a whisper. As with every sound, it came to her ears shrouded by a veil of imperfect silence, obscuring his tone. "What would Zachii want?"

Lindina brought her eyes up to meet his. They were once again soft.

"What would he have you choose?"

"He wants to be in the light," Lindina said. "He wants to be anywhere but those cursed Plains."

"I want your safety above all, Lindina!" Zachii cried. Everyone jumped at this and looked at him. His eyes shot between Haanon and Lindina before locking on her. *"Tell him the truth!"*

"He says . . ." Lindina took her hand from his wing. "'I want you to leave us alone.'"

At this, Zachii merely shook his head. Lindina sighed as deeply as she could with the small bit of air in her lungs. Why couldn't he want happiness for himself? Why did he have to be so self-sacrificing?

"He wants the best for you, Lindina," Haanon said, as if he too could understand Zachii, "as do I. If you continue this path, you will destroy yourself. Consider the regret Zachii would have. You would be forcing him to watch the person he cares for most destroy herself. Would you plague him with that?"

Haanon didn't understand. Yes, it would be hard for Zachii to watch Lindina suffer, but it would be even harder to return to the Plains.

"Are you going to ignore what I told you?" Lindina asked. She knew Haanon would disagree—Jacob too—but it was the truth. "Me and Zachii are the only ones who can stop Baltashazar. The only thing that can kill him is the same darkness he uses."

Haanon frowned. "The Silencers—"

"The Silencers can't do what I can!"

"No. They can do far more."

How could she explain it any more than she already had? Baltashazar had the same powers Dreslen did. Well, he couldn't use the Deep, but Zachii claimed he was as proficient in the Way of the Abyss as Dreslen ever was. Even Mordecai, one of the greatest Sirathim of all time, could not defeat Dreslen. What hope did a group of men in grey cloaks with no powers have against the same power that beat Mordecai? Against such a herald of cold, soundless darkness, the Silencers were nothing.

She looked at Jacob, suddenly remembering. His move to Mortua! Why wasn't he there? Even if he hadn't given up his dream job, he'd still done so much in looking for Lindina. She didn't deserve his help. She didn't deserve anything anymore. Killing someone was unforgivable, and Lindina wouldn't budge on that. She was irredeemable. But so was Baltashazar. Lindina could allow herself to kill him. No, she *had* to kill him, or else he was going to hurt a lot more people. She owed it to the world to kill him.

"Fine." Lindina looked at the ground. She'd need to be quick with her hands, but she needed the pen back. Without it, she was just a frail little girl against a dark lord. With it, she was terror incarnate.

"Fine?" Haanon sounded skeptical. "You'll let the Silencers handle this?"

"Yes."

"Haanon, maybe the girl is right," Ilemek said. That drew a hard look from Haanon. "Obviously it can't be her, but maybe the Silencers aren't strong enough. This is the stuff of legends we're dealing with. Baltashazar isn't a simple Wayfollower. No offense to you, Jacob."

Lindina squinted. Why would that offend Jacob?

"I agree," Jacob said, avoiding Lindina's eyes. "Wayfollowers might be dangerous in some cases, but I've never heard of anything like this. However, I still think the Silencers are our best bet. If they can't stop him, no one else can. Even if Lindina's right, and all the Silencers in Barabus are dead, there are many more in Midor."

"It's settled," Lindina said. "We trust the Silencers. And . . . I'll trust you, Haanon." She turned and stared into Zachii's unblinking, unfathomable eyes. Such beautiful eyes. "Zachii, it's time we said goodbye. You can go back to the Abyssal Plains now. That's a command."

Zachii cocked his head and crowed softly. *"You're lying."*

Lindina nodded. She knew the others couldn't hear Zachii. She whispered back, "Wait outside the forest. That's a command." Thanks to Dreslen's curse, Zachii had no choice but to obey her every order. For once, she was glad of it.

"What did you say to him?" Haanon demanded.

"My last goodbyes. I'm never going to get to see him again, you know."

Haanon looked at her. Hard. He knew, didn't he? She could admit she wasn't a good liar, but Haanon couldn't know her plan. Although, if she didn't start lying better, he might figure it out.

"Goodbye, Zachii!" Lindina forced tears. It wasn't difficult with all the pain gnawing at her skin and insides. Actually, it felt good to cry. "Don't forget me!"

"I'm sorry I have to obey you," Zachii said, spreading his patchy wings. *"For your sake."* As he lowered them and rose into the air, a gust of wind carried to Lindina's face. Judging by how everyone else winced, they felt it too.

As soon as Zachii cleared the top of the trees and started flying away, Haanon breathed in relief. "I fear convincing you was too easy, but I can already feel the forest's gratefulness."

"I'm sorry for not trusting you!" Lindina sobbed. "I want to be healed from this horrible sickness!"

Though the words were a ploy, she meant them. She wanted desperately to be free. Instead, she ran over to Haanon and threw her arms around his waist before he could object. The embrace caused more pain than she expected.

"I . . . am glad you've returned to your senses." Haanon returned the hug stiffly. His hands felt like fire on her back. What must she feel like to him?

"Me too." *This is it.* Gradually releasing her grip, she brought her arms back around from Haanon's waist. Her left hand passed over a fissure in the fabric, and in a smooth motion she sunk her fingers into the pocket and closed around something deathly cold. She would have smiled if she didn't feel so terrible. Haanon didn't seem to notice Lindina's hand go to the pocket of her own dress. Instead, he gazed at her face.

"We shall begin your healing in the morning. For now, I must attend to Zachii's news." He looked up to face his brother—at least, that's how Lindina imagined Ilemek. "Please show Lindina to a hut in the outer lodges. She needs to be among nature as much as possible."

"Of course." Ilemek bowed slightly, then looked at Lindina and smiled. "Shall we?"

Lindina nodded, still sniffling. She wanted to cry all over again, but she'd have plenty of time for that later. After Baltashazar's head was rolling on the ground.

TWELVE

*T*error. *Blood. Death.*

It seemed the Abyss was capable of little else. Not that he complained; it was a simple life, full of its greatest pleasures.

Horror. Flesh. Decay.

Nothing else satisfied him anymore. Gone were the days of feasting, the hours spent in light and love. But what was love compared to ecstasy? No affection for a person was as gratifying as killing. The sheer pleasure of ripping flesh from flesh with his bare hands was incomparable. He was a waste of potential, a student of the shadows who ought to have begun his studies years earlier, practicing before old age caught up to him.

Yet time without end stretched before him if he held fast to the Abyss. If the dravelords could have immortality, Baltashazar could too. All he needed was a deeper connection, to kill more, to conquer, to finish what Dreslen started. It wouldn't be easy, slaying all his enemies, especially the Silencers. But they weren't immortal, and certainly weren't powerful. Just irritating.

The only thing that worried him was that horrible pounding from the north. Strike after strike, flash after flash. A pinprick of light in the distance, enough to distract him. What would happen when he got closer? Dreslen mentioned nothing like this in his book. Perhaps the Silencers were more prepared than he realized.

But no, the Silencers were naïve. They never expected the return of the Way of the Abyss, and now twenty-three of them were dead. He could kill twenty-three more. A hundred more. He'd kill everyone in Atlantia if that was what it took to appease the shadows.

Dreslen could have done it. He could have covered the land in darkness and enslaved the Sirathim like he'd planned, but he was weak. All that power, withheld. After killing Mordecai, his only rival, he stopped trying. History, even the Book itself, couldn't give him an answer as to why. It was the stupidest decision of all time, made by the most brilliant man of all time.

Baltashazar wasn't Dreslen—he never could be. But he would be stronger. Soon, but not yet, wrath would come. Very soon.

He laughed, sipping from his goblet, letting the thick, metallic-tasting liquid satiate his tongue. The soldier across the table watched with a trembling open jaw. They sat in the guards' mess hall, alone. A few torches lined the pillars, illuminating blood-stained round tables and broken dishes.

"Are you going to drink yours?" Baltashazar nodded to Kastor's goblet. It was still full.

Kastor remained frozen and speechless. Good.

"I asked a question."

Kastor shook his head, eyes on the table.

"What if I ordered you to?" Baltashazar set down his cup and rested his elbows on the table, leaning forward. The Abyss yearned to escape his body and kill the man, like serpents twisting between his organs.

As expected, Kastor said nothing.

"Take a drink, soldier. You've earned it. Eight years of serving the king faithfully. I can still remember the first time I told you how to hold a sword . . . Do you remember that day?"

Kastor nodded.

"Being lord of the guard *was* gratifying, but I think this suits me better. You need a king who respects this land's history. After all, Amiroth didn't build this city."

"What if I don't want the promotion?" Kastor whispered.

"I need a captain to lead another expedition. This won't stop until the item is in my hands."

"Why me?"

"Because you've been the silent one all your life. Now that the Silencers are dead, you can finally cast *them* into *your* shadow. How would that feel?"

"I just wanted to protect the king."

"I am your king."

"Not yet. You haven't been coronated, and King Baraz is still alive." He winced.

Baltashazar leaned back and raised his eyebrows. "Oh? Where did you come by this rumour?"

"I . . . didn't. I made it up."

"So there are some still loyal to Baraz. I'll have to deal with that. For now, what of my proposal? You really ought to say yes. Oh, and have you tried your drink yet?"

"I—"

The door to Baltashazar's right swung open, slamming against the wall. A man in a black tunic stood in the doorway, sword at his side.

"What in the name of Amiroth is going on?" he said.

Baltashazar frowned. He recognized that voice. Surely one of his soldiers, but if that were the case, he should be groveling in terror. There wasn't a guard in Barabus who hadn't seen Baltashazar's executions. Perhaps this man could be turned into another example.

"Where is the king?" the man said, stepping forward and drawing his sword. Torchlight illuminated his face better now.

Ah, I remember you. Baltashazar calmed his insides. This man wasn't rebellious, just ignorant. "Sit down, Sorias. I'm promoting Kastor. You can be a witness."

Sorias spat. "Cut the drivel. They told me you murdered King Baraz. That you murdered the Silencers and half the castle guard."

"They were right, and Kastor will be next if you don't sit down."

Sorias stopped walking. Soldiers were so predictable. Ready to give up their own lives yet unable to sacrifice their comrades. Only Hazak had been different. Oh, what Baltashazar would give to have another sadist in his troops.

"Tell me, Sorias, why are you so late in returning? The rest of your squad was here yesterday."

"Tell me why my king is dead."

"The other men told me what happened. A huge lightning strike out of nowhere, nearly burning down the forest. They say it killed Captain Hazak. All the other men rallied around that point and waited for you, but you never came. Why?"

"Tell me why King Baraz is dead!"

"Oh, very well. I wanted the throne."

"That's it? You murdered your cousin, who always respected you, so you could be king for a few short years? We won't stand for this."

Sorias raised his sword again, entering the combat stance Baltashazar taught him. Left foot forward, sword in his right hand, fist in his left. Amiroth form. Aggressive and swift, but reckless against an experienced fighter. Sorias should know better. Then again, Baltashazar did look frailer than he used to. Still tall, but thin and weathered.

"I think you will." Baltashazar turned to Kastor, readying his shadowblade. It accumulated invisibly in the shade beneath the table, lighter than air but lethal as rockweaver venom. Some of the chill left Baltashazar's arm, escaping into the blade. "Isn't that correct, Kastor?"

"Don't try it, Sorias," Kastor said. "Even Rinar and Indring couldn't match him."

"So I've heard." Sorias remained in stance, keeping his eyes intently on Baltashazar. "They call you the new Dreslen."

"Fitting," Baltashazar said. What should he make of Sorias? The man probably needed to watch an execution before he fell into place, but Kastor was too valuable to kill. He'd seen Kastor fight before. A knife in the dark, if ever there was one. Eventually, if he survived being captain, Baltashazar might make him an assassin.

Perhaps Sorias should be the new captain, though. He certainly had the resolve, but his insubordination wouldn't do. "How about this, Sorias?" Baltashazar said. "I'll make you a night patrol officer for the Outer District. If you're still complaining by the end of three days, I'll slaughter three families at random. That's how it works from now on."

Sorias cursed at him, as terrible a curse as Baltashazar ever heard. Contorting his face, Sorias stood up straight and returned his sword to his scabbard. "This won't last forever. The Silencers will come."

"I'm looking forward to it."

Sorias spun around and marched out of the room with a grunt, slamming the door behind him. The impact echoed for long after he was gone, fading into beautiful silence.

"I like that . . ." Baltashazar muttered, looking at Kastor. There was something in his eyes that wasn't there before. Resolve. *Perhaps Sorias does have to die,* he thought. He couldn't have him starting a rebellion. Then again, a coup would be a perfect excuse for an execution. He'd just have to wait and see.

"Captain Kastor, you're promoted. Refuse my orders, and I'll kill everyone in your family and make you drink their blood. Speaking of which . . ." He nodded to the goblet.

Kastor gulped, put his hand to the goblet, and raised it.

"That's an order, soldier."

He took a sip and retched, spraying blood out of his mouth.

Close enough. Baltashazar stood up and left the room, leaving Kastor alone, still sputtering. He'd get used to it eventually.

Screams from the soldiers' training grounds still echoed in Adriel's mind. It had been two days since meeting Dredding in his office. Two days since Syndria was executed. If Adriel had any tears left in her, she would weep, but crying without pause for hours on end did strange things to a person. The doctor in her wanted to figure out how crying for that long was possible; her human side just accepted it. She was living a life worse than any nightmare. If anyone were in her position and didn't cry, she'd call them broken.

It was Midwaning, the second-last day of the week. Half the moon shone over the dark stone, complementing the flickering firelight emanating from the street torches. The night was still young, so many were still out of doors and walking to their destination. Those in the Central District rarely moved when they didn't have to. At least, those who weren't her patients. She recognized a couple she used to treat, now walking the opposite direction of her. They were probably out for their prescribed evening wal k.

Adriel looked at the ground and shielded her eyes, although hiding her face wouldn't do much good. She was one of the few people in the city with blond hair, and hers was exceptionally light no matter which kingdom she went to. Dredding told her he had a plan to keep her alive, but still refused to say what it was. Was he tricking her somehow?

She shook her head. Dredding was a shell of the man he once was, but that shell was still him. He still had some care left, whether he admitted it or not—Adriel was living proof of that. If Dredding hadn't stuck out his neck to stop the soldiers from executing her . . .

Screams. Death. Blood everywhere. She couldn't relive that moment. Years of a being a doctor, performing surgeries many would find grotesque, had not prepared her for such a morbid scene. Baltashazar, tall, thin, and draped in shadow, standing over the bodies and laughing. The cold shadow of a dravelord under the chilling sun.

Even now, she had a hard time convincing herself this was all real. She wasn't a history enthusiast, but knew the signs all too well. Dredding was right—Dreslen had returned. How that worked was beyond her. Did he reincarnate himself? Was Baltashazar being possessed by Dreslen's spirit? Many would call her superstitious, but if they could see what she had seen, they would believe it as well.

There was simply no other way to explain it. Baltashazar used to be a respectable man. Unnerving at times, but always obedient to the king and seeking the good of the kingdom. The creature he'd become was pure madness.

Ignoring the greetings of Patrila and West, Adriel rounded the corner and walked onto her home street. What would she find at her house? She hadn't been there since the day she left Syndria. Knowing Baltashazar's methods, she wouldn't be surprised if she found blood stains. Could she live with the blood of her dearest friend painted on her floor? The grief would kill her more each day until she was no better than Dredding.

The gate leading up to her mansion was open. Unsurprising. There shouldn't be anyone still in there, though, if Dredding was right. He made the Central District Patrol Division forbid entry on this house. If a guard were to see her now, she'd be arrested, but there was no one in the area. It would seem Baltashazar killed too many of his guards to spread them far enough.

Once she reached the end of the pathway, she looked over her shoulder. Good. No one watching. She strode up the steps onto the porch, put her hand to the doorknob, and turned, swinging the door inward and closing it as soon as she was inside. As she moved her hand to the lock, she thought better of it. This house w as *supposed* to remain unlocked. If a guard couldn't get it open, it would arouse suspicion. Better for her to hide if a guard came.

"Great rockweaver, you're alive!"

Adriel turned, eyes wide, and looked at her living area, barely illuminated by the light from the windows. Rising from the couch was a tall man holding something long and thin that gleamed at the tip. *Great.* Maybe he'd kill her and put her out of—

No! She grit her teeth. Becoming like Dredding was *not* an option. As a doctor, she was responsible to uphold all human life. Including her own.

"What are you doing here?" she asked. Perhaps she should maintain her charade of authority. "I ordered all guards to be removed from my property."

"Afraid you don't have that authority, Doctor Adriel." She knew that voice. Where from? "You didn't have the authority to see Doctor Dredding, either. How are you still alive?"

Gib. He'd been at the castle gate two days ago. "That's none of your business."

"If Lord Baltashazar knew, he'd have me kill you. I'd be more careful with my words."

"You wouldn't kill me." Adriel stepped forward. "Not you."

"I could," he said grimly. "As could anyone in the castle guard. Except for maybe Sorias, mind you."

"Don't mention that name under my roof."

"If you'd just listen to him, he—"

"I don't care what he has to say! And I'd watch my back around him, if I were you. I wouldn't be surprised if he was the first to join Baltashazar's new army."

"I know you don't like him very much—"

"Not one bit."

"But he's not *evil*. He's one of the—"

"We're not discussing this now. Stop."

Gib shut his mouth, sitting down again. Darkness and silence overtook the room. Not too long ago, Adriel would have called them her friends. Now they only reminded her of Baltashazar.

"There's only one way we're going to keep you alive," Gib said. "We've got to convince everyone that you're dead."

"I think Dredding is taking care of that."

"And why is Doctor Dredding helping you at all?"

Adriel didn't know the answer. She assumed it was because she'd been better to him than all the other doctors, especially during the death of his wife, but that could only be a piece of it. More likely, he was clinging to guilt and trying to absolve himself by saving her. No one understood how his mind worked, though not for lack of trying.

"Tell me, Gib." Adriel knew the answer, but some hope remained. Foolish, dangerous hope. "Is Queen Syndria dead?"

"Slain by Lord Baltashazar's own hand."

Of course. She didn't expect any different. Why should she? Everyone she'd ever cared about was dead, except for the one who backstabbed her. He was still alive, unfortunately. Despite being a doctor, she was still unaccustomed to death. Whenever she lost a patient, she mourned, but that was nothing compared to losing Syndria.

"He has to be stopped," Adriel whispered. "He can't keep killing people like this."

"He can, and he will. He won't stop with Barabus, either. Midor will be next, then Collabria. Maybe even Dunn. Unless we can find someone as powerful as Baltashazar, there's nothing we can do. It's all about survival now. I'm sorry, but self-preservation is all that matters."

"Then why do you want to help me?"

"Because I'm a guard. It's what I do. I protect people."

"What about self-preservation?"

"I'm smart. I think I can keep us both alive."

"And if you had to choose?"

"Right now, I'd say I'd protect you. But if that moment actually comes, and his terror seizes me like a tightening noose, I can't guarantee it. We can't all be Sorias."

"Thank the Silence for that."

"That's not what—"

"I know what you meant."

He sighed. "Have it your way. I can't convince you otherwise."

"That is correct."

Gib stood up once again, spear pointed upwards. "I should be going now. Stay here, and don't let anyone in. Not even city guards. *Especially* not city guards. If they do come, don't let them see you."

"What about you?"

"If I need to reach you, I'll shoot an arrow through your window."

What good would that do? Adriel thought. Wasn't he trying to keep her alive?

"With a message attached to it." Gib must have seen the confusion on her face. "Remember this: trust *nobody*."

"I won't."

"Not even me."

"That's . . . counterintuitive, but alright. As soon as you leave my door, I'll stop trusting you."

Gib nodded and walked past her, peering through each of the front windows. Without a word, he opened the door and slipped through it, leaving her in dark silence again.

No one to trust, she thought. So this was the end, sequestered inside her own house, alone, while murder ensued outside.

No reason to hope.

THIRTEEN

Jacob tried to snap out of his daze. He felt as though his entire life had been torn apart. Indeed, it had. When he left Midor to seek Lindina, he'd given up everything. The quest had been the only thing holding him up, the one thing giving him purpose. Now it was over. He'd found Lindina, and this was where she needed to stay. Who was he to intervene?

However, her sudden change of heart still itched his head. One moment she adamantly defied Haanon, and the next she embraced healing with tears of apology. Was it genuine?

Likely not, Jairus said. *But it may be so. Regardless, Haanon is better equipped to deal with her than you. Put her out of your mind.*

Jacob tried and failed. Even with Iven rambling beside him as they walked through a lush part of Tahil forest, he couldn't think of anything but those shadow-bound eyes, streaming tears to the blackened grass beneath. The girl he'd tried to save, broken beyond his aid. There was nothing he could do now, but what if he'd acted earlier? What if he had—

"Jacob, are you listening?" Iven said.

"Yes." Jacob turned his head. Iven raised his eyebrows. "No," Jacob admitted.

"Understandable," Iven said tersely. "This is a nightmare for all of us. But nightmares, like many things, are little more than one's imaginings."

"I beg your pardon?" Jacob didn't hide the indignation in his voice. This was far removed from imagination. How dare Iven even suggest it?

"Do not mistake me," Iven said. "I'm sure this is all quite painful for you, but can we agree that non-physical pain is all a matter of perception?"

"Perception? Is that all?" Jacob reached down and ripped a blossoming blue flower from the forest floor. Iven yelped and tried to intervene, but Jacob backed away and held the flower aloft. "Was that simply perception?"

"Jacob, you can't kill the forest to make a point!"

"So, you admit I'm right?"

"No, I said you made *a* point. Frankly, it supports my argument better. I felt pain at the flower's death; you didn't. The only difference is our perceptions."

"Then why did you only feel pain once the flower died? Clearly, the act in itself was painful to you. Perception allows us to feel pain, but is not what causes it. Otherwise, pain doesn't exist."

"But what is existence, anyway?"

"Existence is, well . . ." Jacob stammered. "Iven, you can't *define* existence! It just is."

"Then neither can we objectively define whether something exists. All we can know is what we *perceive*. But that is where the line is most fundamental, I think. Are you familiar with the myth about the tree farmer?"

Jacob shook his head.

Iven smiled. Few others could match that expression of joy. The way his eyes danced with green light, Jacob could have guessed there was actual fire beyond his face. "It goes something like this," he said. "There was once an old farmer, living alone in the forest, who specialized in breeding trees. Oaks and pines, willows and everbirches—"

"Everbirches?"

"That's how I heard it."

"What *is* an everbirch?"

Iven shrugged. "Probably not important. Anyway, the farmer decided to breed a great tree after the likeness of every other tree in the world. A great tower of wood and leaves, a beacon of beauty that would be admired from one end of the world to the other. For years, he worked on the seed in solitude. But old age hastened on him, and he finished the project early and planted the seed before he was sure it would sprout."

Jacob waited for Iven to continue, but he instead let his hands go limp at his sides. Around them, birds chirped quietly, as if discussing the story amongst themselves. Tall grass brushed against his hands, leaves rustled in the warm breeze, and sunlight bathed his face between shadows. Finally, in the silence between Iven's story, Jacob could finally appreciate the forest. No more worrying about Lindina.

Lindina.

"What happened next?" Jacob asked.

"That's the end of the story."

"That's it? Did the tree grow? Did the old farmer die?"

"Oh, the farmer's most certainly dead. That's why the story ended, after all. But you asked the right question: did the tree grow? Did that magnificent tree exist?"

"In literal reality, no. It's just a story," Jacob said.

"Not all stories are lies."

"Is *this* one true? *Did* the tree exist? Or the farmer, for that matter?"

"You'd know as well as I. But let us assume that the farmer existed. What of the tree?"

Jacob knew where Iven was approaching from. Relativism. A denial of objective truth in favour of subjectivity. Back home, the only people who held this belief were those who wanted to live in denial of facts. A rule-breaker or a grieving widow who couldn't accept her husband's death. None of them had been particularly intelligent. Not like Iven.

"The tree may or may not have existed," Jacob said. "We cannot know, because we have insufficient evidence. However, if one were to visit that spot, one might find remnants of the tree and prove its existence . . . or lack of it."

"*If*," Iven said. "*If* one were to visit that spot. But no one has, and no one will, because it is lost forever. Remember, the story ended at the death of the farmer. For the sake of the story, all ceased to exist."

"Then for the sake of the story, the tree doesn't exist. But in reality, it may still exist."

"But you wouldn't have heard of the tree if not for the story. Thus, the story is the basis for the question of the tree's existence in the first place. I'm sure you can put the rest of the pieces into place."

Iven was still wrong, of course, but his argument had some sense to it. Too much sense. "Fine," he said eventually, "let's assume that reality is based upon perception. But what if there was a being that perceived all?"

"An omniscient observer?" Iven looked ahead, stepping over a protruding root and scratching his hair. "I suppose if that were the case, reality would be similar to objective. However, an omniscient being must not exist if it cannot be perceived."

"Now you're using circular reasoning."

"I am, aren't I?" Iven grinned. "It's terribly boring sometimes, not having anyone to debate philosophy with me. Besides Haanon, of course. Thank you, Jacob."

"Red herring." Jacob returned the smile.

"A red what?"

"A statement that has no relevance to the argument."

"Ah. Forgive my lack of terminology. Most of my philosophy comes from my own intuition, you know. I don't have the privilege of vast libraries."

Neither do I, Jacob thought. *Not anymore.*

There's still time, Jairus said. *Perhaps, if you leave soon, you can still fight for your position.*

"An omniscient one . . ." Iven slowed, then stopped. "Would the Deep be considered that?"

Jacob had often wondered about that question. If the Deep was indeed sentient, and it truly flowed through all things, such a fact would be plausible. However, he had no way of verifying anything regarding the Deep. The Silencers banned all texts that spoke of it as anything other than a dangerous force and left it at that. All Jacob knew from texts was that the Deep empowered the Sirathim to create and Dreslen to destroy.

But unlike most Atlantia, Jacob had personal experience with the Deep. Mostly, it was a source of power, enabling him to harness the forces of nature. To guide the wind, to connect to trees, to spark fire . . .

Junia.

Remember the tolling bell? Jacob told himself. The Deep had allowed Haanon to ring the bell, all in order to connect them in a vision and save his life. It seemed to *want* Jacob in Tahil. That alone was enough to support the idea that the Deep had a will.

"I think," Iven said, "the Deep is beyond our understanding, and thus we cannot lean on it for the understanding of anything else, especially for something so rudimentary as existence."

"I thought the Sirathim were devoted to the Deep more than anything."

"The Sirathim are gone. But like them, I hold to the Deep above all."

"Then is it not the lens through which you view the world?"

Iven pursed his lips. "It's complex."

"It needn't be."

"You speak the words of an idealist. Tell me, how devoted are *you* to the Deep, Wayfollower?"

Jacob thought back to the many times he'd renounced the Deep as evil. Even now, his feelings about it were mixed at best. "One could hardly call me devoted."

"And why is that?"

"The atrocities committed by followers of the Deep speak for themselves."

Iven frowned. "The atrocities committed by breathers of *air* speak for themselves. Does that make air any less vital to our existence? Any less worthy of thanksgiving?"

Oh, if only you understood . . . Jairus muttered. *Jacob speaks not of others.*

"You experience the Deep," Iven continued, "but do you know it? Have you felt the majesty of its presence? Have you witnessed its kind touch in nature, its providential hand in bringing about all sorts of good? Have you yielded yourself to it, releasing your dearest secrets, listening for its pervasive voice and clinging for life?"

Jacob inhaled sharply, drawing the wind. Branches bent towards him. Leaves, plucked from their trees, encircled his body as if chained by a whirlwind. His lungs filled with sweet air purified by the trees of Tahil, expanding like a bellows preparing to blow. In that moment, holding his breath, Jacob was powerful, a force of nature holding Iven at his mercy. One who adjured the wind, who commanded the Deep itself, and they obeyed him.

He gusted at Iven. Wind rushed past Jacob's ears in a fury, yet he stood his ground and beheld Iven being thrown from his feet, robe billowing, sailing through the air a short distance before slamming into a tree. He collapsed, and the wind ceased.

All went quiet but for Jacob's heavy breaths and the flutter of small wings. A short way off, Iven stared at Jacob, all mirth gone from his eyes. Mixtures of confusion, anger, and wonder crossed his face.

"Perhaps I don't know the Deep," Jacob said. "But it knows me, and that is enough. Too much, in fact."

"What—"

"The Deep is the only reason I will never find peace. I can't think of a *single* time where it's brought me anything other than grief."

"It led you to Lindina, did it not?"

"To what end? I can't save her!"

"At least you've been granted peace of mind."

Jacob almost kicked him. He instead clenched his fists.

Iven pulled himself up and brushed the loose hair away from his eyes. "I mean it when I say you can have peace here. You know it too, I think."

That was what Jacob feared. This may be the one place left in Atlantia where the Deep wasn't seen as evil. A place without the Silencers. A place where death was a myth, where suffering was only a concept. The place he wished the rest of the world was like.

Jacob looked away and sighed. In the distance, the birds resumed their song. Tahil was everything anyone could dream of, but it was not his home. He belonged in Midor, heralding the wisdom of ages past and present. For Carl's sake, he had to return and tell of Lindina's safety.

Iven seemed to read Jacob's thoughts, for his face fell. "You can't leave, Jacob."

"Is that so?"

"You're not the only one in Tahil who can use the Way of Wind. Finding you would be no small matter."

"Finding me?"

"The wind can be used for more than knocking people over." Iven closed his eyes and took a slow breath, puffing out his stomach. When he released it, the wind circled around Iven like a whirlwind unborn, the seed of a mighty tempest in its docile youth.

Jacob braced himself, planting his feet apart and holding onto a tree.

When Iven inhaled again, the wind returned to normal within a few seconds. "There was no need to steady yourself," Iven said, eyes still closed.

"What was that?"

"A bird approaches from behind you."

Jacob turned around. He saw no bird, only green grass and leaves, deep-brown bark, and a handful of blue and yellow flowers growing from vines in the boughs above. The only creature within view was a squirrel darting across the ground to scurry up a tree.

"There's no—"

"Wait," Iven said. "Perhaps it will still come."

It took only a few seconds before a red jay fluttered from behind a large trunk and came to rest on the branch next to Iven. How had Iven seen it from that far off?

"You wish to know what I did?" Iven said, stroking the jay's feathers with his fingertips.

Yes, of course, a part of him said. Another part of him, the part he'd been trusting for the last three years, warned him of the dangers of the Deep.

Iven went on without prompting. "The Sirathim looked down upon naming the abilities the Deep grants. It encourages the view that the Deep is no more than a source of power. So, I will not tell you what I did, only that it allowed me to connect to my environment better."

"You knew the bird was coming." Jacob stepped towards Iven and looked at the jay. It was bright red, with black crests on the top of both wings, a straight beak, and a white patch on its belly.

"If you stay, I can teach you," Iven said. "I'm sure you'd discover this art on your own, given enough time, but you aren't the patient sort."

"What makes you say I'm not patient?"

"Jacob, your breath *reeks* of haste. Unlike this bird, if Haanon sent you as a messenger, you'd probably come running up to me, panting, and start blurting your message before I even recognized you."

"Messengers are *supposed* to be fast!" Jacob glanced between the bird and Iven, whose eyes shimmered again. "This bird is Haanon's messenger?"

"Along with every other bird in the forest. Shall we hear it out?" Jacob nodded.

The bird took its cue and recited a series of chirps. To Jacob's ears, it was nothing more than an ordinary birdsong. Perhaps to Iven it sounded like Haanon's voice.

Once the bird finished, Iven stared ahead with a blank expression. "Again," he said, squinting. When the bird finished repeating its message, Iven winced and put his hand to his forehead. "Scholar, Haanon."

"What did he say?" Jacob asked.

Iven groaned. "I have no clue. Say it again, slower this time."

The bird recited the message again. Jacob recognized the same pattern of chirps.

"I said slower!" Iven said. "More slowly? You understand that?"

The bird cocked its head and went silent.

"Oh, bother." Iven waved his hand. "The only word I could pick out was 'study'. I imagine Haanon wants me to meet him in his study."

"Could he want me, perhaps?"

Iven glared at the bird. "Slowly. *Slowly*, please. Recite."

The bird blinked a few times then sang again, leaving far more space between chirps. It took almost a minute to get the full message this time.

"I really need more practice," Iven muttered. "Yes, Jacob. Haanon wants you in his study. Best not to keep him waiting; he can be just as impatient as you are."

A cold sweat broke over Jacob. This was about Lindina, wasn't it? Did she try to escape?

Or perhaps it was about Jacob. Haanon already knew he intended to leave, so he might be looking to convince him otherwise. Should Jacob leave now, while Iven was the only one nearby?

Do it, Jairus said. *The old man's a powerful Wayfollower. If he wants you bound, he'll see you bound.*

"Come, Jacob," Iven said as he walked in the direction the bird came from.

If Lindina's in danger, I have to know. Jacob gulped and set out after Iven. If not for the serenity of the forest, he may have gone into a state of panic. But the sweet aroma of blossoming flowers kept him sane. The warm light, reflected off the resplendent leaves, hushed his raging fears.

As he waded through the grass, a sense he couldn't describe overshadowed him. A mixture of peace and anticipation, contentment and foreboding. He basked in life, but something told him it would break soon, and all the terrors of the world would descend upon him like a living nightmare.

But it was only a feeling. For now, he tried to enjoy the bliss of Tahil forest and forget about all that was wrong in the world.

Fourteen

Jacob sat once again in Haanon's study, listening to the rapid scratches of Haanon's pen dancing across the yellowed paper. Aside from that, it was eerily silent. Even after Zachii departed and Lindina left for the outer lodges, the birds had not returned to resume their song, and neither did the trees sway in the same way as before. Tahil didn't feel dead, especially compared to his own forest, but it seemed to be dying.

Haanon's face was turned away at the moment, but judging by his heavy breathing, he was as worried as before. Jacob could still picture his face—wrinkled, weathered, eyes so deep yet so hollow. Even as his right hand carried across the page unwaveringly, his left hand trembled on the desk.

"Why are you here, Jacob?" Haanon said. He didn't stop writing.

"You requested me in your study."

"You were intent on leaving. So adamant about defying me. What changed?"

"A lot changed." Jacob didn't understand it himself. He still planned on leaving the forest, but the urgency was gone. After seeing Lindina and finding out the truth, everything shattered. This young girl, more innocent than anyone else he knew, had partaken in the darkest, most evil essence in the world. If that were possible, what else was a lie? Next thing he knew, the Silencers would turn out to be Dreslites as well. Maybe Dreslen was the *hero*, and Amiroth stained his reputation. Was all life a lie? Was reality no more than a flawed perception?

He couldn't leave until he had a firm grip on the answer. What if he really should stay? The Deep, as much as it pained him to admit, enthralled him, and he'd never be able to properly study it in Midor, even if he was a librarian. Only the Silencers had access to that sort of knowledge.

It seemed he had to choose between the Deep and books—he couldn't have both. But what did he want more? What was more important, not only for him but for the rest of society? If he became a librarian, he could work his way through the ranks and possibly found a library in Tonto, providing hundreds with books and potentially inspiring a generation of scholars. If he pursued the Deep, he could uncover secrets forgotten for centuries, but to what end?

What good was knowing the Way of the Deep if he could only use it within Tahil? He'd spend his entire life with unimaginable power, but could never properly use it. Unless, of course, he revealed himself to the Silencers and effectively waged war on all Atlantia.

The decision was obvious, so why didn't it feel that way? The world needed him as a librarian. It could do without another sorcerer. Yet something pulled at his heart, dragging it down to the forest, keeping him here. The Deep? If it had a will of its own, like Haanon believed, it was likely.

Then allow me to pull you the other way, Jairus said. *You're finally coming to your senses. You can see that, logically, the best solution to this dilemma is to return home. Don't forget Carl, either.*

"Do you trust the Silencers, Jacob?" Haanon said.

"Yes. They give up their entire lives to fight for peace. If anyone can stop this Baltashazar, it's them."

"Do you have peace?"

"I . . ." *No.* He'd never had peace. Ever since he'd discovered his connection to the Deep, he'd hidden from the Silencers in dread. They terrified him like nothing else.

"You do not belong out there, in Midor or anywhere else governed by the Silencers. There was once a time when people were free to practice the ways of the Deep as they desired. There were rules, to be sure, but it was not outlawed."

"Yes, I know. The time of the Sirathim."

"But how much *do* you know, Jacob?" Haanon's writing stopped. "Midorian education is . . . selective, at best. Outright lies at other times."

"How would you know?"

"Many wish to know how I come by this knowledge. There are guesses, some more accurate than others. But I will not reveal it to you or anyone else. The shame I carry is far too great."

"Then I have no reason to trust you."

Haanon turned in his chair. The worry on his face calmed. "Do you see all these books?"

"Of course." Jacob couldn't ignore them. It was the biggest personal library he'd ever seen.

"Could I have written them all myself?"

"No, but I suspect there were others before you."

"True, but you'd be surprised at how many of these books are written by Midorians. Some of them date back to the time of Amiroth."

Jacob raised his eyebrows. He didn't take Haanon for a liar, so he must be mistaken. Amiroth ruled hundreds of years ago. Any writings from that time would be kept solely by the Silencers; either that or under close watch in the Central Library.

"You don't believe me?" Haanon rose from his chair and picked a book from the shelf to his right. Its cover was made from thick, decaying leather, held shut by a fraying piece of string which wrapped around it twice over. "*The Necessity of Silence.* You would know this work as the *Doctrine of Amiroth*, but this is one of the first copies. Some ideals have been changed throughout the years to match society. Quite hypocritical, honestly, but the Silencers are aware of it."

Jacob didn't need to open the book to know it was real. The cracked, discoloured leather spoke for itself. "How did you come by this?"

"Another secret, I'm afraid. My point is to assure you that you can trust my scholarship. I'm not so sheltered as you may think me. By rights, I am the *Bein Jemin*. That's ancient tongue for Great Scholar, used by the Sirathim to mark their leader. In a sense, I am the successor of the Great Scholar himself, the founder of Atlantian civilization."

"What's your point? If I assume everything you say is true, what do you want to say?"

"You must remain in Tahil if you are to achieve mastery in any of the Deep's ways. Apart from training, you can only grow so much. It may surprise you, but I condemn the actions of Wayfollowers in Atlantia. They know the laws of their kingdoms. If they wish to follow the Deep, they ought to do so where it is legal, such as here in Tahil or beyond the eastern border."

"What if I don't want to follow the Deep? What if I want to work towards bringing a library to an illiterate town?"

"Your desire is noble, but you have a responsibility. The Surge has proved you capable of the Way of the Deep. As a part of this world, you are obligated to seek it out."

"I'm also the only one with the will to bring a library to Tonto. Shouldn't I seek that out?"

"If you learned the Way of the Deep, you could teach it to others in Tahil. Either way, your legacy survives, but one may have greater significance."

"Which do you think has more? A well-known town or an isolated forest?"

Haanon raised his finger. "It will not remain that way forever. Do you think following the Deep will always be illegal? The Silencers, like the Sirathim, will pass when the time comes. When that happens, I wish for a great revival. With the Way of the Deep ready to be taught, a glorious new society will ensue, binding the wonders of the past with prospects of the future."

Jacob's breath caught. Was Haanon truly hoping for the demise of the Silencers? The people in Tahil were hidden as exiles. If they had the Way of the Deep, they might be able to resist their oppression. They'd have a weapon to match the Silencers. Was this Haanon's plan? He spoke of waiting for the end of the Silencers, but what if he wanted to cause it?

Remember Dreslen, Jacob told himself. Dreslen, who began as a noble man with a passion for the Deep, who mastered its ways faster than any other and rose until he was forbidden to rise. He slew those he loved in the name of the Deep, awakening dark powers and becoming a tyrant. Dreslen built the city of Barabus for his army of gargoyles, waged war, and sank Atlantia into chaos and death. All in the name of the Deep.

"I can see the shock in your eyes." Haanon put his book back in its place. "You think me a revolutionary. Doubtless you 'remember Dreslen.' I do not blame you for it."

"Is it true?"

"Hardly. But the Silencers have done well at indoctrinating you. Twisting history in their favour. Though I fault them for that, I can see why they do it. They are afraid. Terrified, in fact. Ever since Amiroth founded them, their order has been built on lies. They know this but cannot decipher the truth. To compensate, they do everything in their power to protect. They silence every threat, anything that could become like Dreslen. That includes perpetuating lies and killing Wayfollowers."

"They kill innocents and let men like Baltashazar live."

"Like I said, Wayfollowers are not innocent. They are guilty of breaking laws. As for Baltashazar, I cannot say much. I can only hope that with my letter, they will be able to counter him. Until then, Baltashazar is my responsibility."

"Yours?" Jacob almost laughed. The old man could hardly stand before a dravelord, let alone contend with a powerful Dreslite.

"Yes." Haanon frowned. "I love this world we live in. To love is to embrace responsibility, and love never comes without action."

"But why you?"

"I cannot guarantee that the Silencers in Barabus aren't dead. Since Lindina's word is the only one I have, I must assume it true."

"That doesn't make you responsible for dealing with Baltashazar."

"In the practical way, it does. If the Silencers in Barabus are dead, who will contact Central City to send more Silencers? I doubt anyone would be allowed to leave Barabus at all. Thus, Lindina was the person outside the city who knew of the usurping. Now that she has passed that knowledge to me, I share that burden. I also have the *means* to contact Central City. Thus, my action or inaction alone will determine the fate of Barabus."

"But I know about it too, now. So does Ilemek. Doesn't that make us equally responsible?"

"Perhaps. But I forbade you to leave the forest, and I've appointed Ilemek to watch over Lindina. It must be me, Jacob. I must embrace my responsibility, and I encourage you to do the same."

Jacob looked down at the tea table. No amount of talking would convince him at this point. He was going to leave Tahil. If Haanon was indeed lying and did plan to use the Way of the Deep to overthrow the Silencers, Jacob wouldn't have any part in that. But even if his intentions were true, what of someone else who might learn the power? It was a risky game, one he was unwilling to play. By default, Haanon had lost.

Huh, Jacob thought. *I don't feel conflicted anymore.* Nothing now tied him to Tahil. His will was to return to Midor. But when should he leave? If Haanon knew Jacob intended to leave immediately, he wouldn't make it easy. Better to escape by stealth. Patience. He needed to bide his time. Perhaps tomorrow morning—

As if he'd been stabbed, Haanon clutched his stomach and curled his back, gasping. His pen clattered to the floor and leaked ink onto the ground.

"What happened?"

"I don't know yet. Stay here. Do not leave this study until I've returned." He walked to the door, hand on stomach, straightening his back.

Perhaps this would be a good time to escape, Jairus said. *Once he's been gone for a while, sneak out and flee the forest.*

It sounded too simple. Was this a test? Surely he couldn't . . .

As soon as Haanon closed the door behind him, quick, heavy footfalls shook the floor.

Oh, Scholar, Jacob rose from his seat and rushed to the door. This was about Lindina, wasn't it? Why else would Haanon run? Perhaps the dravelord had returned.

But that couldn't be it. When Zachii first entered, Haanon hadn't reacted this strongly. This was something worse. Deadly. Bad enough to physically hurt Haanon from a distance.

Opening the door, Jacob glimpsed Haanon before he rushed around the corner. The carpet in the hallway was nearly in a pile.

He wasted no time in running after Haanon. Thinking of escape could wait. If this really was about Lindina, Jacob needed to make sure she was safe. Was he responsible for her? By Haanon's logic, no. He may be one of the few who knew of her curse, but he didn't have the means to heal her. Only Haanon, it seemed, could take responsibility, but that wouldn't make Jacob feel any less guilty if something happened to her.

As he leaped out the front door, leaving it open, he paused. His shoes were still next to the porch. The outside world wasn't as well padded as Tahil's soil, so he'd want his shoes when he left. With a grunt, he turned, grabbed his shoes, and darted down the path after Haanon. He could put them on later.

Haanon was nearly out of sight. If not for the houses, Jacob would have a difficult time distinguishing Haanon's robe from the grass or trees. The old man's speed was remarkable. He looked to be in his seventies, perhaps even eighties, yet ran with the vigour of a child. His flowing robe didn't even hinder him.

When Haanon came to the end of the rows of houses, he took a sharp left. That would lead to the outer lodges. If there was any question before, it was gone now. This was about Lindina.

After Jacob cleared the houses, he took the same left and ran into the tree line. He couldn't see Haanon anymore, but he knew his way. It was a straight line in this direction, for about a minute, to reach the outer lodges. Running was more difficult here. Besides trees, the ground was uneven, littered with bushes, and strewn with fallen branches. Shoes would have been helpful, but he couldn't waste time putting them on.

Upon clearing the trees and entering the outer lodges, Jacob nearly stopped in shock. There were more people than he could count. Some ran in arbitrary directions, but most gathered chaotically around a short hut about a stone's throw away. He'd seen something like this before in Tonto, when a crowd had gathered around a man who had a heart attack. In that moment, there were people crying. But in front of him, everyone was silent as death.

There! Jairus brought Jacob's attention to a narrow pathway between the crowd. It was closing up. *That must be where Haanon cut through.*

Jacob ran. He needed to know. Pushing people aside, avoiding their horror-struck eyes, he made his way to the centre of the crowd. What would he find there? His gut told him death, but he couldn't accept it. Lindina wouldn't make her dravelord kill anyone. Unless . . . Lindina was dead. He shook his head. Impossible.

"Jacob!"

Someone grabbed Jacob's wrist as he neared the edge of the crowd. Iven.

"What happened?" Jacob said.

Iven gripped harder. "The girl—your sister—attacked my father."

Jacob gasped. "Where is she now?"

"Gone!" The same panic filled Iven's face. "What kind of monster is she?"

"I don't know." Jacob found himself breathing hard, even though the run hadn't exhausted him. He needed to see what happened.

From inside the hut came a loud cry. Jacob snapped his wrist free of Iven's grasp and rushed to the hut's open door. Nearly everyone else backed away. Inside, Haanon sat on his knees beside a motionless body. Chills ran over Jacob's skin. Lindina . . .

"Lemmy!" Haanon cried, putting his face into his hands. He wept.

"No," Iven's voice broke as he pushed Jacob aside, rushing in to join Haanon. As soon as he saw Ilemek's lifeless body, he staggered, nearly falling out the door.

Jacob stood, frozen, as he watched the two men weep. This was his fault. If only he'd have tried harder to help Lindina . . . if only he hadn't been so self-absorbed, thinking only about his career and living in his daydreams.

Death comes to all, Jairus said. *Learn to embrace it.*

What has she become? Jacob put his hands to his head, reeling. The little girl he'd loved like a sister, who he'd given up his life to protect, had murdered someone. This was worse than being a Dreslite—or perhaps part of it. She was going to become like Baltashazar.

Iven stared at Jacob, ceasing his cries. *This is your fault,* the stare said. *You've killed my father. You're a plague and a curse.*

A fool, Jairus added. Or was it Jairus speaking the whole time?

"Find Lindina," Haanon said between gasps, looking up at Iven. His right hand was in his pocket. "Bring her back."

"She killed my father!"

All was silent for a dreadful moment. Not so much as a breeze filled it.

"I cannot allow her to do it again!" Haanon stood up abruptly. "The girl must be healed!"

"She's gone. She's not our problem."

Responsibility. Haanon's voice echoed in Jacob's mind. *To love is to embrace responsibility, and love never comes without action.* Jacob loved Lindina. Despite what she did, he still loved her. She was his sister. He was responsible.

"Which way did she go?" Jacob shouted, looking around him. Almost everyone stared with glazed eyes. "*Where is Lindina?*"

One man not too far from Jacob, middle-aged with a crooked nose, pointed beyond the hut, hand shaking.

"Thank you." Jacob looked into the hut one last time. Haanon and Iven stared at him incredulously. "Goodbye, Haanon. It's time I embraced responsibility."

With a nod to Iven, Jacob darted around the hut, took a deep breath, and readied the wind.

FIFTEEN

"Iven, don't let him leave the forest!" Haanon's voice echoed.

Without reconsidering, Jacob exhaled and guided the wind, splitting the crowd in front of him with a powerful gust. Tahilites tumbled to the left and right as Jacob dashed through the path, leaping over feet and clearing the ring. It was his first time using the Deep since entering Tahil. Something about this place amplified his abilities, giving him more control, greater ease. For once, it actually felt *right*.

Jacob didn't have to guess which way to go after that. Blackened grass and slashes on huts and trees told him exactly where she'd been. Perhaps it was Zachii or Lindina herself. He'd have to confront them both.

Wind at your back, eyes ahead, Jairus said. *I can't keep you from Lindina, but I can keep you alive.*

Jacob looked behind him one last time before nodding and preparing to windsprint. Iven was still having trouble getting through the crowd.

You have a lead, but it won't last long, Jairus said.

His lungs filled, Jacob started to let the air go, guiding the wind to his back and pushing forward. Dodging the huts wasn't difficult, and the trees weren't dense enough to be a problem. He felt as though he were flying, his feet barely touching the ground as the wind practically carried him. His legs had to move furiously to keep up.

As soon as you reach the tree line, the forest will be too dense to windsprint through.

It wasn't too far off, considering the speed he was moving at. Jairus was right. He'd need to slow down to manage the trees—even more than in the South Midorian Forest. There, the ground was even and the trees relatively sparse. Up ahead, foliage was everywhere and the trees clung to each other for life.

Slow down now.

Jacob sucked in air, stopping the flow of wind. The loss of momentum jarred him, as if time itself slowed. Stumbling, he slowed at the edge of the clearing and stepped onto the trail of blackened grass. Ahead, dark stumps stuck out from tree trunks, as if the branches had been painted black before being torn off.

Iven grew up in this forest—he'll be faster in here. Your greatest advantage is your head start.

Jacob gripped his shoes and shot forward. Thanks to Lindina's rampage, he didn't have to worry about running into branches. His biggest problem was the ground. He could dodge around trees without too much issue, but the grass was tall enough to hide any ridges or fallen branches. One wrong step would send him falling on his face. The only way to ensure balance was to bring his leg up high for each step, anticipating a change in level each time. It slowed him more than he liked, but his overall pace was probably better for it.

Which way was he going? Leaves crowded the sky, and he couldn't look up for long before a tree appeared in front of him. Almost the entire ground was covered in shade, so he couldn't use shadow as a guide. All he had was his memory. If it served him well, he was running southwest, straight towards Barabus. He wanted desperately to stop and check the sun, to prove himself wrong, but there was no time for that.

Why would Lindina do this? All Haanon had wanted to do was heal her. She even admitted it would be for her good. The problem was the dravelord. She'd dismissed it, but whispered something afterward. "Last goodbyes," she called them. Now, Jacob wasn't so sure. Convincing her had been too easy.

But what about himself? He was as guilty as Lindina for disobeying Haanon. Yet what else could he do? Iven wasn't willing to chase after Lindina, and Haanon was too weak. The rest of the Tahilites were too shocked at Ilemek's death to do anything. If Jacob didn't chase her, no one would. She would be lost to her own curse.

"Jacob!" Iven called.

Jairus cursed. *He's far too close.*

"Stop!"

You have to windsprint.

Are you insane? Jacob twisted around a large willow in time to nearly crash into an oak. The black path was straightforward enough, but keeping his footing was like dancing on a giant snake. The trees obscured which way it would turn next, and it occasionally lurched in odd directions.

You're the one talking to a voice in your head, Jairus said. *Between the two of us, I'd call you the more insane. Embrace the madness.*

This is not going to end well. Jacob inhaled through his teeth. His lungs burned from anticipation. When he could hold it no longer, he let it go in rapid bursts, forming gust after gust. Each one lurched him forward enough to allow him to readjust his course, but controlling it became more difficult with each gust.

"You can't leave!" Iven's voice was further away now. Jairus's plan was working.

Of course it's working! It's—

Jacob exhaled too much, creating a gust that sent him sailing into the trunk of a great oak tree. He cushioned the impact with his hands but couldn't stop his cheek from slamming into the rough bark, scraping it as he slumped to the ground.

Head . . . spinning. Legs not working.

Get up, fool!

Jacob blinked. He was lying on his back atop a protruding root, staring at the swaying leaves. Letting instinct take over, he propped himself onto his feet and inhaled.

Before he could gust the wind, a force tackled him from behind. Jacob and Iven tumbled to the forest floor, parting as soon as they hit it. Wind swirled around them, bowing the grass and carrying leaves like spectators. In a fluid motion, Jacob rolled opposite Iven and sprang to his feet, wincing from the new bruises. His cheek still stung. But where was—

Something grabbed Jacob's ankle and pulled, toppling him to the ground. Iven was still in his green garb, blending into the grass, but Jacob could see his face now. Using his free leg, he kicked with his bare foot. Iven groaned, letting go of Jacob's ankle and clutching his face.

It was the perfect opportunity. Jacob stood again, using the wind to lift himself, and looked around for the path. As he started down it, he froze. He hadn't been paying attention to the landscape. Everything looked the same.

Southwest, Jairus said. *Go southwest.*

With a quick glance at the sky, Jacob knew which way to go. He darted as Iven got back to his feet. Unlike before, they were in close quarters. If Jacob didn't use the wind, he'd be caught in seconds. All or nothing.

Using even shorter bursts than before, Jacob windsprinted through the trees, weaving himself like a serpent. He didn't know how he did it. All those years spent as a child dashing through trees, outrunning Carl, were finally paying off. Only now, the fun was replaced by necessity.

He didn't know how long he ran for. His brain told him minutes, his lungs told him hours. Iven was still close behind, judging by his gasps. If Jacob could keep this up, he'd make it to the forest's edge. That seemed unlikely. Windsprinting took a greater toll on his lungs than regular running, and he already felt as though he would collapse. His throat burned with each breath. His heart shook his ribs with every beat. He couldn't keep doing this.

Before he could change his mind, he stopped controlling the wind. The change in speed was stark. His lungs didn't feel any better, but at least they weren't being worked by the force of a thousand winds.

Iven tackled him to the ground once more and this time didn't let go.

"Get off me!" Jacob said, grass filling his mouth.

"Swear you'll go back!"

Jacob rammed his elbow into Iven's stomach. He heaved but didn't let go—in fact, he gripped harder, wrapping his arms around Jacob's stomach.

"I can't," Jacob sputtered. He couldn't get the air he needed. His lungs were going to melt. "I . . . Lindina . . ."

"That monster killed my father!" Iven loosened his grip slightly—enough to let Jacob breathe properly. "She doesn't deserve to be helped."

"Then let me bring her back. If she's out there, she can do whatever she wants. Let me bring her back here, and she's yours." *Not that Haanon will let you do anything,* Jacob thought.

"What do you expect me to do to her?" Iven let go completely, rolling onto his back. "I'm no killer. She's the killer."

"I'm sorry about your father," Jacob said. He wanted to get up, but every fibre in his lungs pinned him down. "I'm sorry she did this to you."

"There's nothing you could have done."

The two lay on their backs for what felt like a long time. All Jacob could hear was the rustling grass, the birdsong, and the pathetic sound of two heaving men. When would he get up? Iven was trying to stop him from leaving the forest—for now, he was succeeding.

"I can't go back, Iven," Jacob said. "Lindina's my sister. Even after what she's done, I can't give up on her."

"You sound like Haanon," Iven said, sighing, "which means you're a better man than I."

"What?"

"I'm selfish. Haanon said I remind him of my Uncle Venet, and he thinks that's a good thing, but everyone else saw Venet as callous and prideful."

"Then don't be like him. Let me go rescue Lindina from herself. We couldn't save your father, but maybe we can save her. Please, Iven."

"I . . . I don't know what to say. I respect Haanon more than any other man, and he wants you to remain here."

"What would Haanon do in my position?"

Iven paused. "He'd go after the girl. There's no question about it."

Jacob propped himself into a sitting position. A faint breeze danced across the top of the grass, cooling his sweat-covered face. The air in Tahil regenerated him more quickly than normal, but it wasn't instantaneous. Magic still had its limits. Now, if only Jacob could recognize his own. His powers could only get him so far, especially if he planned to enter the territory of an Abyss-worshipping madman. But Iven didn't know about that, did he?

Iven sat upright and looked at Jacob. "I suppose I'd have to drag you by force."

Jacob managed a smile. "You're absolutely right."

"You've already proven that would be too difficult. It seems I have only one choice."

"To let me go?"

"Two choices, then. Either that or speed you on your way." He grimaced. "You'll have trouble keeping up with her, I imagine, and even more trouble bringing her back. I've decided . . . to give you provisions."

Jacob tilted his head. Did he plan on returning to the village to gather resources? Lindina already had a head start. The longer Jacob waited, the more hopeless his quest became.

"I appreciate it, but I need to get moving again."

"No, I insist." Iven got to his feet, pulling his satchel over his head and extending it to Jacob. "Promise me you'll return it."

"You know I can't do that." Apprehensively, Jacob accepted the gift. "What's inside?"

"Goldberries. I must admit, I was quite eager to give them to Haanon, but you need them far more."

Jacob undid the gold button on the satchel and raised the flap. Inside were spheres of glimmering yellow, some the size of marbles and others as big as small oranges. Oddly, there weren't any of intermediate size. "Thank you," he said. Since he wasn't hungry yet, he resisted the urge to try them. Why wasn't he hungry? *Tahil air, I suppose.*

"You have no idea how useful those are," Iven said. "They provide nourishment, swift energy, and even pain tolerance. Be careful, though. It might feel like it, but they won't heal you."

"Like an anesthetic."

"A what?"

"Never mind. It's a Midorian word."

"Travel safe." Iven put his hand on Jacob's shoulder. "I give you every blessing I know. May the Deep guide you, and may you return safely with Lindina."

Jacob nodded. "Thank you, Iven." Clasping the satchel shut and throwing it over his shoulder, he turned to the blackened path once more. "I would ask you to join me until the edge of the forest, but I doubt you'd want to keep up with me again."

"Truly spoken," Iven said. "Goodbye. I hope our next meeting will be less confrontational."

"Goodbye."

Jacob started jogging down the path once more, weaving between trees and keeping an eye out for unexpected turns. He decided against using the wind. Although his lungs felt fine, they were sure to flare up the moment he started windsprinting. They needed rest.

Unfortunately, he'd chosen the wrong quest for that. Jacob doubted he'd find rest until Lindina was safe in Tahil again. There might be a few sleeps along the way, but nothing substantial. Like the rest of his life prior, peace eluded him. He'd abandoned any chance of it when he decided to leave Tahil.

It was hours before Jacob finally reached the edge of the forest. When he did, the thin, cold air shocked him. By now, he was wearing shoes—only because he was tired of carrying them, not because his feet hurt. If anything, they felt better than ever because of Tahil's soft floor.

The easy part was over. A flat horizon stretched before him, unforgiving and untended by the Deep. Somewhere in the distance, a city made entirely from stone awaited him. Why Lindina had decided to go there, he couldn't fathom. Whether it was betrayal or heroics didn't seem to matter—he'd get her out of there, regardless. Somehow.

"Shall we windsprint?" Jacob said.

"*Why not?*" Jairus said.

After a long inhale, Jacob pushed out the air and guided it to his back. In not too long, he was flying across the plains.

Sixteen

After becoming accustomed to Tahil's air, the open plains of Atlantia were a shock to his lungs. He'd only been running for an hour, but he couldn't go faster than a jog.

His legs burned, and his trousers seemed to get tighter on his flexed muscles. He was likely to injure himself if he didn't stop soon, but he wouldn't slow down until every part of his body cried for mercy. He'd run for longer than this in the past; he could do it again. After being revitalized by Tahil, he had no excuses.

With every passing second, Lindina moved closer to her demise. Occasionally, he could make out a dark form in the sky flying directly southeast. It could have been Zachii or even Lindina herself. Iven *had* referred to her as a monster . . . It wasn't likely, but it was possible.

She goes to betray us, Jairus said. *After Haanon denied her power, she goes to the only person who will accept her as she is. Tahil will be the first to fall.*

Jacob didn't accept that. Lindina betraying an entire society to a powerful psychopath?

She's a Dreslite.

Yes, but—

She murdered Ilemek.

That was the only part that truly made Jacob reconsider. If she was willing to go that far to escape Tahil, what else would she do to preserve her power? Joining Baltashazar wasn't outside of possibility. Even so, she wouldn't give away Tahil to him—would she?

Jacob didn't want to find out. If he could get to her before she reached Barabus, that would be ideal. At this rate, that wouldn't happen. She'd probably get caught by guards, and he'd have to track her down the hard way. Fortunately, a young girl with light-brown hair should stand out in Barabus. He wouldn't have trouble finding witnesses. The hard part would be actually rescuing her.

You've got to slow down, Jairus said. *You seem to forget that prior to entering Tahil you ran for a day and a half.*

And I plan to again, Jacob said. *It's the only way.*

Listen, fool! It won't be long before—

Jacob's right calf felt like it split in two. He collapsed with a cry, landing on his knees and scraping his hands across the ground. The grass here was nothing like Tahil's—dry, unkempt, browning, and ridden by weeds. The dirt beneath was gravel by comparison. His hands learned that the hard way.

"You win!" Jacob clenched his teeth, clutching his leg. He'd torn a muscle, hadn't he?

You make it sound as though I wanted you to injure yourself.

"Don't you?"

Jairus paused. *If it drives you to return to Tahil, I'll be glad for it.*

"What?" Jacob tried to stand, but his calf exploded as soon as he put pressure on it. "You want me to go back? But you helped me escape!"

Only because I couldn't convince you otherwise. I never actually intended for you to reach Lindina. I needed you in a place where you'd choose Tahil of your own accord.

"But you wanted me to leave Tahil in the first place!"

Curious, isn't it?

Jacob ignored Jairus. Now that he was alone, the Voice wouldn't stop bothering him. It was nice to have someone to talk to, but not if that someone was a hallucinated pessimist. Almost without fail, Jairus disagreed with Jacob if they were alone. If Jacob changed his stance on an argument, so did Jairus. If, by chance, they agreed, Jacob grew suspicious. As he should.

But what about his leg? Resting a few minutes, or even hours, wouldn't be enough. It would be *days* before it was back to normal. He didn't have days. He needed to move *now*.

"The goldberries!" Jacob's hands scrambled to Iven's satchel, fumbling the brass button open and lifting the top. Now that the sun wasn't hindered by the trees, they truly shone like gold. Brighter, even.

He withdrew one of the marble-sized berries, squeezing it lightly between his two fingers. Its skin was as smooth as it was glossy, firm enough to resist pressure. He brought it hesitantly to his lips. Was this how he ought to do it? His calf hurt, not his mouth. What good would eating it do? *Well, I am* tired. *Iven said it would give swift energy.*

He didn't wait any longer. His teeth clamped, bursting it, scattering sweetness over his tongue. His mouth tingled from the juices, and all thirst vanished as it saturated his throat. The sun was more brilliant now, warm rather than cold. His heart slowed, and his breathing relaxed.

Jacob looked at his calf, pulling up the hem of his trousers. It looked perfectly normal but was still throbbing. Perhaps if he waited a bit longer . . .

It won't work, Jairus said. *What you need to do is apply the juice directly to your injury.*

"It's a muscle injury, not a skin injury."

"Cut yourself, then. Pierce your skin, and infuse the juice into your blood."

Jacob pursed his lips. "That might work." Unless he'd dropped it, he should still have his pocketknife with him. The idea of cutting himself wasn't appealing, but it might be the only way.

Jacob took the weight from his left hand and placed it into his tunic pocket. He felt a narrow piece of metal with a switch on the side. It was ovular, rounded on both ends, with an engraving of his name opposite the switch. When he removed it and looked at its black sheen, he felt a jolt of homesickness. It had been a present from his parents on his sixteenth birthday.

No time to think of that now.

As soon as he pushed the flat switch up, the blade swung out from the side. It was almost exactly the length of his little finger and just as wide. He hadn't used it in months. Was it still sharp?

Jacob brought his finger away from the blade's tip with a small bead of blood. "Definitely sharp."

Do it, then. One clean cut.

Jacob sighed and leaned over his leg. It was still burning, but it also felt cold somehow. The pain shouldn't multiply when he made the cut. Skin wasn't connected to the muscle, right?

He brought the tip of the knife to his calf and pressed gently, closing his eyes and inhaling. As soon as he released his breath, he pressed the tip into his leg and drew a crimson line through his skin.

He gasped, pulling the knife away and tossing it to the ground. Blood trickled out of the clean gash, staining his other pant leg. The pain intensified. Perhaps he cut too deep, for the ache in his calf worsened.

Frantically, Jacob reached into the basket beside him, fingering the berries to make sure he didn't pull out a large one. When his fingertips finally closed around a marble goldberry, his arm shot to his leg and squeezed the berry. Cool juice trickled out slowly, at first stinging worse than the knife had. He groaned, clenching his teeth, squeezing until there was no juice left.

As Jacob pressed his hand to stop the blood flow, the pain vanished entirely. Even when he flexed his muscle, he felt nothing.

"Huh." Jacob removed his bloodied hand and looked at the wound. It had stopped bleeding. Hadn't Iven said that goldberries merely relieved pain? Why, then, were they healing him too?

"Tread carefully," Jairus said. *"We still don't know exactly what they can do. Best not to become reliant on them."*

"It's too late for that now." Jacob grunted as he got back to his feet, arching his back, stretching in the warm light. After readjusting his right trouser leg, he started walking in a circle. Still no pain. Was the muscle healed or not?

His knife was still open in the grass somewhere. He felt around for about a minute before he found it, only realizing how stupid that was after his fingers struck the blunt edge of the blade, narrowly avoiding another cut. After wiping the blood onto the grass, he snapped the blade back into its handle and returned the knife to his pocket.

The south horizon looked no less ominous than before. If he kept running straight towards Barabus, he would eventually intercept the edge of the East Midorian forest. Once at that point, it should only be another day of travel before making it into the city of stone. If the goldberries continued to work their magic, he had no worries of hunger or dehydration. All he needed was to reach the city, and he could look for food from there.

With his confidence restored, Jacob ran towards Lindina again. If the muscle in his leg really was still injured, he would need to cover as much ground as possible before the pain sprang up again. He refused to let such a minor setback decide Lindina's fate. If he suffered, it would be for her sake.

⸺◦⸺

Jacob awoke peacefully to the sunrise. He hadn't meant to sleep through the entire night, but his body needed the rest. His eyelids twitched from the light. The grass beneath was cool and wet from the morning dew, gently caressing his exposed neck and forearms. Birds sang in choirs on his right, perched in branches high and low. Their melody chimed like flutes and bells, an anthem of the morning light and the crisp, clean air.

When he inhaled deeply for the first time, his breath was shaky. Every muscle ached, and he felt an intense hollowness inside him, like his belly was sinking down to his back. If he had a stomach at all anymore, he couldn't tell. The hunger pains had not yet begun, but they would soon. Running for half a day with minimal sustenance had its consequences.

He had originally thought to sleep under the cover of the trees, but the grass beside the forest was free of fallen twigs and crusty leaves. There were still a few, but he had brushed them away. Even so, a few pieces of parched leaf rested atop him, only to be blown away and replaced by others.

A breeze danced over his face. Jacob groaned as he lifted his arms from his sides, planting his palms on the ground, pushing himself shakily into a sitting position. His entire midsection contracted painfully, as if preparing for a strike. When he put his hand to his core, he felt the muscles vibrating unnaturally, pleading for him to stop overexerting them. Jacob wanted desperately to oblige.

As he shifted to make himself more comfortable, icy pain seared his right calf. He gasped and relaxed both legs. The injury from the day before was worse than ever, but he didn't have any good options. He kept the pain at bay yesterday by periodically instilling goldberry juice into his leg, but he knew he couldn't keep it up forever. Sooner or later, he was going to have to see a doctor or go back to Tahil. But he was far from either option, stranded at the edge of the East Midorian Forest with no medicine.

Jacob sighed deeply, reaching for the satchel on his right, careful not to put any pressure on his injured leg. It was closed, sitting next to the stump of a small oak tree. He brought it to his lap and undid the button, removing a single marble-sized berry from the pile.

His stomach rumbled, and he instinctively reached for a larger berry. It wasn't as sweet as the smaller one—somehow, that made it better.

After messily eating the berry over a few seconds, his hunger dissipated. He wiped his mouth pointlessly with sticky hands and cleaned off the juices with the handkerchief in his right pocket. He was no longer sore, and his calf didn't hurt much anymore. Perhaps another incision wasn't needed.

When Jacob inhaled this time, his breath came in strong. All weariness was gone, replaced by an unbreakable feeling of strength and life. He almost felt like he was in Tahil again, basking in the warm light and breathing the sweet air of the all-surrounding green. All wear was gone from his joints, and he felt like he could run for hours without tiring.

Rising and throwing the satchel over his shoulder, he ran again. He needed speed more than endurance if he was going to outrun the return of his pain. But then again, if he ran out of energy before the pain returned, he was in no better a situation.

It wasn't long before the trees on the right vanished. He adjusted his course, running along the south edge of the forest to avoid traversing the stone of Barabus more than necessary. Once closer, he'd alter his route to run southwest to the city. As soon as Barabus came into his view, he would change his path again.

He drove the wind forward.

⊷◆⊶

At long last, Jacob crossed into the Barabs. Gone was the forgiving grass beneath his feet, replaced by this dark-grey stone stretching into eternity.

The barren landscape filled him with a sense of dread. This was the land that—hundreds of years ago—was home to the gargoyles. As the tales said, the gargoyles were savage cannibals cursed to wander this wasteland or be turned to stone. Just tales, of course. If there really were gargoyles abroad the Barabs, and they really killed each other, shouldn't he be seeing—

"Never mind," he muttered. The skeleton of some creature appeared beneath his feet, joined soon by others. The bones were decaying, turning brown and crumbling to ash. He was careful to dodge around them as he ran, but he accidentally stepped on a skull as he looked up towards the dying sun. The bone crumbled beneath his foot, and he was not hindered in the least.

It was a marvel that Dreslen broke the Deep magic that chained the gargoyles to the stone. How powerful would he have been—and how twisted that he would enlist those savage creatures in his war? He fought against the Sirathim with no heed for the value of life. Was it his strength in the Deep that drove him to such madness, or was it purely the Abyss?

Jacob didn't bother checking for bones anymore. They were brittle enough to crumble on contact, so they didn't pose as much of a danger as the uneven crags in the ground. He expected the Barabs to be as flat as the plains, but it was nothing like that. Small fissures split the ground, and the stone rose and fell like waves suspended in motion. Everything was the same dark-grey colour. By the time night fell, he wouldn't be able to see anything. The sun was dangerously low, now red, less than an hour from the horizon.

He needed to go faster, but his goldberry supply was more than half gone, and he dared not waste energy. The more he worsened his injury by running, the more berries he needed to subside the pain. If he continued at this rate, he would make it to Barabus with provisions to spare, but not enough to return to Tahil. His only hope was to find a doctor who could tend his injury enough to make a slow journey back.

After a few minutes, he entered a stretch of rock that was flatter than before. Barabus rose menacingly, a massive city silhouetted against the orange sky. When he got closer, he would be able to set eyes on Castle Dreslen. Hopefully, he would never have to enter it, but if Lindina acted as rashly as she did in Tahil, she may already be inside.

Pain seeped up his right leg, and he slowed to a stop. It hadn't been that long, had it? He'd eaten a large berry shortly before crossing into the Barabs. Apparently, it wasn't enough. Slicing himself open wasn't as horrible as it had been the first time, but he still hated the ritual. Maybe it was because Jairus suggested it.

Something was off about Jairus in the last few hours. He'd gone quiet, but Jacob could still feel him lurking in the back of his mind, prying into places Jacob couldn't see.

He rolled up his trouser leg, performed the surgery while standing, and put his knife back in his pocket. The pain surged for a moment then subsided completely. *This won't last forever,* Jacob told himself. *Just half a day more.*

If he used the wind, it shouldn't take him too long to reach the city—an hour and a half at most. The city wasn't walled, so he shouldn't have any trouble finding his way in. Hopefully, he would stumble across someone willing to provide food for him. As soon as he found Lindina and talked her out of her insanity, he would go looking for a doctor.

You're going to die, Jairus said.

Not if I'm careful. Secretly, Jacob was relieved. He wouldn't have admitted it to him, but he actually missed Jairus.

If you follow through with this madness, I promise you will live your nightmare before the end. Do you remember that day when you decided never to use the Deep again? When Junia—

Jacob shook his head. *I don't care to, either.*

If you are going to die, let me have my fun. Let me torment you one last time.

"Jairus, please." Jacob slowed down just so he could have the breath to speak. "Not now." He'd done everything he could to forget that day. But for all the effort he spent, traces of it remained.

Enough to remind him it was there, but not enough to picture it. All he could fully remember was Jairus taking over at the end to help him escape the Silencer.

Turn back, and I'll spare you from the memory.

Jacob said nothing. Even if he wanted to, it was too late for that. He would run out of goldberries before he could make it to Tahil, then potentially die of starvation. As backwards as it sounded, running towards Baltashazar's city was his safest option.

Then you are doomed.

"No." Jacob bit down and hastened. "If you keep us vigilant, we'll stay alive. I don't remember that day, but I know you saved me. You can do it again."

Jairus scowled. *Perhaps. But I stand by what I said. If you die, you will spend your last moments reliving that nightmare. Let this be your incentive to stay alive.*

What other choice did he have? *As you wish.* Lindina almost seemed secondary to survival now. He'd locked away that day for a reason. If he was right about it, it would destroy him as surely as Baltashazar would.

Stay alive, he told himself. *Find Lindina, see a doctor, get out. Don't go looking for extra trouble.*

This shouldn't be too difficult.

SEVENTEEN

Lit by dying sunlight from beyond the southern horizon, Castle Dreslen rose menacingly from the centre of Barabus, its spires piercing the sky like black knives on a dark canvas. The night was void of the moon's glow, allowing the stars to shine all the brighter as the sun's last light faded. In the air above the city, an orange light echoed, flickering as fire's glow.

Jacob knew how big the city was, but seeing it up close shocked him. Although Central City was larger, this was more impressive. Thousands upon thousands of houses and buildings, all created by a single man. A man known for his destruction, not his creation. History could say what it wanted about Dreslen, and it would be right to point out his evils, but this act of pure creation should not be undermined.

Yet as he drew nearer, he noted the crudeness of the buildings. They were all identical—one-story rectangular houses with roofs that slanted in one direction. He passed through the first two buildings. Each had a single window on each of its four walls, about as high off the ground as his waist. Most had shutters, but the ones that didn't were without glass. If he wanted, he could break into a great deal of houses. The crime rates here must be low enough to justify such a lack of security. That, or people resigned themselves to being robbed.

He continued walking through the dark streets, as if on a sea of obsidian. There were tall, thin torches placed at each corner, as well as in the middle of each stretch of road. Jacob avoided the places where the torches had died out. Without the moon, the torches were the only thing separating him from near pitch darkness. What thugs might be waiting in those shaded corners?

The more he walked towards the castle, the closer the buildings were spaced. When he first entered, he could easily stride between two of them; now, the gaps were so small he could barely imagine passing through. Everything here looked the same. Straight, wide streets with slope-roofed rectangular houses rising on either side. Intersections led straight ahead, right, and left. No curves at any po int.

After walking for a few minutes, it occurred to him that he hadn't seen a light in any house. Did they not have lamps? Or were the Barabians bound to a curfew? Even if Baltashazar didn't want people sneaking around the city, it didn't explain why they couldn't at least light their homes. Maybe there was a fuel shortage.

But that couldn't be it. The street lights were lit, weren't they? And if no one but him was outside, what use would they be?

Jacob suddenly heard voices. He froze. The sounds came from around the corner, steadily becoming louder. There were footsteps, too—heavy ones. The stone absorbed every noise, allowing none to echo.

Guards. He'd completely forgotten about them.

"You there!"

Jacob winced and stopped mid-stride. The first of the soldiers was already around the corner, staring him down as two companions came to his side. Under the torchlight, he could actually see their pointed helmets and stiff black uniforms. They didn't appear to be wearing any armour aside from helmets. In unison, they marched towards him as if controlled by a single mind.

Jacob bolted down the street away from them, the pain in his leg worsening. Were it not for that and his exhaustion from wind-sprinting, he would have been confident in his ability to outrun the guards. But pain was a ball and chain. In this case, it was locked to his lungs as well as his leg.

He could hear their heavy boots striking the stone street, quickly and without coordination. Jacob's pain would increase the more he ran, giving him a disadvantage in the long scope of the chase.

But they cannot use the Way of Wind, Jairus said. *You must ignore your weariness.*

Jacob took a deep breath, shaken by his footfalls, and released it into the wind. *Too much.* The pain left unable to concentrate, staggering, pulled down by his impossibly heavy lungs.

Before he could recover, the three soldiers surrounded him in a triangle. One held a bow, another a short sword, and the last bore no weapon at all.

"What is your name?" the weaponless soldier asked. He had a round silver badge on his uniform. "You know what? Let's take you under the streetlight so we can get a better look at you."

The soldiers started walking to the corner, Jacob still in their midst. He could practically feel the point of the sword on his sweating back.

I'm going to need your help, Jacob thought. In the South Midorian Forest, Jairus had used lightning to attack Hazak. The only reason it failed was because he underestimated the other man.

Clearly, Jairus said. *But are you sure you want to give me that much power?*

No, I'm not. Just promise me you won't kill them.

No promises.

The group stopped beneath a streetlight, and Jacob could now see their faces better. The guard without a weapon had a thick jaw covered in a short black beard. His expression, unlike the other guards', was stern, without a hint of uncertainty. The other two looked out of place next to him.

"What's your name?" the bearded guard said.

"Jairus. I'm—" Jacob said.

"You!" The sword bearer cut him off, eyes wide. "You're that Wayfollower who killed Captain Hazak!"

The other two soldiers backed away immediately. The bow trained on him, arrow nocked, and the commander drew two knives from his belt. But the one who recognized Jacob froze, holding his sword beneath his waist.

"I . . ." If Jacob misspoke now, he would find an arrow and two knives in his chest. He couldn't talk his way of this. Not anymore.

"Are you the Wayfollower?" the commander yelled. His arms shook slightly.

Jacob took a breath and closed his eyes. *Any time now, Jairus.* The moment he raised his arms, they would see it as a threat and attack. He needed to distract them for a moment while he brought his hands up and let Jairus shoot lightning. But how?

Jacob met the commander's eyes. Somehow, he had to make him order the guards to stand down. "Are you going to try to kill me?"

"Not yet." His voice was deep. "We'll have to take you in for interrogation."

"No!" the guard with the sword said. He turned his entire body to the commander. "This is the man we need. We can't turn him in to Lord Baltashazar."

"Lord Baltashazar could be listening right now," the commander said. "We may be under the streetlight, but there are shadows everywhere."

"Then he'll already know." The guard put his sword back into its scabbard. He turned to Jacob. "Do you remember me?"

He didn't recognize his face, but the voice was familiar. Sorias, if he remembered correctly. "You were with Hazak. I chased you in the forest, then you tried to kill me."

"And I'd be foolish to try again."

"Whose side are you on, then?"

All was still. Heavy breathing filled the silence, accompanied by the slow crackling of the torch above their heads. Heads turned, weapons twitched. The commander drilled his eyes into Sorias but kept his knives trained on Jacob. What Sorias said next could earn them both death. How loyal was he to the throne of Barabus? Would he betray Baltashazar out of fear of Jacob?

"I can't kill you, and I can't turn you in," Sorias said. "Make of that what you will."

"Treason!" the commander whispered.

"Don't try it, Nor. You'd be dead before you threw the first knife."

Sorias put far too much confidence in Jacob. That incident in the forest was a one-time event. Even if he wanted to, Jacob couldn't recreate it. But if he said that now, Sorias would lose all fear, and Jacob would be dead in a heartbeat.

"This is madness, Sorias." For the first time, the soldier with the bow spoke. All turned to his shaking body. He raised his bow with unsteady hands, aiming it at Sorias. "You'll be executed for this. Me and Nor will be next. I'd rather not take my chances."

All stood tensely, waiting for the imminent death. Jacob had two knives pointed at him, and Sorias had an arrow trained on his chest. Breathing intensified on all sides. If Jairus wasn't fast enough, they'd both be dead in a split-second.

No, they wouldn't be dead. They'd fall to the ground, dying slowly from wounds, listening to each other's agonized groans. Jacob would relive the nightmare.

This should be fun, shouldn't it? Jairus said.

Don't kill them. Jacob pointed his hands at each of the enemy soldiers but kept his arms lowered. *Disable them. Nothing more.* No matter how much he pleaded, he knew he couldn't control Jairus once he took over. If they died, they died. Jacob would have to live with it.

As soon as Commander Nor's hand twitched, Jairus lashed out, laughing as two bolts of blue lightning shot from his fingertips, successfully hitting both soldiers. Commander Nor dropped to his knees, shaking violently and dropping his daggers. The other soldier convulsed, loosing his arrow above Sorias's head.

"Again!" Jairus screamed, casting another bolt at them. This time, the soldiers cried out and fell to the ground, clutching their stomachs and vibrating. Nor moaned as he looked up at Jairus. There was something pitiful about this once-proud soldier who now lay helpless.

But Jairus felt no pity. He chuckled as he trained both his hands on the commander's head, preparing for another strike. The electricity would cling to his metal helmet, charring the skin off his skull, burning the flesh beneath.

The moment before Jairus attacked, Sorias tackled him from behind. He fell hard. Though he tried to brace the fall with his arms, they buckled under the weight of Sorias on his back. He turned his cheek to the ground, grunting as it collided. His arms took the worst hit, now stinging even more than his calf. Jacob's calf.

That's enough. Jacob shoved Jairus away. Through his closed eyes, he saw only chaos. Swirling and flashing shapes appeared and vanished in the blackness of his mind's eye, worsened by the pulsating pain. With Sorias on his back, pinning his chest to the ground, his breath failed him. The metallic taste of stone touched his lips. Or was it blood?

"Get up!" Sorias finally pushed himself off Jacob's back.

Jacob gasped and scrambled to his feet, suddenly aware of his weakness. When Jairus used lightning, he must have channeled the energy out of his body. His knees righted themselves, but the pain in his calf was becoming unbearable. He needed to perform another goldberry surgery.

Both Nor and the other soldier rose as well. Jacob backed away instinctively as Nor reached to the ground for his knives, but Sorias kicked them away before he could grasp them. He then landed a kick to Nor's stomach, sending him reeling.

Jacob dodged as the other soldier threw a clumsy punch at him. He returned the blow, landing it in the soldier's side beneath the ribs. His hand struck against something hard and rough, and he brought it away stinging. There must have been armour beneath his uniform.

Unfazed by Jacob's punch, the soldier prepared to attack again. He clenched his fist, but Sorias came upon him before he could strike. With one quick motion, Sorias swiped his foot at the soldier's, pulling it from beneath him. He tumbled to the ground without catching himself.

"Let's go." Sorias ran down the dark street. After a few steps away from the torchlight, he was nothing more than a silhouette.

Jacob gave one last glance at the recovering guards before running after Sorias. His leg wailed with each step, but he swallowed the pain through clenched teeth. His life had just been saved, and he wasn't about to throw it away.

Behind him, the sounds of boots picked up. Jacob looked over his shoulder and saw both soldiers jogging towards him. Considering the beating Jairus and Sorias gave them, they were coping remarkably well. Jacob didn't stand a chance of outrunning them if his leg stayed like this.

His vision started to go black.

No. He shook his head, and his skull rattled painfully, jostling him awake. Ahead, Sorias took another right—but not around the street corner.

"Hurry up!" Sorias pushed on the door of a house. It was set on the corner, and the street lamp partly illuminated the stone door.

Jacob reached the entrance of the house, bending over his knees before walking onto the doorstep. He panted heavily as he watched Sorias try to push the door open. It didn't budge.

"Stoning civilians!" Sorias said.

Jacob couldn't stand the exhaustion. If it came down to more running, he was going to die. Fumbling with his satchel, barely able to keep his hands steady enough, he opened the flap and took out two marble goldberries. His supplies were more than half gone.

The berries rejuvenated him instantly, even relieving some pain in his calf. That wouldn't last long if he kept exerting himself. They need safety. Now.

"Stupid brain," Sorias muttered, trying the doorknob.

It opened.

"Get in!" Sorias rushed through the opening doorway, glancing worriedly at the approaching soldiers.

Jacob didn't dare look behind. As he stumbled through the door, he felt a sharp pain in his lower back.

Then his upper back.

"No!" Sorias turned around and bounded past Jacob, removing his sword from his scabbard.

Jacob turned wearily, facing the oncoming soldiers. Nor's hands, once clutching knives, were now empty. *So that's what the pain is.* He was certain the only reason he was still standing was the goldberry juice. For that reason alone, he couldn't allow himself to fight. If he drained the goldberry energy now, he'd die.

The bow was left behind, leaving both soldiers defenseless. Sorias planted himself between them and Jacob. "Stand down!" He raised his sword to chest height. "I don't want to kill you."

Jacob didn't know how this would play out, but Sorias clearly had the advantage. Combat skills, no matter how effective, were no match for an armed man. At least, that was what Jacob thought, and by the looks of things the soldiers thought this as well. They stood motionless—shaking, but stationary—while they glared at Sorias.

"You won't have to." Nor reached behind his head and withdrew something from beneath his uniform—a short sword with a single edge. "I don't want to kill you either, but you've given me no options. Either I kill you and the Wayfollower, or I face brutal execution."

Nor bore down on Sorias with a yell. As the blades struck, both Jacob and the other soldier backed away. Jacob considered running inside the house but couldn't bring himself to do it. This man was risking his life to protect Jacob. If necessary, he'd eat another goldberry and aid him in the fight. If Sorias died, it was of his own decision, but ultimately Jacob drove him to it.

The two combatants swung with impressive speed. A strike of metal sounded twice per second, sometimes joined by a scraping. Both men remained stationary. Their only moving parts were their arms, guiding the swords in arcs, jabs, and blocks.

At first, Nor only used one hand to wield his blade, but he couldn't keep up with Sorias's two-handed power. After nearly dropping his sword, he matched Sorias's style. Even then, he staggered from Sorias's overhead blows.

Sorias jabbed, yelling, and Nor stepped to the side. He hit Sorias's sword from above, sending it clattering to the ground. The impact jarred Nor, nearly making him drop his own sword. By the time he brought it up to attack again, he was too late. Sorias swung his fist at Nor's face before stepping back to pick up his sword again.

Nor stumbled backwards, grunting. He released one hand from the sword's handle and wiped his nose.

"Stop this, Nor." Sorias lifted his sword into a ready position, like a coil about to unravel.

"Show me mercy." Nor raised his weapon again. "Make my death painless."

"I don't want to kill you!"

"It would be better than Baltashazar killing me."

Sorias didn't respond. He raised his weapon higher, and Nor made ready to block.

But the clash never came. Sorias's sword clattered to the stone ground, and he backed away with his arms raised. Nor looked back and forth between the weapon and the former wielder.

Sorias said something Jacob couldn't hear. It was barely noticeable in the torchlight, but he also saw Sorias's hands shaking. This was the worst kind of gamble—one with lives at stake. Jacob instinctively reached for his satchel. Sorias didn't realize it, but he was gambling with Lindina's life as well. Jacob had to live. If it came down to it, he *would* let Jairus kill Nor.

"I don't—" Nor started pacing, putting one hand to his mouth. "I can't kill you." He threw his sword on top of Sorias's. The stone prevented the impact from echoing, but it resonated long in Jacob's mind. The sound of steel on steel. Peace.

Sorias and Nor looked at each other for a long moment. Jacob wished he could see their faces, but the darkness was too overwhelming. Grim silence filled the air. Nor had spared Sorias at great personal cost, showing himself willing to suffer the wrath of Baltashazar for his fellow's sake.

"You . . ." A shaky voice came from behind Nor. Jacob looked past him to see the shadowy figure of the third soldier. "You can't let him go . . ."

"What can I do?" Nor looked at the ground. "If I kill him, I'll be no better than Baltashazar."

The third soldier stepped closer and stopped beside Nor. "If there's even a *chance* that he'll mutilate us—"

"We'll flee the city," Nor said sharply. He bent down and picked up his sword, and Jacob tensed. "If that dravelord tries to stop us, we'll—"

"We'll die!" the third soldier shouted. "Do you even know what it is, commander? It's got talons like daggers and a scream that could pierce souls!"

"Then we'll avoid getting spotted."

"You can't do this!" The soldier lunged for Sorias's weapon. Sorias kicked the soldier's hand away, picking up the sword himself.

"You're all going to die." The third soldier gritted his teeth, steadying himself. "I'll make sure of it!" Before anyone could stop him, he took off running down the street.

"Coward!" Nor shouted after him. Everyone listened solemnly as the soldier's heavy footfalls faded, reaching silence as they rounded the corner at the end of the street.

"He'll be going straight to Baltashazar." Sorias put his sword away and turned to Jacob. "You have no *idea* what kind of danger you're putting us in. I swear, if you even lift a finger at me, I'll personally take your head off."

Jacob gulped, nodding. He looked at Nor, who still held his sword. He still didn't trust the man completely. What had made him change his mind? One moment, he was trying to kill them; the next, he defended them. It reminded him of Lindina's trickery. What was he playing at?

"You going to put that away?" Sorias nodded at Nor's sword. Nor returned it to his scabbard a little too quickly. Sorias nodded again then looked around. His eyes settled on the window of the house.

Jacob followed Sorias's gaze and saw two hands withdraw from the windowsill, followed by a faint silhouette vanishing with a rustle of garments. Someone had been watching. Considering the commotion they made, there were probably multiple eyes on them, peering from the cover of shadow.

"Come with us, Commander." Sorias looked at the window a few seconds longer before turning to Nor. "You'll be safer with us than alone."

"Safer with you?" Nor laughed grimly. "Baltashazar will have the entire guard looking for you and the Wayfollower. I'll take my chances with the dravelord."

Sorias tilted his head towards Jacob. "If *he* was able to get in without being spotted, you should be able to get out. Evidently, Baltashazar controls us more by fear than actual power."

"My life depends on it." Nor walked towards Jacob. "Sorry about the knives in your back."

"Don't mention it." Jacob grimaced. In the thrill of the fight, he'd forgotten about the knives. If he didn't get them dealt with soon, there would be no chance of returning to his search for Lindina.

"I know a doctor." Sorias started walking the opposite direction they had come from. "Good luck, Commander," he said over his shoulder.

"Don't get yourselves caught," Nor grumbled. He turned in the other direction and moved down the street.

Jacob followed Sorias. The night ahead was long, and his leg still hurt, but he could wait a few minutes longer. Knowing a doctor was within reach, he couldn't justify using any more goldberries. They were his only advantage. Once they were gone, he would have nothing for another injury.

So he ignored the pain. The dark road twisted ever on, and the streetlights did little to help it. Sorias was Jacob's only hope. The soldier marched forward confidently, as if the identical streets were in fact unique and the way to the doctor was obvious.

Maybe it was for Sorias, but to Jacob it was an endless maze of black stone. All he could do was trust and see where it would take him. Would it be to healing or more pain? Maybe neither, maybe both.

Eighteen

S tone was struck. Metal on stone from below. The sound of her door being knocked. Who might it be? A traitorous lord come to tear bone from flesh, drinking her blood until her corpse was dry?

Don't let anyone in, Gib had said. *If I need to reach you, I'll shoot an arrow through your window.*

It didn't matter who was there. Even if it was a patient, she'd only be putting them in more danger by welcoming them inside. Baltashazar thought she was dead. Dredding had convinced him of that. If he found out she survived, what would he do to Dredding? That poor man had already resigned himself to death, but Adriel wouldn't have it. He was the last person she had left to save. After Syndria . . .

Save the dying; give little thought to the dead.

Adriel couldn't do that. Burying her head in her pillow to drown out the knocking from below, she sobbed silently.

"Do you remember, Syndria? Remember how we used to sit under the full moon and talk until the sunrise?"

The sun always came, but tonight Adriel felt it would be different. Even the moon was gone. What hope was there? The stars were many, but so insignificant against the dark expanse of night. They pierced the darkness, but to what end? Only to remain in it, being eternally surrounded by blackness and void. Endless torture. The stars had no hope for themselves, for only the sun and moon were bright enough to banish the shadows. Now both were gone. Syndria and Baraz were both gone. Who would give light now?

What point was there for her to live?

Save the dying.

Who was left to save? Dredding? When he died, there would be no one left. Her life would be meaningless. Even if she saved Dredding, what was she saving him for? Life under a merciless, brutal tyrant, always under fear of death and pain. Neither he nor Adriel would ever have peace again.

More than any other time in her life, she envied the people around her. They still thought King Baraz was alive. Their views on him might be tarnished because of Baltashazar's curfew, but at least they still held on to the illusion of stability. Some were probably confused, but none—Adriel was sure—guessed the truth. Who would?

It wouldn't be long. The Silencers were gone, the city guard was more pervasive, and the curfews alone were suspect. People would catch on and demand answers from the king. Then, they'd eternally regret it as they watched Baltashazar slaughter their families in broad daylight. If he was merciful, he'd kill them too.

The knocking below didn't stop. She covered her ears and tried to fall back to sleep.

"Idiot," Sorias muttered, relentlessly swinging the moon-shaped knocker on the doctor's door.

Jacob watched from the shadows, frequently looking over his shoulder. Somehow, they made it this far into the city—only a few streets away from the castle—without being stopped by guards. He only had Sorias to thank for that. Jacob still didn't know how Sorias could pick up the sound of footsteps from so far away, nor did he understand how he always knew the perfect direction to hide in. The only time they were close to getting caught, Sorias got them out with a well-thrown rock.

All that stealth came from a man rapidly striking metal against stone to get the attention of a sleeping doctor. He'd wake the entire city if he didn't stop soon. How guards hadn't heard it yet, Jacob had no idea.

"Sorias, this isn't working." Jacob leaned in close, whispering, "You're going to get us caught."

"So you've told me." Sorias brought his hand away. In the low light, Jacob couldn't tell if Sorias looked dismayed or annoyed.

"You said there was another way of contacting her."

"Only one way, unfortunately. I got my friend to check on her, then he went and told her to let no one in, no matter what. Unless, o f *course*, an arrow flew through her window."

"That's . . . odd."

"It's stupid. I've never been trained with the bow, and we obviously don't have any arrows. I guess Gib thought I wouldn't be needing to reach her at all." He sighed. "And he'd be right, if it weren't for you."

Jacob's back still hurt, but against all odds he hadn't bled much. It was a risky move, telling Sorias about the goldberries. But if he hadn't done that, Sorias wouldn't have been able to apply the juice to his wounds. Of course, Jacob lied about where he obtained them. He couldn't have anyone knowing about Tahil. Claiming he'd stolen them from the Silencers' Complex wasn't the most convincing lie, but it fooled Sorias. He still thought Jacob far more powerful than he really was.

He kept the lies to a minimum. Sorias now knew about Lindina, but not her curse. Dreslites were a touchy subject for him. If Sorias knew he was trying to rescue one, he'd probably kill Jacob on the spot. The same could be said if he knew Jacob's true intentions. Once he had Lindina, he'd be gone. The entire point of this journey was to rescue her. If he put her in danger by doing something the Silencers were going to do anyway, he may as well have never left Tahil.

According to Sorias, no one except the city guard and a few others knew about Baltashazar's rise to power. Jacob pretended to be shocked when he heard about it. Of course, he also had to hide his skepticism when Sorias said that King Baraz was dead. According to Zachii, he was locked in the Pits of Todoros—a fate less preferable—but Jacob couldn't betray any knowledge he'd obtained in Tahil or through Zachii.

"What do you suggest we do?" Jacob asked. He could feel some blood trickling from the upper wound on his back. The knives had fallen out as they walked, much to Sorias's dismay. Apparently, they kept the wounds from bleeding. Sorias suggested binding the cuts, but the goldberry juice had been sufficient. *Had* been.

"I'm thinking!"

"With all the noise you're making, you may as well shout up at her window to let you in."

Sorias chuckled grimly. "Trust me, I'm the last person she wants to hear."

"And why's that?"

"Not your problem, Jairus. Not your problem."

"I forgot to mention it, but my name's actually Jacob." He could trust this man, couldn't he?

"As long as you're going to kill Baltashazar, I couldn't care less about your name. Wait a moment!" Sorias ran off the porch onto the stone path amid the lawn. "Jairus—Jacob, get over here!" For once, he whispered.

Jacob did as told, joining him on the grass, following Sorias's gaze to one of the upper windows. The doctor's mansion was as lavish as any Jacob had seen—domed roofs, canopy-covered balcony, upper porch—but what really made it stand out was its plants. Trees dotted the lawn and lined the edges, and thick flower bushes hugged the lower balcony. In a city where everything was made from the same dark stone, it made him feel as though he were back in Midor.

"You can use magic to guide the wind, right?" Sorias asked.

Jacob frowned. He tried not to think of the Deep as magic. Magic suggested something unnatural, but what was more natural than the Deep?

Fool, Jacob told himself. *Remember Dreslen.* He'd become too dependent on the Deep as of late. How would he learn to put it away once this was all over?

"Yes, I can guide the wind," Jacob said. "What good would that do?"

Sorias pointed to the window. "Create an updraft so strong that you fly up there."

"Fly?"

"Why not?"

"Do you have any idea how taxing it is on the lungs to use the Way of Wind?"

"Of course not." Sorias looked at the ground. "Forget it. I remembered when you used your powers to attack me and Captain Hazak, how strong you made the wind, and . . . Yeah, forget it. You need to save your energy for Baltashazar."

It wasn't the first time Jacob thought of using the wind to jump higher. If the Sirathim of old could create tempests, why couldn't he create an updraft? Thinking about it made him breathe harder. He wasn't a Sirathim—he was a Wayfollower. The age of the Deep was over. This was the Silence. The world simply did not permit Jacob to exercise his abilities and become stronger in the Deep. For that, he was thankful. Still, more experience *would* be useful right now. Sorias was right. If he could use the wind to propel him, he might be able to jump through the window.

Perhaps . . .

Adriel lifted her head from her sweaty, tear-stained pillow. That rapid knocking, along with the arguing, was over. The Deep permitting, they were gone—whoever they were. It wasn't likely to be guards. They all thought she was dead. All except Gib, anyway. Unless Gib betrayed her, in which case Baltashazar himself might be at her door.

She decided not to think of that. Last week, she could imagine torture. Now, she didn't have to. Images still burned in her memory. Screams from grown men, some of whom were the bravest in the city. What would Baltashazar do to her if he found her?

Don't think about that! she told herself, looking out the window. The sky was black but for the torchlight rising from the city and the hopeless stars. Should she go and look at the street? Whoever tried to reach her was probably walking away. But should she chance it? No. *Stay out of sight.*

Adriel had moved her bed into the upper living area. That way, if Gib shot an arrow through the window, she'd notice it right away. Although, she didn't even know what he'd be contacting her for. To let her know of imminent danger? By that point, she'd be helpless. To help her flee the city? With Baltashazar's dravelord out there, she may as well walk right up to the castle and request permission to leave. This was all so pointless.

A tremendous gust of wind sounded from outside her window, like a wailing whisper. Odd. The weather had been so docile lately.

It happened again, louder this time. *What in Atlantia?* Adriel sat up in her bed, rubbing her eyes. Was it a trick of her overstressed brain? She hadn't heard wind like that since the giant storm almost a year ago. But there wasn't a drop of rain outside, nor thunder and lightning. What if she just went to peek outside—

No! Adriel clutched her head. *Stay here. Don't let anyone see you.*

Another gust, louder again, filled her ears. She even felt a breeze *inside* the room, wafting over to the window.

Then she saw the shadow. The shape of a head, a few feet away from her open window. Did she imagine it? No, it was as real as the wind. But it vanished so fast! Could it be that Baltashazar was really here?

She waited for the wind to gust again, eyes trained on the window, hardly daring to blink. *Don't come back,* she thought to the shadow. Nothing happened. *Don't come back, don't come back.*

The wind howled. The head appeared, closer this time, joined by shadowy, fingered tendrils reaching for the window.

She screamed.

———◄O►———

Jacob tumbled to the ground once again, this time landing in the bushes, scraping his cheek against a bramble. The amount of pain he'd amassed from attempting this would need another goldberry at least. His legs hurt from jumping, his arms hurt from falling, and, more than anything else, his chest burned with a wildfire. He could hardly take proper breaths. Each one came in shallow and went out full, like he was losing more air than he was gaining.

A stifled scream echoed in his mind. The doctor had seen him, although he didn't give quite the right effect. In the darkness, he must have looked terrifying.

"You were so close that time!" Sorias whispered, rushing to Jacob's side and helping him up. Great Scholar, the man was actually *smiling.*

"It's . . . no use." Jacob accepted Sorias's arm and let himself get pulled up. All he wanted to do was fall back onto the grass and cease to exist.

"What are you talking about?" Sorias dusted off the shoulder of Jacob's tunic, where some leaves had nested. "Come on, one more time!"

"Even if I were to grab the window . . ." Jacob bent over and put his hands on his knees. He must have sounded like a dying old man. "I'd be too tired . . . to pull myself up."

"Fine then. Send me up there."

"What?"

"Create a gust of wind that I can jump into."

Jacob shook his head. "I don't think that's how this works. When I jumped, strength went out from my legs just like my lungs. I think the one who's jumping has to expend his own strength."

Sorias frowned. "Can't you take strength out of me?"

"Like I said, that's not how this works." *As far as I know.* There was much about the Deep he had yet to understand. He supposed that energy transfer between persons was possible, but he'd never experienced it or even heard of it. He'd have to ask Haanon about it when he returned to Tahil.

If he returned to Tahil.

"We've got to change our tactics," Jacob said. "All I did was scare her. Not exactly ideal if I'm wanting her to help me."

"Speaking of which, how are you holding up?"

Jacob pulled a goldberry from the satchel and put it into his mouth. It made the pain manageable. "Not great. This doctor better be as good as you say she is."

"Don't you worry about that." Sorias looked up to the window, rubbing his stubbled chin. "If anything, I've set your expectations too low."

"You speak so highly of her." Jacob stared at Sorias until he looked back. "Were you courting at some point?"

"Like I said—not your problem."

"Maybe it is my problem. If she won't let you in because she has a personal issue with you, then maybe you're putting me in danger by bringing me here."

"First," Sorias said, turning his body to Jacob, "this isn't about you. The only reason I saved your hide from my men is because you're the only one who can kill Baltashazar. I don't give a shade about you personally."

"We're even, then. But aren't you putting the entire city in danger if I die?"

"I'm not lying. Adriel really is the best doctor in the city. Doctor Harold might have contended for that title, but he's a pile of ashes now."

"Makes sense. Go to the best doctor in the city, knowing she'd never let you in, then waste our time as we try to find a *different* doctor who might actually help us. Perfect plan, Sorias." Jacob wasn't usually sarcastic, but getting stabbed twice, having to walk for almost an hour, then getting tossed up into the air and falling to the ground did strange things to a person. Jairus would be proud of him if he were here.

Oh, I'm here, Jairus said. *And I applaud your behaviour.*

Jacob wasn't sure he wanted that. Jairus wasn't exactly a good role model.

"Stone this all," Sorias muttered, leaving Jacob behind as he walked towards the street. He stopped right at the edge of the lawn, surveying the road.

Was he leaving? If so, it was for the better. They were wasting time here. Jacob walked to join him.

"Hey, Adriel!" Sorias turned around and walked back towards the house.

Jacob froze. What in *Atlantia* was he doing?

"It's me, Sorias! I know you don't want to see me, but I've got a guy who took two knives to the back. 'Save the dying', remember?"

"What are you doing?" Jacob hissed, grabbing Sorias by the shoulders.

"You got any better ideas?" Sorias broke away, walking right beneath the window. "I know you're still alive! Gib only checked on you because I sent him. But this isn't about me. Jacob here is a Wayfollower. He's going to help us defeat Baltashazar."

That's enough, Jairus said. *Let me kill him before he goes straight up to Baltashazar to turn us in.*

Jacob struggled to restrain Jairus—not because Jairus's will was any stronger than normal, but because Jacob himself wanted to give in. Sorias was shouting his darkest secret into the night for all to hear. What if a surviving Silencer was nearby? What if one of the neighbours heard?

When silence followed for the next minute, Sorias turned around and scowled. What right did *he* have to scowl?

"So much for your good idea," Jacob said. "Didn't you already tell me that wouldn't work?"

Sorias grunted. "We're not leaving without her help."

"This is just about you, isn't it?"

"I'm trying to liberate the city here! How is this about me?"

"Perhaps because out of all the doctors in the entirety of Barabus, you go to the one who hates you for some reason. I don't know the entire story, but I'm no fool—"

Liar.

"I'm quite certain you two had a relationship of some sort. You're trying to use me to put it back together, aren't you?"

"How many times do I have to say it? *Not your problem.*" Sorias put his hand to his sword hilt. "If you bring this up one more time, stone you, I'll—"

The front door creaked open. Both Jacob and Sorias took their heated eyes off each other and stared. Inside the house was pure darkness, not unlike most of the outside.

Jacob looked at Sorias. "I think I owe you an apology."

"Don't mention it." Sorias's eyes remained on the open door. "Shall we . . ."

"Let's go." Sorias let go of his sword and strode across the lawn, tentatively ascending the balcony steps.

Jacob followed. He was still upset at Sorias, but that wouldn't get him anywhere. If he was going to get any closer to finding Lindina, he needed to work with this man. The more he thought about it, the more he dreaded the betrayal—that was what it was, wasn't it? Lying to Sorias, leading him to think he was going to kill Baltashazar, when all he really planned to do was save Lindina. But it was either that or betray Lindina herself. He'd sworn to protect her. He *needed* to.

"Bring him in," a hushed voice from within the house said.

Sorias looked at Jacob and nodded.

NINETEEN

Lindina was not accustomed to sneaking around, but she had enough natural talent to make up for it. Thus far, no city guards had approached her, and there were no signs of pursuit from Tahil. They *would* follow her, though. At the very least, Jacob would. He was too caring for his own good.

She almost felt guilty for leaving, but it was the right thing to do. Only she could kill Baltashazar. It was a daunting task, but she had daunting power. At will, she could turn into a monster destructive enough to tear up a forest, one in the likeness of a gargoyle but far deadlier. Zachii said Dreslen himself created the pen she now possessed—what chance did Baltashazar have against that?

The castle loomed. It was a sight to behold under the gaze of shadow. Spires rose from its mountainous figure, piercing the stars. The grounds of the castle were easily the size of Tonto, perhaps larger. But it didn't frighten her. She was a Dreslite, at least for the time. This place was crafted by the man who first discovered the power of the Abyss. But Dreslen did not only destroy. From the barren rock of the Barabs, he created this breathtaking city. Were those the actions of a purely evil man?

To Lindina, the Abyss was the opposite of the Deep. If the Deep could be used for evil, couldn't the Abyss be used for good? She thought so. But at the same time, she knew it was killing her. Lindina hated to admit it, but the feelings of death were becoming more apparent each day. If she did not detach herself from the darkness soon, she would fall into a painful slumber and not wake from it.

Haanon was right in trying to heal her. Once this ordeal ended, Lindina would have to let him. But she couldn't give up her power yet. Once Baltashazar was dead, she would hand herself over to Haanon. It would be painful, but she knew he could cure her. He might even be able to cure Zachii too.

She looked over her shoulder at the last group of houses before the castle. They were far too lavish to be the residencies of castle staff members. Beyond those, beyond the rest of the city, Zachii waited for her return. It pained Lindina, but it was simply too dangerous to have Zachii in the city with her. As it was, she could barely get around without being seen. The only thing keeping her alive right now was the shroud of silent darkness she summoned around her.

Lindina knew she didn't need to worry about Zachii. He was undead, after all. Not even an army of the best soldiers could kill him.

But Baltashazar could. The only people capable of killing drav-elords, according to Zachii, were Dreslites and powerful Sirathim. The Sirathim were gone, so the only one Zachii had to worry about was Baltashazar. Lindina refused to let Zachii get near that twisted man, even if her life was at stake. She'd rather be killed than watch Zachii die.

After a long moment, Lindina stepped away from the castle's wall. She strode through the front courtyard, walking quickly, keeping her ears peeled for guards. There were bound to be more here than the rest of the city, weren't there?

Being able to shroud oneself in a cloud of darkness wasn't the only advantage of using the Abyss. All her senses were amplified, allowing her to hear threats from great distances, even if all sounds were muffled. And if she focused *really* hard, she could transfer her vision to another body of darkness, effectively turning shadows into her eyes. For some reason, that didn't seem to work when she shrouded herself. Not yet, anyway.

A sound pierced the dark. Lindina froze, thickening her shroud and breathing hard, waiting for the guards to pass. Normally, her shroud was thin enough to see through, but when it was this heavy, she couldn't see a thing and could only listen.

She heard no more than her own breathing for a few moments, but out of the silence, footsteps emerged, marching in tandem, becoming louder. They might have been walking right towards her. As they reached a spot a few feet away, they turned and continued their march. She didn't dare extinguish her shroud yet; they might look over their shoulders. But how long should she hold it for?

It felt like ages before she allowed light to penetrate her again. Lindina fully dissipated her shroud and looked around, finding no guards in this front courtyard. Part of her was surprised, but Barabus was huge. Baltashazar would have his troops spread thin to be patrolling the entire city, leaving only a few to watch over the castle—which made Lindina's job a lot easier.

She walked to the centre of the courtyard and looked up at the magnificent torch. It almost looked like a chalice with a shallow bowl, made from metal rather than stone. The smell of smoke and death surrounded it. Were there people burning inside the torch? If there were, she couldn't see. There was too much light inside the bowl to transfer her vision there.

"You!" a voice shouted from Lindina's right. She spun and focused on a man she couldn't see. Gradually, her view transferred to the area ahead of her, and she could barely distinguish the shapes of three soldiers. They were walking towards her quickly.

Shouldn't have turned off my shroud, Lindina thought.

"Who are you?" the voice shouted again. Lindina could now see the guards approaching without needing to look from the shadows.

Lindina took out Dreslen's pen from her dress pocket, trembling. A piece of heavy, cold metal. Even touching it made her feel sick.

"What is—" The soldiers came within a sword's distance of Lindina. The leader stopped and looked down at her. He had a gruff voice and an even gruffer beard. "What is a little girl doing in the castle courtyard past curfew?"

"Is the castle unlocked?" Lindina covered the pen with her other hand. "Can I go in?"

"What?" The patrol leader squinted and cast unsure glances at the other soldiers. "No, of course you can't go in! Do you need help finding your way back to your house?"

"Is the castle unlocked?" Lindina repeated. She stared at the commander.

"No, it's not." The commander got down on one knee and looked Lindina in the eyes. "Do you have any idea how much danger you're putting yourself in? If we're *really* careful, I can take you back to your house. Tell me where you live."

Lindina closed her eyes, jabbed the pen into her wrist, and winced. Nausea spread through her blood from that point outward, writhing, eating away at her life. She noticed the guard's eyes train on the pen as she put it back into her pocket.

"I live in . . . in . . ." Lindina trembled. "In . . ." Her knees buckled, and she fell to the ground. Death consumed her from the inside, locking away all strands of life. Her vision blackened, her body went cold, and she felt her hand become stiff and clawed. Skin pulled tighter around her bones. Her back erupted with pain as wings broke through, convulsing as much as the rest of her body. Her monster was here. The soldiers would have to die.

The last thing she realized before losing consciousness was the tolling of a bell.

The inside of Doctor Adriel's house was pure darkness. Windows were shuttered, no lamps burned, and the door was now closed. All he noticed was breathing . . . that and the pain in his leg and back. Oddly, he couldn't feel any fresh blood. When had he stopped bleeding?

"Where are you two?" Jacob said. His voice sounded out of place in this void.

"Here," two voices whispered at once. One on each side of him.

"Sorias, lead him to the second room," the voice on his right said, moving past him and Sorias. "It doesn't have any windows, so I can spare some light."

A rough hand grasped Jacob's arm, squeezing a little too tightly. "Follow me," Sorias said.

Jacob nodded, even though no one could see it, and walked in the direction Sorias tugged. The fact that Sorias knew his way around the place supported Jacob's theory. What happened between them? Whatever it was, it seemed to be Sorias's fault. Why else would Adriel be angry with him? Fortunately for Jacob, she wasn't so resentful that she didn't let them in.

Sorias's tug pulled upwards, and Jacob nearly tripped on a stair. Even after he started ascending, he had trouble with his footing. The steps were so small that he couldn't predict where the next one was, and they curved in an odd direction. He reached out to the right, finding the banister and holding on. Its surface was smooth like glass, but its shape was wavy, like a serpent in motion. More like a rockweaver, probably. He doubted they had any snakes in Barabus.

On they went after crossing the last stair, Sorias's boots drowning out any potential footsteps from ahead. As they rounded a corner to the left, Sorias released Jacob's arm. Jacob heard shuffling and muttering ahead. The shuffling moved about the area, growing quieter, until finally a flame ignited some five feet away from Jacob. It wasn't much light, but it nearly burnt a hole in his eyes.

"The door," Adriel said, looking at Sorias.

"Of course." Sorias reached beside Jacob and grabbed a knob of brass. The door had been camouflaged into the wall until Sorias swung it into its frame.

Meanwhile, Adriel walked around the room, lighting torches on the wall. She was half a head shorter than Jacob, wore a loose dark-green dress, and had dishevelled light-blond hair falling just past her shoulders. Hair that light was an extremely rare trait no matter which region one lived in, but in Barabus it was remarkable.

The room itself was simple. A bed with white sheets in the back-right corner, a dresser and a rolling table next to it, and a long table with a basin on the left side of the room. There was a torch in the middle of each wall, even above the foot of the bed. Jacob would have thought it hazardous, but doctors needed light, didn't they? One torch would have flickered a good deal. But with four the light was near constant.

For the first time, Sorias removed his helmet, revealing shortly trimmed black hair on a round head with a strong, stubbled jaw. He set his helmet beside the door, earning a glare from Adriel.

"So . . ." Jacob needed to start a conversation before things got uncomfortable. "Sorias tells me you're the best doctor in the city."

Adriel looked at the floor. "He's right. But only because Doctor Harold was murdered."

Jacob never asked Sorias how Adriel knew about Baltashazar's rise to power. He could ask her himself, but it didn't feel right at the moment.

"What's your name?" Adriel said.

"Didn't you hear when Sorias was shouting like a lunatic?"

"It wasn't very clear. I only really heard the part about you being wounded."

"And that was enough to persuade you to let us in?"

"I took an oath to protect people. What else can I do?" Adriel narrowed her eyes. "You don't seem like you're wounded."

Jacob turned around, displaying his bloodied tunic. He expected something like a gasp, but Adriel was silent. Perhaps double knife wounds were commonplace in the medical field.

"How did you obtain these wounds?" Adriel said.

Jacob turned around. "City guards. They nearly brought me to Baltashazar, but Sorias helped me fight them off."

"How long ago was this?"

"About an hour, I'd say."

"You should have bled out by now."

Jacob held his tongue. The less he explained, the safer Tahil's secret was. Sorias knowing about the goldberries was bad enough. He didn't need—

"He's got these magic berries that he stole from the Silencers' Complex," Sorias said. "I applied their juice to his wounds, and they stopped bleeding."

Jacob shot Sorias a glare.

"Are you lying?" Adriel asked.

"Jacob, show her."

Reluctantly, Jacob removed his satchel, opened it, and showed it to Adriel. He didn't want to, but the alternative was Adriel arguing with Sorias about lying—or so he figured. He didn't know what was between these two and didn't want to find out.

"What are these?" Adriel brought her hand forward to reach in.

"Not yours!" Jacob pulled the satchel back, closing the flap. It was childish, but they were the only thing keeping him alive.

"And how did—wait! You stole them from the *Silencers' Complex*? Who *are* you?"

"A Wayfollower," Jacob said. Sorias was bound to say it if he didn't.

Adriel's eyes widened. "You're . . . You aren't lying?"

"Didn't you see me using the wind to jump up to your window?"

"I thought that was . . ." Adriel sat down on the bed, head in her hands. "Goodness, first Dreslen returns, now *this*."

"I know it's daunting," Jacob said, "but I need your help. I can't get you in more trouble than you're already in, if Sorias is right. At the moment, I've got two knife wounds in my back, as well as a strained calf."

"I don't know what I can do about the calf, but I'll see to your wounds." Adriel rose. "Take off your tunic and turn face-down on the bed."

Jacob set down his satchel and did as instructed. The blood made his tunic stick to his back, and once it was off, the chill in the room did nothing to comfort him. Keeping a wary eye on his satchel, he laid down on the white bed. It was the most uncomfortable mattress he'd ever felt. Even the one in Tahil had been softer than this. The lack of pillow didn't help, either.

"This is impossible," Adriel said. "These wounds are sealing up—they look hours old!"

"Magic," Sorias said.

Adriel mumbled something about the berries, then turned to the dresser and opened the top drawer. "Water, Sorias."

Sorias took a white cup from the left table and scooped into the water basin. After adjusting the amount, he set it down on the rolling table next to Adriel.

She murmured thanks, pulling a glass jar and spoon from the dresser. "This is a sleeping tonic mixed with a light anesthetic." Adriel opened the jar and levelled a spoonful of powder from within, scooping it into the cup and stirring. "You'll be asleep for a few hours, but you'll still feel pain. It should be manageable by the time you wake up."

Jacob propped himself up to take the cup from Adriel and sniffed the murky grey liquid. It didn't smell like anything, really.

He brought the cup to his lips, took a long sip, and clenched his mouth shut by instinct. If dirt was a liquid, this was what it would taste like.

"All of it," Adriel said.

"Fine, then." Jacob scrunched his face and downed the last of the tonic. He retched and nearly dropped the glass, but at least it was done.

Adriel took the cup and set it on the dresser, returning the jar and spoon as well. "The tonic will take effect in a few minutes."

In the distance, a bell tolled. Had Haanon struck the Tahil bell again? If it rang again, louder each time, he'd know.

The bell tolled once more and went silent.

"You'll have to work fast, Adriel," Sorias said.

"*Doctor* Adriel. We're on a professional basis now. Don't push things."

"Fine." Sorias closed his eyes. "But when Jacob and I dealt with the guards, one got away."

"And?"

"He'll have the entire guard looking for me. That bell? Baltashazar is calling the city guard to the castle. It won't be long before . . ."

"How long do we have?" Jacob asked.

"Hours, I'd say. Four at most."

"Perfect," Adriel said. "Maybe a guard will take me out of my misery instead of Baltashazar himself."

Sorias shook his head. "I'll protect you."

"What if I don't want your protection?"

"You're not the only one who took an oath."

"Yes, but it seems I'm the only one who takes them seriously."

Sorias opened his mouth, then closed it without a word.

"You swore fealty to the king of Barabus, just like you swore loyalty to me," Adriel said. Jacob wished he'd fall asleep soon. "You betrayed us both."

"I'm sorry. I can't count how many times I've told you that."

"Yes, I'm sure you are."

"But how could I have betrayed the king? King Baraz is dead, and Lord Baltashazar has yet to be coronated. I'm still acting with honour."

"And if Baltashazar was king?"

"I'd rebel. Justice outweighs honour."

"What's the point of all this, anyway? You're only going to get us all killed."

"No, Jacob's going to kill Baltashazar."

Jacob opened his mouth to object, then caught himself. The tonic was making him drowsy. All conversation from the room faded into incoherent murmurings, torchlight smudged into the walls, and thoughts ran without sense—all except for Jairus.

Sleep, fool, he said. *You won't die.*

Jacob tried to respond, but even in thought, he couldn't form words.

I won't let you die.

TWENTY

"Wake up, Jacob."

Jacob opened his sticky eyes and swallowed through his parched throat. How long had he been sleeping? A thin blanket now covered him, and as Adriel promised, his body suffered. His calf pulsed like a heavy drum, beating pain through his leg every second. Had Adriel even done anything to it? He felt no stinging on the skin, nor any other evidence of an incision. Even the cuts he'd given himself to apply the goldberry juice seemed to be gone.

His back was a different matter. He felt each wound distinctly, burning into his skin like knives fresh from the anvil. Jacob imagined that without the goldberries, he would have felt this kind of pain when he first received the wounds. Maybe he could ask Sorias to apply some juice right now, granted that Adriel wasn't in the room. He still didn't trust her with the berries—she was far too fascinated by them. Why shouldn't she be? She was a doctor, after all, and the goldberries offered anesthetic and rejuvenation all at once.

Don't trust her, Jairus said. He'd been unusually quiet since attacking the guards.

Why not? Jacob said.

While you were sleeping, I heard someone shuffling around by your satchel.

You heard something while I slept? How's that possible?

"Jacob, wake up." A rough hand accompanied Sorias's voice, grabbing his shoulder and shaking lightly. "We don't have much time left."

He turned his head away from the wall and faced Sorias. "I'm awake," he attempted to say, though he could only manage the vowels.

"What's that?"

Jacob groaned. "Is the doctor in the room?"

"Not at the moment."

"Good. I need you to apply some juice to my wounds."

Sorias hesitated. "You don't have many left."

"I know."

"As in, you only have eleven left. Nine small ones and two large. We should use them only when we absolutely have to."

We. The word resonated in his mind. Sorias already thought of them as a team. What was worse, Jacob did too. Did he really plan to betray him? He needed to rescue Lindina, and that was the end of it. But was it at all possible he could fight Baltashazar as well? Unlikely. Sorias had a skewed image of him. He remembered a man surrounded by flames, blinding light, and trembling earth.

No, Jacob couldn't do what Sorias wanted. As much as it pained him, he could only play along while he got closer to Lindina. As soon as he was forced to abandon them, he would. He swore himself to Lindina. *Nothing* was more important, not even the liberation of an entire city.

"Have it your way," Jacob said. "I'll wait until we're ready to leave."

"Is he awake?" Adriel's ragged voice said from the doorway.

"Yes," Sorias said. "We can go over the plan with him now."

Plan? This wouldn't be good. Considering what Sorias thought of Jacob's powers, he wouldn't be surprised if the plan involved Jacob flying across the city and striking the entire castle with a lightning storm.

"I'm telling you, it won't work," Adriel said. There were two wooden chairs in the room now, one beside Jacob's bed, which Sorias sat on, and the other near the footboard, where Adriel now s at.

"You haven't seen what Jacob can do," Sorias said.

Great, Jacob thought. "Well, let's hear it."

"First," Sorias said. "How much of a showman are you?"

Jacob chuckled. His back did not appreciate that. "Not much. Why?"

"You'll see in a moment."

"Just tell me the plan."

Sorias frowned. "What do you know about the city guard?"

"Next to nothing."

"It's big, and Baltashazar will have gathered them all to the castle. He knows there's a Wayfollower in the city now, and that will scare him if he's smart. I'd guess that he'd have a third of the three-hundred guards looking for us and the rest guarding the castle. Your job is to fight and kill Baltashazar."

"You can't possibly be asking me to fight through two hundred guards as well."

"Exactly. You need to save all your strength for Baltashazar. That's why we need to deal with the guards differently."

"A different way would be nice," Adriel said, rubbing her eyes. "Maybe one that didn't involve a massacre."

"We'll only have a massacre if the plan fails."

"It *will* fail. No one's going to listen to a Wayfollower, no matter how much lightning he can conjure."

Sorias turned back to Jacob, scowling. "In the North City Centre, there's a giant bell like the one in the castle. You can hear it for ages away, but only authorized personnel may ring it. Why? Because it's law to gather there when it's rung two times in a row, no matter what you're doing."

"So you propose to ring the bell," Jacob said. "Drawing the guards away from the castle and giving us a clear path inside?" This plan helped Jacob's goals more than Sorias could know. He needed to get inside the castle, one way or another. If Lindina wasn't there, where else would she be?

"Not quite. Guards aren't required to heed the city centre bells, only civilians. My plan is to gather hundreds of Barabians, rally them for war, and send them to march on Castle Dreslen."

"In other words, a massacre," Adriel sighed. "Barabians are tough, and they might be able to take on the castle guard if roused enough, but there's no way we'll be able to convince them of the truth. Who's going to listen to a rogue soldier, a broken doctor, and a Wayfollower? It doesn't matter how much of a show Jacob puts on. They'll just be scared of *him*, not Baltashazar. For all they know, King Baraz is still on the throne."

"But—"

"They're as loyal to King Baraz as you were, Sorias. As long as they think he's still king, they'll never march on the castle. Everyone will be illegally waiting in the city centre, Baltashazar will find out, and he'll send his guard to slaughter them."

"There's got to be some way to convince the people of the truth!" Sorias stood up, running his hands over his head.

"Even if we proved that King Baraz is dead, that would cast suspicion on the Wayfollower."

But he's not dead, Jacob thought, narrowing his eyes. *Zachii said he's in the Pits of Todoros.* What if . . .

No, that was a foolish idea. Even if the king was alive before, he'd probably be dead now. Probably. But what if he wasn't? What if King Baraz was still alive? If the Barabians were as loyal as Adriel said they were, they'd follow him without question. If the people fought bravely, there wouldn't be a massacre—or so Sorias claimed. Could that work?

"If the people *did* choose to fight," Jacob said. "If they marched against the castle guard, how many people would die?"

"Not as many as Baltashazar killed in the last few days," Sorias said. "And far less than he's going to kill if we don't kill him first."

"What if . . ." Jacob trailed off. What was he doing? If he mentioned that King Baraz was alive, they'd start asking questions he couldn't answer. But if this was the only way, then for Lindina's sake, he had to.

"What if what?"

"If King Baraz was still alive," Jacob spoke slowly, weighing each word before it came out, "would he be able to rally the people?"

"If he were still alive, absolutely. He's the best king Barabus has had in almost two hundred years, and the people know it. But he's dead. There's nothing we can do about that."

"How do you know he's dead?"

"Word of mouth. Besides, Baltashazar wants to be king. He can't be coronated unless the old king is dead."

Jacob gulped and closed his eyes. "King Baraz is still alive."

"You're lying. I may depend on you, but that doesn't mean I trust you."

"No, you're right. I did lie to you before. The truth is, I knew about Baltashazar before entering the city. I knew about the dravelord and the king's supposed death. I even knew about the deaths of the Silencers."

"I remember the shock in your eyes when I told you about all that," Sorias said. "You definitely didn't know that information before."

"The Deep revealed it to me."

Sorias raised his eyebrows.

"Alright, that's a lie. But I truly did know about Baltashazar. And I know the king is alive."

Sorias leaned in close, unblinking, breathing hard. "Tell me how you know this. I'm risking more than my life for you, so don't you dare lie to me."

Jacob tried to push his head further into the bed, away from Sorias, but it wouldn't budge. He couldn't afford to tell the truth, but with Sorias so close, scrutinizing his every word, he couldn't lie.

"Leave him alone, Sorias," Adriel said.

"Tell me the truth," Sorias said.

Jacob winced. "Remember the girl I'm trying to save? Lindina?"

"Yes."

"She knew about Baltashazar before I did. That's why she came here, to kill Baltashazar." *I hope.* There was still a chance that she planned to join him.

"How old is she?"

"Only eleven."

"Dreslen . . ." Sorias muttered. "Is she a Wayfollower too?"

"Worse, I'm afraid. She's—" Jacob stopped himself. If he told Sorias about Lindina's . . . condition, Sorias would try to kill Lindina as well. He could see the rage in his eyes, the pure hatred for the Abyss. This man would stop at nothing, not even a massacre, to kill Baltashazar. He wouldn't give a second thought to killing Lindina.

"She's what?"

"I won't lie to you, but I can't tell you the truth, either."

"Of course!" Sorias almost yelled, standing up. "Why should you tell me the truth? I only risked my life to save you!"

"Sorias," Adriel said, walking over.

"No, it's worse than that," Sorias said. "If I fail, not only will I die a slow, excruciating death, everyone I care about will share the same fate. Do you have *any* idea how much is at stake?" Sorias leaned over Jacob and seized his shoulders. "Do you have any idea the kind of *monster* we're dealing with? Keep lying to me. Fine!

Sabotage the mission because you can't trust me. You'll taste your own blood and grovel for death *long* before he's done with you."

"Sorias!" Adriel grabbed his arms and tried to pull him off Jacob. Sorias didn't budge.

There wasn't anything Jacob could do. All his strength was gone. A bead of sweat fell from Sorias's rage-contorted face, landing squarely on Jacob's nose.

Help me, Jairus.

But there was nothing Jairus could do. No energy to tap into.

"Leave him alone!" Adriel hit Sorias in the face, filling the room with a deafening slap. She clutched her hand and cowered with wide eyes.

Sorias let go of Jacob and spun on Adriel. "What do you want me to say to you? I did everything I could to fix us!"

"This isn't about us anymore!"

"Isn't it?" Sorias kicked the chair he'd been sitting on, toppling it to the floor. "It's always been about us! You couldn't live with the *thought* of me, so you made sure you'd never see me again. You had me stationed on the opposite end of the city, you slandered me to the king, and you made my name a curse in Barabian high society."

"You have *no clue* how much pain you caused me." Adriel's voice broke. "I came to you when I was broken, and you shattered all the fragments I had left. It's been two years, and I still haven't put the pieces back together."

"You're right—I don't know how much pain I caused. All I could do was guess, because you refused to tell me!"

"I *did* tell you. But you never listen! Two years, and you're still the same stubborn, self-centred man."

"Maybe it's because I forgot how to care." He walked right up to Adriel, speaking through his teeth. "Because every time I tried, I was returned with the same hostility. What is caring, anyway? A stupid waste of emotions that did nothing more than hurt me."

"It's not about you!"

"That's the problem: it was only ever about you. I was the soldier, the one who wasn't supposed to have emotions. Since *your* feelings were the only ones that mattered, it was perfectly justifiable to shut me out of your life without a word!"

Adriel hardened her eyes and stared at him. "You're right. It was, and I'm glad I did it."

"You—"

"Because no amount of apologizing will *ever* fix that day. I was wrong about what I said before. You aren't the same man you were two years ago—you're far worse." Adriel turned around and stormed towards the door. "Goodnight."

Without turning around, she slammed the door behind her.

The silence that followed was the worst Jacob had ever experienced. Sorias stood there, hands clenched into fists, breathing heavily. What was Jacob supposed to do? He was good at many things, but fixing relationships was not one of them. Anything he said would be out of place. This wasn't his problem, like Sorias kept reminding him. Why, then, did Sorias insist on having the argument in front of him?

That fight could not have been timed worse. They needed Adriel. Jacob was formulating a plan, but it wouldn't work without her. She was one of the only people Jacob could trust in this city.

"Don't say anything," Sorias said, picking up his chair and falling onto it. He tapped the backboard with his right hand, absently staring at the door as if willing Adriel to walk through it again with a big smile on her face. Jacob almost wished that too.

"I made a mistake two years ago," Sorias said, "one that I've regretted every day since. I tried to forget about it and move on, but she won't listen."

"I know you're struggling," Jacob said, "but this is bigger than you."

"It always is," he muttered.

"I don't believe what Adriel said about you. You saved my life. You're a good man."

"What does your opinion count for?"

"That's up to you. Right now, you need me. And I need you. Can you trust me?"

"I—" Sorias closed his eyes. "I don't know."

Jacob gulped. He wanted so badly for Sorias to trust him, even knowing he would betray Sorias.

No, Jacob told himself. *I will not betray him. This man is the only reason I'm still alive. If I let him fall into Baltashazar's hands, I'm no better than Baltashazar himself.*

But Lindina!

Jacob exhaled. *I have to save her too. I have to do both.*

Then you will fail.

Jacob forced himself to sit up, ignoring the searing pain in his back. "Sorias, do you trust me?"

Sorias looked over, his face sullen. "Can I trust you?"

Jacob paused. "Yes, I swear it on my life. As long as it's in my power, I will help you defeat Baltashazar."

Sorias shuddered. "If I can't trust you, then we're all doomed anyway. I choose to believe you, Jacob, not because I think you're telling the truth, but because I have no other choice."

"Then we need to bring Adriel back."

Silence.

"Sorias, this is more important than anything in your life. Yes, it's not about you. I know you're tired of hearing that. But it's the truth we all need to deal with. If we're going to save this kingdom from Baltashazar, we're all going to have to stop thinking of ourselves. This will be difficult—more difficult than anything you've ever been through. And it starts with bringing Adriel back."

Sorias sniffed, then nodded.

Jacob wished he could get out of the bed to help him, but Sorias was right; he needed to wait until the last minute to use the goldberries. Everything depended on Sorias at the moment. If he didn't get up and go after Adriel, Jacob's plan would fail.

<hr>

Adriel shuddered, staring at complete blackness. Her front door. She couldn't feel. She could hardly think. Every time she thought things couldn't get worse, they did. Syndria lost Baraz, Adriel lost Syndria, Baltashazar slaughtered men before her eyes, and if anyone found her, she would be guilty for trying to help the queen. A fugitive thought dead, forced to drown herself in fear until it finally killed her. *May that day come soon.*

Save the dying.

Adriel was dying, wasn't she? According to her oath, she had to save herself. That was the last thing she wanted to do. All she wanted was to sleep and never wake.

Now Sorias had returned to her, shouted at her for not being good enough, and attempted to guilt her into loving him again. It was nothing more than she expected, but it didn't negate the pain. Secretly, she wished he'd change. She wanted to reconcile with him, but all hopes of that were dashed.

Give little thought to the dead.

No, Adriel wasn't dying—she was already dead. Irredeemable. No medicine or tonic, no bandages or tensor, could repair her. Like Baltashazar had broken the hearts and minds of everyone under his command, he'd broken Adriel—not that there had been much of her left to break—as had Sorias. Now they both harrowed her, unable to let her find rest.

With a blank expression, she reached out and felt the doorknob. The metal was colder than death. Outside, soldiers looked for Sorias and Jacob. They'd know to check here. What would she find if she opened the door? Perhaps they had already arrived. Perhaps she could give herself into their hands and plead for a quick, painless death.

She turned the doorknob as soon as she heard approaching footsteps from the stairwell.

"Adriel, wait!" Sorias said.

Adriel opened the door and stared out at her lawn, taking a deep breath. No soldiers yet. It didn't matter—she'd find them, and she would ask for death.

"Jacob needs you."

She stepped through her doorway, running her hand along the frame for the last time. It wasn't as smooth as she remembered. Perhaps the next owner would take better care of it.

"We need you."

The wind picked up, seeping through her dress and chilling her. There was nothing out here but icy darkness. Shadows danced by the dim light of flames, creeping forward, preparing to swallow her. A crow mourned overhead. Tears fell down her cheeks.

"The night is dark, the shadows deep."

Adriel stopped.

"In every hour, the silence steeps."

She hadn't heard this poem—her father's poem—in two years. All her work of shutting out that grief shattered, spoken by a careless man who claimed to uphold goodness. How dare he recite this!

It's all lies, she told herself, lip quavering. *He speaks of hope when hope is dead. Hope is dead.*

"The dawn is near, but not yet here."

"Till then we yearn . . ." Adriel whispered, turning around, looking at the silhouette of the man who crushed her. The man who scattered the pieces to the wind and burned them. The man who stoked the embers of hope, keeping her father's memory alive.

". . . and embers burn," Sorias finished.

"Why now?" Adriel couldn't sound the words properly. Her lower lip felt useless. From the depths of her soul, a sob rose into her throat. She didn't let it out.

"The night has not yet won. But without your help, it will. We need you. You are our last hope—this kingdom's last hope. A star that will pierce the shade." He extended his hand and walked towards her.

Don't, she thought, holding back her arm. She needed to run, to die, to give up hope.

"I failed you, Adriel. Know that I've regretted it times without number, and that I would do anything to take back what I did. But I can't. Some things are irreversible. If you walk away from this, you can never change that. If hundreds die because Baltashazar was not stopped, you will have to live with that for the rest of your life—like I have to live with my mistake."

"I want to die," Adriel said, breath shaking. "I have nothing left."

Sorias took her hand in his. She didn't resist. "I know you, Adriel. You're as brave as half the soldiers in the guard."

"You're wrong. I'm a coward. A broken, helpless coward."

"You are not a coward. Be strong, like you've always been. Mourn the dead, and save the dying. You can do both. We need both right now."

"I—"

"You have nothing to lose and everything to gain. If you die, so will hundreds of others. We can still save them. We *will* reach the light of day. Jacob needs you. I don't know what he's planning, but without you, he says it will fail."

Adriel found herself nodding, following blindly as Sorias led her back into the house. If she was going to continue in thoughtlessness, she may as well save a few more people. What was it Sorias said? Mourn the dead *and* save the dying? All her training told her that grief was the enemy of effective care. But it was all she had left, all that drove her. Grief for Syndria, and grief for herself. She was dead, but perhaps she could spare others from grief.

When finally they reached the second medical room, Jacob was still on the bed, looking at the ceiling. How far had this young man come to rescue the little girl? How far was he planning to go to save Barabus from Baltashazar? He was far braver than she'd ever been. Braver than Sorias, even. What chance did they really have? Baltashazar would win anyway, and they would all die.

"Doctor Adriel?" Jacob said, tilting his head towards her.

She didn't need to say anything. He could see her.

"Now that you're both here . . ." Jacob propped himself up on the bed, much to Adriel's distaste. He should rest until he ate the goldberries. "I'll go over the plan with you."

"Is it better than Sorias's plan?" Adriel asked.

"An improvement. Sorias, put on your helmet. We're going to rescue King Baraz from the Pits of Todoros."

Sorias's jaw dropped. "The . . . We're going to do what?"

Adriel was speechless. Baraz was really alive? Maybe there was hope after all.

But if Baraz was in the Pits, he was better off dead. Todoros was one of the worst, most horrid places in Atlantia. Maybe Jacob wasn't brave—perhaps he was simply insane.

"You heard me," Jacob said, wincing and swinging his legs off the side of the bed.

"What am I supposed to do?" Adriel said.

"You're going to gather the Barabians. Prepare them for war."

Adriel gaped. *Me?* This man was definitely insane.

"Here's what you're going to do . . ."

TWENTY-ONE

With the sunlight now gone, the Barabs were far more dismal a place. This region, like others, was like hardened sand tossed by a windstorm, creating jagged mounds and sweeping dunes. Everything was black—the ground, the sky, the form of Sorias up ahead—but Jacob's eyes had adjusted to it. The stars gave adequate light to distinguish the outlines of major shapes, but also enough darkness to remind him of the danger he faced.

Out of instinct, he reached into his satchel. Ten goldberries left. Just enough to tend to Baraz, bring them all back to Barabus, and give Jacob enough strength to fight Baltashazar. There could be no complications. If he received another injury, or he miscalculated the time, he might have to face Baltashazar without the goldberries. Could he fight a Dreslite *and* three wounds at the same time? Not if he wanted any chance of winning.

The plan was simple: Sorias would lead Jacob to the Pits, they would both descend, and, working together, would bring Baraz out—assuming he was still alive. He tried not to think of the alternative. If there were guards posted at the entrance, Sorias would talk them into letting Jacob through. In the case they refused, Jacob would let Jairus attack them. Hopefully, it didn't come to that. He could still feel Jairus's bloodlust whenever Sorias mentioned killing.

"Did you know King Baraz personally?" Jacob asked. He needed to think of something other than Jairus.

"I did. When Adriel and I were still on good terms."

"I know you don't want me asking, but—"

"If you know, then don't ask."

"Fine." Jacob looked ahead. Dark stone as far as he could see. It wasn't a wonder Dreslen built his city here—it was the perfect place for a follower of the Abyss. Cruel, unforgiving landscape, cold shadows, signs of death everywhere. Did the Silencers not expect another Dreslen to rise?

Of course they did; they killed Wayfollowers to prevent that. But they were looking in the wrong places. In their obsession with silencing the Deep, they overlooked the place where Dreslen drew his malice. They'd died for that mistake, and the Abyss would have the last laugh if Jacob didn't stop it. Was he really the only one capable?

"Sorias, how did the Silencers die?"

Jacob thought the Silencers were qualified to deal with Baltashazar, but Sorias wouldn't stop talking about how they were powerless against him.

"Various ways," Sorias said grimly. "I don't care to describe them all."

"But did Baltashazar go to each one individually?"

"The dravelord helped with some."

"What about the ones without the grey cloaks? I expect some Silencers would want to operate inconspicuously."

"They're dead too. They all wore medallions of white steel beneath their garments, no matter what they wore. That's how he proved to us their identity. Face it, Jacob. The Silencers here are dead, and if more come, they'll be dead too."

"I don't understand how he could have found them all."

"Neither do I. But he did."

"What else do you know about Baltashazar?"

Sorias set his jaw. "Lord Baltashazar was the cousin of the king and the lord of the guard. A respectable man. He personally trained me—all of us guards. When the White Plague struck

Barabus a few years ago, only King Baraz and Lord Baltashazar remained in the royal family. Baltashazar was Baraz's mentor for most of that time.

"Over a month ago, he went missing without warning. Rumour has it he travelled northwest, but no one recalls seeing him go that way."

Except Zachii, Jacob thought. "If my source is correct, Baltashazar did indeed travel northwest. He spent about a month in the Abyssal Plains."

"That would explain his dark powers," Sorias said. "Did your 'source' tell you where else he went?"

"He did not." If they got out of this, Jacob would have to ask Zachii. It might explain how Baltashazar found the secret to defeating the Silencers.

Sorias went strangely quiet—it wasn't the first time he stopped talking, but even his breathing was softer. Quicker. He looked back and forth between Jacob and the ground, shaking his head. Finally, he sighed and looked forward. "You were going to ask me what I did to break Adriel two years ago."

Jacob wished he hadn't brought it up. "Something along those lines."

"After everything you've done—everything you're doing—you deserve to know."

Jacob waited for him to continue.

"Adriel and I had been courting for five months. Things had been going well until the last few weeks. When the White Plague came, patients flooded her. On the odd chance I got to see her, I always worried it would be for the last time. Being a doctor was the most dangerous profession in those days.

"In my idiocy, I tried to convince her to stop treating patients. To protect herself. I thought I was nobly putting her safety first, but I now realize I was serving myself too. I couldn't bear the thought of losing her. That thought tormented me day after day, driving me to obsession. I couldn't focus on my guard duties.

"It got to the point where I half hoped she would die, just so my worrying would be abated. That's when her parents caught the disease. She put all her other patients on hold to tend to them, willing to sacrifice their lives for even a *chance* at saving her parents. All she did was draw out their deaths.

"While they were still alive, she called me to see her. I refused. It was the decision of a true coward. She'd done nothing against me, but my anger towards her grew. When her mother died, I knew she'd come looking for me, so I hid. I found my place among the drinkers, thinking that if she died, I'd be too drunk to fully take it in. After a while, I realized that I'd feel the pain of her death no matter how much I hid. She was the only woman who had ever loved me, and I couldn't let that woman die. So I decided to end our relationship—the problem was, I couldn't bear the thought of turning her away.

"When her father died, she reached out to me again. I came to her doorstep with another woman at my arm. As soon as she saw us, I kissed that other woman right in front of Adriel. I couldn't turn Adriel away, but I could make her turn me away. By the time I came to my senses, I felt like I was dying. The guilt of what I'd done stabbed me all over, ripping me apart, tearing until there was nothing but pain. I've relived that day hundreds of times, watching helplessly as I broke the one I claimed to love."

Sorias slowed, no longer jogging. "Adriel is right to hate me. Just as I hate myself."

Jacob didn't know what to say. He'd made guesses about what Sorias had done, but none of them were this dark. To betray Adriel on the night when her father died? It sounded nothing less than evil. Before, he gave Sorias the benefit of the doubt. He couldn't do that anymore.

"I'm sorry you have to work with me," Sorias said. "But I'm the only one desperate enough to resist. Like Adriel, I don't have much to lose."

"At Adriel's house, you shouted about losing everyone you cared about," Jacob said. "Is that not much to lose?"

Sorias paused. "I don't care about people—not like I used to."

"You saved my life."

Nothing.

"You aren't the same man you were then." Jacob remembered his courage in fighting off Nor and the other soldier. "Even if you made the worst, most hurtful decision in history, you can't let that decide what you are now."

"It happened. I cannot change that."

"You're right. You're a guilty man, Sorias. Guilty of worse than a crime. But don't let that rob this kingdom of the hero it needs."

Sorias laughed grimly. "I'm no hero. That would be you."

"The kingdom still needs you."

"And I will serve it. But after all this is done, even if things go back to the way they were . . ." He looked at the ground. "But they can't go back. Not after I confronted Adriel like that. My nobility is a lie that I can't put on again." He looked at Jacob, shook his head, and sighed.

They jogged in silence. What more needed to be said? Sorias was right. After everything that happened, things could never be the same. Not for Jacob, not for Sorias, and not for Adriel. Hardships forced people to change. Either you grew or you let the pain break you. Jacob saw both growth and brokenness in Sorias and Adriel, despite only knowing them for a few hours. In himself, he saw something else. Confidence that wasn't there when he searched for Lindina in the South Midorian Forest. Then, he'd been running from the Deep like it was the Abyss itself. Even by the time he got to Tahil, he'd been torn. Was his destiny to be a Wayfollower or a librarian?

Now, he used the Deep at leisure, paying no heed to the long-term consequences. Was that a good thing? Probably not. He might be more confident now, but that made him irresponsible. That Jairus was arguing with him less was suspect enough. He'd always considered Jairus a voice of madness and spite; if they agreed more now than before, what did that say about Jacob?

Ahead, beyond a mound of stone, orange light glowed. It was the first proper light he'd seen since leaving Barabus.

"I know that dune," Sorias said, stopping with his arm raised. "We're here."

Jacob took the signal and halted. Cautiously, they walked towards the edge of the towering dune. It rose high over his head, the side closest to him steep and curved inward, rising to a peak like as sharp as the talons of a dravelord.

"Stay here," Sorias said, walking to the edge. "If you hear one shout, come peaceably. If two, prepare to fight. But *do not* kill them."

Jacob half nodded. It wasn't up to him whether they lived or died. The only way he knew how to attack with the Deep was to give Jairus control. Crackling blue light would stain the air, skin would burn, and screams would echo long into the vaults of death, crying for mercy from a being that fed off malice. If Jairus were given form, he would be no worse than Baltashazar himself.

Sorias vanished behind the dune, leaving Jacob alone.

"Are you afraid of me?" Jairus whispered.

He'd always been afraid of Jairus. The Voice seemed like its own being, separate from Jacob, possessing him to do what he did not wish. To kill. Each time Jairus took control, Jacob was near helpless, watching from the subconscious, wondering whether he'd ever rule his body again. A time may come when Jairus did away with him for good. It could happen in a few moments, for all he knew.

"Yes, I fear you," Jacob said. "Because of you, I have to worry about the safety of those around me. And my own."

"It is my purpose. To be the nightmare that haunts your waking hours. The dark torrents of despair. The shadows of madness."

"Yet you still wish to keep me alive. Why? Just to torment me?" Jacob leaned forward as if Jairus were in front of him. "I've felt your emotions, Jairus. You actually care."

"I do not."

"You seem to forget that we share the same mind."

"I only 'care' about you enough to keep you alive. If you die, we both do."

"No." Jacob shook his head. "No, you're lying. You do care. Somewhere deep down, even if you can't see it, you have some decency. How do I know? Because you're a part of me. And I'm not all evil, am I?"

"We shall see."

From beyond the dune, Sorias gave two shouts in rapid succession. The signal to prepare for attack. To give Jairus control.

Listen to me. Jacob walked around the left side of the dune. *If you kill anyone, I'll find a way to punish you.*

How amusing.

Jacob struggled to keep from shouting at Jairus. When would he get him under control? It could make the difference between whether someone lives or dies.

Ahead, a round hut rose from the ground in unnatural perfection. Horns protruded from the top and both sides, curved upwards like knives aimed at the stars. In front of the entrance, two thick poles supported torches. Chained to the poles were two soldiers, restrained by their ankles, carrying longswords. Each wore a large breastplate, a helmet, and chain-mail sleeves for their arms and legs. Firelight glinted off the metal like red stars fallen to the earth, punished for rebellion.

The guards turned their gazes from Sorias and looked at Jacob with blank expressions. Their swords hung by their sides, unwavering. He couldn't help but pity them. If they were chained here, this had to be punishment. Did they know they were standing guard against their true king, or were they deceived as well?

"Time is short." Sorias backed up next to Jacob. "Make it quick."

The guards shook, eyes widening. Did Sorias tell them what was going to happen? Why didn't they speak? Their jaws rose and fell violently, but their lips remained sealed. They were cursed, weren't they? The first curse Jacob had seen since witnessing Zachii.

Jacob closed his eyes. *Please,* he thought. *Don't kill them.* They were terrified. He wished they would say something, anything to convince Jairus of their humanity. But nothing came. Not even panicked groans.

"I'm sorry," Jacob said, giving up control.

Jairus emerged before Jacob could change his mind. He laughed, bringing up his arms and pointing one at each guard. *"Perish!"* he shrieked. Streams of blue lightning shot from his fingertips, latching onto the guards' armour and holding fast. Crackling filled the air, overshadowed by Jairus's laughter.

Both guards jolted where they stood and fell to the ground without catching themselves, still gripping their swords. As loud as Jairus's laughter was, it couldn't mute the sound of their armour scraping on the stone as they writhed, finally dropping their weapons as he relinquished his power. The Sirathim called this the Way of Light—utter foolishness. Lightning was far more than that. It burned. It bound. It seized the body and mind, holding them in agony until Jairus released them. With more practice, he could do it for longer. Perhaps he'd gain more control of what type of lightning he used.

He lashed out again.

Behind him, Sorias yelled. Jairus spun around to see the soldier striding towards him without a weapon. Fool. Did he expect to tackle Jairus to the ground with his bare hands?

Raising his arms to Sorias, he lashed. Sorias's eyes went wide with shock and pain. He stood there, convulsing, groaning like a useless old man. Sorias had already stopped Jairus before—he wouldn't ruin his fun this time. Now that he finally had control of Jacob's body and mind again, he would hold them as long as possible. He'd kill Baltashazar and Lindina alike. The Silencers would fall next, and the world would descend into chaos.

Yes . . . chaos. Madness. There were no greater pleasures than these.

"Did you trust me?" Jairus said, ceasing the bolts. Sorias fell to his knees. *"Did you truly think I'd help save your pitiful life?"* With a single bolt from his right hand, Sorias tumbled onto his hands.

"You . . ." Sorias could hardly raise his head. "Why?"

"It is my purpose." Jairus tried to crouch in front of him, but the pain in his calf was too much. No matter. He saw what he needed to see—pure fear in his eyes. *"Can the world have chaos without agony and—"*

Sorias lunged, grabbing Jairus's leg and pulling. His balance faltered. Before he could right himself, Sorias pulled again and toppled him to the ground. His back hit the rock with a thud. Both knife wounds cried out, as if drilling deeper into his back. His head wasn't much better.

Sorias got to his feet and reached for his short sword, his face contorting. Anger now mixed with the fear—a deadly combination, if harnessed correctly.

Jairus tried to stand, but Sorias kicked him in the chest. The back of his head collided with the stone ground, and his vision swarmed. He could hardly see Sorias, let alone his emotions. For the first time since the South Midorian Forest, he felt pain. Jairus's entire head felt as though it was being crushed on all sides.

"What was all this for?" Sorias yelled, waving his left arm in the air. With his right, he trained the tip of his sword on Jairus's throat. "Answer me!"

Jairus raised his left hand to cast lightning at Sorias, but bashing his head on the ground had weakened him. The best he could summon was a few sparks between his fingers.

He was out of tactics. If he didn't give consciousness back to Jacob, Sorias would shove a blade through his neck.

Sorias brought the sword's tip against Jairus's throat. The point was so small he could hardly feel it compared to the throbbing in his skull, but if he so much as swallowed, he was sure it would pierce his skin. Sorias narrowed his eyes. "No more lies." His tone was soft and gravelly at once.

Jairus didn't dare speak. *Help me, fool!* he screamed at Jacob.

Jacob blinked and lifted his eyes. Sorias breathed heavily, but the sword was as steady as the stone. "Please," Jacob muttered, closing his eyes. Saliva built up in his mouth, threatening to trickle down his throat. If he coughed, he was a dead man. He raised both his palms in the air.

Sorias inhaled deeply, holding still. Eventually, he grunted and retracted his blade. It still pointed at Jacob, but it at least gave him room to breathe comfortably.

Jacob gasped and sputtered. He tried to prop himself into a sitting position by straightening both arms behind him, but Sorias brought the sword closer again.

"I don't want to kill you," Sorias said. He withdrew his blade and inserted it into his scabbard. "You're our only hope."

Jacob nodded, his eyes still wide. He remembered Jairus's attack as if it had been his own, but only now did he feel the pain. His head throbbed every second. He'd felt worse, though. He might recover quickly without a goldberry.

"I'm sorry," Jacob said. He gulped again. "I promise, I lost control."

"Sure." Sorias averted his eyes from Jacob, looking towards the entrance to the Pits.

Jacob got to his feet, shaking. "It was the only way to attack them."

"What?" Sorias turned around. "You had to attack me in order to attack them?"

"No—"

"And the laughter? You *enjoyed* that!" Sorias reached for his sword again but stopped his hand before he withdrew it. He closed his eyes and swore, letting his grip go.

"I . . . can't cast lightning." Jacob looked down at his hands. "I have a voice in my head. When it takes control, it—"

"Stop." Sorias raised his hand and took a step towards Jacob. "I don't care if you're being possessed by *Dreslen*! Get it under control!"

Jacob opened his mouth to speak but thought better of it when he saw Sorias's face. His eyes were uneven and twitching, narrowed with raised eyebrows. Rage given form.

"You done? Then let's go." Sorias spun away from Jacob and walked to the entrance.

Both guards lay motionless on the ground. Sorias crouched beside one and put his hand to the guard's neck.

"Dead?" Jacob asked. He already knew the answer.

Sorias nodded. Rather than turning to Jacob, he ventured inside the gaping mouth of the horned mound. Jacob couldn't follow. Not yet. Slowly, painfully, the gravity of what he'd done set in. He killed two men. It may have been through Jairus, but Jairus was a part of him. A piece of his deepest thoughts. Jacob had no one to blame but himself.

"No torches in there." Sorias emerged from the entrance, bent over with both hands on the doorway, panting hard. "Can you summon fire and hold it in your hand?"

"No." Jacob didn't know why, but Sorias's suggestion chilled him. Fire killed, especially fire from the Deep. As long as he lived, he would never use the Way of Fire again. Memories burned, crawling through the depths of his mind, wailing against the door. Screams. They'd never get in. No amount of fire could destroy the door he'd created.

But Jairus held the key. Upon the moment of death, it would open.

"Well, we can't go in the dark." Sorias crouched beside a dead guard, inspecting beneath the breastplate. "Help me take this off. We'll wrap his uniform around my sword and use it like a torch."

It was arduous, unstrapping the guard's armour and taking it off the body. Worse, there was chain mail beneath it. Once all that was off, Sorias untucked the rigid black top from the belt, unbuttoned it, and transferred it onto his own sword. He bunched it up near the top, holding it in place with the guard's belt.

Sorias raised his makeshift torch to head level and immersed it into the flame of the torch-post. At first, the fire licked around the sword, creating bulges on its sides. After a few moments, the fabric ignited, growing fiery tendrils.

"You're going to be the one to carry it." Sorias drew the flaming sword away from the torch-post. "I don't trust you enough to have both your hands free."

"Why give me a sword, then?" Jacob reached out and took the blade. It was heavier than he expected.

"You'll go in front." Sorias beckoned for Jacob to walk through the doorway. "That way, I can keep an eye on you."

"Sounds fair." Jacob walked ahead of Sorias into the dark hut. Empty racks mounted the wall, all covered in rust. Most seemed fashioned for weapons, but some had round inserts that could easily hold a torch.

On the floor in the centre of the room was a crudely shaped hole. Its dark mouth gaped, steaming forth the scent of a hundred rotting corpses. Jacob doubled over and retched, nearly dropping the torch. Now he knew why Sorias had been panting when he came out.

"Breathe through your mouth." Sorias walked into the hut.

"I know." Jacob brought the torch closer to the hole. He could now see bars of rust on the side of the hole closest to the door—a ladder. As hideous as it was, it at least gave Jacob the comfort of knowing he would not have to jump down.

"Jacob, I trusted you."

That cut Jacob like a sword. Jacob had trusted himself too, but then he tried to kill the person he swore to fight alongside. After that, could honour ever be repaired? He imagined that as long as the Voice loomed over him, it was impossible. Any promises he made would be hollow when Jairus could thwart them at any time.

"Maybe you shouldn't trust me," Jacob whispered. He half hoped Sorias wouldn't hear. "I can't even trust myself."

Sorias looked at his feet. "Neither of us have a choice. I don't think you should tolerate me, and you don't think I should trust you. But we both do anyway."

Jacob nodded slowly, peering into the pit. It was like staring into the Abyss itself.

"If we fail each other, this was all for nothing. Our entire lives . . . for nothing."

"I won't fail you." Jacob meant it, but could he follow through? "As long as it is within my power, I will not betray your trust again."

"Then let's go." Sorias looked at the hole. "The king is waiting."

TWENTY-TWO

Jacob took a deep breath through his mouth, seized his muscles, and stepped onto the ladder. The decayed metal was rougher than sand, scraping against his left hand, while his right arm struggled to hold the torch whilst descending. Step after step, the entrance rose higher above his head. After the first few rungs, the descent became a blur of terror.

His muscles ached and trembled, threatening to collapse with every step lower. But they held, just like his breath. The growing stench made him gag.

From lower down, clicking noises echoed through the shaft. Sometimes ratcheting, other times slow and deliberate, like careful clicks from a tongue. A hiss of steam and the thick dripping of tar soon joined the sound. Above, Sorias climbed onto the ladder, making the rusted metal groan all the more.

The air heated. Sweat poured from every fibre of Jacob's body, saturating his clothes, doing nothing to cool him. Shortly above his head, the flaming sword licked the narrow walls of the shaft, brushing the tar's hard residue and setting it aglow. He'd have to be careful once he got to the bottom—if he dropped the torch or put it too close to a wall, the entire tunnel might go up in flames.

"You almost at the bottom?" Sorias called from above.

Jacob stopped, switched which hand held the torch, and looked downward into blackness. "Doesn't look like it." Even if they made it to the king, getting back up may prove difficult. Jacob had a large berry to spare for Baraz, but depending on his condition, even that might not be enough to bring him up the ladder.

The clicking got louder; some even sounded like hissing.

Jacob looked up. Sorias was only a few rungs away. "What's that noise, Sorias?"

"Spiders."

Jacob's blood chilled. "Are you sure?" Spiders were one of his few fears. Small enough to hide, vicious enough to bite, and more grotesque than any other monster, real or legend. Judging by the volume of the clicking, these spiders weren't as small as he was used to—nor were they few.

"My father's a miner," Sorias said. "According to him, that's why this tunnel was abandoned. Got infested."

"You didn't want to tell me before?"

"And make you change your mind? Now that you're here, there's no going back."

Jacob cringed as a click sounded next to his head. *Don't look at it.* If he didn't engage them, they wouldn't engage him. Only . . . they were spiders. They didn't care. He could prepare them a lovely meal and still they would crawl over him and hide until he slept.

Above, the clicking turned into a screech. He looked to see a small creature raise all its legs from the wall, losing its grip and tumbling to the depths. Jacob shivered despite the heat. How much longer until he could go back to the surface?

Minutes passed in much the same manner, until finally Jacob's foot squelched into a sticky substance, sinking past his ankle until it reached solid ground. Lowering his torch, he could see nothing on the floor but blackness and a faint reflection of the firelight. The walls were wider than before, and though they were of the same dark stone as the surface, they seemed a light grey compared to the tar.

As he stepped onto the ground with his other foot, he noticed something moving nearby. A spider the size of his hand swam through the tar, propelling itself with all eight legs, slowly drawing nearer. Jacob yelped and tried to step to the side, but the tar proved too much for his injured calf. With his uninjured hand, he opened his satchel, took a small goldberry, and consumed it. Due to his hand touching the ladder, the berry's outside tasted of rust.

But it worked. The juices gave him the energy he needed to side-step right before the spider latched onto his leg. Now off balance, Jacob reached for the ladder with his spare hand to steady himself. Instead of the ladder, he caught Sorias's leg.

"What is it?" Sorias said.

Jacob ignored him. The spider was still swimming for him, covered in tar-stained grey hair with a fleshy patch on its abdomen.

"Get back!" Jacob pointed his flame at the spider. The creature screeched, raised its legs, and sank through the tar, unable to maintain motion.

"Back?" Sorias asked.

"No!" Jacob would *not* be alone down here. "I saw a spider. It drowned."

"Drowned? In what?" Sorias let go of the ladder, his feet squishing into the tar at once. "This isn't right. The tar shouldn't be nearly this deep."

"Who defines what 'should' happen in an abandoned dungeon?" Jacob hated it. Hot tar seeped through his shoes, sticking his toes together and nearly burning his skin.

"That's only legend," Sorias said. "Dreslen may or may not have used this as a prison."

Jacob tried walking again. Without a spider lurching towards him, it was easier. He found the best way to move was to raise his legs straight up; once his foot cleared the surface, he'd move his leg forward and repeat. Clicking surrounded him on every side, but with all the echoes it was impossible to tell where many of the spiders actually were. The torch was bright enough to illuminate both sides of the tunnel, revealing some spiders perched on the walls. If Jacob brought the fire too close, they'd raise their legs, freeze, and fall. Most were dormant, but some crawled along the wall in arbitrary directions.

What worried Jacob most was when they crawled upwards. The ceiling was uneven enough that it was difficult to tell the spiders' locations. They might be right above his head, and he'd never know until they fell onto him. For that reason alone, he kept the torch low. It obscured the ceiling more, but it was better than getting a spider on the head.

"Sorias," Jacob said, shivering. He couldn't shake the feeling of legs skittering over him. Any distraction would be nice. "What are you going to do when this is over?"

"I'll probably move to Midor and become a farmer."

"You? A farmer?"

"Anything to get away from all this stone. I've had it with this place. Perhaps I'll get the attention of the Silencers and they'll recruit me, if I'm lucky."

Jacob had intentionally kept his mind off the Silencers. They were supposed to be the ones to fix this, not Jacob. And what if he succeeded? If Baltashazar died, there was little chance of the Silencers accepting Jacob as a Wayfollower. They'd see him as someone powerful enough to kill a Dreslite—assuming he could do it—and execute him for the danger he posed. It was the system that kept Atlantia safe.

But it wasn't safe anymore, was it? The Silencers failed. Had they allowed the Sirathim to continue, Baltashazar would have already been stopped. There might be smaller conflicts at a greater rate, but the excess of Sirathim would make sure they never escalated. Of course, Dreslen lived in an age like the one Jacob described. That didn't stop *him* from nearly ruling the world.

Perhaps the Silencers were right. Jacob almost hoped they were, despite his own suppression. It was the not knowing that drove him mad. The question posed in his mind repeatedly, day after day. Peace for the faithful of the Deep, or peace for the general population?

Was Jacob faithful to the Deep now? At a glance, he had to say yes. If he rescued Lindina, he'd bring her back to Tahil, and he intended to stay until she finished her healing. What would he do in that time? Exactly what Haanon wanted. Study the Deep, grow his powers, and perhaps, if he were diligent enough, learn the Way of the Deep.

"Jacob, look," Sorias said. "The walls."

Jacob snapped out of his thought and saw that vertical, rusted iron bars replaced the rough stone walls. Beyond the bars, darkness loomed.

"Well, this confirms it," Jacob said, bringing his torch near the wall and dropping a particularly large spider. The cell showed nothing more. "It's definitely a prison."

The ceiling was higher now—or were they getting lower? Regardless, the torch wasn't bright enough to illuminate all of it. If there were spiders waiting in ambush, he wouldn't know. But the cells were showing up now, so it shouldn't be too long until—

"Sword!" Sorias cried.

Jacob twisted in place to look at Sorias. He was further behind than he should have been, though not by much. Above him, an enormous spider—triple the size of the one that assaulted Jacob—descended on a string from the ceiling. Its mouth had five sharp pincers set in a circle, clicking as they moved in and out. The creature stretched out its front legs towards Sorias's head.

He didn't know how to toss a sword, let alone a flaming one, but the spider didn't care. So, with a grunt, Jacob heaved the fiery stick of metal through the air. Its blade turned to the ground, but Sorias grabbed it by the handle before it could fall into the tar. In the same motion, he leaned back and jabbed his sword into the spider's abdomen.

The spider screeched, curling its legs and catching fire. Sorias swung the blade—spider still attached—to the tar below. The spider slipped off, but so did the flaming cloth. Both rested on the tar's surface, hesitating for a moment.

"No!" Sorias lunged with the sword, trying to hook the cloth. Too late.

The fire extinguished, leaving them in total darkness.

The next moment, the clicking grew louder. Without light, Jacob and Sorias had nothing to stave off the spiders. It could be only a second until hundreds of hairy legs writhed over his body, accompanied by dagger-encrusted mouths. A few moments of terror, some flashes of pain, and he'd be dead.

And there was nothing he could do about it.

"No . . ." Sorias said. "No, no, no."

Jacob was breathless. A spider already clung to his shin, slowly crawling up his leg. Since he couldn't shake it off, he swatted with his hands. It held firm, using the tar to help it stick. Soon, he felt legs on his shoulder. He screamed, punching it off, hopefully to its death.

You're going to die, Jairus said. *You know what this means.*

"No!" Jacob grit his teeth and grabbed the spider on his leg. It writhed under his grasp, holding fast to his hand. Eventually, he shook it free, but only as two other sets of legs skittered onto his shins.

Embrace madness and fall.

Pain seared into the side of his leg. With a cry, he seized both spiders and shook them off his hands, but not before being bitten on the finger. A mass fell onto his head. Legs scrambled for a grasp, but the fall's momentum didn't give the spider enough time. It tumbled in front of his face, scratching his cheek with something sharp.

"Jacob!" Sorias's voice was on the verge of screaming. "You're a Wayfollower. Do something!"

There was nothing he could do. The wind wouldn't save them, and if Jairus took over to cast lightning, he'd only kill Sorias and escape without the king—assuming he had enough energy. Either way, Sorias would die, Adriel would be without aid, and Baltashazar would win. Lindina would fall to the Abyss. She would die because of Jacob.

"Make fire!" Sorias said.

No. Jacob convulsed, swatting over his body frantically. They kept coming from the tar and the ceiling, clinging to his shoulders, shins, and thighs, skittering along his back. They bit, tearing out bits of clothing and skin. On his arm, he lost a piece of flesh. Fire could kill these monsters, but Jacob could not make fire. He *could not.*

Then fall. Die.

Images formed in the darkness—trees, raging light, and smoke.

"Stop!" Jacob flailed around, focusing on the spiders. *Anything, even being eaten alive by spiders, was better than that nightmare.*

Relive your greatest failure and die.

Jacob wept amid his screams. It was his fault. His sister was dying right now, and it was all because of him. If only he'd done better, if he would have committed more, he could have saved her!

Before he knew what he was doing, he started snapping his fingers, trying to make a spark. Fire would save them. Fire would kill them. *He* would kill them. But the sparks didn't come.

"Please!" Sorias's voice broke into unintelligible cries.

Save them, Jacob thought, snapping his fingers. No sparks. Why couldn't he make fire?

You're not trying, Jairus said.

"I am trying!" A spider bit into his upper back. He focused on the terrible image of fire and snapped, to no avail.

"Embrace your nightmare!" Jairus screamed.

Jacob could do no more. *I've failed her.* He closed his eyes and resigned to death.

Fire raged everywhere around Jacob's shivering body. Crawling up the trees, catching leaves, whirling in the wind. Though he lay in the midst of them, the flames consumed him not. Instead, they drew heat from his dying body, rising higher into the air, staining the blue sky with flickering orange mountains.

From those mountains, smoke poured, falling to the ground and saturating the air, burning his eyes like a cloud of tiny knives making invisible incisions. He coughed, further aggravating the wind, which already swirled like a storm. Every breath felt like an intake of poison. He had to get up.

Somewhere amid the roaring fire, he heard weeping and scream-ing. Sometimes, he heard his name.

I'm coming, Jacob wanted to say, but he was out of breath.

Fool, Jairus laughed. *Oh, what a fool you are! Now she will die. She will burn in agony, wailing for you to save her. Well done, fool. You've earned your sister a gruesome end.*

Jacob sat up, convulsing. He was so cold he could hardly feel any part of his body. The Deep betrayed him. Everyone told him to stay away from it, but he pursued it anyway. In secret, he practiced the Ways, learning all he could from nature. The Silencers were right—he'd become Dreslen. What had he done to earn this?

"I'm sorry!" Jacob sobbed, clutching his face. His breath came as coughs, smoke mixing with the tears. He should never have engaged the Deep. It was evil—pure evil. Because he refused to listen to those wiser than him, Junia was dying.

"I trusted you!" he cried to the Deep, falling to his knees. Power went out from him, fuelling the fire against his will. Blue light flickered in the deepest parts.

Junia wailed Jacob's name again. In the howling wind, her voice sounded far off. Broken beyond repair.

I'm coming. Jacob tried, and failed, to stand. He couldn't feel his legs. *I'm coming, Junia.*

"Lies," Jairus said. *"All lies. You'll stay right where you are."*

"But I . . ." Jacob's breath failed him. Though lit by fire, the world turned black, silencing itself. Was he dying? If only. No, he'd wake up and find himself in a blackened forest, weeping over the body of his dead sister. His only sister.

"Fall!" Jairus said. The flames grew bluer. *"Did you really think you could protect her from yourself?"*

Jacob had thought that. When Junia first caught him practicing magic in the forest, he'd refused to show her any more. Each day, she pestered him more, begging him to use the Deep. "Just a bit of fire," she said. "Just a little!"

Months passed, and she didn't stop. Only when she threatened to reveal his secret did Jacob give in. Just a bit of fire. He'd done it many times before, never with ill consequences. What could go wrong if he did it for Junia? It wasn't fear that made him do it—it was the look in her eyes. The excitement, the pure joy that filled her when he said yes. If fire could give her more joy, then why withhold it?

Her smile at the flame in his hand turned to horror as it leaped out, covering the grass and spreading to the trees. She tried to run, but the wind knocked her down, stealing the air from Jacob's lungs. They were both trapped—Junia burning, Jacob freezing. In panic, he tried to stop the flames with a heavy wind. That only strengthened and spread them.

Now, he sat on his knees, powerless against this storm of death, cursing the Deep. It truly was what the Silencers claimed. It betrayed people like Mordecai and gave victory to Dreslen. It killed and destroyed. It created bundles of sticks covered in oil, disguising them as shelters. Jacob had fallen for it, even so foolish as to bring someone else in.

It was your decision, you realize, Jairus said.

Jacob clenched his fists. Jairus was right. It *was* his decision. And he was going to make it right.

Though he couldn't feel his legs, he remembered what it was like to stand. So he did. Focusing on every sensation he could, drawing heat back into his body, he put pressure on his legs, propping himself up with his hands. When he was high enough, he let go of the ground and straightened his knees. He might have been standing, but he hardly felt any different from when he was lying on the ground.

Where are you? Jacob looked around, but all he saw was fire and smoke. The screams and wails seemed to come from every direction.

Leave her! Jairus said.

"Where are you?" Jacob took a step towards where he thought the cries originated. "Junia!"

"Jacob!" Junia's scream drew out, shrill and painful. "Help me! Please!"

I see you. Jacob closed his eyes, subconsciously connecting to the forest. The trees were nearly dead, but they granted him some vision in exchange for his life force. Nausea aside, he saw a writhing form on the ground about ten feet from him.

Jacob pressed forward through the fire and pretended he could feel his legs. One foot after another, stumbling over roots, until he stood over a figure on the ground. At the first sight of Junia, he lost all resolve and collapsed beside her. All that was left of her dress was alight with fresh flames, and the skin underneath was red in some places, black in others. In some spots, she didn't have any skin left.

I'm sorry! I'm so sorry! I'm—

A Fool! Jairus stood up. All around, the fire turned blue. Jacob was beaten. That fool couldn't even control his own mind, let alone his powers. He deserved *all* of this. Pain. Yes, sweet pain!

The Silencers would be here soon. If he was still here when that happened, he'd share the same fate as Junia. As much as Jairus relished death, it terrified him. That was the thrill. But if death claimed him, it would be ages until he could enjoy it again. He needed to keep Jacob alive as long as possible.

Grunting, drawing the fire back into his body, he reclaimed some of the lost heat. Jairus needed to leave some behind, of course, to cover his tracks . . . and to finish off anything that might pull Jacob back once they were clear. Junia would die, and that was tragic, so tragic Jairus would have laughed if not for the smoke. Really, he should take better care of himself. *Oh well.*

"Please!" Junia's final scream was the loudest. Usually, Jairus enjoyed those kinds of noises—but something about this one was different. It ripped at his heart, almost bringing a tear to his eye.

Now you're the fool, he told himself, chuckling. *Stay focused. Chaos. Madness. This is our chief end.* Paying attention to a dying girl was something Jacob would do, not him. And yet, he could have saved her . . .

Finally, he stepped out of the last blue flame, basking in the untarnished forest. It would burn soon enough. For now, he had to get away from here. Junia would be dead now, and the Silencer wouldn't be far behind. That smoke would be visible for miles.

Have fun, Jacob, Jairus said.

Jacob gasped as he returned to consciousness. Where was he? The last he remembered, spiders were eating him in a dark tunnel while he waded through tar.

Lindina.

Junia.

Both were dying. Jacob turned around and looked at the orange flames. Even if he wanted to run into the fire, he couldn't move his legs. Junia was dead, wasn't she? The screams were gone.

"You've failed her," Jairus said, walking out of the fire. He appeared as a figure of blue flame in a dark, hooded cloak. His face had no features but two dagger-like eyes and a wicked smile. *"Because of your incompetence, your sister is dead."*

"Lindina?"

Jairus frowned. *"She will be soon."*

Jacob fell to his knees. He didn't care how much it hurt. "How do I save her?"

"Embrace your nightmare."

The nightmare. Junia's death. Fire. But how? Whenever he tried, nothing happened. Not even a spark.

"You're holding onto your guilt." Jairus turned to look at the fire. *"Let it go. Embrace the nightmare. Embrace madness."*

The fire in this memory had killed Junia. What was he supposed to do with that? Use it again? All it did was bring pain and death. Junia, his only real sister, died for it. Now Lindina was all he had left. He needed to save her, to absolve for what he did to Junia. He couldn't use fire. It was . . .

"Insane?"

Yes, insane.

Jairus turned around and smiled. *"Then fire you shall have. Embrace your madness, fool. Face your guilt—kill it if you have to! You won't die today. We won't die. Now, show me who Jacob of Tonto truly is. Do what you must!"*

Before Jacob could object, the world collapsed.

TWENTY-THREE

Jacob's eyes snapped open—not that it made any difference. Pitch darkness saturated the tunnel. Spiders still crawled over him, clinging with tar-covered legs to everywhere but his face, sometimes biting. The pain was minor compared to the horrid feeling of the legs and the ratcheting clicks. From Sorias's direction, metal rang out, accompanied by his frenzied shouts. Jacob hoped Sorias didn't accidentally hit him with the sword.

Embrace your madness.

It was time. Because of fire, Junia died; because of fire, Lindina would live. Jacob had to listen to Jairus. *Face the guilt—kill it if you have to.* He accepted responsibility for Junia's death. That day, he vowed to never again use the Way of Fire. But no more. Now, in this darkest of nights, light would fill the tunnel, and all would burn.

Jacob focused on his body heat. For the first time since entering the tunnels, he was glad it was hot down here. It had been a few years since he last used the Way of Fire, so he would be able to create little more than sparks. Fortunately, he needed nothing more. There must be dry tar everywhere, perhaps even coating some spiders.

Shifting his focus to his arms, he raised his right hand and prepared. *Madness.* Lightning a tunnel on fire. But they were going to die anyway, so what did they have to lose?

Without another thought, Jacob snapped, concentrating the heat in his fingers. Orange sparks flew, vanishing less than a second later. It wasn't much, but it was light. Hope.

Do it again! Jairus said.

Jacob couldn't make fire from sparks alone. His face contorted as he reached for his stomach, pulling off a hefty spider and gripping it tight. It thrashed between his fingers, but he held firm. With his other hand, he focused the heat again and prepared to snap. *This better work . . .*

Once the sparks caught the spider, it lit up in flames, giving the appearance that Jacob held pure fire. Seeing it filled Jacob with horror—this was what killed Junia. He was doing it *again*. Memories pounded at him. The screams, the smoke, the weakness. The guilt.

Madness!

"You're doing it!" Sorias shouted.

Embrace it.

Jacob needed to listen. There was no time for guilt. Lindina was dying—Sorias, right next to him, was dying! So he smiled. At Jairus's unspoken guidance, he poured his fear into laughter, emptying all emotion until he was filled with pure, twisted, terrified joy. Though the fire remained orange, he imagined it turning blue. Was this Jairus, or was it himself? The lines blurred, but he held fast to control. He was in charge, and he was what Jairus made him.

He ran his flaming hand over his body, stunning the spiders and dropping them into the tar. Some caught flame, but their light extinguished the moment they drowned. Oddly, Jacob's clothing didn't burn.

By the light of the flaming spider, he could see what danger they faced. Hundreds of spiders crawled on the walls and the ceiling, screeching from the light. On the tar's surface, some still swam towards him. Sorias waved his sword without method, striking the walls, clearing the spiders off his body. His eyes transfixed on Jacob's flaming hand.

"Save me!" he said.

Jacob took three steps through the tar, holding his light low. He could clear the spiders off Sorias in the same way he did himself.

As soon as he raised his light to stun Sorias's spiders, the flame died. Screeching intensified as the darkness returned. Soon after, spiders fell onto Jacob's shoulders, scurrying over his body before he could swat them away. They kept coming, like a rain of monsters, wasting no time in biting him. Beside him, Sorias screamed.

Jacob forced himself to laugh. Rather than ignore the terror, he used it. It made him sweat and overheat. Grabbing a spider with its fangs sunken into his leg, he sparked it with his other hand and swung it around his body. Every spider, save one, fell. The one that remained clung to his torso with claws at the end of its legs, tearing into his tunic and skin.

Forget the pain, Jacob told himself, ripping the spider off his stomach and setting it alight. Now he had two flaming hands. With them, he drew near to Sorias and purged the spiders from his body. Those with claws weren't so easily dropped, and Sorias had to use his sword to kill them.

"Come on!" Jacob turned around and trudged through the tunnel. Sorias wasted no time in following Jacob.

It wasn't long before he could feel the fire dying again. This wouldn't work. He was bleeding all over from spider bites, and if he didn't leave the tunnel soon, the spiders would grow accustomed to the light and attack him anyway. There had to be another way!

Yes, of course. The clawed spiders didn't drop when they saw fire. But what if they were *on* fire?

Jacob hurled a flaming ball of legs and ash at the ceiling. A few spiders lit up but immediately dropped and extinguished. Now he only had one fire left. He breathed deeply. The spiders with claws didn't drop when light was nearby. If he could ignite one on the ceiling, it would spread its flame to the others simply by scurrying along. However, if his fireball *didn't* hit a clawed spider, he'd be in darkness again.

He threw it. To his horror, all the spiders that lit on fire let go of the ceiling and plummeted to the tar.

You can do better, fool! Jairus said.

Jacob shot his arm to the ceiling, snapping as it reached its apex. Sparks flew, some of which ignited spiders. None of them had claws. He tried again and again. Both arms, flying into the air, shooting sparks, draining the heat from his arms. Around him, fiery spiders fell into the tar with pained screeches, like a hailstorm of light, while orange sparks rose and fell like dying stars cast from the heavens.

One spider, on fire, remained on the ceiling, scrambling to get away. As it crawled, it lit other spiders, dropping them. Though the light persisted, Jacob didn't stop sparking. It could die at any moment, and he didn't plan to be in darkness when that happened.

Forward they went, Jacob launching sparks and Sorias avoiding the falling flames. As more clawed spiders burned, the fire spread of its own accord. It wasn't long before the light stretched ahead of Jacob, illuminating the rest of the tunnel.

"Help me!" a voice echoed, rising above the tumult of screeching.

Jacob laughed. King Baraz was still alive.

The smile didn't last long, though. The flame spread to the end of the tunnel, revealing a wall of iron bars covered in black webs. A gargantuan spider—half the size of Jacob—sprawled in front, rapping its pincers together. Grey, overgrown hair covered its many-jointed legs but failed to hide the fleshy patch on its abdomen. Smaller spiders swarmed around it—Jacob couldn't tell if they were defending it or seeking protection.

It was the most ghastly thing Jacob had ever seen. How was he supposed to kill that thing? Even if he did set it on fire, it could easily kill Jacob before dying. Maybe fire wasn't enough. Perhaps Jairus could—

No! If Jairus escaped him, he'd kill Sorias and perhaps King Baraz too. He had to find another way.

Oh, Dreslen. Jacob froze. The spider was moving. Bending its head to look at Jacob, curling its legs, walking from the wall to the ceiling. Aside from the flaming spiders, all the screeching and clicking stopped. When the large spider clicked, it pierced all other sounds, low and sinister.

"Sorias?" Jacob stuttered. "I need your help."

"What? Are we almost—" His sword stopped swinging. "Glorious name of Amiroth . . ."

The huge spider quickened, stepping between the spiders beneath it—or above, depending on how one looked—avoiding any that flamed. It screeched, only moments away from Jacob.

"Sorias!" Jacob turned around. He hoped Sorias could see the panic in his eyes, because he needed help *now.* "Your sword!"

Sorias swung at a spider falling in front of him, looked up at the approaching monster, and nodded. Keeping the blade straight up, he hefted the sword through the air.

Jacob caught it but didn't anticipate the weight. The blade swung down, landing in the tar. He pulled, but it was stuck. Above, the spider slowed, looking down at him. It reeled on its back legs and reached for his head.

Jacob ducked, but not before a claw scraped his scalp. With a yell, he stood upright and yanked the sword from the tar with both hands, swinging with all his strength at the legs nearest him. The blade sliced clean through, chopping off three claws.

The spider screeched, lifting its legs rapidly, but still held onto the ceiling. Good. If it fell, it would land on Jacob.

It fell.

The next moments were pure terror. Legs and claws latched onto Jacob, sticking unnaturally, clinging and writhing at once. Jacob dropped the sword out of alarm and wrestled with the beast. It was pointless. He only had two arms, the spider had eight—five, if he only counted the full ones. It crawled to his back, wrapping its vibrating legs around his stomach and setting its pincers on the back of his head. A flash of pain erupted.

The spider writhed again—more this time—and stopped biting him. Jacob turned to see Sorias grabbing hold of it and pulling. Soon, it came off, but now it latched on to Sorias's arm and crawled onto his torso before he could shake it off.

The sword. Jacob looked down to see the piece of metal sinking beneath the tar, barely visible in the dying light. He grabbed it and had to pull hard for a few seconds before it came loose. When he freed it and held it aloft, dripping thick tar, Sorias screamed. Jacob didn't think about what he was doing. He yelled, sticking the front of the sword into the spider's fleshy abdomen and twisting.

The spider screeched, completely letting go of Sorias. Jacob swung the sword into the tar—spider attached—and held it down. After some thrashing, all was still.

Jacob sparked the ceiling to renew the little light they had, though his tar-covered fingers made snapping difficult. It was less effective now, since many of the spiders had fled at the appearance of the giant. Fewer spiders meant less light.

"Are you alright?" Jacob handed the sword back to Sorias, who took it with a nod, grimacing.

"Been worse." He rubbed his upper chest. When he took his hand away, Jacob could see numerous bloody marks in a circle.

"We have to hurry." Jacob turned back to the end of the tunnel and trudged through the tar. When he came to the end, a few sparks were more than enough to dissipate the spiders on the bars. The fire even caught onto the webs, which vanished in seconds.

When he backed away and looked at the bars more closely, he could see the shape of a door, outlined by a metal rectangle with hinges on the left side. No lock and no handle.

Jacob put his hands to the rusted bars and pulled. Nothing happened. There might have been a secret lock he couldn't see, but he suspected it was because the bars descended beneath the tar.

"Sorias, give me a hand."

Sorias drew beside Jacob and grasped the metal. Together, with much slipping and grunting, they made the old door budge. It groaned every second the hinges scraped against each other, eventually creating an opening large enough to walk through.

They stood back as if waiting for another monster to crawl out and devour them.

"Who goes in?" Sorias said.

"I have the goldberries."

"Be careful."

Jacob didn't need to be reminded. After everything that happened in the last few minutes, it was impossible not to be paranoid. He still felt legs crawling over him.

How was that? Jairus said.

Horrific. Incredible. Something I never want to do again.

I meant the madness.

Jacob still felt it. Laughter, welling up from his fear. It was liberating. The laughter meant he didn't have to care what happened. Pain turned to joy, fear turned to mirth. All became meaningless in a strange blur.

But madness dominated Jairus—and all it did was turn him into a sadistic monster. If Jacob continued to embrace it, what would he become? Would Jairus fully overtake his mind?

"Help . . ." The sound poured from scarred vocal cords, dripping with death.

Jacob sparked the wall. Somehow, his first try caught a clawed spider, giving enough light to see Baraz. He sat in the tar, legs invisible, stringy black hair sagging around his bowed head. His garments were torn and bloodied. If Jacob didn't have Zachii's testimony, he would never guess this man to be a king.

"I'm here." Jacob stood beside him and removed a large goldberry from his satchel with sticky fingers. He hoped the tar wasn't so poisonous that the goldberry couldn't counter it.

"Help . . ." Baraz said again.

Jacob bent down and held the goldberry in front of Baraz's face. It glinted softly in the light of burning spiders. The king's eyes lifted, near lifeless.

"I need you to eat this. It will—"

"Jacob!" Sorias shouted. From the tunnel, the clicking intensified, worse than ever before.

"Please eat this," Jacob said.

Baraz didn't move. Didn't speak.

"Eat the stoning berry, Baraz!" Sorias said.

Jacob forced Baraz's mouth open and shoved the goldberry in. This was no way to treat a king, but leaving him to die was no better.

The moment the juice entered him, his eyes lit up. He swatted Jacob's hand away and finished devouring the berry himself. "What in Silence did I eat?"

"Not important." Jacob ate a small goldberry and reached under Baraz's arms, heaving him out of the tar. Baraz didn't complain. It took precious seconds, during which light died, clicks intensified, and Sorias's muttering grew tense.

Jacob grabbed Baraz's wrist—he was still in a daze—and led him out of the cell. Sorias guarded the door with both hands on his sword, looking in all directions. The fire was almost dead.

"Take this." Jacob gave a goldberry to Sorias. After all the spider wounds he must have taken, he may need it.

Sorias looked unsure, but the hunger in his eyes got the better of him. When he ate it, he looked more worried than before. "That's one less for you."

"I can manage."

"Can you?"

Jacob didn't know, but he nodded anyway. "I need you to guide Baraz so I can light the way."

"Careful, Jacob. Sounds like there are a lot of spiders ahead."

"I'm counting on it." Jacob gritted his teeth and walked ahead, appraising the darkness. Spiders once again swam in the tar. The ceiling swarmed.

Time to embrace the nightmare.

Jacob stomped forward, took a deep breath of rancid air, and sparked the ceiling. The screeching resumed at a greater volume than before as countless spiders lit up, spreading the fire amongst themselves and falling into the tar.

"Is he . . ." Baraz said.

"Yes, he is," Sorias said. "Come on! Are you complaining?"

"Of course not! I'm just shocked."

Jacob ignored their arguing. At first, he'd been happy about the excess of spiders. More spiders, more light. But now that his arms grew cold, he wondered whether he'd be able to keep up the sparks. If he stopped, they'd be in a dire situation. They needed speed more than anything.

He looked behind. Sorias stabbed his sword at the ground. Good. At least he wasn't killing the spiders on the ceiling.

How much longer would it be? Every passing second put their lives at risk. Jacob could handle a flaming spider falling on him, but if either of the other two were hit, they might burn to death.

"Keep up, Baraz!" Sorias said from behind—too far behind.

"*Both* of you keep up!" Jacob shouted. His arms felt like tubes of ice, hardly able to produce sparks anymore. He didn't know how to transfer heat from one part of his body to another. The tar was hot; his feet burned. If only he could use that heat, they'd be out with no problems.

Eventually, they passed the iron bars. The walls were once again dark stone—but this time they were covered in spiders crawling over each other. Jacob turned his attention to the walls, lighting them up. The flames held better here. Good thing, too. His arms limped, completely void of heat.

Jacob grabbed a spider from the wall before it could plummet. Try as he might, he couldn't absorb the heat. At least it gave him immediate light.

The fire spread faster than they could walk. After about two minutes, the end of the tunnel came into view. But the darkness returned, creeping from behind. It wouldn't be long until blackness enveloped them. Sorias and Baraz were about three paces behind Jacob—he'd slowed for their sake as much as his own. His calf burned like lightning, hardly able to lift itself through the tar.

"Almost there," Jacob said as a small spider fell onto his head, scrambling down to his goldberry pouch. He knocked it away, and, to his horror, the pouch's flap opened. He'd forgotten to button it up. As he reached to seal it, a spider gripped his leg from below. He jolted, knocking three goldberries out of the satchel. They fell onto the tar's surface and remained there.

Jacob stopped in his tracks and reached for the berries before a spider could seize them.

"What are you doing?" Sorias pushed Jacob a moment before his fingers closed on the goldberries.

"Stop!" Jacob shoved back, keeping his eyes trained on the same spot. A spider was on top of the berries now.

"We need to get out of here!" Sorias said. Indeed, the light was almost all gone. Only a few small fires remained. Even after the spider moved from the goldberries, Jacob could see them no longer.

"Fine," Jacob said, pushing forward. Every step was a nightmare . . . so he embraced it. He laughed, and it gave him the strength he needed.

"What are you laughing for?" Baraz shouted.

Jacob only laughed harder, reaching for the ladder and looking up. Spiders swarmed the shaft.

Ready? Jairus said.

Jacob heaved himself up, struggling to hold on with his chilled arms. Step after step, he climbed, ignoring the spiders crawling onto him. *Embrace the terror.* He felt every bit of it, every leg, every pincer, every hair. He heard every click and every screech. The horror—it heated him.

When he was five rungs from the bottom, he shook his right arm free of spiders and snapped hard. Sparks sprayed, lighting every spider nearby. He grabbed one and used it to clear the rest of the spiders on him, dropping them onto—*oh no.*

Sorias and Baraz were beneath him. While Baraz clung to the ladder, Sorias swung his sword at the falling spiders. There would be more still. They might burn on the way up.

Jacob shook all his spiders free and turned his attention to the walls. If there was enough light, no spider would dare attack. He sparked rapidly, rendering his right arm near useless after a few seconds. But it worked. The fire spread up and down, lighting the entire shaft. It was like ascending a giant pipe made of fire.

He looked down. Baraz was still climbing, and Sorias had stepped onto the ladder. Above Jacob, any remaining spiders scurried at him. He grabbed a flaming spider and held it while climbing, careful not to touch any of the ones that fell. If only the spiders on the wall burned, Sorias and Baraz would be safe.

Step. Lift. Burn. Inhale the scent of tar, smoke, and death. He didn't know how long it lasted. It could have been minutes, could have been seconds. It felt like hours—no, eternity. An eternity of screeching and roaring fire.

Then it was over. The next moment, he was out of the hole, stumbling outside the entrance hut with a flaming spider in his hand. He collapsed beside one of the guards he'd killed, panting.

Baraz and Sorias emerged moments later.

The king was on fire.

Images of Junia burning in the forest filled his mind. It was happening all over again. Baraz screamed, clutching his body, dying. He was dying.

Jacob stared. His mouth trembled. What could he do?

Help me! he cried to Jairus.

Jairus chuckled. *This is what madness brings.*

Jacob looked at his tar-covered hands. He'd done this. It was all his fault. The king was dying, and—

"No!" *Face the guilt.* He stood up and looked at Baraz. Sorias tried in futility to quench the flames by hitting them, but they persisted.

When Jacob tried to save Junia by using the Way of Wind, he'd only made the fire worse. Air nourished fire. The attempt to save her accidentally killed her.

Embrace madness, he told himself, inhaling. This was a bad idea. It was absolutely *insane.* "Embrace madness!"

When his lungs could hold no more, he gusted the wind at Baraz with all his might.

TWENTY-FOUR

All was quiet in the North City Centre. No guards patrolled the area, and the sun was still a few hours beneath the horizon. Flickering firelight touched the ground, searching for the people who once walked the streets of Barabus. The only signs of life came from Adriel—the one woman foolish enough to disobey the curfew.

Adriel's feet scattered a few small rocks across the road. The gentle wind carried them for a few seconds, determining their ends for them. Adriel wished it would do the same to her. To be relieved of the weight of choice, the burden of right and wrong. Every decision she ever made seemed to break her. Trying to save her parents? They died anyway, and so did countless others she could have saved. Becoming a doctor in the first place? She healed some, but they would die just like anyone else. What was the point?

She was starting to think like Dredding. It was so much *easier* that way. Wallowing in misery, ceasing to care about anything or anyone. That was what she wanted. But Sorias cast the burden of hope upon her. The pain of believing things might turn out alright. They wouldn't. They *never* did. Even Sorias, the one she'd trusted more than any other . . .

Adriel still couldn't fathom why he'd done it. All she did was ask for help, and he deliberately betrayed her at her most vulnerable moment. She wanted to forget. If ignorance was bliss, she wanted it. But life was not so simple as that—it was a twisted, dark labyrinth of snares. You could choose a path and follow it with all your heart, drinking its joys and being embraced in love. Then the path would turn, and you would never find your way back. She was lost. She was so hopelessly lost.

A crow sounded, followed by the flapping of wings. Adriel didn't look up. She shook her head and bit her lip, fighting back tears. *Why, Sorias?*

Another crow mocked her. The entire city mocked her with silence. Here was a woman who put her trust in a well as dry as the Barabs. A woman who—with all her heart—put her hope for happiness in sources that could never satisfy. Her parents failed her by dying, and Sorias . . .

Adriel let her knees fall slowly to the stone. Her dress folded around her legs, its hems now tarnished by the filth of the road. A tear shuddered down her face. *Every single time I try to care . . . Father, Mother, Syndria, Sorias . . . They always break me.* Her hands collapsed to her sides. She was through with the illusion of composure. She was a doctor, so why couldn't she save anyone she cared about? Why couldn't she save *herself* from those she cared about?

Without warning or permission, Sorias strode back into her life. A fearless soldier, the only one with the mettle to confront Baltashazar. Sorias was once again risking his life for the greater good. She knew what a great man he was. He laid down his life for everyone, asking for nothing in return.

And still he betrayed me. Adriel sobbed. Her body heaved in time with her cries, hunched from the weight of her heart. Her breath wavered, as if uncertain where to go. To mingle with the night air, or to return to the mouth that set it in motion? It didn't belong in this world. Adriel didn't belong in this world.

Before her was the great bell of the square. Its dull sheen wrapped itself in low torchlight, oblivious to the darkness. Though it towered over her, it gave comfort. There was something larger than herself, something meaningful to fight for. Her short-comings did not dictate the world.

But she would change it. Sorias had offered Adriel a role in the redemption of Barabus. By ringing the giant bell, she would gather the oppressed to this square, the hopeful and the despairing, the strong and the weak. All who answered the call and listened to Sorias would partake in the noblest story of Atlantia—nobler even than Amiroth's quest to slay the gargoyle king. With Jacob at the helm, they would bring light to this darkest of nights, and hope would reign once more.

Or darkness will claim us all, Adriel thought. What was the point? She knew what Baltashazar could do, and Jacob was no match for him. He couldn't even jump through her window. But whether she lived or died, she *would* fight for this. It was all she had left to do.

Adriel stopped her cries and wiped her nose. Sniffling, she got to her feet and looked around. The area surrounding the bell was a circular path wide enough to fit her mansion. Unlike most roads in the city, the ground here was cobbled, and though worn by centuries of use, still retained some of its smooth shine. Dreslen may have been the evilest man to walk Atlantia, but he knew how to build a city properly.

Buildings surrounded the road, matching its curve. The bell in the centre stood on a slab half as tall as Adriel. Two posts at its sides suspended it. During the day, she had seen the immaculate inscriptions which covered its face. It was a work of art, but under the cover of night, she saw nothing but its outline and the rope dangling from its centre. It occurred to her that she would have to stand *inside* the bell to ring it. People could hear this thing for miles away—what would that do to her ears? Perhaps she should return home and grab some earplugs.

That would be risky, though. The timing had to be perfect. By Sorias's estimate, their mission to rescue the king would take four hours. On a New Moon night, it was impossible to tell time accurately. Her instincts, though, told her that two and a half hours had passed. If she was right, she still had an hour to wait. Once she rang the bell twice, civilians would crowd around the city centre—after that, soldiers would arrive.

If Jacob and Sorias didn't bring Baraz with them, all was lost. The people wouldn't believe them until the city guards came—by then, it would be too late. Adriel didn't know if Baltashazar would slaughter everyone or only her, Jacob, and Sorias. Either way, they failed.

＊

Jacob raised his arms, winded, and prepared for impact. Sorias tackled him to the ground for the third time that night, pinning his shoulders. All Jacob felt was breathlessness and the pain in his skull.

"You killed him!" Sorias spat on Jacob's face, seething. "You stoning, Abyss-cursed son of a rockweaver!"

Jacob took the blows as they came. He deserved every single one. More pain. Blows to his face, bruises to his chest. It wasn't enough.

Death. He wanted death.

"We were so close!" Sorias cried. "We brought him out. He could have lived!"

Jacob wanted to say he was sorry, but even if he could find the strength, it wouldn't bring the king back. The last Jacob remembered, he had blown Baraz with a gust of wind so strong that it knocked him back into the hut. It extinguished the fire, but it also sent Baraz toppling through the hole, some fifty feet into the blazing tar pit.

This is what madness brings, Jairus said solemnly. *I am sorry.*

How can you be sorry? Jacob's head tossed as more punches hit his cheeks. *This is what you wanted. For him to die.*

No. I wanted Baltashazar to die.

"You were laughing in the tunnel," Sorias said. "You planned this, didn't you?"

"I didn't know . . ."

"There is no little girl to rescue, is there? You've been working for Baltashazar this whole time!" Sorias stood up, kicking Jacob in the side. "Even after you murdered these guards, I trusted you. After you tried to *kill me*, I still trusted you! What kind of idiot am I?"

Jacob closed his eyes, preparing, *longing*, for more pain. He did what Jairus said. He embraced madness. Now he was in the same nightmare as he was all those years ago. King Baraz, up in flames, now dead because Jacob tried to help. Lindina, locked somewhere in Baltashazar's castle, doomed to fall prey to the Abyss.

Guilt. Jairus told him to let it go, to face it. He didn't deserve that luxury. For all the people who died because of him, he deserved all the guilt he felt, and more. He would let it crush him. Death would be too great a mercy. Better to suffer first then die painfully.

Junia, dead.

Baraz, dead.

Lindina, dead. There was nothing he could do to save her now. Without the king, they couldn't build an army to breach the castle guard. Baltashazar would kill them all.

Hundreds more, dead. Because of his foolishness! Embracing madness may have gotten him out alive, but to what end? To kill the one he risked his life to save?

"You're done here," Sorias said. He didn't strike again.

Please, Jacob mouthed, *don't let me live.*

"You were our only hope. Right now, Adriel is preparing to gather hundreds of innocents to fight a battle they shouldn't have to fight. Without their king to lead them, they will *all die*." He looked across the barren landscape towards the city. "I would have no integrity if I didn't die with them. Fighting for them. Goodbye, Jacob. May your insanity lead you to ruin one day."

Don't go . . . Jacob tried to reach out, but his arm wouldn't move. So he watched, unable to speak, as Sorias stomped away, disappearing beyond the rock dunes. *I can still help.*

But could he? Every time he tried to help, he made things worse. If he hadn't tried to "help" Junia, she might still be alive. If he hadn't pursued Lindina, she might not have fled Midor. If he hadn't come to Barabus and encountered Sorias, Adriel wouldn't be gathering hundreds of innocents to await their deaths.

He created those problems, and he wanted no more than to erase them. To reverse time and to throttle himself until he abandoned the Deep. But here he was, sitting in a sea of stone, useless.

Why? Jacob asked. To whom, he knew not. He received no answer, not even from Jairus.

A bell tolled. *Probably Adriel signalling the beginning of the massacre.*

Again. *Sorias said it needed to ring twice.*

Again it tolled, coming from every direction. Could it be . . . the bell of Tahil? If it was, it didn't grow in volume like last time. No surge of powers, just sweet ringing metal.

Jacob of Midor, a voice said. It sounded neither young nor old, neither low nor high. It was simply a vessel of words. He couldn't tell where it came from.

Who are you? Jacob thought. Was this real? It could be another voice like Jairus.

Rise, Jacob of Midor. My light is little, and I can help you no further.

"Who are you?" Jacob groaned.

Rise. The Night of Shadows must pass. I did not save you to let you die at the mouth of Todoros. My light is little. Rise, Jacob . . .

"Who are you?"

The bell faded into the wind; only echoes remained. Was he going mad? Well, yes. There was no question about that. But did he imagine that voice?

I heard it too, Jairus said.

Of course you did. You're me . . . I think. I don't know anymore.

What was he to do? That voice—if he didn't imagine it—told him to rise. How could he? Pain, weariness, and guilt weighed him down. The first two, he could overcome with a goldberry. But he *deserved* to die miserably. For all the pain he'd caused others, he ought to remain and suffer.

Face the guilt, kill it if you have to. Jairus's words. The words that got Baraz killed. Words of madness. Did he dare consult them again? Should he try one last time?

Your guilt is unmerited, Jairus said. *Let it go.*

You're wrong. I killed Baraz.

Why won't you let it go?

Because I deserve to suffer.

I couldn't agree more. But what of Sorias? What of Adriel? Lindina, for Amiroth's sake?

They're going to die because of me.

"No," Jairus spoke out loud. "*Rise, Jacob of Midor. If you let go of this guilt and allow yourself to try, you may save them.*"

"What if I make things worse?"

"*You, fool, have already made things as bad as they can possibly be. I cannot think of a single thing that is within your power to make worse.*" Jairus moved his right arm to the satchel. "*Perhaps you deserve the guilt—perhaps you don't. If you ask me, it's a luxury, not a punishment. You* want *to feel guilt. Do you deserve to get what you want? Stop thinking of all the mistakes you've made and start making them right!*"

"Since when do you care?"

"As of right now." Jairus fumbled with the button but eventually managed to get it open. Goldberries spilled onto the rock beside him. So few left.

"I can't, Jairus . . ."

"I don't care what you can do." He reached for the last large berry and brought it near his mouth. *"What matters is what you* will *do. I leave Lindina's fate in your hands."*

Jacob didn't move. The last time he trusted Jairus, someone died. Who was to say it wouldn't happen again? If Jacob lived, it meant Jairus did as well. Jairus *would* kill again if given the chance, Jacob was sure. But . . . what if Jairus was right? What if things were as bad as they could be?

Embrace madness.

No, he was done with that. But he was also done running from what he'd done. He looked into his memory, gazing upon Junia's burning figure. No amount of self-pity could bring her back; all it would do was kill Lindina faster. He faced the guilt, grabbing it with both hands and forcing it to the ground. Above him, the nightmare loomed. Jairus said to kill one and embrace the other.

Instead, Jacob let go and walked away, coming back to his senses. No more looking at the past. If he saved Lindina, there might be time for that later—but not while she was dying. Guilt, he now realized, was selfish. It was time to let go.

He put the entire berry into his mouth and bit down.

It was time to save Lindina.

TWENTY-FIVE

For the first time in hours, Baltashazar looked up from his book. His hands were sweaty, as much from his frustration as his worry. Days had passed. Days spent enthralled in the Book of Dreslen, searching, failing to find what he wanted. Could it be that Dreslen never faced this problem? Why was there no solution?

Light. Horrible, pounding light from the north. Not too long ago, it had gotten worse for a few moments. During that time, he actually felt *pain.* Not the pleasant kind that came from death, either, the kind that seared into his skull and scorched his heart. Light. Life. The stuff of nightmares.

What if this book was a fake? He remembered the meeting in Torania. The strange man in the dark cloak, giving Baltashazar a book he never knew existed. One so powerful that it could rival the forces of the so-called Silence. No, it couldn't be a fake. The ink itself glowed with darkness. But why didn't Dreslen mention the light from the north?

Baltashazar stood from his chair and screamed. He didn't care if anyone outside the room heard him. If his scream reached the guards, they would only be more careful about not disturbing him. Already, they feared his malice. How much more would they fear his rage?

At least he had this . . . device. The pen taken from that girl in the dungeons. The pen he'd sent Hazak to seek out in the South Midorian Forest, now brought to him by another. If it was indeed the one described in the Book of Dreslen, it may give him his greatest advantage yet. Still, he couldn't risk it. The transformation was supposed to be temporary, but what if it wasn't? What if, after he stabbed himself, he remained a gargoyle for the rest of his life?

He'd need to test it on someone else first. Being a monster wasn't *entirely* unappealing, but he valued his hands. Claws would make reading rather inconvenient.

A low sound pierced his skull, a soft and booming toll that scratched at the inside of his forehead and resonated in the room for at least five seconds. Baltashazar knew that noise. Someone had struck the bell in the North City Centre.

Baltashazar began taking long strides towards the doorway, a rush of curses pouring from his mouth. *Of all times, must it be now?*

The double door was fashioned from thick steel and engraved all over with images of gargoyles and curved scimitars. Some were stained a deep red, even in their metal depictions.

At the base of the door, human heads were etched into the metal. Some were crushed, some severed, and others torn, but all were dead. The largest of the heads was suspended by the hand of a gargoyle, who grasped its long beard. Mordecai, the last Bein Jemin, the one who Dreslen himself killed in a duel.

Baltashazar turned the handles and pulled them as one. The two guards standing in the hall turned their heads. Straight backs, square shoulders. No tremors. Good soldiers.

Still, a show of fear would be nice. Baltashazar walked to the one on the right and let the doors swing closed behind him. The guard—Baltashazar didn't know his name and couldn't care less—sweated, a hint of perspiration on the forehead.

But where were the shudders? Was this man not terrified of him? Surely he'd seen Baltashazar torture the other soldiers. If this guard thought himself safer than any other, he was as much an idiot as the floor he stood on.

From his pointed helmet to his spiked boots, black armour covered him. Swords, spears, and bows would have little effect against it. The only exposed skin he had was his face and the top of his neck.

"What's your name, soldier?" Baltashazar asked, leaning forward. He had yet to find a soldier taller than himself.

"Haldric, sir. Is there something—"

Baltashazar brought his hand up to Haldric's throat and squeezed.

Haldric gasped, groping for his short sword, but Baltashazar's fingernails had already pierced skin, and the darkness had seeped in. By the time Haldric had his sword in hand, he fell to the floor, writhing. He wasn't dead yet—that was the fun part. It would still be about an hour of agony before he expired.

"What are you doing?" The opposite guard stared at Baltashazar, eyes wide. He was already gripping his sword with white knuckles. Finally, some proper terror.

"Are you going to kill me?" Baltashazar grinned and rapped his fingers on his legs. He was quite certain the soldier would back down, but just in case he began accumulating solid darkness beneath his sleeve.

"No . . ." His idiotic lips faltered, shaking almost as much as Haldric.

Baltashazar wanted to kill the other soldier as well, but someone rang the North Bell. If it meant what he thought, he had a revolt on his hands. He needed all the men he could spare.

"Stop looking at me!" Baltashazar screamed, running past the guard. The dagger blade had fully formed within his sleeve, and he would have shot it towards the guard's face if he hadn't run away. "Who rang the North Bell?"

Baltashazar descended the staircase. It wound to the right with no rails to give balance and no torchlight to give direction. Though he could rely on the darkness for sensing his environment, it wasn't always ideal.

A deep toll saturated his ears again. He heard himself screaming. He was insane, and he loved every bit of it.

"My King!"

As Baltashazar leaped from the last stair, he emerged into a large balcony with a railing that overlooked the throne room. Near the stairwell's entrance, two fully armoured guards and a man in a black robe stood. It was he who spoke, and he who would die if he gave the guards permission to ring the bell.

The title of lord of the guard was a something that Baltashazar let go of begrudgingly. As he prepared to become king, he had other things to worry about. Politics with other kingdoms, plots against Central City . . . the pounding light. He simply didn't have time to administer the guards. The man standing before him, short and bald, was one of the smartest men in the city. More important-ly, Baltashazar trusted him.

"Who rang the bell?" Baltashazar lunged forward and grabbed Lord Goldor by his robe's gold collar. "Have I not made it clear that *no one is to ring it?*" Spit flew from his mouth as he spoke.

"I haven't a clue, My King!"

"Why was it not locked down?"

"We had not the time! You told me to bring every soldier to the castle immediately because of the Wayfollower and the rogue."

Baltashazar clawed himself in the face. In his preoccupation with the pen and the light, he'd completely forgotten why he fortified his castle in the first place. His troubles were mounting steadily, but his defences remained the same.

"Then it means rebellion!" Baltashazar let go of Goldor.

"Shall I send out a division?"

Baltashazar smiled. "No, this revolt can't be allowed to spark others. It's not enough to beat them—we must *crush* them. Slaughter them all, and a few extra for good measure. I want all three divisions sent to the North City Centre. Distribute the Silencers' metals in a ring around the area, just like we prepared."

"But the Wayfollower—"

"I'll deal with him." But how? He wasn't keen on fighting the man himself. Perhaps Uroku could prove useful. Or better yet . . .

Yes, if he pressed both advantages, this Wayfollower wouldn't stand a chance. What was one follower of the Deep compared to a lord of the Abyss and his deadly servants?

"Shall I give the order, My King?" Goldor asked.

"Not yet. Come, Goldor. I have something to show you."

⸺⟡⸺

The crowd gathered in the North City Centre was bigger than Adriel's expectations—and she was expecting a lot. Citizens of all ages, in garments varying from nightclothes to work uniforms, pressed around the bell pedestal on which she stood. For a throng of soon-to-be rebels, they were awfully quiet. Some muttering, but nothing more.

It had taken ages for her head to stop ringing, but she could finally see again. Ringing the bell was the most painful thing she'd ever done. After the first time, she thought she was dying. Forcing herself to toll it again was torture.

But here she was, standing, waiting. Had she timed it wrong? What if the guards got here before Sorias and Jacob? She kept looking over her shoulder. Still no guards. Still no Sorias.

She imagined how ridiculous she must look to the crowd. A dishevelled woman in a green dress, unable to remain steady, standing on the bell pedestal and watching them all. No one asked questions—it wasn't like the Barabians to do so. They showed their strength through patience and stubbornness. That didn't stop people from giving her strange glares, though.

"Bad news," Sorias's voice erupted behind her back. She turned, shocked, to find him standing on the pedestal, watching her with a grim expression. Thick, drying tar covered his soldiers' uniform. The crowd quieted. Perhaps they thought Sorias was arresting her.

"What? Did . . ." Adriel looked around. Realization settled in. "Where's Baraz? Jacob?"

Sorias bit his bottom lip. "Jacob's gone. He tried to kill me once, then he toppled King Baraz into a flaming pit . . . *after* we almost died rescuing him."

Adriel raised her hand to her mouth. "No." There were hundreds of people—perhaps over a *thousand*—gathered here. Without Baraz, Sorias couldn't rally them. And without Jacob . . .

"We have two options," Sorias said grimly. "I can tell these people you illegally rang the bell and send them all home, or I can try to prepare them for battle."

"We have to send them home." Adriel looked around. Had *she* really done this? "I can't let them all die."

"There's a problem, though. The city guards could arrive at any moment. If the civilians aren't prepared, they'll go into a frenzy."

"Then prepare them!"

"What do you want me to say? 'Go back to your homes, because you're all about to be slaughtered'?"

"Tell them the truth."

"They won't believe the truth. They're Barabians. As long as they think Baraz rules, they won't even consider otherwise."

Adriel wished Sorias was wrong about them, but she'd grown up here. She knew their mindset. If Sorias started proclaiming they all believed a lie, they would easily disregard him as a rebel.

"We can't beat Baltashazar without Jacob," Adriel said. "If you make them fight, they will *all* die."

"And if we don't," Sorias said, "most will still die. But do you know what else will happen? No one will *ever* rebel again. They'll see how Baltashazar's forces defeated us without contest, and they'll lose all hope. But if we can damage his army, it might inspire future rebellions. Enough of those, and he *will* eventually fall."

"Why do you care?" Adriel felt like crying but didn't know why. Maybe it was because of the imminent slaughter, maybe it was because she was about to die. Perhaps it was because of her hand in all this.

"Because someone has to." Sorias turned from Adriel and regarded the crowd. "People of Barabus!"

All muttering stopped, heads turning to Sorias. Adriel noticed him shaking.

"I don't know how to say this, but you've all been deceived. Your king, Baraz, was murdered. Lord Baltashazar reigns in his place."

More than a few protests sprang up.

"I saw him only a few days ago!"

"Why should I believe you, soldier?"

"The Silencers assured us he was alive!"

Sorias's shouts did nothing to settle the din. He looked at Adriel, eyes hopeless. They both knew this would happen. But was Sorias giving up? If he walked away, the people wouldn't know what to do. They might go back to their homes, they might not. The bell had finally given them an excuse to be out during the curfew.

"You have to try, Sorias," Adriel said. *Don't give up on them. Don't treat them like you treated me. Please.*

"Listen to them," Sorias said. "Why should they listen to me, really?"

Adriel needed to encourage him. She opened her mouth to respond, then stopped. Something was coming. A large silhouette, running under the streetlights at impossible speed. Coming towards the crowd.

"Sorias, look." She pointed over his shoulder. It wasn't coming from the castle, so what was it?

Sorias turned around and nearly fell over from shock. "That son of a rockweaver!"

"What is it?" Adriel peered forward and caught her breath. The large figure split into two humans. *My goodness...*

<hr>

"Can you walk from here?" Jacob said, panting. Finally, he could take a break.

"Do I have a choice?"

"Your people need to see you strong."

Baraz grunted. Jacob took that as permission to let go. He'd been carrying Baraz on his back for over half an hour—all while windsprinting. Even with the goldberry's help, he was near winded. His legs hurt. His lungs burned. His arms and back ached. But he was here; they weren't too late.

Baraz slumped to the ground behind him and groaned. "That was some ride."

"Don't count on it happening again."

"After what you did, I'd say you owed me."

"After saving you, I'd say we're even."

"Fine." Baraz grimaced. "Clear a path, and I'll follow."

Jacob nodded, still gasping, and turned to the crowd. Those on the outside edge regarded him with puzzled expressions. If Jacob could guess, they didn't recognize their king. Covered in tar, clothing torn, and crownless. But they would recognize his voice; Baraz guaranteed that.

"Make way for the king!" Jacob pushed forward, shoving people aside when he had to. They were in chaos. Shouts of anger and confusion hopped from mouth to mouth. Accusations of lies, words of rebellion, the occasional yell of "imposter." Once he exited the main road and walked into the city centre, he could see the middle of the commotion. Sorias and Adriel stood on an elevated platform with a giant bell, both watching Jacob with eyes bigger than their skulls.

What would Sorias say to Jacob? Would he turn him away because of his madness? Would he thank him? Both?

"Move aside!" Baraz said from behind. The stories were true—his voice, when commanding, was as great as the Grim Mountains.

Jacob smiled. When he rose after eating the goldberry, he was about to run straight for Barabus, but a thought wouldn't leave him. What if Baraz, against all reason, was still alive? He couldn't tell if he was embracing madness again, but it didn't matter. Climbing back into the Pits, he felt dread and assurance at the same time. Even if Baraz was dead, as supposed, Jacob wouldn't give up.

At the bottom of the ladder, Jacob found the dying king, saved from the fall by the tar that once held him captive. There was enough light around him to stave off spiders, but the fire wasn't close enough to burn him. Incredible.

The next decision was the most difficult. In the end, Jacob gave up the last of his goldberries to save Baraz and renew his strength. Baraz, understandably, punched Jacob in the face after that. So far, Jacob didn't regret a thing. The coming moments might change that.

Jacob pushed aside the last few people and climbed onto the pedestal. Sorias stood, frozen, as Baraz followed.

"What . . ." Sorias said.

"It's a shame you didn't check whether I was still alive," Baraz said.

"But you fell. It had to have been at least fifty feet!"

"Into a thick layer of tar."

"How are you standing?"

"Magic berries. Now, may I take over? It appears you're doing an *excellent* job here, but the people want their king."

Baraz surveyed the gathering with dark eyes, commanding more silence with each passing second. Remarkable, considering his beggarly appearance.

Baraz turned to his right, speaking far louder than necessary, "Sorias, give me your sword." More heads turned to the bedraggled man with the authority to command a city guard.

"As you wish." Sorias drew his short sword from its scabbard and held it up to the torchlight for the crowd to see. After an unnecessary hesitation, he tossed it blade upwards to Baraz, who spun it with a flourish.

Nearly everyone's eyes fixed on the bell pedestal now, but murmurs still passed between them. The night was late, and though the sun had not yet risen, its glow crept over the horizon, mixing with the torchlight to illuminate the crowd. There was fire in their eyes; whether a reflection of torches or ferocity, Jacob couldn't tell.

By now, even the whispers were dying. Aside from the calls of the crows, the loudest sound to be heard was the crackling of the torches' fire. Hundreds of men and women on all sides waited tensely to hear from their king.

"Gather your weapons!" Baraz bellowed at the top of his lungs. The veins in his neck became visible as he opened his mouth. "Plunder your own city to find anything you can use to fight!

"I am Baraz, your king! My cousin Baltashazar betrayed me and cast me into the Pits of Todoros. My guard has been overtaken and used to inflict a curfew on you, my people. Get up! March with me on Castle Dreslen and help me throw down Baltashazar the tyrant!"

The crowd erupted as if the ground beneath them turned to fire. Their shouts mingled and distorted one another, accomplishing only chaos. The volume steadily rose as everyone fought to be heard above the din—but it was hopeless. There were no distinguishable voices.

Ah, pandemonium, Jairus said. *The sweetest noise of all.*

Baraz gripped his sword with both hands, took a step backwards, and pivoted his entire body as he swung the blade like a club. It struck the bell, yielding a sound so deep and piercing that it cut through the crowd and sent a wave of pain into Jacob's head.

The sound did more than hurt his ears; it penetrated his very being, inhibiting his thought and reasoning. Even Jairus reacted to the psychological onslaught, spewing sounds without form and meaning. For a moment, Jacob forgot who he was and why he was here.

Focus— Jacob shook his head, rattling his already aching brain. *Focus, Jacob.* He was regaining thought and perception. Somehow, Baraz didn't seem the least bit bothered by the bell. He stood with a straight back and a battle-ready posture, gripping the sword given to him by his only loyal guard. His eyes fixed upon the crowd, who had finally given up their clamour.

"Who am I?" Baraz shot his voice into the city square like the bell toll before it. He stepped forward, away from the bell, lowering his sword below his hips. The way his head turned when his eyes swept over the crowd made Jacob cower.

"Am I not your king?" Baraz stepped forward again so that he stood at the edge of the pedestal. The crowd looked amongst themselves and muttered, most not daring to look up at their leader. "Are you not my people?"

Sorias stood tall. "Listen to—"

Baraz raised his hand at Sorias without looking. "Are you not the Barabians, the bravest people in all Atlantia? Are there any others with the sheer resilience to overcome the challenges of living in this stone wasteland? Are you not—all of you—soldiers, fighting against the very ground on which you stand in order to survive? Are you not?"

"We are!" the singular voice of a boy rang out. All whispers disappeared. Baraz was in full control.

"Have you not the courage of this boy? Is he truly the bravest among you? Let him come forth, and I will bestow on him honour upon honour. If anyone would match his strength, I offer you a prize greater still: freedom. Join me in my rebellion against the tyrant Baltashazar, and I shall restore to you the kingdom you once had."

"Hear him!" a woman shouted. "Do you see what . . ." Her voice trailed off as she realized she was the only one speaking. But unlike the boy, she lifted her voice again. "I pledge myself to you, My King!" And with that, she kneeled.

It was a simple act. At first, it was only one head lowered below a sea of many others. But one by one, those surrounding her followed her action. They lowered themselves onto their knees, some raising battle cries and lifting their fists. By lessening their height, they increased their stature into men and women of war, uniting under the sword of a king whose resilience outmatched the Pits of Todoros.

Jacob held his breath as the kneeling citizens rippled outward, infecting their neighbours with the plague of courage. Even behind him, where the king's back was turned, the people gave their allegiance. The fear and confusion that once filled the air evaporated, burned by the fire that grew from Baraz's spark. This was the mark of a true king.

Within moments, no one remained standing. All heads were raised, looking upon the man in the tattered garments. Though some muttered, Jacob knew it was not because of disinterest. These were sounds of reverence. Even the crows scattered from the square, away from the bane of darkness that stood so confidently with a sword in hand, ready for the coming battle.

"You are the Barabians!" Baraz walked around the bell, facing the opposite half of the crowd. "Men and women of strength, courage, and spirit! We will march on Castle Dreslen, and we will take back the city that is ours!"

A shout of approval rang out from the army. Though their bravery was admirable, Jacob couldn't help but think about what would become of them. Even if they had half the strength of a city guard, the only weapons they had were kitchen knives and frying pans—assuming they had the time to gather such items. More than a few people would die before the sun rose, all to give Jacob a chance at defeating their true enemy.

And what if he failed? What if Jacob, or even Jairus, was not strong enough to defeat Baltashazar? All these men and women, and even some children, would have died for nothing. The battle cries of the throng should have emboldened Jacob, but all they did was fill him with worry. His only hope was Jairus, a volatile being guided only by self-regard.

Not today, Jairus said. *Today, I fight for you.*

Jacob looked over the crowd to the north sky, where the sun would soon rise. Though not bright enough to give light, the sky lightened into a dark blue, blotting out the remaining stars. It was from this direction that light would come—and with it, victory.

Baraz still gave rallying cries, raising his sword, receiving the clamour of a battle-ready army. Jacob didn't doubt their courage, but could they fight? Could they possibly stand up to Baltashazar's own army?

"We march!" Baraz said. "No matter the force that comes upon us, we will storm Castle Dreslen and pave the way for our Wayfollower. Do not give up, even if Baltashazar himself comes to smite us. I am afraid, and you should be as well. But I have something greater: courage! Courage is not the absence of fear but the power to overcome it. I say, what is stronger?"

"Courage!" the crowd replied almost in unison.

"Then lead on, and worry not about weapons. With our numbers, we can easily pin down a soldier and take his sword for our own." Baraz turned south and pointed his sword to the horizon. "We march now!"

TWENTY-SIX

Baraz turned away from the castle and walked towards Jacob. The crowd—now an active rebel army—didn't wait for their leader. They did as commanded, marching towards the dark heart of the city, where the first battle in centuries was about to take place.

"We're behind schedule," Baraz said, coughing, "but our chances are still good."

"Yes, I think—" Sorias stopped, frantically looking around. "Where's Adriel?"

Jacob scanned the crowd. No short blond heads anywhere. He was sure he'd seen her when approaching the pedestal, but . . . what after that? Did she leave?

"I don't blame her," Baraz said. "This is about to get bloody."

"She's no coward," Sorias said.

"War makes fools of us all."

"Do you really think they can win?" Jacob had to raise his voice to be heard over the army. It got rowdier by the second. "Didn't Baltashazar himself train the guards?"

"Yes." Baraz looked over the army with darkened eyes. "The castle guard is too powerful for them to defeat without considerable casualties."

"What?" Jacob raised his eyebrows and looked at the marching throng. They seemed so fearless, walking towards a deadly army. Did they know their true danger? Baraz had given them courage—and now he told Jacob it was false courage.

"He's right." Sorias drew alongside Baraz as he returned his sword to his scabbard. His eyes were larger than Jacob had ever seen them before, blinking rapidly and casting the reflection of firelight. With his empty hands, he tapped his legs and stretched his fingers. Here was a man who had trained for war all his life yet never tasted it. Could it be that Sorias was actually looking forward to the bloody encounter?

"They can't win this fight," Sorias went on, locking his eyes on Jacob. "But you can. Whatever madness you have bottled up inside of you, it's powerful enough to rival Baltashazar's. Once he falls, so does his army. All you have to do is get to him."

"But in order to do that . . ." Jacob looked between Sorias and Baraz. The plan was clear—the army had to defeat the castle guard *before* Jacob could approach Baltashazar. He couldn't save them.

"We'll stay at the back of our army, letting them pave the way for us," Baraz said. "We need them to advance enough to draw out the remainder of the castle guard. Once that's done, you can go ahead to the castle. He'll be waiting there, I'm sure. He won't risk his life on the battlefield."

"We're putting the helpless, weaponless rebels in the front lines to contend with a force you know they can't defeat?" Jacob stared at Baraz. Was this really the same king who gave such a message of hope and courage?

"It is the surest way to get victory." Baraz's voice deepened. "And they know the risk. They may—no, they *will* die, as sickening as the thought is. But Baltashazar *must be killed*. Do you understand?"

"But your people will—"

"Do you understand?" Baraz yelled, freezing Jacob in his speech. "We can't win this without bloodshed, but I can assure you, if we lose, Baltashazar will do more to Atlantia than shed its blood." Baraz breathed hard, clenching his shaking fists and looking Jacob directly in the eyes.

Jacob looked away. He knew what Baraz was doing—looking out for the good of Atlantia rather than the life of a few commoners—was right. It was a perfectly rational decision. In actuality, it would be quite foolish to value a few individuals over thousands of Atlantians.

But it didn't *feel* right. The act of consciously sending people to their deaths, however necessary, felt like an act of evil. Baraz was killing his subjects in order to kill a greater threat. Where should the line be drawn? Should Jacob change the plan, potentially ruining everything, or should he follow through and consign hundreds to death?

Think, fool! Jairus yelled. Battle cries rang in his ears, the sound of false assurance uttered by the foolishly brave. Soon, they would turn to screams of pain, then to silence.

"I can't do this," Jacob said quietly enough that neither Baraz nor Sorias heard him.

"What was that?" Sorias said.

Jacob looked up at the soldier who had saved him both from city guards and Jairus himself. Sorias was a noble man. How could he follow this plan? Going against Sorias was almost the hardest part. Then again, was their trust repairable at all?

"Change of plan." Jacob raised his voice and walked backwards. "I'll go ahead and fight Baltashazar before—"

"Are you insane?" Baraz shouted. "That's impossible! The castle guards will slaughter you before you even get to him!"

Fool! Jairus screamed. *Utter, utter fool!*

"He is insane." Sorias grit his teeth and looked at Jacob. "You can't do this. I'll hold you back if I have to."

"But the people are—"

A cold screech, coupled with a deep croak, pierced the air. It immediately sent pain to Jacob's ears and a wave of nausea down his throat, chilling his insides and burning his skin. Unexplainable terror gripped his legs, bringing him to his knees.

The screech lasted for seconds. Jacob knew what kind of creature made such a sound. He had seen one only yesterday, nestled like a bloody knife in the folds of beautiful cloth. Zachii.

Baltashazar's dravelord was attacking.

"No . . ." Baraz put his hands to his ears and shook his head violently. "No, no, no, no!" His groans continued, rising in volume and intensity, peaking in a scream almost as terrifying as the dravelord's. "No, no, no!"

Jacob scrambled to his feet and locked eyes with Sorias, whose face quivered like a child about to weep. Why hadn't Jacob anticipated this? The dravelord could paralyze their army. Even the king, supposedly the bravest, screamed in horror at the mere sound of the creature.

The rebel army, once thrilled with the prospect of noble combat, went silent with dread. Their march stopped, and their eyes flew in all directions, searching for the source of the terrible noise. They had no idea what they were about to face, did they? Once it came upon them, they didn't stand a chance.

He had to leave now. The only way to stop the dravelord was to stop Baltashazar. Jacob could still picture Zachii's talons; curved like a sickle, crude as a stone, and black as the Abyss. They would tear through the rebels like a knife through bread. Jacob had never seen Baltashazar's dravelord, but if it was anything like Zachii, it was a threat far more pressing than any army.

Jacob spun away from Sorias and looked towards the castle. He couldn't see the dravelord, and its sound had vanished. That was a good sign. If the dravelord focused on the ground, it might not notice Jacob.

Running through the army wasn't feasible, and going around would take too long. He had to go over them, across the rooftops. If he windleaped onto the nearest building, he could do it. The darkness would make judging gaps difficult, but as far as he could tell, it was the fastest way.

Then again, he'd never successfully pulled off a windleap.

Jacob took a deep breath and ran.

"Jacob, no!" Sorias shouted.

Jacob leaped off the pedestal, closed his eyes, and focused on the air rushing around him. For a moment, the clamour of war vanished. He heard nothing but his own heartbeat. Then he exhaled.

The wind rose between his fingers and flashed into his ears, but his descent had already started. Heaving the last air from his lungs, he gathered the wind from all corners of the square, siphoning it into a geyser that moved fast enough to chill his skin. Half a second later, Jacob was no longer dropping, but he was barely ascending. The updraft was enough to keep him at roughly the same level as he flew towards the stone wall of the upcoming building.

Jacob reached out and grasped for the roof's ledge, catching it the moment the updraft vanished. His lungs felt as though someone had taken a torch to them, splashed acid on the edges, and shoved salt down his throat. It didn't help that he was dangling, stretched out, from a roof.

Pull up! Jairus pushed. *Push the pain aside and rise!*

Jacob felt his fingers slipping. A drop from a one-storey building wouldn't hurt much, but it would cost precious minutes and risk his legs. He *had* to get to the roof.

Jacob grunted painfully, forcing his shaking arms to bend. Inching his hands forward, he reclaimed his grip on the cold stone as his fingers found an inner ledge to grasp. Breathing was near impossible. Every gasp was like seizing a support that wasn't there.

Rise!

With a final heave, Jacob pulled his body up and stretched his arm onto the rooftop, gaining enough leverage to hoist his leg over. He rolled onto his back and collapsed. Air once again entered his lungs, but it would be a few seconds before he could run again.

Jacob turned his head to look at the bell pedestal. Sorias crouched down next to his king, putting an end to his screaming.

He looked up at Jacob and shook his head, shifting his gaze to the south—towards the source of all this darkness. Jacob closed his eyes and took another deep breath. He didn't have time to stop.

Right before he attempted to get back to his feet, a chill ran through him.

The dravelord screeched—this time from Baraz's direction.

Terror gripped him as he turned to see the descending black nightmare. Its wings, not even fully spread, were like a black canvas in the sky, so full of darkness that even the dying night seemed a glorious day by comparison. It cast no shadow, for the sun had not risen, yet it made no difference—the dravelord *was* the shadow.

On the bell pedestal, Baraz stared upwards, sword at the ready. Whatever Sorias had said to him worked. Yet even as the king stood—be it from bravery or foolishness—Jacob could see him tremble. Baraz knew his peril. Why did he fight?

With a loud rush of air, the dravelord flapped its massive wings to slow its descent as it reached out with its talons and seized the bar suspending the bell. With no sound but the internal screaming it caused Jacob, the dravelord lowered its crooked head and looked at Baraz. Though no longer airborne, its wings remained outstretched, slowly retracting to its sides.

"No!" Jacob shuddered, scrambling to his feet. Sweat poured over him, doing nothing to warm his chilled insides. He could barely think straight.

The dravelord croaked a long, deep note, leaning downward at Baraz. Shaking even more, the king held his ground, raising his sword higher.

Fool! Jacob thought. He wanted to jump in and save him, but he couldn't reveal his presence. Baraz might be the king, but Jacob was this city's only chance of salvation. If the dravelord discovered Jacob, all was over.

Sorias! Jacob shifted his gaze past the bell, where Sorias stood frozen. He was weaponless, having given his sword to Baraz. Why didn't he do something? He was the only one close enough!

Not the only one, Jacob thought. All he needed was to cast some of his powers, and the monster would turn his attention from the king. Jacob could save him.

You've already saved him twice, Jairus said. *But by all means, do it again! Commit suicide!*

Insane, isn't it? Jacob looked at his hands and took a deep breath. A simple gust of wind in the dravelord's direction was all he needed.

Come on! Jacob grit his teeth hard enough to bring pain. Why couldn't he do it? At this very moment of inaction, the dravelord leaned closer to the fear-frozen king, raising its wings for action. It would only be a second before the king was dead.

What did Baraz even plan to do? Stab the creature with his little sword? Did Baraz even know it was cursed to be deathless?

Jacob closed his eyes and took one final intake of air, readying his hands to push the wind. *Embrace madness, Jairus!*

As the wind rushed past Jacob's ears, it sucked the air from his lungs. Pain, fear, and suffocation clouded his vision, but even through the blur, he could see the ruffled feathers of the blackness atop the bell. It let out a short screech and snapped its eyes away from Baraz, settling on Jacob.

Now Jacob knew for certain why Baraz hadn't moved. Under the watch of those eyes, so dark and so pale at once, he felt as though in a nightmare. Screams welled up inside him, pleading to be released to call for aid. But terror clenched his throat shut, and all that left his mouth were stifled whines.

Help me! Jacob's face contorted, stretching out in agony, wanting to look away but unable to. His legs did nothing. Blood boiled inside him. Skin froze and quivered. All he could long for . . . was death, anything to be free from this torture of the body and mind.

The dravelord lifted its wings and let out a long croak. It penetrated Jacob, striking through the centre of his being. All it passed through—body, mind, and soul—it left in turmoil. Even Jairus cried in agony.

Suddenly, pain hit Jacob's ears. The dravelord screeched, lurching straight into the air in no particular direction. The toll of the North Bell filled the night, low and high at once.

As soon as the dravelord broke its gaze from Jacob, he was able to think again. The scream finally escaped him, though it was outmatched by the resonance of the bell. What now? The dravelord thrashed in the sky while the bell resonated.

Sorias stood next to the bell, helmet in his hand, shaking. Baraz was still frozen.

Before Jacob could consider rushing to their aid, the dravelord fell from the sky next to the bell pedestal. By now, all the panicking rebels had cleared out of the square, either running towards the castle or fleeing in any direction that could get them away from the winged horror. Only Jacob, Baraz, and Sorias remained with the dravelord, which lay prone on the ground.

Jacob looked at Castle Dreslen. Baltashazar had sent out his best defence, and the rebel army was already halfway to the castle. If Jacob left now, he might time the attack perfectly. If he stayed, there was little chance he'd have any strength left to fight Baltashazar—assuming he survived the dravelord.

Idiot! Jairus said. *Why are you still waiting? Go now!*

I—

The dravelord raised its wings, convulsing. It turned its head to Jacob.

"Alright." Jacob turned and sprinted across the rooftop towards the castle. If he could build enough speed by windsprinting, he might have enough momentum to jump across the rooftops for the entire way. Windleaping, while possible, was too taxing.

Taking deep, rapid breaths, Jacob channeled the wind forward, pushing it against his back. The first gap came easily, since the buildings were close together. The roof ahead was across an alley-way—a narrow one, but a considerable jump.

Jacob huffed and forced his legs to move faster. They burned, especially his left calf, but his fear of being overcome by the dravelord was greater than any discomfort.

With a brief cry, Jacob sprang across the void. Air rushed all around him, spurring him on and holding him back at once. He couldn't help but look down at the alley beneath him. Once again, Jacob was flying. This time, he kept his limbs from flailing.

The dravelord shrieked halfway through his jump. All it did was fill him with adrenaline. The next thing Jacob knew, he was running again, trying to right himself to avoid falling on his face. Clearing the first large gap was the first victory won. Many more lay ahead.

Jacob stole a backwards glance, twisting his neck towards the dravelord, which rose with its wings spread. It had not yet begun to pursue Jacob, but it wouldn't be long. Sorias and Baraz weren't at the pedestal anymore. Hopefully, they were in the army and—

Look ahead! Jairus shouted.

Jacob snapped his eyes forward in time to catch the next gap between buildings. This one was far narrower, but the next building was two storeys high. He needed to windleap.

Jacob took a painful gasp and pulled the air beneath him. It whirled up through his garments, once again rushing into his ears and impairing his hearing. Leaping, he reached out to clutch the rooftop of the next building.

His body collided.

At first, he felt no pain. His vision blackened and he felt a sudden weightlessness, but no pain. A moment later, his legs crumpled beneath him. His head hit the ground right after. No breath.

Oh no. Jacob blinked rapidly, struggling to stay conscious. Looking up, he could see the declining night sky between the two buildings. Legions of black stains swarmed his vision, shifting and swirling in a dance of darkness. Light faded.

No . . . Jacob clutched his head, pulling his hand away wet. Was he going to die? *I can't. Help me, Jairus.*

Silence.

I have to get up. Jacob shifted his body into a sitting position, still looking at the sky. All at once, pain flooded into him from all directions. His head throbbed in the front and back, his legs stung like they never had before, and his chest felt like it had an anvil over it

.

The pain did two things. It gave him a desperate desire to give up and lie down again, to succumb to suffering. There was nothing he wanted more than to die. But the pain sharpened his vision, clearing away the dark streaks—all but one.

The dravelord, which hadn't been following him moments ago, hovered in the air between the two buildings, unable to pass between them. It looked down. This time, Jacob was too stricken from his fall to feel any actual terror.

Get up, Jacob! Jairus said, distant. *Think of this city. Think of Lindina! Please don't give up.*

"Lindina," Jacob muttered. He remembered his vow. He had run through forests, sprinted across grasslands with little food, and survived in Atlantia's harshest environment for this long. He had battled soldiers and faced the Pits of Todoros themselves. That couldn't have been for nothing. Yet the creature above him was so terrifying, and his hurt so great, that Jacob had little choice but t o—

"Get up!" Jairus forced his voice through Jacob's mouth, burning his lungs from the sudden exhalation.

Jacob knew what he needed to do.

The dravelord circled and croaked in frustration. Still, it made no motion to change either tactics or target. It was waiting for Jacob.

What was Jacob waiting for?

Grunting, he began to get to his feet. All his movement felt slowed, as if he were submerged in water. Even his thoughts seemed to lag compared to the world around him. The ground beneath his hands was rough, painful, but helpful because of the friction. The contraction of every muscle hurt, every breath laboured. Teeth ground against each other in an act of defiance; Jacob would not let pain defeat him. He had overcome pain before and would overcome it again.

In one swift motion—which seemed to take seconds—his legs straightened, and Jacob stood once more. He had done it! Now all he had to do was walk towards the castle through two battling armies, find Baltashazar, *fight* Baltashazar, and deliver the city to Baraz . . . all while being pursued by a dravelord . . . while injured from his fall.

I can't do this, Jairus. Jacob put his hands to his head, which felt lighter than air and heavier than a rock at the same time. The task ahead of him was impossible. *Impossible.* There was no way he could complete what was required of him. Baltashazar would remain undefeated, and the city would fall. If Lindina was lucky, she would be killed quickly.

He had failed.

A sharp cry sounded from the dravelord. Jacob looked up, his gut wrenching, and witnessed it fly towards the street. It must have seen something—surely not the king. If they were smart, Baraz and Sorias should be a good distance from here right now. But there wouldn't be anyone else in the street. What else could possibly make the dravelord turn its attention on—

Adriel! Jacob saw her as she passed in and out of view of where Jacob stood. She ran in her green dress and appeared to be carrying something. What in Amiroth's name was she doing here? Now, of all times! The dravelord would catch her and tear her flesh in a matter of seconds!

Time to go. Jacob limped forward, readying his hands to cast lightning at the dravelord. He knew he wouldn't be able to kill it, but it might be the only thing that would draw its attention from Adriel. All he needed was Jairus's agreement.

Absolutely not! Jairus said. *If we turn that monster's attention on us and drain our last energy all at once—*

We're going to die anyway. Jacob stepped out from between the two buildings and onto the main road. The dravelord had already caught up to Adriel but hadn't attacked yet. In fact, it landed on the ground in front of her and spread its wings, screeching. Adriel froze at the beast's presence.

Why was the dravelord so interested in Adriel? And why wasn't it killing her right now?

You're asking me for madness! Jairus said. Inside, he forced a smile.

"Then give it to me!" Jacob shouted out loud. At once, numbing cold washed over him. The dravelord looked over Adriel's shoulder, trying to meet Jacob's eyes. Jacob snapped his shut before it could paralyze him. "Run, Adriel!"

"Jacob!" Adriel screamed. "Open your eyes!"

Was this a trick? Had Adriel turned to the dravelord's side? Why on all the face of Atlantia would Jacob open his eyes and make himself vulnerable to the dravelord's gaze?

The dravelord screamed with a heavy flap of wings. It was flying to him now, wasn't it? He couldn't see Adriel, but he could only hope that she was running. *If I die and she doesn't take the opportunity to escape, I'm going to kill her!*

"Open your eyes!"

Why?! Jacob finally let his eyes snap open and immediately wished he hadn't. The dravelord landed directly in front of him, spreading its wings and screaming like it had done to Adriel. Horror enveloped him. Jairus's panicked mutterings stopped. All he could even think about was the terrible scream ringing in his ears.

But there was something else. In the top of his peripheral vision, he saw a glint of gold flying across the sky, bright enough to draw his eyes from the dravelord. He didn't know what it was, but it seemed to give off a light of its own. It could have been a star, coming down from the heavens to lend aid against the battle against darkness.

As the gold spark began to descend, Jacob realized what it was. He backed up quickly, stretching out his hands towards the sky, and waited. Even the dravelord turned its attention to the source of Jacob's distraction, lowering its wings halfway and closing its beak.

When Jacob caught the goldberry, it was too late for the dravelord to intervene. *Now, Jairus!* Jacob shoved the berry into his mouth, bit into it, and extended his arms. *Save us!*

Jairus needed no more prompting. Pure energy shot through Jairus's entire body as the sweet juices saturated him, removing pain everywhere it went. He felt like he could have been made entirely of lightning. The fear was still there, but the thrill of power overshadowed all of it. He knew he couldn't kill this creature, but he could deliver a blow it would remember for the rest of its undead life.

With a loud cry, Jairus sent a long bolt of lightning out of each of his fingertips. The dravelord screeched and reared back, falling over and extending its wings at once. It writhed on the stone road, giving a mixture of screeches and croaks. Its noise matched the crackling lightning and the sound of searing flesh.

This was the most powerful Jairus had ever felt. He wanted to keep going, to see this bird as a pile of scorched feathers. Oh, the power! He *was* power. What marvellous things goldberries were.

Don't use up all our energy! Jacob said.

Jairus knew that if they were going to make it to Castle Dreslen and fight Baltashazar, Jacob was right. But if he could continue for a few seconds longer . . .

"That's enough, Jairus!" Jacob broke into full consciousness and stopped the lightning, raising his steaming hands into the air. The dravelord was on the ground, unmoving but for a few twitches in its wings and talons. Somehow, against all probability, Jacob defeated it.

Looking up and past the beaten dravelord, Jacob saw Adriel standing there, frozen, with eyes as wide as a full moon. "How?" She put her hand to her head and looked to the unmoving form of the dravelord. "That was . . . unbelievable."

"Thank you, Doctor." When Jacob spoke, it almost came as a surprise that his voice was strained. He felt better than he had in hours thanks to the goldberry, but he was still very much injured.

"You look like a corpse," Adriel said. Then her expression re-laxed, and she laughed. "But you're alive!"

He was indeed.

Jacob smiled, then frowned. "Where did you get a goldberry?"

Adriel looked at the ground. "I stole it from you. I thought I might have been able to use it to save someone else if I lived through this. But when you came back with the king, and I saw how *ghastly* you both looked, I knew you needed it."

See? Jairus said. *I told you not to trust her.*

So you did.

"It doesn't matter anymore," Jacob said. "You need to get to safety. Baraz expects a brutal onslaught from the enemy soldiers, so our men will need a good doctor when this is over."

"I'm not leaving."

Jacob sighed. Barabians. "You really are all this stubborn, aren't you?"

"You'd be correct."

"Stay safe." Jacob looked at the dravelord. Almost motionless. "And get away from here. I don't know how long it will be until this thing gets up again."

"You didn't kill it?"

Jacob shook his head. "It's undead. The only way to stop it is to kill Baltashazar." He flexed his fingers. *And with the goldberry in my body, I have the strength to do that.*

"Right." Adriel looked at the dravelord again, taking a deep breath. "Do you know where Sorias is? King Baraz?"

"They're both with the rebels." *I hope.* Jacob stepped over the dravelord's outstretched wing. Travelling by rooftop was out of the question based on how he handled it last time. He would have to go by the road and take his place at the back of the army.

Adriel looked like she was about to cry.

"We're going to win this," Jacob said, stopping next to Adriel. He was probably going to regret saying this. "And when we do, I'll make sure you get things sorted out with Sorias."

Adriel looked up, shocked. "I wasn't . . ."

"Get yourself to safety." Jacob walked away from Adriel and the dravelord's body. "As for me, I'll do quite the opposite!"

Taking a deep breath, Jacob prepared to run. It wasn't far to the back of the army. If he windsprinted, he could get there in seconds.

Now you're getting the hang of it, Jairus said. *Running towards absolute danger like a true madman.*

Jacob smiled. *I thought you didn't like danger.*

Turns out I can change.

Jacob ran headlong. It was time to make the most of his insanity.

TWENTY-SEVEN

The back of the army was eerily quiet. Those who weren't frozen with fear darted their eyes in every direction, looking for a way out of the coming onslaught. Jacob didn't blame them. This rebel army was large but nearly defenceless. Against trained soldiers, what hope did they have? At least the ones in the back had a *chance* of survival.

Despite their terror, they stood their ground. Alleys and roads opened to the right and left, offering an escape from the soldiers ahead and the dravelord behind, but the Barabians marched on, likely towards their death. What could inspire such courage in them? Baraz's rallying was powerful, but it was mere words. This was something else.

And what of those at the front of the army? They proved themselves braver even than the king himself. Baraz may have proclaimed courage, but the leaders of this army took it to heart. Jacob would soon join them.

With goldberry energy pulsing through him like a radiant heartbeat, he felt unstoppable. What were a few soldiers compared to a Wayfollower? Even without Jairus's lightning, he could handle them. Probably.

"Where's the king?" Jacob forced through the back of the rebels. Anyone who looked at him promptly looked away. Perhaps they didn't recognize him as the one who stood at Baraz's side on the pedestal. More likely, it had to do with his grisly appearance. Tar still coated him, now drying, and some blood stained the side of his head from when he fell from the building.

"Where is King Baraz?" Jacob grabbed the shoulders of a tall man wearing a brown vest. He kept his composure better than those around him.

"He went ahead." The man backed away from Jacob. His eyes widened. "Are you the Wayfollower?"

Right. Baraz did mention that, didn't he? That might make it difficult to hide his powers after this ended.

"Thank you." Jacob turned away and continued through the army. Nobody seemed to mind him getting ahead.

"Wait!" the man said. "Are you a Wayfollower or not?"

Don't answer, Jairus said. *They'll all know soon enough.*

Jacob tried to ignore the shouting ahead, but after a few distant cries of pain, he decided to absorb them. These were, in a sense, his people now. He fought for them in a way he'd never fought for Midor. If Haanon were here, he might say Jacob was responsible for them, being the only one with the means and opportunity to contend with Baltashazar. If the Barabians suffered, Jacob wouldn't turn a blind eye. Rather, he allowed the sounds of chaos to fuel him.

Finally, Jacob heard Baraz's unmistakeable iron bellow above the din. "Well fought, soldier! You, in the red cap, come here!"

Jacob pushed forward. Those surrounding him now were less unnerved. Unlike those at the back, these rebels kept their heads forward, eyes level and steady. They shook, but it was more of a twitch than a tremble. Careful, controlled fear.

"Move out, men! We need more!" Baraz called out again. "Red cap, what's your name?"

"Pitt, sir!" a gruff voice said. "At your command!"

Jacob shoved between two overeager boys and finally got a good view. A group of three men and a woman held down a helmetless castle guard who bled from his temple. Beside them, Baraz faced a burly man in a pointed red cap. *Great Scholar!* His arms might have been thicker than Jacob's legs.

"Do you have experience fighting?" Baraz asked. He tried to stand up straight, but his back hunched more than when he gave his speech. If the goldberry ran out before he could get medical attention, he would be in serious danger.

Jacob reconsidered his resentment of Baraz's decision. Yes, a king should lead by example. But this was a special case. Baraz was the only thing driving the people forward, and he was dying. If he fell, what would become of the rebels? Without their leader, they might lay down their arms and scatter, only to be hunted down later and killed. In moving to the centre of the army, Baraz had proven his courage enough.

"Yes, sir!" Pitt said. That voice was thicker than Sorias's skull.

"You, boy!" Baraz pointed to a young man holding a short sword. He had been one to restrain the soldier, who was now unconscious. "Give that sword to Pitt."

The boy's crestfallen eyes lowered to the sword in his hand. After a second passed, the fire relit in his eyes, and he tossed the blade upwards to Pitt, the same way Sorias had done to Baraz.

Pitt caught it in his left hand and raised it to Baraz—probably a salute of sorts. "Your orders, sir?"

"Get to the front line. Once you incapacitate a soldier in any way, send his body back here so we can arm more fighters. March!"

Pitt bowed tersely, turned, then ran through the advancing army with a terrifying battle cry.

Baraz looked in Jacob's direction, glanced away, and turned back with wide eyes. "You're still alive?" His mouth hung open like a box with a broken hinge. "The dravelord chased you! And . . . what happened to your head?"

"Ran into a wall." Jacob stepped towards the king. "Where's Sorias?"

"Out in front," Baraz coughed. His hands, which once made firm fists, hung loose by his sides.

"King Baraz, there's something I didn't tell you," Jacob said. "The goldberry didn't heal you. From what I guess, it puts injuries in a stasis, allowing them to heal naturally without worsening. If the effects are already waning, it won't be long—"

Baraz raised his hand and stared Jacob in the eye. "I know I need medical attention if I'm going to stay alive."

Jacob raised his eyebrows, faltering. "You do intend to stay alive, don't you?"

Instead of answering Jacob, Baraz merely turned towards Castle Dreslen. Built by the most powerful man ever to walk Atlantia, now the fortress of a new dark lord. It was closer than ever. Jacob could already make out its many spires, piercing the dying night sky and the rising hope.

Jacob guessed that it was fear more than hope that drove Baraz to take this revolutionary action against Baltashazar. And he was right to fear. But this fear, though it might drive him, was going to kill him.

"You need to go find Doctor Adriel." Jacob grabbed Baraz's forearm. It was crusty from the tar dried on to it and far thinner than it ought to be. "She's somewhere past the back of the army."

"And if we fail?" Baraz drilled Jacob's eyes with his own, stepping forward. They were wild, dark reflections of Jacob's own doubts, radiating with terror. "If we fail, he'll do worse than kill me. You know what he did before."

Jacob gulped. He knew exactly what end awaited Baraz if this mission failed. What did he have to say to that? What words could possibly counter the prospect of being sent *back* to Todoros to live with the spiders and eat the tar from the walls? Some part of Jacob knew Baraz was justified, but another part wouldn't have any of it.

"We're not going to fail!" Jacob said. "I'm going to kill Baltashazar and put you back on your throne. You think I'm out here risking my life so that someone loses theirs? The *king*, no less?"

"My life is my own," Baraz growled, stepping back from Jacob and averting his eyes. His face looked grimmer than it had this entire journey. "As is my death."

Jacob gave the king a hard look, but it was not returned. *Fine*, Jacob thought, turning to the castle. *Be a coward*. It might not have been his fault, given the torture he endured, but it was his character, nonetheless. Whatever courage might have formerly rested in Baraz was crushed by the hands of Baltashazar. Now, Jacob would crush Baltashazar.

He started running, pushing aside those who marched at a slower pace. His gaze was set, his fists clenched, and his eyes narrowed. Anger at what Baltashazar did to Baraz and this city pushed him forward. Fear at what would happen to everyone if he failed spurred his legs. The hope of victory kept his eyes open, and his trust in the strength of the Deep kept his head up.

Looking back on how he was in Tonto, he almost laughed. Who was that man on the watchtower, blatantly ignoring the past and terrified of the Deep? Certainly not the same man who ran through an army, embracing as much madness as he dared, preparing for a duel with the greatest threat since Dreslen. The Deep was his greatest strength; no more would he hide from it. This was who he was. Jacob, Wayfollower of Atlantia.

But the Deep had blessed Mordecai, too. The strongest of the Bein Jemin, who trained for years upon years, had given every effort to put an end to Dreslen. But who emerged victorious? The herald of darkness. The lord of the Abyss.

This will be different, Jairus said. *Baltashazar is not as powerful as Dreslen was.*

But the darkness is the same. Jacob started guiding the wind from his lungs to propel him forward and push others to the side. *And I am hardly as skilled in the Deep as Mordecai was.*

Do not count the coming battle as one between two men. You and Baltashazar are merely vessels used by forces greater than we can comprehend. Whether you succeed or fail will not be in your hands. This is between the Deep and the Abyss.

Still feeling the adrenaline from the goldberry, Jacob mustered his strength to windleap again. A rush of wind gathered at his feet and propelled him upwards.

What power! This time, the windleap didn't completely exhaust him. Flying over the heads of the rebels sparked something—he might have called it joy, if not for the fact that he jumped towards a Dreslite. Even as his arc began its descent, he couldn't help but feel happy exhilaration.

He could do this.

Oh no. As soon as Jacob hit the ground, he realized he was no longer in rebel territory. Shouts mixed around him. Furious rebels on one side, terrified soldiers on the other. One such soldier, wearing full metal armour and wielding a short sword, took notice of Jacob and swung at his neck.

Jacob ducked into a crouch and tried to push the soldier with a gust, but windleaping had drained his air. Looking up, he saw the soldier bring his sword around, preparing a downward strike.

Jacob gasped and jumped to the side, landing on his stomach and scraping his hands on stone. The gasp gave him enough air to gust at the soldier, but his prone position granted no opportunity.

Using the wind, Jacob rolled himself onto his back in a swift motion as the sword struck the ground with the sound of a hammer on an anvil. Jacob craned his neck upwards to see the soldier hesitate with wide eyes at Jacob's sudden maneuver.

Extending his arms towards the soldier, Jacob pushed with all the air in him. The man nearly dropped his sword as he went flying backwards, tumbling into another fighter—whether it was a rebel or a castle guard, Jacob couldn't tell.

Scrambling to his feet, Jacob inhaled deeply. It was his best defence at the moment, given that he wouldn't let Jairus take over his mind. In front of him was a small space unoccupied by fighters, surrounded by a battlefield with raging rebels and soldiers. Baraz's forces, as planned, outnumbered Baltashazar's, but they were still without weapons or armour. Many lay slain on the ground, trickling streams of blood onto the rough stone and tickling the feet of those who still fought.

A clang sounded behind Jacob, and he instinctively spun around and extended his arm, preparing to gust.

"What are you doing here?" Sorias yelled, blocking an overhead strike from a soldier. Sorias moved his sword with forceful momentum, and the other soldier swung his blade as if weightless, gaining him speed but losing power. He managed a quick hit on the side of Sorias's midsection, but it glanced off Sorias's chain mail.

Jacob gusted, this time with less power, at Sorias's opponent. The soldier staggered, giving Sorias the opportunity to make a jab to the man's thigh. The sword pierced with little resistance, sliding quickly in and out of the soldier's heavy trousers and coming away bloodstained.

"Thanks." Sorias held his sword to the side and planted a firm kick in his opponent's chest, sending him falling to the ground. He turned to Jacob, panic setting in the moment their eyes met. "Behind you!"

Jacob didn't need to prepare. Spinning around, he forced the wind at the oncoming threat, effectively stopping the soldier and stealing his balance. With a sharp inhale, Jacob rushed forward and did just as Sorias had, kicking the man in the stomach.

Unlike Sorias's opponent, this soldier did not fall to the ground. Rather, he doubled over and swung without aim at Jacob, slicing him on the arm. Wincing, Jacob rushed at the winded soldier and tackled him, grasping for his sword as they both tumbled to the ground.

Jacob underestimated how much falling on top of an armoured man would hurt. Buckles and metal plates dug into his skin, revisiting old bruises and reminding Jacob that he was not, in fact, invincible. The goldberry wouldn't last forever, and getting beat up like this would only shorten its effect.

On the positive side, the stunned soldier's sword was now in Jacob's hand. Before the soldier could react from the fall, Jacob raised the sword and smashed the pommel between the soldier's cheek guards on his helmet. Something on his face cracked, making the soldier cry out and clutch his face. The act wrenched Jacob's gut, but in the heat of battle, he couldn't manage sympathy.

"You need to get to the back of our troops!" Sorias reached for Jacob's arm and helped him up, simultaneously fighting off another soldier. With another gust from Jacob and a kick from Sorias, he was easily disarmed.

"That dravelord is going to wake up any minute now, and it won't stop attacking until Baltashazar is dead!" Jacob tried to swing his newfound sword at an oncoming guard, but he underestimated its weight. Instead of slashing towards the soldier's midsection, it travelled in a low arc near his legs. The soldier knocked Jacob's sword away with ease, leaving him prone.

"Well, what do you propose?" Sorias lunged in, and with an upwards sweep of his blade, he blocked the strike descending upon Jacob.

"I have to get—" Jacob gusted at the soldier and staggered from the loss of air.

"You have to get to Baltashazar *alive!*" Sorias brought his sword down on the attacker's right arm. Everything from the elbow downward fell to the stone, further staining Sorias's weapon.

Jacob heaved, trying to get air back into his lungs. Every time he emptied them, it took longer to fill them again. He didn't know how much longer he could go before he was winded for good. "I don't see any other way. We have to finish this quickly or it's all over. I can't fight the dravelord, no matter—"

"Save your breath." Sorias grabbed Jacob's arm and pulled him away from an attack.

"Cover me!" Jacob dodged another blow, staying near Sorias. "I have a plan!" It was a rather foolish one. For it to work, he needed all the air he could get. Sorias would have to do without his help for a while.

Gathering air while dancing around blades and spears proved more difficult than expected. As he focused on gathering breath, he realized he'd been subconsciously guiding the wind before, allowing him to move more nimbly. That was gone, now, as he made deep inhalations and slow breaths out. If not for Sorias's incredible fighting skills, he'd have been stabbed and slashed a hundred times over

.

Sorias hardly seemed to notice Jacob as he spun in every direction, exchanging blows, dodging at the last moments, and incapacitating soldiers. He did not kill. Every sword thrust was aimed at a limb, usually towards its end. Jacob could only guess why Sorias could best all the other soldiers. They fought out of terror and obligation, while Sorias fought from calculated determination—his level face revealed that much.

Jacob looked at the castle. Every minute, the rebels pushed the soldiers back more, suffering heavy losses. The ground was so slick with blood that Jacob found it difficult to keep his footing. A smell like decaying metal rose with the screams, mingling with the hot sweat clouding his face. The chill of night was lost to the heat of battle.

What makes you think this will work? Jairus asked.

Because it has to work! Jacob spared a breath to dodge out of a spear in time. The sudden movement caught the soldier off guard enough for Sorias to clip his forearm.

Almost time, Jacob thought. Anticipation welled up within him, spurring the wind against his will. The wind was *his.* A force of nature, pervasive as the earth itself, under his command. He did not deserve this gift. Who did? All he could do was use it for others, and, perhaps in the future, he would earn it. For Lindina, for the king, and for all Barabians, Jacob would embrace the Deep and win t he day.

"I'm leaving!" Jacob said with a brief glance at Sorias, who didn't look over from his assailants.

Jacob blinked rapidly, clenched his fists, and ran. The soldier ahead of him readied his spear to thrust it, but Jacob had already stopped with bent knees. A moment before the spearhead found his gut, Jacob sprung, the wind shooting him up and forward as it did before. Flying over enemy ranks was hardly the same as leaping over allies. When he landed, he didn't know if his foot might find the tip of a readied sword.

Landing, fortunately, came easily. As he hit the ground in a wobbling crouch, soldiers around him either didn't notice or were too surprised to act. They must have heard of the Wayfollower working with the rebels, perhaps even of what happened to Captain Hazak. They ought to fear him, even though he had no intention of attacking.

The first windleap was unexpectedly easy, but even so, he didn't have the strength for a second. Jacob cursed internally. The plan had been to make two consecutive windleaps then run through the castle gate. With all the soldiers crowded around him, there wasn't enough room to get a running start or even recover his breath properly.

Jacob watched three soldiers lower their weapons at him and prepare to strike. As Jacob made to dodge, everyone froze.

A shriek cut down all the sounds of the blood-stained night, filling Jacob with a nauseating terror. *Not again.* The dravelord's cry came all too soon. It was looking for him, wasn't it? Even if Jairus had enough energy, he needed to save as much of it as possible. Attacking it again might win the battle but lose the war.

Jacob wasn't the only one affected. Every other person surrounding him went pale. A few dropped their weapons. Whether these men had encountered the dravelord before made no difference. There must have been some magic in that screech for it to petrify an entire legion of soldiers.

Move! Jairus screamed. *It's coming!*

Jacob broke free from the stupor. He'd been struck by the dravelord's cry before and walked away. This time, he was faster. It didn't take much to weave through the guards in front of him. Yes, he was almost running. Almost ready—

"Stop there!" A shaking voice accompanied the point of a spear in front of Jacob's chest. Wielding it was a thin soldier without a helmet, revealing a patch of closely shaved black hair on a young head. Even when the dravelord screeched again and everyone cowered, this soldier didn't let down his guard.

"Get out of our way!" Jairus lashed out from the depths of Jacob's mind and shot lightning at the soldier. Electricity bounced between his armour plates as he let out a stifled yell, dropping his spear to the ground but staying on his feet. Jairus was being merciful.

"Get him!" someone else bellowed.

Jacob didn't think. Before any gloved hands could seize him, he expunged the air from his lungs and gathered the wind beneath him, jumping forward into the newly created updraft. Up he flew, over the heads and swords of Baltashazar's army. Even at this small height, he knew he would land near the edge of the soldiers, only a few feet away from the entrance to the castle grounds. The problem wasn't landing—it was trying not to get killed when it happened.

His feet struck the ground first, narrowly avoiding the head and shoulders of a fear-frozen guard. As he rolled onto his side to brace the impact, he inhaled and looked above him. Startled faces blurred in and out of view for every moment of that painful second, watching him as his shoulders took the worst of the impact. Even his chest couldn't take in enough air and felt like it was being ripped apart.

When he finished rolling, Jacob lay prone on his back amidst a group of enemy soldiers.

Dreslen.

They stalled, eyes wide—either from Jacob or the dravelord. Taking the opportunity, Jacob forced his lungs to work. It was painful, inhaling after that jump, but without immediate air he knew he would pass out. For all he knew, he could pass out anyway. If it weren't for the goldberry, he would be *dead*. And if he didn't get moving, the juices would run out and the mission would fail.

Jacob made one final inhale as the soldiers reached for their weapons. Then, letting go of his fear, he pushed the wind as hard as he could towards the guards on his right.

As prepared as he was, the pain still shocked him. Every part of his chest burned like wildfire, working its way up his throat and into his head. Light faded, falling into a sea of grey and slowly darkening. He knew he was gasping, but all he heard was the ringing in his ears.

Get up, fool!

Someone was shouting. Many people, actually. The shouting got louder, carrying a voice Jacob recognized—the burly fighter Baraz had given a sword to. Pitt.

"Get out of his way!" Pitt roared. "Let him pass, men. He goes on his way, or you all fight me!"

Jacob could hardly believe what he was seeing. Pitt wore a helmet and breastplate, carried a *longsword,* and glared at everyone like he was in charge. Stranger still, the other soldiers obeyed and left Jacob alone.

"Get up, Jacob!" Sorias said.

Sorias? Jacob tilted his neck to the left in time to see Sorias emerge from the back of the army.

"Are you deaf?" Sorias grabbed Jacob's wrist without a warning and pulled, stretching the skin on his forearm painfully. It was enough to snap Jacob back to full consciousness.

"What happened?" Jacob scrambled to his feet and pulled his arm back from Sorias. His head still felt like it was being pounded with a mallet, but at least he could see and think clearly again. On one side were Sorias and Pitt; on the other were three guards standing at the ready. The open gate to the castle grounds loomed beyond, at the centre of which was the most terrifying building he had ever laid eyes on.

"Pitt used to be our captain before Hazak came along. He still has their respect . . . and fear."

When the dravelord cried out again, Jacob barely flinched. He was transfixed on the majesty and terror of Castle Dreslen, with its black spires and twisting towers. No torches lit the windows of the castle anymore. All was dark, as was fitting.

Dawn broke. Jacob found himself shielding his eyes as he turned around to look at the radiance. The sun was brighter than he ever remembered after enduring that dark night, and it spread its brilliance across the helmets and swords of the Barabian soldiers. Where there was light, there was hope—and there was no greater light than this.

"Wish me luck." Jacob nodded at Sorias one last time before turning and running past the blinded guards. With the light of day on his back, nothing could slow him. Nothing could drench the hope he had. They were going to *win.*

TWENTY-EIGHT

Jacob couldn't bring himself to walk—not with so much at stake. He ran at a full sprint, though not with the wind. The goldberries could no longer alleviate his internal injuries and skin wounds, yet still those wondrous juices sustained him. He knew he didn't have long before their effect ran out completely, but he couldn't conserve his energy. Baltashazar wouldn't stay holed up in his towers forever. Soon he would join his soldiers and reinvigorate them.

The outer courtyard of the castle grounds was impressive. Statues were littered everywhere, on the ground, atop immaculate pillars, and within the pools of the many fountains. Some statues depicted men in fierce armour with horned helms, grasping weapons from longswords to spears, but most statues bore the likeness of gargoyles.

Jacob had never seen an image of a gargoyle before, aside from his own imagination when reading about them. They were slenderer than he expected, with skin that seemed to act as a mere coating for their skeleton. Their height varied greatly. Most statues hunched, their claws either digging into the ground or preparing to slash a victim. The ones that stood upright, which became more common as Jacob advanced further into the courtyard, were far more intimidating. Some were of greater stature than the tallest of men, with tails that wound around their legs like a serpent and webbed wings almost as large as a dravelord's.

You seem . . . relieved, Jairus said.

They're all dead. Jacob looked around. No guards anywhere. *Dreslen used gargoyles, but Baltashazar can't.*

Do not be eased, for a creature far worse than gargoyles awaits you. I can only imagine what Baltashazar has become.

Jacob stopped to catch his breath. He'd already passed the Victory Torch, so he was more than halfway there. Directly ahead, blocking the path, was a fountain with the statue of a headless man holding a staff. Red-tinted water poured from his neck and many holes in his torso, emptying into the basin and swirling around the figure before being drained into the ground again. It wasn't the only broken statue, but this one was especially grotesque. Why would Amiroth have allowed it to remain?

Walking to the front of the fountain, he looked down at the basin for an inscription. There, set in a plate of silver, were the words:

Bein Mordecai
Slain by Dreslen in 434
"May your downfall be your own doing."

Mordecai. Dreslen's arch-foe and the leader of the Collabrian forces against the gargoyles. The last Bein Jemin, the head of the Sirathim, and the one who dared confront Dreslen himself in a duel. The one who failed.

Jacob staggered. Even in the morning light, fear cast its shadows on his faltering hope. Mordecai had the full blessing of the Deep—or so it was said—when he duelled Dreslen. He died anyway. What chance did Jacob have when Mordecai, who trained for *decades*, failed against the Abyss?

Perhaps none. Jacob strode past the statue solemnly. *Perhaps it is my doom to fail.*

Yet he would fight anyway. He was done doubting. The road, terrifying as it was, couldn't be clearer.

It wasn't long before he approached the castle's entrance. Two guards stood next to the massive doors, their armour gleaming in the sunlight. They looked far more intimidating now than they did in the shadows.

"Who goes?" a guard called, his voice raspy.

"The Wayfollower Baltashazar's so afraid of." Jacob may as well be honest. If they resisted him, they were going to find out anyway. Better that he intimidated them into submission.

The guards looked at each other, then kept their eyes fastened on Jacob. Both held spears and had long scabbards attached to their belts. The one on the right looked thicker than he might expect from a guard, but he was nearly half a head taller than Jacob. The left soldier had a pointed, greying beard, and he rapped his fingers anxiously on the shaft of his spear.

"Is Baltashazar inside?" Jacob looked at each guard, scowling.

The bearded guard looked to the other, nodded, and drew his hand into a pouch on his belt. Jacob prepared for danger, readying Jairus, but the man simply withdrew a key. He inserted it into a hole in the left half of the double door, turned, and created an unexpectedly loud latching sound.

"Unlocked," the guard said, nodding at Jacob. His jaw trembled.

"You aren't going to stop me?" Jacob asked. *What are you playing, guard?*

"Lord Baltashazar is expecting you." He leaned closer to Jacob and dropped his voice to a whisper. "It's a trap, sir Wayfollower."

"I might have guessed that." Jacob tapped his foot and tried to ignore his writhing guts. *Now* he felt afraid. He hoped to the Deep it wouldn't cripple him.

"You go in, that monster kills you," the larger guard said.

"You've got it backwards." Jacob stepped towards the door.

The bearded guard crossed his spear ahead of Jacob. "You think he's scared of you? He emptied the castle of every soldier but us two. That's what a man does when he's cocky, but Baltashazar ain't never been one to gamble like that. You're no more than a fly to him."

Jacob paused, studying the man. Yes, he definitely trembled more now. So did the other one. Were they trying to help Jacob or trick him into leaving Baltashazar alone? Whichever it was, Jacob didn't have a choice. Even if Baltashazar confidently awaited Jacob, he had to be dealt with, and Jacob had to be the one to do it. Strength trickled away with every moment. The time was *now*.

"Out of my way." Jacob shoved the spear aside and reached for the ringed doorhandles. The doors themselves stood about nine feet tall, engraved all over with images of gargoyles and men, all bowing their heads in reverence to a hooded figure in the centre. Dreslen—or so Jacob guessed—held out his hands and clutched the two rings that made the doorhandles.

As Jacob's fingers closed around the metal, a sudden wave of cold and weakness spread through his body. The chills of death, not those of a bitter mist or heavy wind. Darkness, too. Somehow, he could *feel* the darkness.

"You're doing exactly what he wants you to," the bearded guard said. "You go in there, you ain't walking out. If you're lucky, he'll kill you quick."

A large part of Jacob agreed with the guard, but he forced those thoughts down. No doubts. If he was insane, so be it. At least he was insane for a good reason.

Pushing through the necrotic weakness, he pulled the door rings with all his strength, splitting the image of Dreslen in two and opening the black mouth of the castle. Beside him, the guards muttered indistinguishably.

Beyond the doors stretched a large hallway, which started out narrow but widened and grew taller further on. Unlit sconces lined the walls, visible by the few streams of sunlight that crept through the doors. At the end of the hall, another door towered to the ceiling, easily two stories tall.

Jacob walked inside and let the doors close behind him. Silence reverberated eerily in the dark hall, echoes of soundless whispers and the coming dread. Though the place was neither hot nor cold, he shivered.

He put his arms in front of him and broke into a long stride. Cold grew around him, licking at his fingers and stiffening joints. Was that darkness he felt? The shadows seemed to have *substance*. Even in the utter blackness, he could sense an even deeper darkness. Hearing clouded, touch went numb. Even the growing pain in his leg faded for a time, replaced by . . . nothing. Utter nothingness.

Finally, his hands came up against cold metal. As he ran his fingers over the door, he could feel the engravings. The ridges were wider and less often, so Jacob assumed the images were larger. Even now, he marvelled that Dreslen had created all this by his own hand. This castle alone would have been near unbelievable, but an entire *city*? Something wasn't right about that.

Remember Dreslen. The phrase spoken almost as a maxim for the Silence. Why Dreslen? Why give so much thought to the villain instead of, perhaps, Amiroth or the Great Scholar? True, it showed what to avoid, but why not look at a figure to emulate? The more he thought about it, the more resentment he felt towards the Silencers.

Now's not the time, Jairus said.

Jacob grasped the rings, pulled with all his body weight, and forced it to slowly groan open. Flickering light entered the entrance hall. His gut churned. Baltashazar knew he was coming and may well be waiting beyond this door.

"*He's prepared,*" Jairus whispered, "*and so am I.*"

With trembling legs and a burning calf, Jacob walked into the vast room. Darkness and sheer height obscured the ceiling, but chandeliers descended from the shroud like statues in a sea of shadows. They were unlit, but their many facets of glass and precious metal shimmered with firelight from below. Pillars rose on either side of the walkway, bearing lit sconces about ten feet from the ground, rising to the ceiling to be devoured by darkness. They not only lined the walkway but continued on both sides, as if part of a forest of giant trees, lined perfectly in rows.

The floor, for the most part, was made from polished grey stone. But the walkway, which was wide enough for two to walk abreast, was made of a material Jacob couldn't quite place. It was utterly black like obsidian but also reminded him of glass in the way it reflected light. The walkway led deeper into the great hall, rising up a small set of stairs and ending at the throne in the distance. The throne was made of a similar substance as the walkway, with two horns atop it and a large purple gemstone set in the back.

Seeing Dreslen's throne made Jacob feel sick. The man didn't deserve to be remembered. That throne didn't deserve to stand. If Jacob failed, it would once again act as the seat for a dark lord.

Darkness flashed. For a brief moment, all the sconces went out, then resumed burning as if nothing happened.

Baltashazar is here.

Jacob walked forward warily, looking in every direction. Baltashazar could be hiding behind any of those pillars. He was a cunning man, by all accounts, and would probably have no issue stabbing Jacob in the back.

Even thinking about that reawakened the knife wounds. They weren't as bad as they could be, but if he was stabbed again, there would be no recovery. He was out of magic. All he had was the Deep. *May that be enough.*

"So he has arrived."

Jacob looked around for the source of the low, sinister voice. It seemed to come from everywhere all at once.

"The one who killed my captain. Sorias told me so much about you, Jacob."

Jacob stopped. *Sorias?* No, he wouldn't. Sorias hated Baltashazar even more than Jacob did. Unless it was an act. It couldn't be . . .

"Show yourself!" Jacob yelled, spinning around.

"The man from Tonto," Baltashazar continued, "who gave up everything to search for his friend's sister. Who entered Tahil forest and stole its secrets. Yes, I know about Tahil. Lindina has been quite talkative."

Suddenly, the weight on Jacob's shoulders doubled. If he failed, not only would Barabus fall, but so would Tahil. The worst part was that Lindina gave them away. Perhaps she did join Baltashazar. Ever since leaving Tahil, Jacob carried the hope and let it drive him, allowing himself to believe that Lindina could be redeemed. But if she willingly sided with Baltashazar, she may resist even after Baltashazar fell. *If* Baltashazar fell.

"Do you realize what you've done?" Baltashazar said, chuckling. The lights flickered. "In coming to Barabus, you've sentenced *thousands* to their deaths. I would have been content to let them live otherwise, but I cannot stand rebellion. Once the rebels are dead, I'll find their families and slaughter all of them."

"Coward!" It was all Jacob could think of to say. He had to get Baltashazar to reveal himself.

"No." Baltashazar's voice changed, lowering in pitch and filling out in tone. It was hardly the same as before. "I'm merely cautious, that's all."

The lights went out. For more than a few seconds, Jacob felt only his breath in the darkness. Tendrils of shadow wrapped up his legs. He stepped back with a long-echoing cry, and the tendrils vanished.

The sconces relit themselves of their own accord, and Jacob looked ahead. His jaw almost fell off. There, on the throne of Dreslen, sat Lindina, watching him with an unwavering gaze.

Jacob rushed forward.

"Stop!" Lindina's voice was on the verge of shattering. "Look up."

Jacob lifted his eyes and found a balcony he hadn't noticed before. A silhouette in a robe looked down, leaning on the banister.

Baltashazar. He had to restrain himself from trying to windleap up and throttle the man. The distance was simply too great.

"Please save me," Lindina said, crying now. "Don't let him hurt me anymore!"

"How tragic," Baltashazar said. "Go ahead, Jacob. Try to loose her bonds. She has robbed the lord of the Abyss of his rightful heirloom. All the suffering she endured, and will yet endure, is deserved. Pray to the Deep that your own death will be less miserable than hers."

Jacob clenched his teeth and fists. What could he do? Lindina seemed bound to the chair by a curse. Her stillness was uncanny, especially when paired with shuddering cries. The noise chilled him, but Baltashazar's laughter filled him with such fury that all cold vanished.

"Fight me, Dreslen!" Jacob said. "Come down here and claim that name for your own!"

"Very well, *Mordecai.*" Baltashazar spread his arms. When Jacob squinted, he noticed something in his Baltashazar's right hand. Before he could catch what it was, Baltashazar jabbed his left arm with it, sunk to his knees, and convulsed.

Jacob watched, horror-struck, as Baltashazar rose and screamed, raising clawed hands into the air. Crude, misshapen wings stretched behind him. He looked down at Jacob, his head no longer round, and made a guttural screech. He'd only heard that noise once before. Similar to a dravelord's cry but distorted and mangled. It was the sound he heard when rushing into the South Midorian Forest to look for Lindina.

That wasn't Zachii you heard, Jairus said.

That vision in the forest, when he saw the winged monster . . . That wasn't Zachii. It was Lindina. He remembered Haanon checking his pocket then falling in despair. He took something from her, didn't he? Something that she stole back before leaving

Tahil. Something that transformed her into an unspeakable beast. Something Baltashazar now had.

The winged creature jumped from the balcony and lurched to the top of the stairs, directly in front of the throne. It stood tall, casting its robes aside, revealing the skeletal figure Jacob had seen all too well in the courtyard. A gargoyle, with a winding tail, claws like knives, and wings so hideous they distracted from the other features. It lowered its bent, triangular head and groaned softly. Darkness swirled around it like sand in a whirlwind.

All went black. Jacob waited, breathless, for the sconces to reignite.

They did not.

TWENTY-NINE

"What in Amiroth's name are you waiting for? Get inside!" Adriel walked over to the frozen old man. A few moments ago, he had been running along with the rest of the crowd towards the open door of the apartment building, but now he stood idly looking up at the sky in horror. Panicked rebels pushed past Adriel and the old man, some of them nearly knocking her over.

"Get moving, or there won't be any room for you in there!" Adriel grabbed the man's wrist and yanked him towards the building. His legs buckled for a moment, but the shock was enough to endow his eyes with life and grant movement once more. He stumbled after Adriel as fast as he could muster.

Adriel breathed hard, brushing strands of hair away from her sweaty face. The dravelord was merciless and terrible; with one swipe of its talons, it could fell two rebels in the space of a second. Sometimes, it would lurch its prey high into the air to drop to death on the streets below. Even its screech could paralyze the bravest of them.

"Get in, quickly!" Adriel shoved the old man through the doors and started walking against the current. All these people—young and old, men and women—had volunteered their lives in order to liberate the city that was taken from them. King Baraz had warned them of the strength of Baltashazar's army, assuring them victory, but he withheld the knowledge of the great winged terror that now decimated them. What hope was there against such a fiend? Why had Baraz allowed them to give their lives to a cause doomed to fail?

All she could do now was usher as many people as possible to safety. With many of Baltashazar's soldiers now on their side, it made sense to crowd people into buildings until Jacob could deal with the dravelord. After all, they were untouchable there. The only real danger would come from the few enemy soldiers who were still loyal to either Baltashazar or the dravelord—the ones who had no issue with killing their own people. But they, at least, could be dealt with. The dravelord could not.

Screams of horror erupted all around her as the dravelord screeched once again, sending Adriel onto her knees in a daze. Vomit erupted from her throat and filled her mouth, but she clenched her lips together and forced herself to swallow it again. The vile taste, the burning tissue, the pained coughing—it was the physical feeling of all her emotions.

She had to fight it and swallow. No amount of inner turmoil should be enough to stop her from this fight. She was a doctor, a woman sworn to protect the lives of others as much as any soldier. Until everyone else was secure, she would not allow herself to rest in safety.

Standing on her shaky legs, Adriel looked around for anyone unable to run. The rebels were less crowded now, but she could still barely see anything with her blurred vision. The sky brightened still, turning from a radiant yellow to a clear blue.

If it weren't for the sun, she would have lost hope long before this point. The light was more than just hope—it was the only thing keeping them alive. Not light in any metaphorical sense, but the very essence of what weakened the dravelord. It was a being who preyed on darkness, absorbing it for power. But if the darkness scattered, wouldn't the dravelord be weakened?

"Doctor Adriel!" A frantic voice came from her left. Adriel turned to see a helmetless soldier jogging towards her, a sword hanging from his left hand. The radiant sun behind him, it was impossible to determine his facial expression.

"What is it?" Adriel took a step backwards, unsure of the soldier's intent. He addressed her by name, which meant he probably intended no harm. Indeed, as he drew nearer, she recognized Gib's face.

"You have to get to safety! If you die, there won't be nearly enough doctors to tend to the wounded." Gib drew up to her with a swift halt, wiping his brow with the back of his empty hand. "Did you hear me?"

"Yes, I heard you." Adriel turned away from him, more for avoiding the sun's glare than anything else. "But there are plenty of other doctors if I die."

"None who are as good as you, Doctor." Gib stood next to her. "Harold's dead, Dredding's no good anymore, and the other doctors will be too shocked to act."

"I'm not leaving!"

"If you don't, you'll—" He gasped.

"What?" Adriel followed the thunderstruck soldier's gaze and almost wished she hadn't. Not too far off, the dravelord lurched in place with a body suspended in the throes of its talons. Unlike all its other victims, it didn't throw this body to the ground, instead holding it up as a display.

The body moved.

"Oh my goodness—" Adriel put a hand to her mouth. *Baraz.* Their king was defeated but still alive, painfully grating against the edge of death under the wings of a monster. They had to save him. *She* had to save him!

"Doctor!" Gib grabbed Adriel's shoulder as she started to run. "Did you not hear a word I said?"

"That's Baraz! Our king! *Your* King!"

"I don't care who it is!" Gib gripped her arm tightly and forced her to look at him. "If you run to that monster, you'll die. Think of the wounded! Think of the people you have the power to save."

"Then *you* go!" Adriel shook her arm free from the soldier's grasp and rubbed it. "Do your job and protect the king!"

Gib opened his mouth to answer, but it did not close. Instead, his trembling groan faded into the dying clamour of the streets. His face, once resolute, was pale, and he dropped his sword to the ground. Finally, his mouth moved enough to shudder one word. "Look."

Adriel felt the same terror wash over her body. The sky darkened and became cold once more, drowning all sounds in a low, ghostly drone. It all centred on one point next to the dravelord, covered in a shroud of darkness thick enough to block all vision and understanding. From that point emanated all the feelings of dread and despair that the dravelord's cry had given, and all it took was to look at it.

But she couldn't turn away. The terror that froze the rebels petrified her once more, but there was something else. Something about that mass of darkness reached inside and pulled at her heart, twisting it as if beckoning her forward. Wordless whispers penetrated her, issuing commands she felt but did not understand. The darkness wanted her to *kill*. It didn't matter who, as long as she wrung her hands at someone's throat and suffocated the life out of them.

Then came something she did understand, a deep and drawling voice. *"Your king is better off dead than in my hands again. By the time I am finished with you, you will wish you had died in your mothers' wombs. By this you shall learn never to defy me."*

Adriel tried to breathe but found it nearly impossible.

Baltashazar was here.

———◦O◦———

RUN! Jairus screamed.

Jacob forced his frozen legs to move, darting to the right. The gargoyle's leathery wings beat the air, accompanied by a guttural shriek. *There's just one,* he told himself as he bolted between the pillars. All was dark. The only thing guiding him was memory. Eventually, he would collide with something.

They say Amiroth killed hundreds of these, Jacob thought. *He wasn't even a Wayfollower.*

His self-encouragement was futile against the horrid sounds behind him and the raging panic in his mind. He may be a Wayfollower, but he was no warrior. A warrior like Amiroth would turn around, draw a sword, and swing with precision, felling the monster in one stroke.

Jacob didn't have a sword, but he had Jairus.

I can't see it, idiot! Jairus said. *How do you expect me to do anything useful?*

When the gargoyle's wings sounded mere feet away, Jacob darted to the right again and readied the wind. As he inhaled, he consciously drew the room's air to himself. When it filled him, something odd happened—he could *feel* where the wind had travelled. His vision didn't change, but somehow, based on the wind's path, he knew where the pillars were.

It didn't last long. As soon as he finished inhaling, the air ceased rushing around him and became still. Every sense of his environment vanished like smoke in a breeze. He couldn't even recall what it felt like.

Iven! Jacob remembered. Iven had used the wind to connect to his environment, allowing him to sense where the bird was. Was this the same technique?

Instead of windsprinting, Jacob swirled the air in a large circle when he exhaled. Rushing wind surrounded his ears, blocking out even the gargoyle's wings. This time, when he inhaled, he did so slowly, intentionally keeping the air in motion.

Yes, there it was again! He sensed the pillars as hazy objects, lined in their perfect rows. He even felt his own shape, cutting through the wind like a knife, being pursued by an airborne figure not too far from him.

Jacob used the air to rush forward this time, windsprinting across the walkway into the opposite side of the room. It was impossible to focus on keeping the air moving *and* windsprinting, so every few seconds, he'd slow his pace to sweep the environment.

It worked well for the first while. The gargoyle seemed to have no issue navigating the pillars, but it also couldn't match Jacob's speed while windsprinting. Even in this small success, terror threatened to chain Jacob down. If he so much as tripped, this would all be over. His calf hurt, his air was going to run out eventually, and the gargoyle might outmaneuver him. This was an endurance match, so long as he kept running, and he couldn't win that contest.

The next time he windswept, he nearly froze in shock. The gargoyle was right in front of him. He lurched to the right, but it was too late. Three clear lines of cold, distorted pain shot into his shoulder as the gargoyle hissed. Jacob windsprinted without direction and managed to escape another attack, but the slash had staggered him. With the wind pushing him, he barely caught himself before he tumbled to the ground.

He had no idea where he was now. There could be a pillar seconds away from his face, and he wouldn't know until he collided. Worse, the gargoyle sounded almost as close as before.

Do something, Jairus! Jacob pleaded.

Jairus took control, grimacing as he came to a stop, and turned around. Cracking blue light shot out from his hands, travelling in a spontaneous line in the gargoyle's general direction. As bright as the lightning was, it did little to illuminate the environment. A strand of it hit something flying towards him. The gargoyle screeched, but apart from a brief hesitation it seemed unhindered.

It's too dark! Jairus said, giving control back to Jacob. *I can't aim properly.*

Jacob grunted, windsweeping, and ducked as the gargoyle swiped a claw at his head. He darted off towards the opposite end of the room again, favouring his injured leg.

This isn't working! Jacob grimaced in frustration as he barely missed running into a pillar. The pain in his shoulder worsened, seeping deeper into his arm and infecting it with cold weakness. This wasn't a normal wound, was it? The gargoyle must have injected his skin with a sort of poison when it slashed.

Use the Way of Life! Jairus said.

I don't know how! Jacob windswept, changed directions, and windsprinted.

Yes, you do. The tree, remember? When you used its vision?

Right. When he'd touched the tree in the South Midorian Forest and been granted a vision of Lindina in gargoyle form. He knew little about the Way of Life, but by the sound of its name, it could heal.

He let go the wind for a daring moment and focused entirely on the chills roiling in his arm. It heated as he concentrated life energy into it. Whatever he was doing hurt more than the poison itself, but it seemed to be working. After a few moments of tensely running without the wind, the cold sensation vanished. The skin wounds remained and his entire body nauseated, but the dark poison burnt up.

This isn't the first time I've done this, he realized. The goldberries didn't heal him—they gave him energy enough for him to heal *himself.* Subconsciously, of course, and only enough to stay alive. Even now, he couldn't do any more than get rid of the poison.

A screech from right behind dropped him to the ground. He rolled as claws clattered to the stone beside him, getting to his feet impossibly fast with the wind's help.

The gargoyle was only a few feet away. If he kept running like he'd been doing, he would eventually wear out and fall. It was time to change tactics.

This better work. Jacob windswept, gathering air to his lungs, and bent his knees. A pillar was right next to him. *Perfect.*

He exhaled and jumped, siphoning the air into an updraft. His lungs felt like they took a hit from a battering ram. As he ascended, he ran his hand along the pillar. It clipped the edge of something jutting out from the side. The sconce.

Once he reached the height of his jump, he focused on the heat in his arm. He snapped—nothing happened. His fingers were too sweaty to create enough friction.

He started descending, and he rubbed his hand on his tunic. Then, with a yell, he snapped harder than ever before, shooting three giant sparks towards the pillar. Two bounced away, but one found its target and nestled in the embrace of the metal sconce, smoldering dimly.

Jacob didn't hit the ground—instead, his feet found something moving and uneven. He tumbled off the gargoyle, hitting the stone hard. His right shoulder, the uninjured one, took the brunt of the fall. Next to him, he heard claws scraping on the ground and hisses. A windsweep revealed the shape slowly moving closer to Jacob. *Where's that blighted firelight?*

A claw grabbed his arm, squeezing tight. Jacob used the Way of Life to prevent any poison from entering, but it drained his body of life force. Nausea swept through him and intensified as the gargoyle crawled on top of him and brought a clawed hand to rest on his face.

Goodbye, Jairus. Jacob winced and braced for death.

Light erupted above him in a near-blinding flame. The gargoyle howled, clutching its head, and released Jacob. He took the moment to roll to the side, use the wind—

But of course, there was no wind. The windleap had drained all his excess air, forcing him to get to his feet without help. He backed away from the thrashing gargoyle, hesitant to run. The torch may have been dim under ordinary circumstances, but after being surrounded by blackness, it cut through like the sun itself. The gargoyle writhed in the other direction, trying to get away from the light. Jacob had to stay nearby. The fire was his only shield. More than that, it revealed his target.

"Now, Jairus!" Jacob said, getting his arms ready.

The fire in the sconce turned blue.

Jairus took over, forced himself to laugh maniacally, and channelled electricity into his hands. Blue lightning crackled between his fingers before launching in a single bolt towards the gargoyle, who now recovered from the light. It screamed upon impact, extending its arms and falling. Jairus lashed again. And again. Energy drained from his body faster than ever before.

When he took a moment to gather his power for a fatal bolt of lightning, the gargoyle stretched out its hand to the fire and shot a distorted black bolt. It hit the flame, exploded in shadow, and extinguished the light.

Stone it! Jairus couldn't risk expending his last energy on a shot that might miss. *Back to you, Jacob.*

Jacob regained consciousness and gulped. He had enough heat to spark a few more times, but without enough air for a windleap, it wouldn't do much good. The only comfort was that the gargoyle, groaning and hissing, still struggled to move.

He'd found a way to beat it. Now, if only he could pull off that feat again.

When he started running, his lungs burned. All he dared use the wind for was windsweeping, since it didn't cost him any more breath than a regular inhalation. Unfortunately, when he didn't exhale with the wind, he couldn't swirl the air. Any sensations the windsweep gave were limited and littered with gaps. He could still catch most pillars, but there were more than a few blind spots where the gargoyle might be hiding.

Where was Lindina in all this? He hadn't heard a single noise from her since the gargoyle descended. He expected screams of terror or at least some expressions of worry. It would have at least helped him place his position in the room. *No time to think about her now.*

Jacob's worries of the gargoyle hiding in a blind spot were abated as soon as it screeched. An extended windsweep revealed it to be about fifteen feet behind him. Far enough that he wasn't in immediate danger, but close enough that he couldn't outrun it for long without windsprinting.

You don't have to jump as high as before, Jairus said. *The sconces are only about ten feet off the ground.*

A seven-foot jump should work, then. Jacob's hand still needed to be close enough for a good shot. He didn't have much control over where the sparks went after they left his hand.

It's getting close!

I don't have enough air yet.

That monster doesn't care how much air you have, fool!

Jairus was right. He windswept, ran beside a pillar, then windleaped straight up, limiting his jump this time. It did some good, but the pain didn't vanish. Once he reached the apex, he felt around for the sconce, found it, and snapped his fingers directly over it. Both sparks caught.

The fire sprang up quickly this time. Jacob landed on his feet and braced himself for the oncoming gargoyle, but it stopped in place and writhed from the light, raising its arm to shoot out the light again.

Oh, no you don't! Jacob thought. *Kill it, Jairus!*

Something's not right.

"What?" Jacob shouted, wasting precious air. "Kill it!"

I'll explain later. You deal with it.

You good-for-nothing hallucination! Jacob tried to convert his energy into lightning, as Jairus did, but accomplished nothing more than strained grunts. When he looked up from his fingers, both the gargoyle's hands stretched towards the sconce. Darkness gathered between its claws, growing in a blurry sphere before launching upwards and consuming the flame.

Before Jacob could react, the gargoyle slashed his tunic open, making three shallow cuts on his chest. No poison this time, but the gargoyle was still far too close.

Jacob gusted with all the air he had left. It must have worked, because the gargoyle cried in surprise, sounding further away from Jacob. The wind must have caught its wings. Why didn't he think of that earlier?

Because it's useless, he thought. *All I did was push it back. It'll be at me again in a moment.*

He dashed away. His leg hurt too much. His lungs were ready to give up. Jairus had used so much energy on the lightning. Why was he still alive? Even his life force seemed to be at the breaking point, bordering on nausea. All he had left was heat. But without the air to windleap to a sconce, he couldn't spark a flame.

Then don't spark it, Jairus said. *Embrace the nightmare.*

Of course, the nightmare. As if he wasn't already living in one! Nevertheless, he thought back to when Junia died and pictured himself standing in the flames, shivering from cold, trying to find Junia.

Earlier.

Jacob hesitated. He could deal with the aftermath, but recalling the action that killed her was still difficult. *Madness,* he reminded himself. Then he clearly saw his arm outstretched in the forest, palm upwards, holding fire. Real, substantial fire, not just sparks.

Do it again.

How? Jacob dashed around a pillar and held his back to it. When the snarls of the gargoyle drew near, he braced himself. It moved to the right, so he went left.

Remember.

Fire needs air to grow. Jacob could almost feel it before he started the process. *But it also needs a substance to catch on.*

You're a Wayfollower, fool. Do not underestimate the ubiquity of the Deep. Its power is everywhere.

Jacob knew what to do. The gargoyle switched directions and began to round the other side of the pillar, but Jacob remained still and breathed, closing his eyes—not that it made a difference. When he exhaled, he compacted all the air in the immediate area into a spot above his outstretched right hand. Then he sparked with his left in the same spot.

Fire erupted in his palm. The gargoyle screeched. Jacob yelled, closed his right fist, and brought the flame in a straight punch towards the gargoyle's head. Light flashed on impact, but it drained an immense amount of heat from his arm. Fortunately, the gargoyle fell to the ground from the blow and clutched its face.

Jacob smiled despite his fear. He had a *flaming fist*! Sadly, his arm felt more like ice with each second. It was time to finish this.

He launched himself to the writhing creature on the ground, clutching its throat with his flaming hand, and blocked out all senses. The cuts on his arms didn't matter, and neither did the piercing screams in his ears. He flared the last heat from his arm, letting it go limp, and scorched the gargoyle's throat.

The gargoyle brought up its legs and kicked Jacob off. How was it still fighting? Before it could follow up the attack, Jacob compacted air in his left fist, prepared his right arm to snap, and—

His right arm wouldn't move. No matter how hard he tried, he couldn't lift it. It may as well have been dead.

The gargoyle's claws ripped into his chest again. He screamed, raising his left hand in a last effort, and snapped. The surrounding air burst into orange light, and he *grabbed* it and seized the gargoyle's face. Its last cry was the most terrible of all, threatening to shatter more than Jacob's eardrums.

But his body held firm, as did the fire, and he found himself screaming as he clenched his hand around the monster's face, bringing the flame to a brilliant flare and banishing almost all the heat from his body.

All went dark.

All went silent.

THIRTY

Jacob thought he was dead. The very act of thinking revealed quite the opposite, almost to his disappointment. His chest and arms burned from the gargoyle's scratches, his calf throbbed, and his breath came painfully. He wished his arms were still numb, but, cold as they were, they had some heat in them again.

He groaned and raised his head. Heartbeats pounded in his ears—everything else was incoherent. The room was dark and cold, though quieter now. When his hearing cleared up, he listened intently for the gargoyle. Nothing. It had to be dead.

I killed Baltashazar, Jacob thought with amazement. *Not Jairus . . . me.* It was all over. All the dread, not knowing whether he was strong enough, proved futile. The fighting outside would stop. The dravelord would cease its slaughter. King Baraz would sit on the throne once more, and under his reign, nothing like this would happen again. Jacob was more powerful than the dark lord.

He marvelled at his hands, though he couldn't see them. The power of fire was his now. Setting his fist ablaze was nothing compared to the Sirathim legends, but it was still remarkable. And it *worked.* Though he'd never been taught, he knew how. He had recovered the ability. *I wonder . . .* he thought. *If I forgot this ability after Junia's death, what other powers are hidden beyond my memory?*

More importantly, why didn't Jairus kill Baltashazar when he had the chance?

Something's not right, he had said. *I'll explain later.*

Time to explain, Jairus. Jacob pressed his arms beneath him and propped himself up. The pain in his calf was near unbearable, but he bore it anyway and stood, staggering, on both feet. He needed light, even if just to check that Baltashazar was truly dead. The last thing he wanted was to save Lindina, walk out of the castle, then fall dead from a set of claws.

He wouldn't windleap anymore. Without the gargoyle chasing him, he could take his time with the sconces and light them from the ground. Since a pillar was right next to him, he windswept it to find the sconce. The sweep returned blurry, as always, and did little good. He should have expected nothing less—he'd only learned this technique in the last . . . few minutes? How long was it between defeating the gargoyle and waking up? Hours could have passed for all he knew.

All the more reason to finish quickly. He shook his arms, trying to restore some heat to them, before shooting them upwards and snapping his fingers. Both sets of sparks bounced off the ridges of the pillar and disappeared. He tried again from a different side, and this time one spark caught the reflection of metal from above.

It took the better part of a minute before a spark actually lit the sconce. By then, his arms were nearly numb again, but at least it mitigated the pain of the cuts. Oddly, he wasn't bleeding. He must have subconsciously healed himself while resting after the fight—which would explain the nausea. The goldberry was probably spent by now, but it didn't matter anymore. It served its purpose.

The light grew, illuminating the immediate area. A figure lay motionless beside the pillar. Jacob walked over slowly, keeping his hands forward in case he needed to attack again. The gargoyle was gone, replaced by a man in his undergarments. He was bald, shorter than Jacob expected. Jacob couldn't imagine this stout man being anywhere near intimidating, especially with the horrible burn on his face.

His chest rose.

Jacob staggered back, putting his hand against the pillar and willing heat back into his arms. It didn't work. Wind would have to do.

Hold! Jairus said. *He's still unconscious.*

It could be a trap. Jacob leaned closer for a better look. Baltashazar's eyes were closed, his breath coming too slowly to be anticipating anything. No, he wasn't dangerous at the moment.

I knew something was wrong, Jairus said.

What's wrong?

Tend to Lindina first. You'll have enough time before he regains consciousness. Even then, he'll be too injured to attack.

Jacob hesitantly stepped away from Baltashazar, trying to conceive what Jairus knew that he didn't. Jairus shielded his thoughts well, but Jacob sensed that it terrified Jairus—enough to make him relent from killing Baltashazar.

With the light from the sconce, Jacob found the walkway and followed it towards the throne. Soft whimpers came from that direction, echoing around the vast throne room. At least she was still alive. She sounded so brittle, so . . . empty. Like everything she ever loved was taken from her. The fact was, it was the opposite. *She* turned away everyone in favour of the Abyss.

Jacob intended to turn that all around. He'd make sure she healed in Tahil. Then, whether Haanon approved or not, he *would* bring her home. Everything she lost would be restored to her, and Jacob would finally . . .

He sighed, shaking his head. Yes, it would bring him uncountable joy to see Lindina restored, but would he truly have peace? He was a guilty man. Nothing, not even saving Lindina from herself, could erase Junia's death. Forget the fact that he was a Wayfollower—he was a killer. He knew the risks of showing Junia the Deep, and he did so anyway. Even if, by wonder, the Silencers stopped hunting Wayfollowers, he'd never escape that harrowing

day. Madness alone allowed him to face it, and that was far from p
eace.

A life of madness, Jacob thought. He walked slowly, crippled by despair. *Is this my doom?*

It has always been so, Jairus said. *But it is not so bad as you think.*

And you aren't so bad as you were. Perhaps there's hope for both of us.

Jairus hesitated. Jacob felt his pain, but couldn't quite put it into words. It was gloom and longing, sorrow and guilt, but more than that.

Perhaps, Jacob. Perhaps one day.

Jacob stopped beside the last pillar before the stairs and lit the sconce. This time, he used the wind to guide the sparks, and he found success on his third attempt. The sconce lit the stairs and the throne, revealing a frail girl in a torn yellow dress leaning against an armrest and sobbing quietly, her face buried in her hair and arms.

As Jacob ascended each of the five steps, memories struck him like a hammer. A man, afraid of the past, running into the South Midorian Forest to rescue his sister from the Silencers. The world unravelling as the ground shook and the Deep manifested its glory. The forest of Tahil, once pure, now defiled by Lindina's presence. A tunnel of terror, teeming with spiders, lit ablaze by madness and nightmares. Jacob, standing at the hand of the king as he led an army into the first battle of the Silence.

He reached the top step. His journey had led to this. It wasn't about facing the past or even saving a kingdom. Every trial Jacob faced had been for Lindina, a rebel of the worst sort who needed saving more than any other. Could he give it to her? He'd faced an army and defeated a dark lord, but that sort of power would do nothing if Lindina didn't want to be saved.

"Lindina," Jacob whispered, stepping next to the throne.

He'd never seen anything more tragic. Her hair, once wavy and golden, was frayed and spotted with black patches. Tears ran through her arms, making the armrest shimmer, but even they were touched by shadow. The girl before him was nothing like the one he'd accepted as a sister. Could she ever be again?

"Lindina, I'm here."

"I . . ." Lindina raised her eyes to Jacob, then wailed and covered her face. Like the waves of the sea, her voice rose and fell with every breath, washing against Jacob and spreading her sadness to the shores of his soul. With every sharp gasp and shudder, Jacob's heart lurched with affection for this broken child so long bound by the shackles of darkness.

With a tear seeping from his eye, Jacob touched her arm and immediately withdrew it. She was colder than death itself. The feeling of the gargoyle's poison was present on her skin; even touching her was enough to feel it.

You care . . . too much, Jairus said. *But I will not hinder you. Your life is your own.*

"Jacob," Lindina said between cries, "I'm sorry. I'm so sorry!"

What did Jacob say to that? All he had were tears. Could he forgive her for what she'd done? Perhaps for the wrongs she'd committed against him, but no more. Her debt to others was too great; she was one of the guiltiest people Jacob knew. The Abyss might have driven her to it, but with every chance to fight, she instead embraced it.

Please change, Jacob silently urged, resting his hand on the armrest beside hers. "Lindina, I—" His voice choked, and his lip quavered. Words came out numbly. "I wish I could have helped you sooner. But I'm here now. Lindina?"

Her hand moved to Jacob's own, and darkness rushed into his arm, replacing warmth with nausea. Instead of pulling away, he grasped her and held firm.

"It hurts," Lindina shuddered. When Jacob tried to let go, she strengthened her grasp. "Don't let go. Please don't let me go."

Jacob swallowed a sob and nodded. Instead of concentrating on the death entering his arm, he focused on his life, then *channeled* it into Lindina. His arm felt like a void—a feeling far more terrible than either numbness or pain. But as he forced his life through his arm, the void vanished, replaced by cold and sickness, a mere lack of life.

The rest of his body gave up its warmth to compensate. His injuries burned like fire, but that fire could not rival his love for Lindina. If he died to heal her, so be it. In the chaos of the battle outside, she could slip away unnoticed.

"Find Tahil," Jacob said, wincing from the pain. "Promise me you'll get healed and return to Carl and your father."

"I'm not leaving without you!"

Jacob relented to his tears and wept. He leaned forward and pulled Lindina into an embrace, trembling like never before. Her thin frame was as chilled as her hand, heaving and shaking with violent sorrow. For a while, they held each other in that unsteady embrace, breathing raggedly and shedding countless tears. The warmth of life from all over Jacob's body began to leave, seeping through to Lindina. Feelings of illness, like nausea in every fiber in his body, replaced it, swelling with every second.

I'm dying. Jacob could not dismiss the thought. Nothing else could describe what now washed through him. Despite being so near to death in the last few days, he never truly contemplated it. What was death? Was it just cold pain and weakness, gradually rising until you ceased to exist? Or was it the end itself, when his body failed? What happened after? Such questions should have been important, but they never seemed that way. No one came back from death. It was final, and it was sure. What point was there to worry about something that claimed all creatures?

He almost lost all sensation, but he forced himself to hold on. Her tear-stained hair clung to his cheek, blowing . . . yes, blowing in the wind. It swirled around them in a circle, its rhythm matching

Jacob's dying breaths, watching. Who was he, that he could command the wind? Perhaps, when he died, he would become like it. A presence ever flowing, ever guiding, ever dancing. Peaceful. The wind was free, like fire and light, answering to none but the Deep itself.

But he was not the wind. He was a waste of a man that could have been, giving the last of his essence to a broken child, hoping she may live. He could have served the Deep so much more, but he gave his life to books instead. They didn't seem all that important, now. Nothing seemed important in the face of death. It all just . . . faded.

Weakness overtook him, and he let go of Lindina and fell to the ground.

"Jacob!" Her voice seemed distant, though stronger.

Who am I, Jairus? Jacob looked into the shadows above, unmoving but for his chest, which rose and fell slowly to his ragged breaths. Now separated from Lindina, warmth threatened to return. He closed his eyes. It seemed death was the only peace he could find, but even death eluded him. Feeling spread out from his heart, washing further with each beat, until he felt with clarity the cuts and injuries he'd endured for so long.

"Jacob, please wake up!"

She will care too much, Jairus said. *Do not rob her of yourself, lest you both pass from life.*

That doesn't sound so bad, Jacob thought. *Perhaps death is what we're all looking for, even if we don't realize it.*

Lindina lives. Get up, fool! For the Inheritor's sake, get up! You know that life is more valuable than death. For what is existence but to be experienced? Life gives meaning to the world, and without it there is no purpose. I may be the face of madness to you, but even I know better than to embrace death.

That didn't stop you from killing others.

Yet it will not hinder me from saving you and Lindina. Go, both of you. Flee!

"Please!" Lindina wailed. He heard her rush off the throne and crouch next to him. She put a hand to his chest. Through the rips created by the gargoyle's claws, he could feel her skin, and it was no longer cold like before.

All is now accomplished. You've done what you set out to do.

I have, haven't I? Jacob had defeated Baltashazar and left him prone. Sorias could finish the job if necessary. He'd found Lindina, and now he'd healed her. He *saved* her.

Not yet, Jairus said. *You have yet to bear her to Tahil.*

And so I shall. Jacob forced his eyes open, accustoming to existence again. Lindina's face lit up against her tear-stained cheeks, and he saw something in her he hadn't seen for over a month. True, uncompromised joy. That sight alone gave him the strength to rise. Warmth from her precious eyes flooded him, and when she rushed to embrace him, all sorrows vanished like mist in the wind. His injuries still hurt, of course, but physical pain couldn't be less important.

"Thank you!" Lindina said, squeezing harder. "Thank you so much!"

Jacob let a tear slide down his cheek, falling onto Lindina's ragged head. *You're welcome, Lindina.* He pictured the look on Carl's face when they returned, and laughed. This joy was only the beginning.

"What now?" Lindina said.

"We leave the castle, proclaim Baltashazar's defeat, and end the fighting outside. Then we'll grab something to eat and leave for Tahil right away."

Lindina pulled back and looked up at Jacob. A shadow passed over her eyes.

"What?" Jacob asked.

"Where's Baltashazar?" Her voice dropped to a whisper when she said his name.

"Unconscious by one of those pillars."

Swallowing, Lindina cast a furtive glance to where Jacob pointed. "Show me."

Jacob took her hand and led her down the stairs, across the walkway, and towards the room's only other lit sconce. All the while, doubt brewed in his mind. *Something's not right . . . why? Why didn't Jairus kill Baltashazar?*

When they arrived at the spot, Baltashazar's body lay just as it did before.

Lindina paled. "That's . . . That's not Baltashazar."

It took a moment for Jacob to comprehend her. When her words settled, they brought a dread far colder and heavier than ever before. His insides felt dead. Muscles trembled, breath quickened, heartbeats became irregular. All the while, his thoughts formed incoherent screams, urging him to fight, to hide, to do anything but stand still. Baltashazar could be anywhere!

Yet he couldn't move.

You knew! Jacob thought. *Why didn't you tell me?*

"That's the man Baltashazar talked to so much," Lindina said. "I think his name was Goldor." She looked up at Jacob, jaw trembling.

How did you know? Jacob spun around and paced. This was a nightmare. Was Baltashazar hiding in the shadows? No, he would have killed Jacob by now. *Jairus!*

I knew because of how weak he was, Jairus said. *And I'd hoped to keep it a secret from you until you left the city.*

"Do you think I wouldn't have found out anyway?" Jacob shouted. He didn't care if Lindina heard.

"Jacob . . ." Lindina said.

"If you face him, you will die!" Jairus said. *"You both will!"*

"Why are you talking like that, Jacob?"

Jacob clamped his jaw and stared at the giant door. Baltashazar was out there, somewhere. Possibly on the battlefield, slaughtering Baraz's army. Jacob was the only one who could stop him. It was his *duty*. He doubted even swords would be much good against someone who drew strength from death itself. Only the Deep could rival the Abyss.

You're weak, Jairus said. *Look at yourself. You came to Barabus for a single purpose: to rescue Lindina. Rescue her, not just partially heal her!*

"Come on, Lindina," Jacob said, striding towards the great door.

"What are we going to do?" Lindina said.

Jacob didn't know. He really was too fragile to fight Baltashazar, especially if Jairus thought the *gargoyle* was weak. But his doom, whatever it may be, lay beyond the doors. This could be the beginning of a happy ending if he fled the city with Lindina or the bitter end of everything he'd worked for.

Engraved on the giant double doors, an image of Dreslen watched him with calm mockery.

THIRTY-ONE

There was nothing Adriel could do. The streets had been in chaos even before Baltashazar arrived. Without Jacob's intervention, the dravelord ravaged the rebels without contest, but at the arrival of its master, pure, bloody chaos ensued. Terror increased tenfold, panic rose to the blackening sky, and people died every second, staining the air with agonized screams.

Every door she tried to open was locked. The very people she led to safety now turned their backs on her. She didn't hold it against them. If she was in their position, she would have done the same. Her concern for others vanished with the appearance of the darkness in the sky.

"Please . . ." Adriel hyperventilated, struggling to stay conscious against the fear eating her mind. "Let me in!" Banging on the door did nothing, and neither did rattling the handle. Darkness closed in from all directions, blocking out nearly all the sun's light. It was difficult to see fifteen feet in front of her.

Gib was dead. It all happened so quickly that she hadn't quite processed it. From what she remembered, he was impaled by a crude black spear with no metal, which vanished as soon as he fell to the ground, sputtering blood. Without a building to hide in, Adriel would be next, but even buildings presented danger. What if Baltashazar broke down a door? What if the people inside started killing *themselves*?

"*Let me in!*" Adriel grasped the door handle and throttled it. Her throat clenched as full despair set in, siphoning the heat from her skin and nearly stopping her heart. There was no way out of this.

Unless I get out of this area! Adriel's mind raced. Leaving Baltashazar's dark expanse was the only way to escape, if that was even possible. She had no choice but to abandon her duty and escape Baltashazar's terrible nightmare. She was right to label herself a coward.

Letting go of the locked door handle, she set off down the main road, away from Baltashazar. Beneath her feet, bodies crawled from the darkness into her sight, some covered in blood-stained garments and others rotting from vile black patches spreading across their skin. On both sides, panicked rebels pummeled at doors and screamed for admittance. Moments ago, Adriel would have helped them, but she could not save both herself and others.

She was not the same woman. No longer did she look with compassion upon the afflicted, and no longer did she carry any lament for Sorias. All that now filled her was adrenaline and pure dread. She couldn't even feel her feet, which ran across the stone road faster than ever before. The only sensations were the screams in her ears and the dead bodies forming obstacles in her path.

Even breathing hurt. Her abdominals felt stabbed and cramped with each stride. Exercise, a habit as important as eating or sleeping for her as a medical professional, had no effect on her now. Perhaps it was Baltashazar's dark magic, or perhaps it was simply fear. Regardless, she didn't know whether she would make it to the edge of the darkness.

"Hear me, you rebellious subjects!" Baltashazar's deep, thin voice called out from every direction. *"I have not begun to display my power. But before I unleash the full wrath of the Abyss, I offer a chance of life. Present before me the heads of four others, and I shall spare you. Know that there is no escape!"*

Those last words pounded against Adriel's skull. Did he mean it, or was he just trying to keep people from leaving? And . . . he had said to bring the heads of four rebels in exchange for life. She suspected some would overlook the heads of the dead bodies.

The ones who formerly screamed at the doors broke into a wild fury, turning on the closest person they could find. Even Adriel wanted to throttle someone and bring their head to the dark lord, begging for forgiveness. But she had nothing to sever a neck with, let alone kill someone.

"Stop it, Adriel!" she shouted at herself. What was she thinking? She was a *doctor*. If anyone should be able to resist the urge to hurt someone, it should be her. Yet here she was, contemplating murder like an ordinary thug.

"You!" a woman screamed, rushing at Adriel. Although shorter than Adriel, her weight made them roughly equal in size. Her eyes flashed like the red flares of the sun on a scorching evening.

Adriel screamed back, though no words escaped her mouth. Terror guided her every movement. She couldn't think. Adriel punched the shorter woman's head instinctively and kicked without hesitation. Adriel pummeled the wretched woman, and all she considered was her own survival.

The entire ordeal was an extended blur until Adriel planted her boot in the woman's face and knocked her to the ground, likely unconscious. All around her, doors hurled open and streams of people ran out. The battle between the Barabians had resumed, but this time there were no sides. Every single person, including Adriel, thought to kill anyone within their grasp. It wasn't rational, but it was necessary. There was no escape.

"Let me live!" Adriel bent down and swung her fists in random directions. She lost all control to the horror of the Abyss. "*Let me live!*"

Thoughts ceased as the cry of the dravelord cut through the clamour. It reappeared in their midst, diving into the anarchy and piercing the shoulders of the unlucky ones who crossed its path. Adriel looked up at it, frozen in a crouched position with a gaping jaw. It circled high into the air with a dead rebel in its talons, dropping the body to the ground before vanishing into the shroud of darkness above. *This is where it ends.*

A sudden yearning manifested in Adriel's mind: the desire to die. It was strange, wishing for so horrid a thing to happen to one's self, but she could not suppress it. Any fate would be better than this chaos. With death, all would be over in a matter of seconds, then she would be handed over to eternal slumber. There was nothing left for her here but pain and horror.

"Take me." Adriel stood up, looked into the black sky, and spread her arms wide. A breath escaped her lips, calling for the bird to collect her. It must have heard, because a moment later it emerged from the shadows and began gliding towards her.

All was silent as she awaited her doom. Adriel closed her eyes and exhaled. As the dravelord screeched, she braced herself for the sharp impact.

Make a decision, she told herself. In this moment before death, fear evaporated.

Adriel didn't hesitate. *I forgive Sorias.*

Finally . . . closure. Here, at the end of all things, my burden is lifted.

But death didn't come. Instead, the screech was followed by another, then overlapped by yet another. When Adriel finally forced an eye open, she dropped her jaw halfway to the ground. The dravelord lay on its back, wings outstretched and talons flailing, as *another dravelord* hurled its own attacks. *There were two.*

"What's this?" Baltashazar's voice echoed over the din of the duelling birds, and for a moment the darkness lifted. Light streamed into her eyes, illuminating the treachery of her violent actions and the hope she still had. Baltashazar's dravelords had turned against themselves.

Mordecai's final words, uttered before Dreslen severed his head, came to mind. *May your downfall be your own doing.* Could it have been prophetic? Here, at Dreslen's return, his own forces collapsed against each other.

"This is not the end!" Adriel dusted off her dress and looked at the stunned rebels. They had ceased their mindless frenzy to look upon the two birds, and despite the darkness, their eyes reflected what she felt in herself—something she hadn't felt since Syndria died.

Hope.

All burdens vanished. Syndria's death turned into fuel. She saw her face in each of these rebels, scared to death of Baltashazar, willing to do anything to escape him. She saw Sorias in herself—the warrior of wonderful determination and defiance in the face of despair. A hero.

Forgiveness . . . was that really all it took? The betrayal would never erase—she would bear it forever. *That's the difference,* she realized. *I'm bearing it now, not pinning it on him.* Somehow, she found the strength to carry it. By concentrating on others more than herself, she hardly felt the weight.

She had loved no one since Sorias betrayed her. *That changes now.* These rebels, the Barabians, were her family. She grew up among them, tended to their sick, and joined in their life. She loved *all* of them.

Love will only make their deaths hurt more, a voice inside her said. *Care requires pain.*

Then I will suffer like no one before me. Her eyes looked at the floating, distorted sphere of pure darkness. Baltashazar was there—she was sure of it. Hiding like a coward and spreading a plague of fear. Adriel would have none of it.

"We will fight!" Adriel said, looking around. Darkness painted the sky again, banishing the light from the rebels' eyes. "Look at me!"

Many eyes turned. Some bore sparks.

"With our last breaths, with all our being, we will fight Baltashazar! I can't die attacking my people. Can any of you? Maybe we're doomed, and this is all pointless. But don't you see what he's doing? He could kill us all himself, but that's not enough for him. He thinks he can break our resolve. Do *not* give Dreslen the victory he so viciously desires! We will die with *honour*, and they will remember us like Mordecai himself!"

Silence.

Then a boy, no more than twelve, raised his fist with a shout.

A tumultuous cry of agreement arose from the surrounding people. They reached down to help up those who they had attacked, almost doubling their numbers. Women and men, young and old, took up arms once more, not weapons of silver or steel but fists of hope. Indeed, hope was now something to be grasped.

Adriel turned in time to see the dravelords rise into the air, locked in a lethal aerial dance. Talons swiped and beaks stabbed forward, loosening feathers to the ground and invoking cries of great terror and hope. Neither bird seemed to be winning, but their lurching wings bore them towards Baltashazar. If the rebel dravelord emerged victorious against the evil one, it may stand a chance against Baltashazar.

Where are you, Jacob? If only Sorias hadn't sent him into the castle, he might be able to finish this. All Adriel could do was buy him time.

"To Baltashazar!" Adriel raised her arm and took up running again. The pain in her abdominals was gone, replaced by flames of courage. They couldn't kill Baltashazar, but they will have died fighting him rather than each other. Even that was a victory in its own regard.

———◆◇◆———

The morning was darker than Jacob remembered. But then again, there hadn't been an enormous dome of pure darkness either. The border reached the castle gate and extended a mile on each side, surpassing any building Jacob had seen. The dome's edges were undefined, as if drawn by a fountain pen, only to be smudged multiple times. Even as he observed this, they shifted again, always averting his expectations of what *should* be there.

"That's him, isn't it?" Jacob kept his eyes forward while talking to Lindina. The blackness obstructed any direct view of the sun, but its light still warped around the dome and granted visibility. He couldn't imagine what it must be like inside that space.

"That's him." Lindina's voice was flat.

Thank the Deep she's still alive. He looked at her and sighed in relief—probably for the twentieth time. Perhaps Baltashazar had used her as bait for Jacob, or perhaps he wanted her for a nefarious future scheme, but it played into Jacob's hand in the end.

"What are we going to do?" Lindina finally looked up at Jacob with near lifeless eyes.

Jacob bit his lip. Part of him longed for the restoration of the city and the defeat of Baltashazar, to be the hero the kingdom—and Atlantia—needed. But now Lindina was with him, and he couldn't confront Baltashazar without breaking his vow to protect her. If he was going to fulfill his first oath, they had to leave the city undetected.

"I can't stay and fight," Jacob said. Lindina's mouth opened, but Jacob cut her off as soon as the first sound escaped her mouth. "No, listen to me. I made a promise to your brother. I *promised* to do everything in my power to bring you home safely. If I stay and fight, you may not make it to Tahil alive."

"I'm not leaving until he stops killing people!" Lindina pointed at the darkness. "I came here to stop him, and I let you down. If he kills anyone, it'll be . . ." Her voice broke. Scrunching her face to hide the tears, she sniffed and wiped her eye with the back of her hand. "It'll be my fault, Jacob. I already attacked that old man in Tahil. I can't leave until I make up for it."

"Out of the question!" Jacob's heart dropped. Did she believe she had a chance against Baltashazar? *Without* her dark magic pen?

"Well, then I won't ask!" Lindina started walking away from Jacob towards the dome. "Either follow me or abandon me."

Foolish girl! Jacob gritted his teeth and walked after her. The palace grounds were completely deserted except for Lindina and himself, but in the presence of all these statues and memories, Jacob couldn't help but feel watched.

"Lindina, stop!" Jacob put a hand on her shoulder. He may as well have touched a serpent, because her arm came whipping about towards his face. Her attack missed pitifully, but her sharp eyes struck true.

"That's all anyone's told me since I entered Tahil! Does it look like it's doing anything?"

"If you would have stopped when we told you to, neither of us would be here!" Jacob no longer averted her gaze. "If it weren't for you, neither of us would have to decide between our own lives or the lives of everyone else!" Jacob pointed to the dome but kept his eyes fixed on Lindina.

"Well, we are here!" Another tear slid down her cheek. "And we do have to decide. I'm sorry for my choices . . . but there's nothing I can do about it now."

"But there is, Lindina. Let me bring you back to Tahil—let me fulfill my oath!"

"This isn't about you and me anymore. I'm sorry I did this to us—to you. I'm really sorry. But there's a man over there who wants to kill everyone—and I mean *everyone*—in the whole world.

He won't stop until either he wins or someone puts an end to him. Jacob, you're the only one powerful enough. I've already tried, but you have to decide whether Atlantia lives or dies. If this world you love becomes covered in darkness, it will be *your* fault."

Gah! Jairus cursed. *Oh, that you had died in that castle, girl!*

Jacob closed his eyes and took a deep breath. He now heard the echoes of a multitude of screams, all suffering from the cold screeches of a dravelord. Lindina was right; they were all going to die. Once Baltashazar killed the rebels, where would he stop? He truly was the most powerful and dangerous being in the world—far surpassing Jacob. Sacrificing his life for a pitiful strike on Baltashazar was foolishness, yet it was the only course of action that felt *right* to him.

I can't let Lindina die, Jacob pleaded with himself. *But no matter what choice I make, I have blood on my hands. Do I care more about Sorias and Adriel and all the rebels, or do I care more about Lindina?* Jacob looked at Lindina with blurring eyes. She was his sister, like Junia had been. He couldn't lose her.

You are too weak! Jairus said. *We must not listen to her. Bring her back to Tahil and spare your lives, only do not go into that black night for so hopeless a cause!*

"Why?" Jacob cried out and fell to his knees, covering his face with his hands. He didn't care if Lindina thought him a fool—he knew he was one.

"You can save us, Jacob." Lindina put her hand on his shoulder. Though not as chill as before, it was still cold. "Please, you're our last hope."

I made a vow to Sorias, too, Jacob thought. *Must I choose between honour and madness?* He recalled listening to the strange voice outside the Pits of Todoros. *The Night of Shadows must pass,* it had said. The night was over, but the shadows remained. Jacob was the only one capable of dispersing them.

But you aren't capable! Oh, that I had never planted the seeds of insanity in your mind.

They've sprouted, it seems. Determination took hold. He'd made his decision.

Then do it. Jairus's voice was bitter. *Apparently, I cannot stop either of you. Lead onward, fool.*

Jacob stood and put his hands to his sides. With firm, aching shoulders, he looked towards the ever-shifting dome of darkness. Already he could feel the pain of the conflict, but he let it fuel him. Madness was his only advantage. Like Baltashazar, he would draw power from chaos. Even if he couldn't, he would fight until standing was no longer feasible—then he would fight on his knees until the last breath was ripped from his lungs.

"Stay out of sight," Jacob said, taking the first steps forward. His legs throbbed, but his mind stayed sharp. "No matter what happens, I want you safe. Don't try to help."

"I'll do that." Lindina had to jog to keep up with Jacob. Energy filled her voice, but her face couldn't have been more solemn. Was this right for a child? To have the grave mindset of a soldier prepared for war? If ever there was a soul worthy of lament, it was Lindina.

With every step, the screams of the people and the dravelord became louder—or perhaps it was just Jacob's reaction. The feelings of dread returned with a vengeance, but nothing would abate the surety he marched with. He faced fear and death itself; ignoring the terror was not an option. He had to feel it and face it.

"Do you feel that, Lindina?" Jacob felt a pull on his skin, dragging him towards Baltashazar's dome. The pull drained his heat, similar to the life transfer with Lindina but less powerful. By focusing on his body heat and consciously retaining it, he could resist the pull, though he couldn't erase it.

"Feel what?" Lindina didn't slow for a moment.

"The pull? The freezing dread? The heat escaping your body?"

"Oh." Lindina brushed back a few strands of tangled hair from her face. "A little bit. But this is the warmest I've felt in hours."

Jacob stared at the approaching gate. The dome now covered part of the wall, leaving only the top of the grand arch visible. It was only a stone's throw away, and every internal voice screamed for him to stop. *At least slow down and delay our doom!*

"Can you see inside the darkness?" Jacob looked down at Lindina. Her gaze was set and unwavering.

"Yes." Lindina squinted. "I see people running everywhere, panicking and—" Her eyes widened, and she gasped. "Baltashazar isn't even fighting them! They're just . . . killing each other!"

"What?" Jacob stopped. Hadn't Sorias been on the verge of ending the fight when Jacob left? The rebels couldn't *possibly* still be fighting the soldiers. "Who's fighting?"

"Everyone." Lindina stopped a short way ahead of Jacob, still looking into the darkness. "Everyone is attacking everyone else. It's like they're killing for the sake of killing!"

Jacob had to swallow hard to suppress his cry of despair. How could it become any worse? The people he fought alongside couldn't aid him if bloodlust consumed them. It would be Jacob against all the forces of Baltashazar and the insanity that devoured the Barabians. Hope was gone.

"It's over, then," Jacob breathed. He turned to Lindina, who met his gaze. "We have to go back, Lindina. There's no—"

"Wait!" Lindina snapped her eyes back to the dome. "I hear the dravelord, but—"

"Perfect," Jacob muttered.

"No, listen! I hear two!"

Jacob lifted his eyes.

"I told him to wait outside the city, but Zachii's in there fighting Uroku!" Her shoulders dropped. "He's going to get himself killed."

Jacob blinked a few times to get his head in order. If Zachii won against the other dravelord, he might turn his attention to Baltashazar and give Jacob an advantage. Could it be that hope remained?

Ever since Tahil, I've let responsibility drive me. Jacob thought, catching Jairus's attention. *But that wasn't my true motive, was it? I've justified every step with a sense of duty, saying that I was the only one capable of saving Lindina.*

And you were, Jairus said.

But I didn't save her because I was responsible. He looked up at the towering dome and the swirling darkness around it, absorbing the chill, eerie breeze. *Not a single person does things for responsibility's sake.*

You did.

No. I only paid any attention to my responsibility because of guilt, because of what I did to Junia . . . even if I denied it each second of the journey. No more. My responsibility remains, but this time hope drives it. We can win, Jairus. Let's see the light for once, and perhaps we can realize it.

Hope is a madness in its own regard, Jairus said. *The greater its strength, the greater your anguish when that hope is not fulfilled. This hope of yours, that we can defeat Baltashazar . . . I have seen few that rival its folly. Are you ready to suffer, Jacob?*

Against every line of reasoning that crossed his mind, Jacob ran. His burning feet traversed the stone, bringing him closer every second to imminent death. Focusing on his body heat no longer, he let his warmth be vacuumed into the pull of the shadows, embracing the cold—embracing the nightmare.

"Jacob, wait!" Lindina cried.

I'm completely insane. He gave no heed to Lindina. Only two things drew his focus: the fall of Baltashazar and the hope of the morning. Everything else became a blur. His entire life passed into the shade, lost to the shadows of madness that fueled him forward.

A moment later, the blackness was directly in front of him. Then he was through it.

THIRTY-TWO

Jacob couldn't have anticipated the chaos within the dome. Everywhere he looked, the shrouded forms of men and women darted about, screaming, colliding, and raging against each other. Deathly cold air seeped inside him, chilling his insides and making sweat pour from his skin. All sound muffled and terror returned, fuelled by the cries of both dravelords, the encroaching darkness, the maddened citizens, and of course his imminent confrontation with Baltashazar.

We should leave! Jairus pleaded.

"No!" Jacob pushed forward, nearly tripping on one of the many scattered bodies. All kinds of people—soldiers, children, elders—were strewn about. At another time, this scene would have made him cower in revulsion, but Jacob was no longer the same man. This wasn't the first time he'd faced death in a horrid environment. He may be a stranger to war, but it was he, in part, who instigated it. He was about to finish what he started.

As he moved further from the edge of the dome, the crowd grew thicker. On the other side of the dome, the sun poked through the veil, casting dim red light onto the battlefield. It was hardly enough to see, let alone prepare for oncoming attackers. To make it worse, none moved predictably. One would come at him with thrashing fists in a straight line, while another grabbed at his arm from the side. With most, he could escape with sharp movement or light force, but fending off multiple at once proved difficult.

Jacob swung his fist down on the arm of a young man who had grabbed his right wrist. The boy only snarled, his eyes sparking with rage, and launched another punch at Jacob's face.

Jacob ducked to avoid the blow, but pain erupted in his right shoulder. As if by instinct, Jacob brought his left arm sailing towards the boy's stomach—and missed. His knuckles came hard against his ribcage, and the boy released his grip on Jacob. Neither stopped to regard each other before moving.

Jacob darted away, clutching his left hand and fixing his eyes on the ground. He didn't know if the boy pursued him, but he needed to move quickly regardless. With every moment he spent here, his fear escalated. It wouldn't be long before it crippled him; either that, or he would become like the lunatics on all sides.

"Get off!" Jacob swiped away the arm of a middle-aged woman, jumping to the side to avoid collision. Bad idea. By dodging out of the way, he tripped on a body and tumbled to the ground next to a lifeless suit of armour.

As soon as he began to stand, a man with a short sword ran into view, swinging his weapon without aim and bellowing curses. In seconds, the blade slashed the woman's back, dropping her with a scream.

Jairus, lightning! Jacob sprang upright. Every part of him shook and heaved from the prolonged strain, yet somehow he found strength to stand.

"I will not waste my energy on these fools!"

Jacob grunted. Jairus was right. As much as it pained him, he couldn't save everyone. But he could save some.

Where are you? Jacob crouched and looked around, staying hidden. Baltashazar had to be here somewhere, fighting or—

There. Jairus lifted Jacob's head to a distorted mass of darkness floating in the sky. Even looking at it felt like staring into a dravelord's eyes.

That must be him, Jacob thought. *He's just . . . watching.* No, it had to be more than that. These people can't have driven *themselves* to madness. Baltashazar must be fueling their fear and holding the dome in place. How much strength would that take? Jacob didn't know how the Abyss worked, but Baltashazar must be expending considerable energy to maintain such a wide effect.

That will leave him vulnerable, Jairus said. *And concentrated.*

We can only hope. Jacob started running again, carefully watching both his feet. The dead bodies were fewer, but the volume of people made it impossible to move without being struck by a stray fist or colliding with someone.

Baltashazar was still far off, and beyond him, two other dark forms danced in the sky, steadily moving nearer. One was hope, and the other doom. He stopped running to watch the dravelords exchange blows. For such morbid creatures, their movements were graceful. One would swipe, and the other would swoop and rise on the other side with a counterblow.

Then the larger one—or so it seemed from this distance—dove with ferocity upon the other, ripping into its back and holding on. They struggled, attached, as the attacker rapidly pelted the smaller with its beak.

Both fell screeching from the sky, but only one rose. The larger, whoever it was, was victorious. If it wasn't Zachii, Baltashazar had already won. Jacob couldn't face Baltashazar *and* Uroku. But whether or not he was doomed, he had no option but to move forward.

Suddenly, the sky flashed with light. All ceased fighting, frozen with shock, and looked for the cause. In that moment, hope was real. The madness lifted from their eyes long enough to renew Jacob's vigour.

As quickly as it appeared, the light vanished, and with it the still silence. Chaos ensued. Multiple lunatics ran at Jacob, one carrying a short sword. He windsprinted away, drawing ever closer to the floating shroud of Baltashazar.

"Kill the Wayfollower, or I will kill all *of you!"* The deep voice came from every direction, bearing the same effect as a dravelord's.

Baltashazar knows I'm here. Jacob looked around frantically, and so did everyone else. No one knew he was a Wayfollower, did they? That would change when he used fire or lightning. He'd have to time his attack perfectly.

"Grey tunic!" Baltashazar said. *"Tar-stained, untidy hair, south side!"*

Jacob cursed. Everyone nearby looked at him with hatred then rushed in his direction. He was low on breath, but at his current speed, he outran them. The closest anyone came was to jab his satchel with a spear. He took it off and dropped it to avoid distractions. *Sorry, Iven.*

Pitt came into view, and Jacob scrambled to a halt. The burly ex-soldier turned to him with loathing, raising his longsword to the side. He roared and swung.

Jacob windleaped directly up and felt a sharp pain in his toe. From the elevation, he had a clearer view of the street. Further north, a force moved towards him with frightening speed, pushing aside anyone in their way. The dravelord, which had been circling above them, now sped southward, looking straight at him.

He descended, breathless, and hit the ground hard, surrounded by people who wanted to kill him. They hesitated, likely shocked by his jump. It wouldn't last long.

"Get back!" Jacob said, spinning around and attempting to light his hands ablaze. Nothing but a few sparks came out.

Pitt was the only one with a weapon, but everyone was crowded so tightly that he couldn't swing it properly. Fists pummeled into Jacob from all sides, forcing him to his knees. A woman grabbed his neck and squeezed, but she was shoved aside by another who wanted to attack.

Jacob grit his teeth, trying in vain to gather his breath for a gust. All he felt was pain. Everywhere, in every way, pain.

Then his ears erupted with a shriek. Everyone froze as the dravelord descended upon the ring, talons pointed down.

Goodbye.

The wind beat down with fury. Screams rose all around him. The dravelord hovered in place with its massive wings, cutting down everyone above him, spraying the air with blood. Pitt raised his sword to strike the creature, but it lurched forward and grabbed him by the shoulders, dragging him into the air.

It . . . didn't attack me. It was *protecting* him. *Zachii.*

Jacob stood up, dazed, and pushed through the screaming throng. They clutched their faces and scattered, while others who weren't hurt hurried to flank Jacob. He didn't get far before they surrounded him again.

Pitt fell next to him, landing atop an old man with a knife. Both toppled, motionless. Jacob ducked as Zachii swooped down, slicing his talons along a line of people, cutting their shoulders and heads. He came back around with a screech and made a circular pass.

Almost everyone tried to get away, but a black-clad soldier held Jacob fast. He clawed at Jacob's face, narrowly missing his eyes.

Jacob lashed out with the wind. The feeble gust didn't even distract the soldier. *Thank the Deep he isn't armed.* Jacob punched the soldier in the nose and felt a *crack*. He couldn't tell whether the nose or the hand broke, but the soldier groaned and let go of Jacob.

Zachii's help wasn't enough. People came at Jacob from every direction, rendering movement impossible. Zachii dealt with any who had weapons, but even those without were vicious enough to kill—though perhaps not smart enough. They moved like animals, looking for a way to hurt without any strategy. If they would only work together, they could pin him down and strangle him.

But they didn't. Their madness, as much as it wanted him dead, kept him alive.

As fists pounded his head and his consciousness drifted, a sound rose above the din. Short, tumultuous shouts with regular intervals, almost like a chant. Each shout was the same, only louder than the last. A word.

He strained his ear and fell to his knees as Zachii cleared his attackers away.

"Hope!" The chant rose from the north. "Hope! Hope!"

"Finish him!" Baltashazar screamed. A streak of black shot out from his shroud, sailing towards Jacob.

He rolled to the side the moment it struck the ground. A spear made of pure, solid darkness. It vanished a second after impact.

Oh, Dreslen. Pitt was up again, bleeding from both shoulders and standing over Jacob. He held the same longsword as before.

"Traitor!" Sorias's voice preceded the tip of a sword jutting out from Pitt's stomach. Pitt dropped his weapon, eyes wide, and crumpled to the ground.

Sorias pulled back his short sword and wiped the blood on his uniform, nodding at Jacob.

Jacob stood up and looked around. The chanting crowd surrounded him now, hope ablaze in their eyes. They moved in tight groups, tackling the lunatics, rarely killing. Adriel walked among them, leading the chant for hope and reaffirming their goal to defeat Baltashazar.

"Get up, soldier!" Sorias grasped Jacob's wrist and pulled him to his aching legs.

"I may need backup," Jacob said. After that beating, even *speaking* hurt.

"No kidding. Lead the way, Mordecai."

Jacob didn't know if that was supposed to be encouraging, but it didn't help. Mordecai died. He ignored Sorias's comment and trudged through the streets, stepping over casualties into pools of blood, dodging around the savages who Adriel's army had not yet subdued. With Sorias and Zachii's help, he made slow progress towards the centre of the dome, where Baltashazar hovered and watched with chilling fury.

"He's weakening himself," Jacob said, "but once he breaks his concentration on the dome, he'll—"

"What dome?" Sorias said. Both of them had to raise their voices to be heard above the battle.

"We're in a giant black dome. Baltashazar's using it to block out the sun."

"I thought the entire sky had . . ." He trailed off and shook his head. "When he stops sustaining the dome, what happens?"

"He'll focus on me. We have to hit him hard and fast, otherwise his strength will return."

"How do you know?"

"Instinct."

"We'll have to knock him out of the sky first. Any bright ideas?"

Jacob looked at his hands and regarded Jairus. "Quite bright." As exhausted as he was, his adrenaline kicked in. That should be more than sufficient for Jairus to deliver a significant bolt of lightning.

"Get down!" Sorias pushed Jacob to the side, knocking him to the ground.

Where he stood previously, another dark spear streaked through the air and stuck into the ground.

"You have no hope!" Baltashazar said. *"Give up and die!"*

He's afraid, Jacob realized. The revelation was like a thousand candles lighting a dark room. Jacob may be weak, but so was Baltashazar—weak enough to fear defeat. If Baltashazar feared it, that meant it was possible.

He doesn't know how weak you are, Jairus said. *He may expect a surge of power.*

Then we'll give it to him! Jacob forced himself to stand. Another spear bolted from Baltashazar's shroud, flying straight towards his face.

A giant mass of black feathers hit the ground in front of him, spreading its wings and shrieking. Zachii fell backwards, the spear still in his chest.

"Come on, Jacob!" Sorias said.

No time to grieve. Jacob jumped over Zachii's fallen body and ran alongside Sorias, dodging spears as they rained from Baltashazar. They were poorly aimed, and most found targets in the backs of Adriel's army. Even if Jacob wanted to, he couldn't lament their deaths. The thrill of terror surged in him, driving him forward, adrenaline tingling beneath his skin.

"Your plan?" Sorias shouted.

"I'll hit him with lightning. When he falls, you take his head off!"

"That's not going to work."

"It will have to!"

As they approached the intersection Baltashazar hovered over, the air pulsed like a heartbeat. Jacob recognized his own heart beating to the same rhythm, but he wasn't creating the pulse. Baltashazar's shroud, larger than before, convulsed in tandem with the wind, emanating the unmistakable sound of a heart. Deep and pervasive, as if the entire dome was his body. As if the wind was his breath, and the surrounding screams were his own.

The spears stopped, replaced by piercing whispers of a tongue Jacob didn't understand. Each word ripped at his insides, causing *physical* pain. He clutched his stomach and halted, groaning through his teeth, face contorted.

It's time, Jairus. Jacob looked up and raised his trembling hands towards Baltashazar's shrouded figure. Torrents of cold sweat slipped down his armpit. His pain was mounting, but all weariness vanished. The stinging in his back and arms, the rips in his stomach, and the burning in his calf only filled him with vigour.

"Jairus!"

At that, Jairus unleashed madness into his fingers. Lighting sparked, growing into a barren tree of blinding blue and rising, ever ridged and terrible, into the folds of Baltashazar's shroud. When the crackling bolts pierced it, the shroud turned clear as fog, revealing the silhouetted form within.

It was hideous. The right leg was three-jointed and at least a foot longer than the left. Baltashazar's back was bent beyond recognition, sprouting bones at the neck, closely resembling a fat serpent with a mouthful of crooked sticks. His hands, raised above his misshapen head, were twice the size they ought to be, and the fingers varied in both length and shape.

All this was not so horrible as the scream. Cold, broken, deeper than the sea and shriller than a knife, it penetrated him more than the dravelord ever had. Madness, in its purest form. Jairus's greatest fear and former source of power. In its immediate wake, he could bear the lightning no longer, and he dropped his hands to clutch his ears.

The shroud dispelled, but Baltashazar still hovered in the air, convulsing from the lightning. The scream stopped, giving Jairus a chance to regain his bearings. Both he and Sorias trained their eyes on the figure in the air, waiting, avoiding the savages around them and occasionally fighting back.

"This is your last chance!" Baltashazar rasped, reforming his shroud. *"Kill the men beneath me, and I'll spare you all!"*

"Stone it!" Sorias's shout led to clashing steel. Jairus turned to see him locked in combat with two other soldiers at once. That left Jairus on his own.

Without half a second's hesitation, Jairus mustered his insanity. *"Burn, all of you!"* Lightning flew from his rapidly moving hands, paralyzing everyone nearby. He didn't have time to kill anyone. Not that he wanted to, anyway. Strange, that. Here, at the end, he was finally changing.

You fool! Jairus told himself. *Don't forget who you are!*

I am what he makes me. We abandoned ourselves long ago.

"Not the people, Jacob!" Sorias yelled. "Don't kill them when there's a monster—"

"I'm getting to him, imbecile!" Jairus trained his lightning on Sorias's opponents and crippled them. There were only a few left to deal with in the immediate area, but Adriel's army stepped in to help.

"Then do it!" Sorias leaped over several bodies to cut off the closest offenders. When they saw the bloodied sword in his hand, they backed away, stumbling over their own. Pitiful.

"Focus," Jairus told himself, looking up at Baltashazar. Madness belonged to *him.* He ruled it once—he need only rule it once more. How *dare* Baltashazar assert his authority over it!

"This time, your screams will only fuel me," Jairus screamed at Baltashazar. *"I urge you, cry out!"* He lashed, once again piercing Baltashazar's shroud and revealing his form. This time, he didn't stop. Though his energy drained by the second, he continued sending the crackling light upwards. He had to burn Baltashazar or fall.

The pain came. He felt as though robed in a garment of icy needles from his head to his soles. His entire vision clouded in a black mist—not only that, but his feeling and hearing too, lost to a sea of silence, a well of deathly chills. It was as if he was fading into the Abyss itself, where intense pain, both physical and mental, ruled. Every fibre of Jairus's being told him to stop attacking. His knees gave way, and one by one his fingers fizzled out of lightning.

"No!" Jairus shook his head and replanted his feet, gritting his teeth. There were no words for how weary he was. Jacob would have collapsed in the same situation.

The pain continued to rise, seeping through his skin. Every shaky breath let poison into his lungs, and every blink brought fire to his eyes. More and more, his senses darkened as only a single bolt of lightning emanated from his finger. Holding it was agony, but he could tell Baltashazar was suffering as well.

When the pain neared its climax and Jairus was about to die, he surged a final burst of lightning and relented. He fell to the ground, hitting his shoulder, and waited for the pain to subside.

"Zachii!" a painfully familiar voice shrieked in the distance. "Please, no! Zachii!"

Fool of a girl! Jairus opened his eyes and searched for Lindina. The throng made finding her impossible.

"Get up, Jacob!" Sorias pulled Jairus up by his forearm.

With reluctance, Jairus accepted the help and got to his feet. Despite being in less pain, he had no energy left. Using lightning again was out of the question, but what else was there? He was too cold to create fire, and wind would only annoy Baltashazar. That only left one more thing . . .

"Look!" Sorias hit Jairus on the shoulder and pointed to Baltashazar with his sword. The creature stopped writhing in the air, went silent, and plummeted to the ground.

Do you know what needs to be done? Jairus said.

It's the only way, Jacob said.

Then take control and do it, fool. Jairus closed his eyes and felt one last time the breath of life. He didn't know how long it would be until he breathed again. Then, with a sigh, he gave up his being. *Goodbye, Jacob.*

Jacob snapped back into full consciousness. Jairus was gone, perhaps forever. Beside him, Sorias stood in tension amidst the bodies strewn on the ground. Ahead, Baltashazar rose, slow and shaking, from the ground. Beyond him, a great crowd of people watched as the light of day threatened the dome.

"What are you waiting for?" Jacob said.

"It won't work," Sorias said, trembling. "He draws power from death itself. We can't kill him."

Baltashazar regained his footing and looked at Jacob. His eyes—if one could call them that—were entirely black, blacker even than the shroud that enveloped Baltashazar previously. It was like staring into something emptier than nothingness, attempting to drain every notion of hope. But no dread could claim him, for he already knew the worst would happen.

"I have a plan." Jacob looked at Sorias, his ally. His friend. It was at this crucial moment that attachment filled him. He didn't want to leave these people, least of all Lindina, but there was no other choice. There was only one way to stop Baltashazar and save the kingdom. Only one way to save Lindina, Sorias, and Adriel.

One way.

"He's weak, Sorias! We have to act *now*."

Baltashazar limped forward, growing a dark rod out of his hand and breathing menacingly. He still upheld the dome, but it was wavering.

"Sorias!" Jacob seized him by the shoulders and shook him. His eyes were wide and clouded, unable to focus.

"All for nothing . . ."

"I forgive you!" Adriel shouted from behind. "Sorias, I forgive you!"

At once, Sorias's eyes lit up, and Baltashazar thrusted his black blade. With a step to the side and a wave of his arm, Sorias deflected the blow. The two faced each other, weapons in hand and feet ready to spring. Baltashazar heaved like a wounded hound, but the fury on his face crushed any hint of resignment.

Jacob's plan depended on Sorias's ability to hold off Baltashazar. While they fought in a rapid dance of blades, Jacob breathed deeply, hugging himself for warmth, and focused his thoughts on Lindina. She would be safe after this. After Baltashazar died, she'd travel to Tahil, enjoy tea and warm weather, and drink life from the forest. Then she'd return home, and Carl would embrace her, weeping tears of joy. Jacob will have fulfilled both oaths.

"Regret training me?" Sorias's voice snapped Jacob out of his thoughts. He brought his sword down hard on Baltashazar's head, but Baltashazar blocked it. Both held the stance in a contest of strength.

"I should have killed you," Baltashazar said. The shadows weakened, and so did Baltashazar's stance. Sorias had the advantage, but he was right—a sword couldn't kill Baltashazar. Only Jacob could.

Sorias punched Baltashazar in the stomach and brought his hand away black. The blow staggered Baltashazar, but Sorias's hand shook uncontrollably.

Baltashazar raised his sword.

No! Jacob gusted at Baltashazar, holding back too much air. Sorias dodged Baltashazar's blade, getting only a graze on the left shoulder. Nevertheless, he staggered and clutched his shoulder with his sword hand.

"The Abyss take you!" Baltashazar ripped the sword from Sorias and tossed it away, pushing Sorias to the ground. Sorias groaned and tried to rise, but Baltashazar planted his foot on his chest. He looked at Jacob and smiled. *"Would you save him?"*

Jacob was low on air and barely had the strength to stand, so he did the one thing he could: he rushed at Baltashazar and tackled him to the ground. Even coming in contact with the creature filled him with crippling revulsion—like embracing a giant, hairy spider.

As soon as they struck the ground, Jacob rolled to the side and scrambled to his feet—but Baltashazar was faster. He rushed at Jacob with empty hands and grabbed both his shoulders. Icy poison seeped through, and even when Jacob writhed out of Baltashazar's grip, the poison leaked deeper into his arms. He did exactly as he'd done when the gargoyle attacked him, focusing his life energy into the poison and eradicating it.

Baltashazar took his eyes off Jacob and staggered towards Sorias. As soon as Jacob rushed forward to cut him off, Baltashazar turned around and shot towards him, grabbing his neck and snarling with crooked fangs.

Jacob flailed his arms in panic. When he tried to grab Baltashazar's arms, they twisted free like oily serpents. Baltashazar was getting stronger. Jacob needed to make his move *now*, but he couldn't if Baltashazar had control.

"*Yes . . .*" Baltashazar backed Jacob against a wall and seized his neck with both hands. *"You're not as strong as I thought. I think I'll take my time with you."*

Then the piercing came—though not where he expected it. His stomach felt the intrusion of a blade, yet both Baltashazar's hands were on Jacob's neck. Baltashazar looked similarly surprised. His mouth and his eyes opened, and black sludge seeped from behind his lips. Jacob winced at his own pain, but Baltashazar's grip weakened.

Jacob shifted his head to the side and looked behind Baltashazar. There was Sorias, his sword thrust into Baltashazar's midsection and barely protruding into Jacob's own stomach. With a jolt, he pulled Baltashazar back from Jacob and tossed him to the ground, sword still embedded in his back.

"I guess the sword worked." Sorias looked at the blood seeping through Jacob's tunic. He cursed.

"It wasn't deep," Jacob strained, looking at Baltashazar's body. He wasn't moving, not even writhing in pain. By the looks of things, he was dead.

"Stay alert, Sorias," Jacob said. "It's a trap."

"I know." Sorias grabbed his shoulder again, grimacing. Black steam rose from a bloody gash. "How do we beat him?"

Jacob clenched his jaw. "He draws power from death. His entire being *is* death. The only way to finish him for good is to imbue him with life."

He remembered Lindina's reaction in the throne room, when Jacob started the life transfer. The life actually *hurt* her. Lindina still had some humanity left, and that was why she could be healed. But Baltashazar was something else entirely. The Way of Life couldn't save him because he was already dead.

"Imbue him with life?" Sorias said. "What do you—"

A crackling bolt of darkness shot from Baltashazar's hand and hit Sorias in the torso, sending him flying against the wall. He crumpled to the ground, soundless.

Baltashazar aimed at Jacob, struggling to stand.

Jacob dodged the bolt with a twist in the wind, then gathered his life force and tackled Baltashazar. With a grunt, he pulled the sword from Baltashazar's back and cast it aside. Black blood seeped from the wound, staining Jacob's trousers as he kneeled atop Baltashazar.

He grasped both Baltashazar's wrists and held tight, putting his body weight into pinning the monster down. When he thrashed, Jacob almost vomited from disgust. Every instinct told him to let go, to free himself from this curse. To survive. But there was only one way to save Lindina and the kingdom. Only one way to fulfill his oaths.

Give me strength, Jacob reached out to the Deep and focused on his life energy. As he had done in Castle Dreslen, he channeled the life from his own body into Baltashazar, who thrashed beneath Jacob and cried out with a stretched voice. Jacob whimpered, tears flowing freely from his eyes, biting his tongue hard enough to draw blood. Pain like never before shot through his arms as death itself crawled through him. Baltashazar's moans gave little encouragement.

As his life began to depart, Jacob felt an overwhelming emptiness, as if he hadn't eaten for months. The nausea wasn't contained to only the stomach—it spread throughout his entire body, starting with his hands and creeping up to his head and toes. Then the cold came, starting from his core and extending to the rest of his insides. The innermost parts of his body were ice, and the rest was poisoned water, churning violently and crying out to the ground to be consumed.

Jacob welcomed death for the second time that night. Baltashazar was moments away from it as well—he could feel it. True death, not the Abyss's false life. The Abyss held onto Baltashazar, ripping at Jacob with excruciating pain. This was nothing like the peaceful departure from life he'd experienced with Lindina.

He could sense Baltashazar's weakening state, and he knew all it would take was the rest of Jacob's life—no more, no less. One life to end another. With a last push, it would end.

Goodbye, Atlantia. Jacob shut his eyes. As he prepared to wrench the last bit of life from his heart, radiant warmth spread across his arm. Snapping his eyes open, he looked to his right to find the cause of this change. *No . . .*

"Let . . ." Jacob could hardly speak. "Let . . . go." Tears blurred what vision he had left. *Anything but this.* Jacob tried to calm his breathing to quicken his death. He had to die *now.*

"No." Lindina brought her other hand to Jacob's arm and filled him with twice as much warmth and light. She crippled, falling to her knees and gasping with a pained expression. Tears of her own fell to the ground as sobs poured from her mouth. "It's . . . my . . . fault." A desperate breath separated each word. "You saved me. Now it's my turn."

"Please!" Jacob couldn't manage the plea above a whisper. He felt Baltashazar's strength leaving, but Jacob's own life only grew. The chill nausea subsided, and he could once again feel his beating heart. But Lindina grew colder and darker. Every breath she took filled her with shadow, eating at her strength and loosening her grip on Jacob.

She cares too much, Jacob thought. It was what Jairus would have said. That was how she now saved him, how she would kill herself if she followed through.

I have to finish this. Jacob turned his attention to Baltashazar and gathered his life force. With a scream, he poured his remaining energy into the creature beneath him. Cold shadow overtook him again, and the nausea returned. He was dying . . . but not dead. Baltashazar, on the contrary, no longer moved, either in breath or heartbeat. Jacob released him and fell onto his back.

It's done. Jacob opened his eyes and looked into the sky. Black turned to grey, which dissipated quickly and revealed a blue brighter than all the jewels beneath the earth. Silence lifted from the air, and the songs of crows reached his ears along with victorious shouts from the people. A gentle breeze graced his face, though it carried the scent of blood. Lindina's frail hands no longer touched his arm. He had defeated Baltashazar, but had he won?

"Jacob!" Adriel's face came into view as she bent down to examine him. When she saw his blinking eyes, her worried eyes turned joyful. "You're still alive!"

"Help." Jacob could manage only the single word. Pain still touched his entire body—injuries, hunger, strain, and the final life transfer. Life held him by a thread, and it could break at any moment. Yet he held firm. After what Lindina did to save him, he had to.

Adriel clutched his hand, pulling him up, but Jacob couldn't stand. He fell to his knees, dazed. Never would he have imagined that relief would join such pain. He had faced death itself and survived. The world was safe from Baltashazar's plans of chaos, and he could bring Lindina to Tahil for healing. He looked around the pressing crowd for her. She couldn't have gone far.

"Where's Lindina?" Jacob finally managed to stand, though his legs felt like crumbling pillars.

"The girl?" Adriel asked.

"Show me."

Adriel took Jacob's arm and led him through the crowd, pushing people aside when necessary. Blood marred everything, from streams on the ground to stains on clothes. Blood spilled by the Barabians' own hands.

"Is Sorias alive?" Jacob said.

"He's still breathing. Doctor Dredding is attending to him."

At last, they came to a gap in the crowd. After all the carnage Zachii caused, the survivors were justified to stay away from him—all but Lindina, who stood next to his fallen body with a hand on his feathers. Her skin was paler, her hair darker. She crouched by Zachii's head, whispering, then put both hands on him.

Dark smoke rose from Zachii's beak, and he shook his head, scattering some feathers.

"Lindina!" Jacob stepped forward.

Lindina finally turned her head, slowly and mournfully. Her tangled hair blew in the wind, covering her face and falling into her open mouth. When her eyes met Jacob, he lost his breath—they were blacker than night.

No. Jacob fell to his knees again, knocking them against the hard stone. *No . . .*

"I'm sorry." Lindina's voice was stretched like Baltashazar's, both deep and shrill. With a final breath, she leapt onto Zachii's back and gave a cry. Zachii shrieked and spread his wings. The dravelord lurched into the sky with Lindina on its back and bore her away, beyond the crowd and towards the rising sun.

Jacob looked on and felt himself falling. Why did she save him? He was supposed to save *her*! What victory was this, if his one goal was unfulfilled? All was meaningless now. He'd done everything in his power to save her, and still it wasn't enough.

"Jacob?" Adriel's hand rested on his shoulder. It stung. "Can you walk?"

Jacob took a deep breath and rose painfully to his feet, shrugging off Adriel. This wasn't over yet. He would find Lindina, and he would save her. As long as she existed, Jacob had an oath to fulfill.

"Yes," Jacob said, looking into the distance. He had a long journey ahead of him, but he needed to rest and regain his health. Even now, he felt as though he could lie down and die if he wanted. A journey to Tahil might be necessary for a complete recovery, but he needed rest here before making that passage.

"I won't abandon you," Jacob whispered to the north. "As long as I have breath, I won't cease to search for you and cure you."

"Who is she?" Adriel matched Jacob's gaze into the north sky.

Jacob took a deep breath. "She was my sister."

"And you're going after her?"

"I am." Jacob's eyes burned from the sun's radiance, but he looked ever onward. "And I'm going to bring her home."

THIRTY-THREE

⎯⎯⎯◆○◆⎯⎯⎯

Nearly two weeks had passed since the Night of Shadows. During that time, much had happened. The first was the communal effort to bury the dead, who either died valiantly defending their home or fell prey to the madness of Baltashazar. Even the treacherous soldiers deserved better than to lie rotting in the city square. The community tombs were opened wide and filled past their suggested capacity.

Hundreds died, and hundreds more were wounded. Every doctor in the city, with Dredding at the helm, worked without break for a week. After seeing Baltashazar defeated, the royal doctor had a change of heart, becoming one of the most enthusiastic people in the city. Jacob knew little about him but heard he was a different person now. Many were. One did not walk away from a mass slaughter unchanged.

Jacob had not been present during the cleanup, but from what he heard, it was near as bitter as the actual battle. Friends wept for their close companions, fathers cried for their daughters, and sons shed many tears for the blood of their mothers. When they found Baraz's body, the spark of hope snuffed out. None knew whether their king died a coward or a hero, but all witnesses agreed Baltashazar killed him by his own hand. Whatever his final intentions were, he had given his life to save his city. It was he, not Jacob or Sorias, who roused the Barabians to oppose Baltashazar, and though he did not lead the charge, he marched to war as one of his own.

When Baltashazar died, Baraz's last living relative passed from the world, leaving him without a proper heir. Despite rumours of a secret will, officials found nothing after days of searching. Even the king's counselors, who would have known best how to govern the city, were slain when Baltashazar rose to power, leaving no one to fill the impossible gap as king—no one, according to the law and tradition of Atlantia.

Jacob inhaled deeply and winced. Without goldberries, the strain from two weeks ago proved persistent. Adriel advised him to keep moving, but in the current situation that was impossible. People pressed around on all sides, giving him no room to stretch his worn limbs. Worse still, his view was partially obstructed.

As the saviour of Barabus, the new king offered him an honorary spot at his right hand, which Jacob declined. And when urged to take a spot at the front row of onlookers, he resisted the invitation. If news of his disappearance from Tonto reached the Silencers, they may be looking for him. Indeed, many were present in this throne room, and he didn't need them interrogating him. Best to stay hidden.

"At attention!" A strong voice cut through and dissipated the chatter of the crowd.

All heads turned to the back of the room, where the magnificent doors groaned open. Trumpets sounded as the first soldiers marched into the throne room's central aisle, their hands on the hilts of their swords. Each step was in perfect unison, like the drum that accompanied the trumpets' fanfare. Their armour caught the light of the sun streaming through the upper windows, but the darkened look on the soldiers' faces confounded it. It seemed they could not yet see past their decision to side with Baltashazar, but eventually, in the presence of a new king, they would forget their guilt and look ahead to all the good they might accomplish.

Once the first set of soldiers passed through the gates, the trumpeters stopped. All held their breath as they awaited the coming of the king. Jacob didn't feel the joy that everyone else exhibited. Intellectually, of course, he was excited. This country would have a new leadership, one that would not back down from danger, and one that would look to raise up the lowly. But he didn't *feel* anything. In his heart, all was hollow.

Are you there? Jacob had been asking that question every day since the battle, with no response. Jairus was gone. This absence of his closest companion contributed to the void, but it did more. It perplexed him. Was Jairus truly gone? In the days leading up to the battle, Jacob had developed something of a friendship with Jairus. It made little sense, befriending a psychotic phantom that didn't exist, but Jairus still felt real to Jacob. He was changing, too. But if Jairus was indeed gone, he would never know for sure. *Where are you?*

Jacob snapped out of his search for Jairus and looked at the doors again. Through them marched Sorias, covered in shining black armour adorned with gold, inlaid with rubies and amethysts. A cape of rich purple trailed behind him, long enough to assert his majesty but just short of touching the ground. His face was stern, and his eyes fixed ahead, yet they shone with the light of two suns. It was a marvel that Adriel nursed him back to health after Baltashazar's magic struck him, yet here he was—fully restored.

At his side was Adriel herself, the soon to be crowned queen. Gone was her simple doctor's uniform, replaced by a gown of gold-embroidered green. The dress reminded Jacob of Tahil, and though Adriel shone brighter than the sunlight, she couldn't compare to the splendour of that forest. Even so, her graceful steps were the perfect complement to Sorias's assertive stride.

The two had been wed the previous night and now walked arm in arm. After the Night of Shadows passed, Adriel reconsidered her forgiveness of Sorias under less pressure. It didn't take long for her to confirm it. Sorias was skeptical, but he didn't object. After seeking forgiveness for two years, it might be a while before he could accept it. Nevertheless, he accepted Adriel. He devoted himself to her, and she to him. Together, they would rule the kingdom with wisdom and courage to rival the kings of old.

Behind Sorias and Adriel, a second group of soldiers marched through the doors, and the trumpeters resumed their song. Everyone should have been tired from the wedding, but the festivities had lasted all day and kept them in high spirits. It was the perfect foil of Baltashazar's storm of terror; a rain of joy produced by no supernatural means, healing all and giving hope. All was right with the world—or so everyone but Jacob believed.

It wasn't just Lindina who worried him, although she was his biggest care. After the battle, he'd returned to the castle to account for Goldor, but he'd vanished. They'd recovered Dreslen's pen and given it to the Silencers, but if Goldor still had some Abyssal power left, he may prove another threat.

Sorias was unconcerned about it. The Silencers' early intervention would prevent the situation from getting out of hand. Probably. Jacob would listen for updates as much as possible, but the Silencers were rather secretive about . . . everything, really. For all he knew, they had already apprehended Goldor.

They might fail, Jacob thought in Jairus's voice. *If that happens, you must ignore it. If the world must burn before you save Lindina, so be it.* That was probably something Jairus would say.

I trust them to learn from this failure, Jacob thought. *The Silencers are frighteningly efficient.*

On that note, it would be unwise for Jacob to stay longer than necessary. Likely, he would set out for Tahil tomorrow after a good rest. The king and queen had offered him a cart and mule for the journey, but he declined it. Secrecy was a necessity, both for Jacob and for Tahil itself. As long as Sorias and Adriel kept their oath of discretion, Jacob should be able to reach Tahil without giving away its existence, so long as his provisions lasted him.

As Sorias and Adriel ascended the staircase leading to the throne, Jacob finally *felt* it—joy. He had every reason to be sorrowful, but he couldn't help but empathize with the surrounding people. The day was won. Sorias and Adriel were about to be king and queen, and fear no longer hung over the city like a dark blanket. For these precious moments, Jacob allowed himself peace and rest. Tomorrow, he would start his journey; today, he celebrated.

"All hail!" A tall Silencer wearing his traditional light-grey cloak walked onto the stairs leading up to the throne's podium, facing the crowd and standing in front of Sorias and Adriel.

"Hail!" the Barabians said in tumultuous unison.

"Hail Sorias." The Silencer motioned to Sorias with a raised hand. "Soldier under King Baraz and the bane of Baltashazar!"

"Hail Sorias!" the crowd yelled. It was not painful for Jacob to give up his title as the saviour of Barabus. Many of those assembled had seen Jacob fight Baltashazar—people who agreed to lie about the events of that day. As much good as he'd done, the Silencers would still see him as a threat. They could not, in congruence with their ideals, allow him to live if they knew the truth.

"Hail Adriel." The Silencer lowered his right arm and raised the other to Adriel. "Doctor of the first order and the spark of hope that broke Baltashazar's curse!"

"Hail Adriel!" This shout was even louder than the first. Many of these people were turned from their madness by Adriel during the battle, and more still had known her as a doctor beforehand. She was a well-known public figure, one who deserved her reputation.

The Silencer lowered his hands and nodded to the other end of the hall. A small boy and a girl, a few years older, walked down the walkway. Each carried a crown. The first was made from reflective black metal, with gold embellishments and amethysts set in the front. The second was wrought of radiant silver, set with emeralds in gold sockets. On both crowns, the rims rose and fell in sweeping peaks like waves on a stormy sea, yet were poised in perfect symmetry.

When the children reached the Silencer, he took the black crown from the boy and walked up the stairs to Sorias.

"Kneel, Sorias," the Silencer said.

Sorias did as commanded, coming to one knee and resting his arm atop the other, bowing his head. The Silencer took the crown and placed it atop his head with care, taking a step back when finished. "Rise, King of Barabus!"

The king stood and looked at his people. He looked like a hero of old, clad in shining black armour and a royal helm. Surely Amiroth, even in his hour of glory, was inferior. Sorias's gaze was firm and joyful, his posture regal.

The Silencer walked to the girl with the crown and took it gently from her. Then, returning to the place where he stood before, he looked at Adriel. "Kneel, Adriel."

Adriel knelt on one knee as Sorias had done, without bowing her head. The Silencer placed the silver crown on her light hair and stepped back. "Rise, Queen of Barabus!"

When Adriel rose, the sun rose with her. Beside the dark confidence of Sorias, she was the radiant hope. Never had a queen been crowned like a king in Barabus until this day. The assembly erupted into silence to look upon the majesty of their king and the beauty of their queen, and for a moment Jacob lost himself to pure wonder. To see his companions exalted like this was a joy he could never have asked for, far more rewarding than if he himself had been exalted.

"Hail the King and Queen of Barabus!" The Silencer raised both his arms to Sorias and Adriel, bowing his head.

"Hail!" the assembly shouted, raising their hands.

Hail, Jacob thought, smiling. *May your reign be ever guided by the Deep, and may your love hold to each other until the passing of this world. May you find peace, and may your people find rest through you. And may you ever be happy, Sorias and Adriel. May you ever be filled with joy.*

Jacob finished his blessing, took a long, deep breath, and joined the crowd in their cheers.

Epilogue

Rise. The Night of Shadows must pass. I did not save you to let you die at the mouth of Todoros. My light is little . . . Rise, Jacob . . .

What did it mean?

Haanon shuddered, hugging his cold chest, while Iven sat across the room with a pained expression. Two weeks had elapsed since Lindina and Jacob arrived and departed. Two weeks since Ilemek's passing—the first unnatural death in Tahil since he lost Venet.

"You're unwell," Iven said, swallowing hard.

"So you've told me countless times," Haanon coughed. Iven had every right to be worried. In Tahil, lasting sickness was nearly as bad as death itself. Most people could simply use the Way of Life to heal themselves.

It wasn't old age that bore him down, either. At eighty-two years old, he should have at least twenty left to live. He may be fatally old by Atlantian standards, but in Tahil a death at this age was unheard o f.

This was something sinister: Gloomheart, he hypothesized. The same illness that claimed Venet's life, caused by contact with the Abyss. Haanon had carried Dreslen's pen in his pocket for a short time, but that may have been enough. If it was indeed Gloomheart, he didn't have much longer.

He needed to find out what caused the *Tiris Adelon* to ring. And that voice . . . What was it?

Sending scouts revealed Baltashazar was defeated, although no witnesses referred to the event as the "Night of Shadows." If Jacob or Lindina struck the final blow, they didn't take credit for it. A wise decision, in Haanon's opinion, but it made finding the truth all the more difficult.

For his entire life, he'd pondered the *Tiris Adelon*. Who built the bell? Why? What was its purpose? His experience two weeks ago added more questions than it solved. The first time he rang it, he experienced a vision of Jacob. The second time, he received word of him from the strange voice. Haanon knew Jacob was important, being capable of the Way of the Deep, but he had a difficult time grasping it. All these centuries, the Way had been lost. Now, as he neared death, it returned in Jacob.

Unless Jacob was dead.

Jacob had assured Iven that he intended to bring Lindina back to Tahil, but after two weeks, there was no trace of them.

You were supposed to live. Haanon rocked on the couch, closing his eyes.

He knew the air was warm—it always was. But today, like the last few weeks, all he felt was chills. Worse was the despair and dread pulsing with each heartbeat. One day soon, it would claim him, and he would cease resisting death.

"You said this is how Uncle Venet died," Iven said. "Yet you won't tell me *what* this is."

Haanon shuddered. "In your uncle's case, curiosity killed him. In my case, protectiveness did."

"This is because of that girl, Lindina, isn't it?"

"It is."

"Why? You knew it was dangerous, so why didn't you turn her away? It would have saved you and . . ." His eyes fell. "And my father."

"I acted according to compassion. Though I perish, I regret nothing."

"How am I to lead when you're gone?"

Haanon smiled. "Just like this. Ask questions, seek wisdom, and live according to it."

"That's exactly what Uncle Venet did, yet everyone disliked him. Everyone but you, of course."

"There were others, but I must agree. To most, he wasn't like-able. I loved his character, but he had faults, as we all do. He was different because he didn't hide his faults. For that alone, he was the most respectable man I've ever known."

"How am I supposed to be like him *and* be valued by the community?"

"You already are, Iven. You'll make a fine elder."

"But—"

A knock on the front door cut Iven off.

"Great Scholar," Iven muttered, getting off his chair. "This had better be urgent."

Haanon sighed. It would be a worried visitor at best, an urgent messenger at worst. He didn't want to deal with either. Unless the *Tiris Adelon* rang again, he didn't want to get up from his couch at all.

The door creaked open, and a breeze rushed into the house. To Haanon, it was frigid. Birds chirped outside, leaves rustled, and sweet scents drifted in. Even with his impaired senses, Haanon could still appreciate the comforts of the forest.

"Is he here?" a familiar voice asked.

Haanon straightened, craning his neck. *Scholar!* He still couldn't see out the door.

"He's . . ." Iven glanced at Haanon, eyes wide. "Yes, but . . ."

"Here's your satchel, by the way."

Haanon didn't wait any longer. He sprang off the couch, darting to Iven's side to look out the door. Blood rushed to his head from the sudden movement.

Jacob stood there, well-worn satchel in hand, wearing a dark-grey cloak with the hood down. He nodded at Haanon and smiled. "Good morning, Elder. I think it's time we began my training."

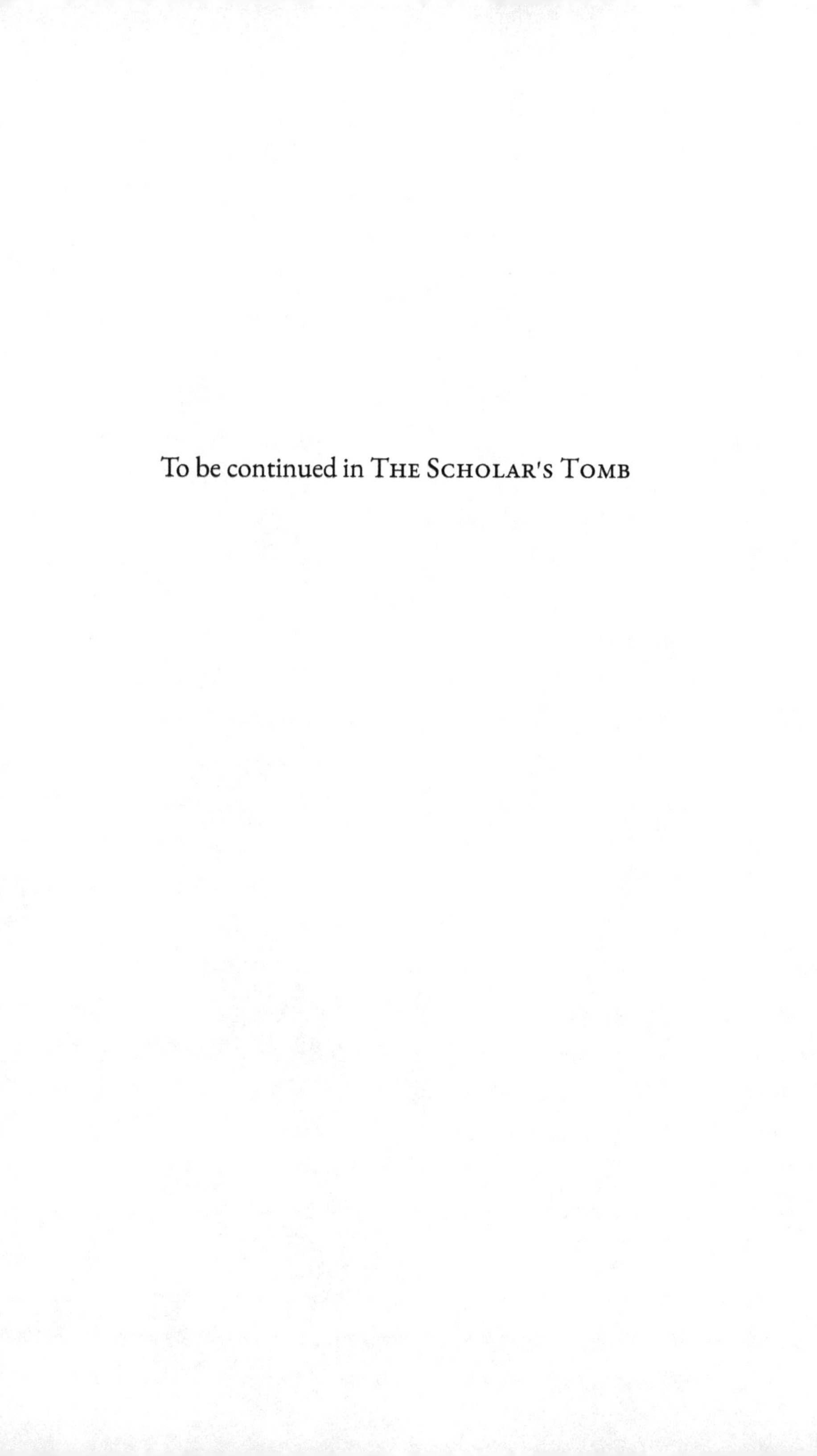

To be continued in THE SCHOLAR'S TOMB

Author's Note

Thank you, dear reader, for reading *The Night of Shadows!* This project has been my dream for many years, undergoing countless changes and refinements to become what you now hold. If you enjoyed this book, would you consider leaving a review to help others find it? It would mean the world to me!

I hope I've swept you along with Jacob on his journey, given you questions to ponder, and made life a little more enjoyable. May you always find hope in the darkest of shadows.

With words,
MB

ABOUT THE AUTHOR

Hailing from the Canadian Prairies, Markus Bitner is the author of The Night of Shadows, the first instalment in the Secrets of Silence trilogy. Aside from reading and writing fantasy novels, he occupies his time composing music, performing piano wherever he can, and pondering life's most enigmatic questions.